Mersey View

Ruth Hamilton is the bestselling author of twenty previous novels set in the north-west of England. She was born in Bolton and now lives in Liverpool, and she writes about both places with realistic insight and dramatic imagery.

For more information on Ruth Hamilton
and her books, see her website at:

www.ruth-hamilton.co.uk

Also by Ruth Hamilton

Mersey View

Ruth Hamilton

PAN BOOKS

First published 2010 by Pan Books
an imprint of Pan Macmillan, a division of Macmillan Publishers Limited
Pan Macmillan, 20 New Wharf Road, London N1 9RR
Basingstoke and Oxford
Associated companies throughout the world
www.panmacmillan.com

ISBN 978-0-330-50753-0

1 3 5 7 9 8 6 4 2

A CIP catalogue record for this book is available from
the British Library.

Typeset by Set Systems Ltd, Saffron Walden, Essex
Printed and bound by CPI Mackays, Chatham ME5 8TD

Once again, I dedicate this piece to Avril Cain, my very best friend.

Not only does she live very close to the setting of the book, but she also handles multiple sclerosis like a master. Mentally, she outruns every doctor and therapist who tries to talk down to her. She is, as locals put it, sound as a pound.

On days when she can't walk, she paints and draws; on days when her hands don't work, she helps me by giving me ideas, characters and locations for my work.

Some aspects of Moira, one of the lead characters herein, are taken from the soul of Avril Cain, who is an example to all of us. Avril's secret is that she remains young and laughs at the various stupidities of her ailing body.

Av, you know I love you, hon. Linda/Ruthie xx

AUTHOR STATEMENT

To the people of North Liverpool, I apologize for messing about with the map and moving the location of Mersey View to a rather grand promenade of Georgian houses near our marina. Liverpool has been my home for thirty years, so I am now part-Scouser and I hope that allows me a bit of leeway.

Acknowledgements

I thank my family, whose members urge me on and keep me smiling.

Gill and Billy, you know I couldn't do any of this without you.

Sadly, I say goodbye to my ex-father-in-law, the best man I ever knew.

Fudge, who is enjoying an Indian summer after a near-brush with death, is now Labrador King of Moorside Park, where he manages and chides all dogs and owners.

Treacle, my baby Lab, you have to lose weight, as must I.

One

At the age of forty-five, Lucy Henshaw ran away from home. The decision to go had been reached neither lightly nor suddenly, since the urge to clear off had existed for about eighteen years, but Lucy believed in duty, so she hung in there until the time was right. It was now or never, so it was now. The millennium had happened, and a new beginning seemed appropriate.

Nevertheless, a degree of trepidation accompanied the proposed exit, since she was leaving behind roots that went deep, and she found herself hoping against hope itself that she might survive without nutrients whose values were beyond the limits of ordinary calculation.

Another difficulty was the suspicion that she might be running from, rather than towards. A new beginning? No. It was merely an ending, a cutting away of rotted flesh in an effort to save what was left of her normal, original self. She now knew where she would be living by this afternoon, and there was a vague idea of how she might occupy her new persona. Beyond that loomed a vacuum, since her children were grown. 'Sometimes, I wonder whether you are really sane, Lucy,' she told herself. Yet it had to be done, quickly, quietly and with as little fuss as possible.

Tallows was not just the matrimonial home; it had been in her family for four generations. 'I was born here,' she told a photograph of her parents. 'You already know that, Mother, because your attendance was compulsory.' She placed the item in a carrier bag, where it joined photos of her twin sons and her daughter. At last, the children were old enough. Would they understand? Advised by her only friend to explain to them in full every detail, Lucy had refused. She didn't want her offspring involved in war. Because Alan would throw several fits and would take no responsibility for his wife's behaviour. He was a ruined man, and their mother had caused all the damage. She would go softly. Since she had done most things quietly thus far, she would be acting in character; no one would be surprised by her lower-than-ever profile.

So Lucy had sent them simple messages just to say that she was leaving, and that her reasons for this were not easy to explain. They had busy lives, plenty to do, friends all over the country. They would endure the blow. These thoughts chased one another across her mind as she walked for the last time through the house she loved.

Her dolls' house was in the attic. Lizzie had played with it too, had grown out of it, and the large, fully furnished treasure had been returned to the top storey for future generations. 'I wish I could explain, Lizzie. But I can't be the means of destroying the love you have for Dad.' It would all come out eventually, and Lucy was used to waiting.

She stroked the rocking horse. Its mane, made from real horsehair, had been depleted by several children who had hung on to it, and it needed repair. But she couldn't save these important things, because she trusted no one enough to allow the removal of mementos. 'Sorry,' she said to Dobbin. Dolls, teddy bears, dartboards, story books, toy soldiers, cars and jigsaw puzzles were piled on shelves. It would all go. Once the receivers moved in, there would be nothing left. If the receivers moved in. According to Lucy's lawyer, the house would remain Lucy's property, but nothing in life was ever absolutely certain. 'I couldn't risk a removals van, because I need not to be noticed, so I have to abandon you to the winds of fate. I hope you'll all be loved by someone.'

The estate was a large one, and its legal owner made her way towards the grounds for a final wander through her family's domain. She looked again at her apple trees, the vegetable plot, her raspberry canes, and at the swings on which her offspring had played. Father's rose beds remained. Lucy had tended them, sprayed them, dead-headed and cut them back. Carp in the fish pond had no idea that life was about to change. Would he feed them? Would the gardener feed them? How was the gardener to be paid?

She stood in a kitchen where she had cooked thousands of meals. The cleaner had been and gone, so it was tidy, at least. The library was the place that hurt most. All Father's leather-bound books were here, and the only item she would manage to save was the family Bible. Still, the situation could not be helped. No matter what, she had to go, and she could take very little with her in an ordinary car.

However, there was a tenuous plan. The house, if he pushed for a settlement and won, would possibly go to auction and, in that situation, Lucy's representative

3

would attend. It was likely that Alan would sell the contents in an effort to bluff his way out of bankruptcy, but his bills were large. She hoped to save the building, and that had to be enough. It should be hers anyway, because she had signed nothing when loans against the house had been taken out. In the legal sense, she had little to fear.

He would win no settlement, surely? So why was her heartbeat suddenly erratic? Why were her palms so hot and moist? Did she fear the man she had married, the one she sometimes referred to as the big mistake? Alan had never been physically violent, though drink made him angry, and he was now married to whisky. He drifted from woman to woman, though each female in turn saw through him, got bored by his drinking and passed him on to the next victim. 'Now or never,' Lucy advised herself.

Where was the cat carrier? Where was the cat? Then the phone rang. She picked it up. 'Hello?' She sounded breathless, as if she had run a half-marathon. It was him. For better or worse had been mostly worse. For richer for poorer – he knew how to make a partner poor.

'I'll be home in about an hour,' he said, cutting the connection before she had chance to reply. Smokey, like the carp, would have to be left to chance. Shaking from head to foot, Lucy reversed her car into the lane and drove off. Once her knees belonged to her again, she managed to control the vehicle. She was gone. She was travelling to Liverpool.

So, she left behind two sons, a daughter, a cat, and a drawer filled with unpaid bills. And a husband. He occupied the lowest place on the agenda, because he'd caused all the difficulties right from the start. In a sense, she should be blaming herself, because she'd married beneath her. Lucy had fastened herself to a man who, after landing her with three children, would spend twenty years forging signatures, remortgaging property and bleeding her dry of her inheritance. But now, the worm had turned, and she was in a new place.

'Then why do I feel so bloody guilty?' she asked an empty room. Her children were all in further education, they had survived, and she had done her best. It had been a waiting game, because she hadn't wanted to ruin their lives, and so she had sat back while he had stolen her inheritance, first to start the business, then to further broader commercial interests; also to gamble, and to spend on other women.

'Tit for tat,' she muttered. 'And he was so used to getting his own way, he never noticed what I was doing.' These words were offered to a bin bag that contained a fraction of her revenge. How would he build an estate of twenty detached, exclusive, executive residences now? That was how he had advertised the project, and land in Bromley Cross hadn't come cheap. But Lucy now held the wherewithal for bricks, timber, glazing, sand, cement, wages and other essentials in a shiny black plastic bag and in a bank account created by her friend and solicitor, Glenys Barlow. The bag was recyclable, of course. One had to do one's bit for the planet these days. She allowed herself a wry smile.

It had taken months. Little by little, she had relieved her husband of all 'his' money while the purchase of the land had been negotiated, while plans had been drawn, rejected, redrawn, accepted. His fatal mistake had been the holiday he had taken in Crete with one of his women – a hairdresser from Rivington. During those fourteen days, Lucy had taken full advantage of her position as company secretary, and she had ruined him.

Over a period of years, she had learned to copy his signature and, after taking private lessons, she had conquered computers. Her lawyer held in a strongroom all evidence of Alan's past misdemeanours. If he wanted to fight back from a legal point of view, he would be riding the wrong horse, since his wife, Louisa, once Buckley, now Henshaw, had merely retrieved money to which he had gained access fraudulently. Confident of his wife's supposed stupidity, Alan Henshaw would not have believed her capable of doing so much harm. Furthermore, she had taken into account inflation, the current value of the money that had been bequeathed to her, and she had left him in a mess. Her children were not in a mess, as she had opened accounts that would see all three through university.

He had been mistaken, because his wife had never been stupid; she had been patient and anxious for her children. Even so, this was a big thing to have done. She looked at her watch. He would have been home for hours by now. She lifted from the refuse bag a copy of a letter printed out this morning at home. No, not home – she didn't live there any more. He could well be reading it now. He would have kittens even before reaching the final paragraph.

Alan,

For a very long time, I sat back and watched while you stole from the joint account. I saw money disappearing from my own personal account, and landing in yours or in the company's records. I also know that you forged my signature several times to remortgage the family home, which was left to me by my parents.

Evidence of your misdeeds is in a safe place, and my representatives know exactly what you have done over the years, so I would advise you to hang fire – go for bankruptcy and take the pain, just as I did.

Why did I wait so long? Because Paul, Mike and Lizzie deserved a chance, and they will have that chance. I have lost a house I love, have abandoned my children, and have left you all the unpaid bills. They are in your sock drawer. It's very full, so your socks are in the dustbin.

You could never recompense me fully for the agonies I have endured for so long a period of time. Don't bother trying to find me, because I shall make sure it all comes out if you attempt to harass me in the slightest way.

Louisa Buckley

Powerful stuff. And how she had shaken when typing it. Had she attempted to write by hand, the letter would not have been legible. It was done. It was all done, and there could be no going back.

Right. Here she sat, waiting for carpets and furniture. As she had bought from a local firm, they had agreed to deliver out of hours, and she might be semi-furnished by ten o'clock tonight. With the exception of holidays and stays in hospital, Lucy had never slept away from Tallows, that large and rather regal house built on the outskirts of Bolton by an eighteenth-century candle-maker. She had been born and raised there, had been loved by parents and grandparents, and by a wonderful sister who had died suddenly after being thrown by her pony.

So alone. In this hollow, musty house, there was just Lucy, suitcases in another room, a rickety chair, and a pile of money in a bag. The rest of her fortune was abroad somewhere. Glenys, her only friend, was in charge of all that. A marriage like Lucy's had attracted few visitors, and she had confided in no one beyond Glenys Barlow. 'I'm a millionaire,' she advised the ornate marble fireplace. Yet she felt poor. The bulk of her fortune had been salted away, but Glenys trusted whoever had handled the money, and that was good enough for Lucy.

She stood up and walked round her seven-bedroom terraced mansion. It overlooked the Mersey, a solid house that was huge for one woman. But she wasn't going to be idle. She needed just one bedroom and a tiny boxroom for an office. So there were five spares, an en suite bathroom for herself, and two further bathrooms for guests. Bed and breakfast, she had decided. Perhaps she would install a few more en suites, but that wasn't important yet. Or she might live downstairs – there were enough rooms to create a bedroom and an office on the ground floor, plus a shower room that would take a corner bath at a push. A fresh start, people in and out of the house all the time – that was a wonderful prospect. Also, it was a beautiful house.

Its listing was Grade Two, and a planned fire escape for the rear had been approved. It was an adventure, she told herself repeatedly. How many women her age got to have a brand new experience, a fresh start? She must remain positive, needed to stop looking over her shoulder, because the bad times were gone. 'You have moved towards something,' she said quietly. Even softly spoken words bounced back in this hollow house. It would be all right. It had to be all right.

She didn't know where the shops were, had no real idea of the community into which she had moved. Crosby was supposed to be posh, though she had already heard Liverpool accents thicker than her grandmother's porridge. The few people she had dealt with had been straight and businesslike, so she wasn't worried about living here.

It was just lonely. 'You're used to loneliness,' she told an ancient, pockmarked mirror. 'You've always been lonely.' Yes, the real poverty in her life was isolation. To attempt a new start in an unfamiliar place in her fifth decade seemed a mad thing to be doing, but there was no alternative. The children might have talked her round. Especially Lizzie, who had occupied from birth the position once held by Diane, Lucy's dead sister. While Lizzie loved her mother, she adored her dad. And Lucy almost worshipped the daughter she would miss beyond measure. A shining light at RADA, Elizabeth Henshaw was beautiful, gifted, and had a promising future in the media. Diane had been like that – singing, dancing, writing little plays. Lizzie would live the dead Diane's dream of performing in theatre, and—

A huge van arrived from Waterloo Furnishings. For the better part of three hours, Lucy leapt from room to room while carpets and other floor coverings were laid. Upstairs was to be left for now, as most of it needed painting and decorating, so the decision was made – she would live downstairs.

At the end of it all, she threw herself into an armchair and opened a bottle of red wine. After a couple of glasses, she made a decision and picked up the phone. She had changed her mind, and she burdened Glenys with a terrible chore. The cat was to be kidnapped.

Glenys Barlow was very taken with Stoneyhurst. 'It's palatial,' she declared after dumping Smokey on a brand new leather sofa. 'All the mouldings and cornices are definitely original – just look at that fireplace! This is Georgian at its grandest. There's a summerhouse – and have you noticed the light on the river? Oh, this is simply spectacular.'

But Lucy was too busy nursing her cat to reply. Until he settled, Smokey needed to regress and return to the cat litter of his youth. He was a Bolton cat, a Lancashire cat, and he might not understand the mewlings of foreign felines from Merseyside. Smokey, a pedigree blue Persian, was only too well aware of his superiority. At Tallows, he had enjoyed total freedom, since the estate had been big enough for him to come and go as he had pleased – would he get used to being downgraded to a mere terrace? 'Poor puss,' Lucy whispered. 'But I'm here. We'll get used to this, I promise.'

'You're not listening,' Glenys accused her.

'Sorry.'

'He was pissed.'

'Who was?'

'Your husband. He was sitting outside near the conservatory, and there were quite a few empty cans on that wooden table. He was talking to himself. I saw his lips moving.'

'I can build a wire roof over the back garden. Then at least I'll be sure you're safe, old lad. I know you've had more space, but this will turn out to be a good move, just wait and see. At least you'll get your dinners. Just you and I, eh? The two musketeers.'

'What?' Sometimes, Glenys failed to hold Lucy's attention.

'He wouldn't have fed Smokey,' said Lucy. 'And with Lizzie and the boys away for the summer, I thought I'd better have him here with me. I should have brought him with me yesterday, but I was in too much of a hurry to look for him. Alan had phoned to say he was on his way. Sorry, I wasn't listening.'

Glenys shrugged. 'No problem – I'm used to you. You owe me for the cat carrier – he wasn't too happy about being shut in there, by the way. He was sitting on a gatepost – I think he was waiting for you – so he was easy to catch. I had a quick shufti down the side of the house and saw Alan in his cups. He was away with the fairies, in a right mess.'

'Did he see you?'

Glenys chuckled. 'The state he was in, he wouldn't have noticed Big Ben on wheels, let alone a little fat woman with a cat carrier.'

Lucy nodded thoughtfully. 'This is where it gets difficult, Glen. Can you write to the children? Get the letters posted in London or Birmingham or somewhere – anywhere but up here. Don't sign. Or get a clerk to do it – you're used to fooling people, it's your job. Tell them Smokey's with me, and they aren't to worry. Don't use your letterhead or the kids will mither you to death. I don't want them going back to Tallows and searching for the cat.'

'The kids are your weak spot, Lucy.'

'I know. I sent notes to tell them I was going, but I didn't give much of a hint as to why. I posted them to

11

where they're spending their summers, but I also left copies at Tallows. They say one thing and do another, these students. They could arrive home any time, so I had to cover all possibilities. It's tricky.'

'You really should keep your distance for months, if not years. Well, you shouldn't – you know how I feel about that. They ought to have the complete truth, you know. He'll fill their heads with nonsense, paint himself in shining armour and blame you for bankruptcy, abandonment, theft and just about anything short of murder. You'll come out of it blacker than hell, while Alan's going to–'

'I know,' Lucy repeated. 'And when they've all finished with exams and what have you they can be shown copies of the truth if I so decide. Until then, it's enough for them to have an absentee mother – the rest can wait. I don't want them confused. Let them blame me for now.'

Glenys disagreed, though she had voiced her opinions too many times. The Henshaws' offspring should be told everything right away. Even now, Lucy was placing herself on a shelf marked *Unimportant*, was allowing herself to wear the villain's hat. But the urge to speak overcame Glenys yet again. 'What if Lizzie leaves RADA to come home and look after her dad? What if Paul gives up pharmacy and Mike abandons his history degree? That husband of yours can't even boil an egg. One or all of the kids might decide to stay at home to take care of their father.'

'They won't give up their education.' Lucy placed the cat in a brand new basket bought this very afternoon from a place on St John's Road. The shops she had discovered were brilliant, the people had been helpful, and life had worn a pretty dress today. This was a good place. It had welcomed incomers for centuries, and all were treated the same. She had been told how to get to Bootle Strand, to Sainsbury's, to a Tesco on the Formby bypass. 'Yer'll be all right, queen,' one old lady had said. 'We've our fair share of criminals, like, same as everywhere else, but you'll settle.'

'So you're going to live downstairs?' Glenys asked.

'I think so. I can let six rooms, but the boxroom's like a big cupboard. That can be for linen – towels and sheets and so forth.'

'Right. And you won't go back to nursing?'

Lucy smiled and shook her head. 'I'm hardly up to date with current practices, am I? If I returned to hospital nursing, they'd need to retrain me for years – not worth it. And I don't think I could stand the noise. No. I'll live and work here, and I'll employ a couple of locals.' A tanker was drifting into port. The new owner of Stoneyhurst stood at the window and watched the scene. 'I'll be fine here,' she said. 'When I stuck that pin into the map, God must have guided my hand. The river's so peaceful.'

Glenys Barlow made no reply. The Mersey was a notoriously changeable body of water. It had swallowed whole houses in its time, but there was no point in mentioning that. She had done her best to persuade this client and friend to be more open about her intentions, to sue the bastard she had married, but Lucy was stubborn enough to stick to her guns. At least she held the guns, and all were fully loaded. With that, the lawyer was forced to be satisfied.

*

Lucy decided to make her apologies before chaos began. She penned notes to neighbours on both sides, informing them of her intentions and promising that noise would cease by five in the afternoon, and would not begin until after nine o'clock in the morning. Since they had raised no objections when advised by Glenys of Lucy's plan to open a guest house, she hoped they wouldn't be fazed by the promised disturbances, but she was determined to be polite. As an invader, she needed to be courteous.

After posting the notes, she returned to Stoneyhurst, pausing for a moment to admire the heavy front door. This was a well-built house, which description could scarcely be applied to the flimsy structures her husband had erected all over Lancashire. He was a cheat, a liar and a fraud, and she was by no means his only victim. Once his houses started to fall down, he'd be up to his neck in the smelly stuff. He would kill himself, though not quickly; he would drink until he fell into the grave.

So here she was: new beginning, clean sheet, to hell with him. Bed and breakfast was no easy option, though. Already, there were fire regulations, a possible inspection of the kitchen, and a list of dos and don'ts as long as her arm. She could do without upsetting the neighbours, and—

No sooner was she back in her own hallway than the doorbell rang. She turned, re-opened the door she had just shut behind her and found a tall, handsome man outside. Without saying a word, he grabbed her hand and pulled her down the steps. Was she being kidnapped? Was the cat shut safely in the kitchen? But no, Lucy was dragged into the house next door, so it wasn't kidnap. At last, the man released his hold. 'Can you deal with the top half?' he asked breathlessly. 'It was a pretty bad fall. I'll get her legs. There's nothing broken.'

A woman lay on the parquet floor. Nearby, a walking stick had fallen next to a coat stand, while slippers had clearly parted company somewhat abruptly with feet and with each other, as one was near the cane, while the second had landed against a door in the opposite wall. The woman was sweating profusely, and her spectacles, their lenses misted over, were perched at a rakish angle on her face. 'Hello,' she said. 'I'm Moira.'

'Louisa, but usually Lucy. I take it you've fallen downstairs? How many stairs?'

Moira nodded. 'Four or five. He can't manage me any more. Not by himself, anyway. He's getting older and I'm getting fatter. It's the bloody steroids.'

The he in question sighed heavily. 'She won't do as she's told, I'm sad to say. She just wants to make me look a failure, don't you? Why don't you shout when you need help?'

Moira giggled like a child. The sound didn't match the body on the floor, as this was a woman well into middle age, yet she acted like a young girl. Lucy thought she knew the reason. It was, she suspected, an attempt at bravery, a stab at separating the illness from the sufferer. Moira wanted to be seen as a person rather than as a bundle of cells attached to some disease, so she giggled and tried to stay young and well in her head. Sometimes, life was excessively cruel.

Between them, Lucy and the man dragged the patient to a sofa. 'Dump her here,' he said almost cheerfully. 'I'll nail her to the blessed couch – it's the only way, I'm afraid.' He stood back and placed a hand on the mantelpiece. 'Lucy,' he said, 'thank you for the note. Feel free to make as much noise as you like, because you'll keep this one awake during the day, then I'll get some sleep at night.'

'Cheeky bugger,' said Moira. 'It was you kept me awake when we were first married, eh? It's the other way round these days – and no sex, Lucy. Who wants sex with a woman who's doubly incontinent?'

The intruder felt her cheeks reddening. Scousers, she was discovering fast, were very open. They called a spade a bloody shovel, and if someone disapproved, they could dig with their bare hands. 'I . . . er . . .'

'Multiple sclerosis,' said the husband. 'I'm Richard Turner.'

'Dr Richard Turner,' announced his wife, who was still prone on the sofa. 'But he can't cure me. Can you, Rich?'

There was tension in the room, and Lucy sensed it more acutely with every passing beat of time. It was as if Moira blamed her husband for her condition, yet . . . yet there was a kind of love here. But physical love could no longer be expressed, and the woman was upset, while the man was probably frustrated.

'Surgery and waiting room are at the other side of the hall,' he explained. 'I have to work from home, since Moira can't be left to her own devices.' He glanced at his wife. 'You can see for yourself what happens if I close my eyes for a moment.'

'What about your home visits?' Lucy asked.

'A nurse comes in sometimes to cover for me,' he replied. 'And we have a cleaner built like the *Titanic* – though I can't imagine any self-respecting iceberg daring to confront her. She's fierce. She's also retiring soon, because this one has probably worn her out. Even the

Titanic goes down. She was a powerful woman till she came up against my wife.'

'Deadly,' agreed Moira. 'Drags me round like a piece of jetsam dumped to make room for something better. You're not from these parts, are you?'

Lucy hesitated. 'Lancashire,' she said.

Moira marked the pause. Because she was confined to a wheelchair, she watched life rather more closely than most, and had become a collector of people. This woman was in trouble. She might well cause trouble too, since Richard seemed quite taken with the new neighbour. Lucy was tall, elegant and well dressed. And she tried unsuccessfully to conceal a chest that was probably magnificent. Richard was handsome, lonely and, at the moment, hormonal. After twenty-seven years of marriage, Moira knew her man well. He needed sex and was attracted to Lucy, who would be living next door. 'Husband?' she asked.

'Deceased.'

The invalid noted the lie. Lucy's eyes betrayed her, which probably meant that she was an honest woman who had been forced into a difficult position. 'Children?' was her next question.

'Grown and flown.' Lucy folded her arms. Over the years, she had been forced to become used to people staring at her upper body. She usually wore loose clothes, but this attempt at disguise could not save her from unwelcome scrutiny. Even the doctor was having trouble pretending not to look at Lucy's 34E breasts. Well, if everyone could experience for just one day the nuisance caused by large mammaries, they'd think again. Bras needed wide straps, because narrow ones dug channels in her shoulders. She suffered backache,

17

neck-ache and even face-ache if she tried to smile through the discomfort. Had she not feared the knife, Lucy would have got rid of her extra flesh years ago.

'Have you registered with a GP?' Richard asked.

'Not yet. But I'm used to a female doctor.'

'My partner's a woman,' he said. 'Celia. She's part time. Not a part time woman, a part time—'

'Doctor,' Moira chimed in.

'Oh. Right. I'll think about it.' Lucy fled the scene and bolted her front door. 'What happened there?' she asked the cat when she reached the kitchen. The cat simply twitched his tail and began a long monologue that was probably a complaint of some kind. 'Oh, Smokey.' Lucy picked up the heavy animal. 'What are we to do?' She didn't want a doctor so close, was worried about having a doctor at all, because they all knew each other, didn't they? And her notes, from Bolton, would very likely say more than Lucy wanted anyone to know.

Next door, Richard Turner stood with his back to Moira and his gaze fixed on the river. He felt as guilty as sin, because he could no longer show love to the woman he had married. She had been a beautiful, tiny girl with a waist so small that his hands had spanned it. The more ill she became, the more he was forced to retreat. He could not manage to desire a person whose soiled underclothing he was sometimes forced to change. And the way she behaved was often embarrassing, as she carried on like a spoilt only child with doting parents who allowed her all her own way. Yet he did love her so much . . . Oh, what a bloody mess.

'Richard?'

'What?' He didn't turn.

'She's got magnificent assets.'

18

'Who?' He knew that the skin on his face had reddened.

'Lucy.'

He lowered his head. He had loved Moira for as long as he could remember – since his teenage years. 'Behave yourself,' he said eventually. 'And stop trying to find concubines for me.' At last, he turned. 'I love you. There's more to life than sex.' That was his brain speaking, but the rest of him craved ... oh, well. Best not to think about all the other stuff. Like the warmth of a woman, the sweetness emerging from between parted lips, his hand on a breast, on a belly– 'There's more to life,' he repeated.

'There has to be,' she replied sharply. 'Because you can't make love to a woman in a nappy. So how have you been managing?'

He shrugged and, as ever, was honest with her. 'A few one-night stands with women I've met online. And a quick fumble with one of the temporary practice nurses – it came to nothing. But it has to be somebody for whom I only feel desire – no more than that. I can't get involved.'

'Why?'

He walked across the room. 'Because you're my wife in sickness and in health, you daft cow – it's in the bloody contract. Because we have three children and, with luck, we'll be grandparents in the fullness of time.'

Moira struggled to sit still. The shakes had started again, and there was no way of controlling her hands. 'I can't feel anything any more, Rich. Only pain, no pleasure. Even if I'm clean, it must be like making love to a side of beef. I don't need to remind you that secondary progressive means no more remissions.' She swallowed with difficulty. 'You're relatively young, and you need to sort this out, prepare for the time when I'm no longer here.'

'Stop this. I mean it, Moira.'

She laughed. 'Is there nothing like a pizza parlour? You know how people phone if they want food – don't they deliver thin crust or thick crust women with or without anchovies?'

When she wasn't being childish, she was priceless. He saw the crippled woman, heard the clever soul within. 'With or without chips?' he asked.

'Without. Get a side salad. So, you want a busty woman with good legs and an undressed salad. Keep your figure, love.'

Sometimes, he needed to weep and scream. He wanted his Moira back, and he knew he would never get that. These days, she was barely capable of swallowing food, and he feared that she might choke to death. Her breathing was impaired and she couldn't walk any distance without becoming completely exhausted or falling on the floor.

'I'll love you just as well if you take a mistress, Richard.'

He was definitely a breast-and-legs man. Lucy Henshaw had two of each, and all four seemed to be in excellent condition. She also wore the air of a woman who had not been touched for some time. Children grown and flown? She didn't look old enough for—

'Rich?'

'What?'

'I just want you to be absolutely sure that whatever, whoever or wherever, I'll understand. But be careful. There's a lot of disease out there.'

'I know.' He closed his eyes and pictured his beloved wife in her wedding gown, plain satin, yellow and white flowers dripping from her hands all the way to her shoes, hair loose in heavy waves down her back. He hadn't wanted her to put it up. The severity of her clothing had served to emphasize that hourglass figure. She had been and would always be the most beautiful bride in the world. It was so damnably clumsy, this wretched disease. Steroids had affected her badly, and she had gained weight at a terrifying rate, so those particular drugs were used only in the direst of emergencies. The problem lay in the fact that emergencies were frequent these days.

Sex had been important to both of them, and fate had now removed any chance of physical closeness. It felt akin to bereavement, because a vital part of their marriage had been killed off by an enemy that could not be defeated.

'Richard?'

'Yes?'

'Don't.'

'Was I thinking aloud?'

She shook her head. 'Only I can hear it, darling. The rest of the world is deaf.' If she tried now, she might manage. Sometimes, her hands were almost cooperative, and she could just about find the strength to use pestle and mortar. Anyway, the coffee-grinder would make short work of it. The happy pills. A sheet of eight was all she needed, but she'd take a damned sight more – who wanted to survive with a buggered liver? They'd need to be crushed, as swallowing was hard and needed concentration. Everything did. People breathed without thinking, ate without thinking, walked and talked without worrying. Sometimes, she didn't even have control of her speech.

She looked at him. Love was a strange thing. It meant needing to die before he did, knowing that she daren't choose an obvious way of self-disposal, because that would break him. Yes, her suicide would kill him, too. And with him being a doctor, the powers could blame him, pin murder via overdose on him—

'Moira?'

'What?'

'Stop it.'

It worked both ways. She could almost hear his thoughts, but he was similarly gifted – or cursed. When it came to theory, Richard was of the opinion that every man and woman owned his or her own life. Suicide was not always wrong, and he was of the school that approved of assisted and heavily supervised exit.

But when it came to Moira, he was seriously prejudiced and out of his depth. He knew that the time had come – he would have to hide her drugs. And he suddenly thought again about the theory of dignified death. As long as it was someone other than Moira, it was a good idea. Yet all those someones had relatives who didn't want the sufferer to kill him or herself. He'd been wrong. Again.

'I don't want to die in Switzerland,' she said. 'Or to endure a life in a wheelchair with my head clamped back so that it won't droop, and a tube into my stomach, and oxygen on tap—'

'I know, love.'

He didn't know. No one could possibly understand the dread that accompanied her from day to day along the pathway to perdition. It was hard work pretending not to care, carrying on as if she'd never felt better in her life. Only another sufferer would have an idea of the thoughts that circled in her head like buzzards searching for carrion. And there was more than one way to skin a cat. It didn't need to be pills, didn't need to be here. But it had to be soon, while she could still drive her motorized chair. The Liverpool–Southport line had three or four level crossings nearby. No one would blame him if she arrived home squashed. It needed to look like an accident. He would accept an accident.

'Don't leave me, Moira.'

She grinned. 'Remember the first time I went out in my trolley? I ran over a traffic warden, a woman's shopping and a post office. Mind, the post office hardly had a dent in it. I wish I could say the same for the warden's foot and that poor woman's eggs.'

He left the room. She could hear him sniffing back tears in the hall. Then her eyes closed and she was gone. They were running into the sea in Cornwall, chasing waves, being chased by waves. Every night in that huge hotel bed, talking, loving, talking again. And all the time, something followed them. Sometimes it was a shadow, a pale thing that hung back whenever she turned. But it grew. It came closer, its colour darkened and consumed her, and she was back in Liverpool with the children and . . .

'Moira?'

She woke. He gave her a cup of tea. Well, half a cup, because she spilt so much if the cup was full.

Richard averted his gaze, because he didn't want her to see the fear in his eyes. She wasn't simply falling asleep any more; she was losing consciousness, and occasionally she stopped breathing. There was no help.

Men walked on the moon – there was money and research enough for that. Moira walked on planet earth scarcely at all, and any possible cure or remedial treatment for multiple sclerosis would be paid for mostly by charities. Somewhere, someone had their priorities wrong.

The rage lasted for more than three days.

Cheated and abused by his own wife, Alan Henshaw tore up the few clothes she had left, burnt the wedding album, dug up her old man's roses, contacted his daughter, and drank himself into near-coma. His wife would come back, he told himself in rare brighter moments. Lucy had nobody apart from her children, and she would be back. The woman hadn't the guts to go it alone – she would need to come back.

Wouldn't she? He had made her money grow – what the hell did it matter whose account was whose? As for the rest of it – his wanderings and his mistresses – what the buggery had she expected? Since the birth of Elizabeth, his wife had been as warm as a butcher's freezer, as responsive as a corpse. And he liked younger, firmer flesh, which was quite normal in his scheme of things. Successful men needed variety, because variety was the spice of . . . something or other.

But, on the fourth day, when all the booze had gone, and he returned to a more normal frame of mind, he had to admit that he was beaten. Her solicitor, contacted by his, had outlined the whole damned mess, and Alan had no leg to stand on. The house was hers, as were the heavy mortgages he had obtained via fraud. Except they weren't hers, because she hadn't signed for them. Three handwriting experts had declared Lucy Henshaw's signature to be forged, while a neighbour who had witnessed one of the documents admitted that Lucy had not been present at the time.

It was the end of the road for Alan. If he fought, she would walk all over him. If he didn't fight, he might as well be dead. Could the children save him? How much of the stolen money had she given to them? It wouldn't be enough. All he owned were twenty plots of land in Bromley Cross, a set of plans, and the clothes in his wardrobe. She, of course, would get away with the crime of forging his signature if the case went to court. She was a lady who had married a rogue, and the forging of his signature had been necessary so that she could take back her own money.

At the back of his mind lingered the suspicion that the land and the plans might well belong to her, so he'd have to find out about that, too. If he tried to sell to another developer, Lucy might decide to relieve him of everything.

A letter arrived. He tore it open so viciously that he had to piece together its contents in order to read them. She was being magnanimous. He could hang on to the Bromley Cross project and find investors, or he could sell it on. How kind of her. *The bills are in your sock drawer* ... and his socks had been salvaged. That had been no easy task, since he had never before used a washing machine, even when sober. The socks proved one thing, though: she was capable of playing dirty. That quiet housewife had a temper. She wasn't perfect.

The bills are in your sock drawer. It was a large drawer. As voluntary company secretary, she had always dealt with bills. Jesus, he was probably in debt to every supplier within a twenty-mile radius. Even if he could sell on the plots and all approved plans, he'd probably still be penniless. A clever bitch she'd turned out to be, little Miss Top Heavy with her high-priced clothing, perfume, footwear and designer handbags.

He should go and see Mags before the shit hit the fan. She was his kind of girl, reed-slim, small-breasted, a teenager's body with the brains of a businesswoman. Three shops she owned outright, and she was only thirty-odd. London-trained, Mags also had franchises in department stores all over the place, because she was good at what she did. Yes, she had borrowing power. When it came to competitions, her firm had won cups in every area of beauty, from hairdressing to make-up and nails. She was his only chance.

It was time to clean up the act. He stank of sweat and whisky. So he bathed, then showered, shaved, dressed and came downstairs to think a little further before turning for help to his current paramour. There would be a divorce, of course. Unreasonable behaviour leading to breakdown of marriage, and he could not contest it, so he'd just have to grin and—

Elizabeth ran through the hall. 'Daddy?' she shouted. 'Daddy, where are you?'

Oh, God. This was all he needed. 'Library,' he called.

She almost fell through the doorway. 'What's happened?' she cried, throwing herself into his arms. Her world had shifted on its axis. Lizzie now realized that Mother had been both anchor and safety net, and she wasn't here any more. Whose fault was it? What had caused her to disappear so suddenly and without warning?

He placed her in a chair. 'Your mother's buggered off,

26

that's what's happened. She's left without so much as a by-your-leave.'

'Where? Why?'

Alan shrugged. 'God knows. I told you on the phone to stay where you were, because there's nothing any of you can do. I don't know where she is, don't know why she did it. There's no money – she's taken the lot.'

Lizzie swallowed. 'All of it?'

He nodded.

She could scarcely believe this. Mother had always been scrupulously fair and honest. Perhaps she was having some kind of breakdown. Women of a certain age seemed to suffer until they got through the menopause. 'She's set up an account for me. And she's paid my fees and my rent for as long as I'm in London. The boys will be finished at uni in about ten months, so they probably got a little less. She's always been like that, Daddy. Always fair.'

Lost for words, he simply grunted.

'The house?' she asked.

'Hers, and mortgaged.'

Lizzie's jaw dropped slightly. 'But she would never risk Tallows, Daddy. That's totally out of character. This house was in the Buckley family for generations—'

'It had to be done, Lizzie. The firm was going under. There was no alternative.'

She sat perfectly still for several seconds. 'Where is she?' she asked again. 'What have you done? Daddy, I demand to know where my mother is. What have you been up to? Is it another of your women?'

Heat flooded into his face. 'What on earth are you talking about?'

She tutted. 'Daddy, everyone knows – it was the talk of our school, especially when you started messing about with the chemistry teacher. I'm not apportioning blame, but Mother wouldn't just go off like that. It isn't in her nature. She'd put up with just about anything – she has put up with an awful lot just to keep Tallows. I'm not daft. I know it's partly, if not totally, your fault.'

He mumbled something about Lucy having changed.

'We all change,' came the reply. 'Otherwise, I'd still be in a pram, while you'd be existing in a two-up-two-down at the wrong end of Deane Road. But my mother is not a bad woman. She wouldn't steal and run unless she had a damned good reason. What happened?'

He offered no immediate reply.

'Daddy, no matter what, I'll always forgive you.'

She wouldn't. He was damned sure she wouldn't. 'Lizzie.' Her name arrived on a sigh. 'I can't explain. I came home early after a meeting, and she'd disappeared with most of her clothes. The cat was still here, but that disappeared the next day . . . or the day after . . .'

'You've been drunk.' This was not a question. 'And you haven't fed him, so—'

'A letter came,' he said. 'She has the cat. There are letters for you and your brothers, too. Posted in Bristol. She wrote in my letter that she'd sent copies to wherever you were staying, as well. Aren't the boys in Chester with Billy Maddox? Weren't you in Somerset?'

'Yes. I got mine. It said very little. Then we spoke on the phone and you were drunk again, so . . .' She paused. 'But Mother wouldn't go as far as Bristol. She's a northerner to the core. She wouldn't even move across the Pennines, and well you know it.'

'No, but she'll have made sure they had the wrong

postmark. It'll all have been done through Glenys.' As soon as the words were out, he wanted to bite them back. Lizzie knew Glenys – the whole family knew her. 'Though I think your mother may have gone to a different firm,' he added lamely.

Lizzie walked to the window. 'Grandfather's roses,' she said. 'Why have you dug them up?'

'Temper,' he admitted.

'That was a wicked thing to do.' She turned and glared at him. There was more to this than he was willing to admit. Her mother was neither a bolter nor an adventurer – she was a reasonable, quiet and fairly gentle soul who looked after everyone except herself. 'Is Tallows to be sold?'

'I expect so.'

She sat down again. The man who had been a wonderful daddy was clearly a poor father. Those golden days of childhood, the memories she treasured, were untrue. Because he was untrue. Something enormous had happened while she'd been away in Somerset, and she intended to get to the bottom of it. 'No matter what, I shall always love you,' she said softly. 'But I fear I may stop liking you.'

'So you're on her side?'

'It isn't a case of sides, Daddy. It's to do with trust and truth. This was Mother's house long before she was born – it's been in her family for a very long time. She would have sold every stick of furniture before mortgaging Tallows. It would be out of the question.' The contents of Tallows were worth a small fortune.

He could not meet the gaze of his own daughter.

'Well?' Her fingertips tapped on a table. 'Well?' she repeated.

He looked at his watch. 'I have an appointment,' he announced. After planting a kiss on the top of her head, he left the room.

'I'll find out,' she called after him.

The only reply was the slamming of the front door.

She stayed where she was for almost half an hour, then she picked up the phone. Some kind of decision needed to be made, and she was the only one here, so it was up to her. When the connection was made, she spoke briefly to Glenys Barlow.

'But you can't,' Glenys said, when she had finished.

'I must. Find somewhere, Glenys. I mean it.'

'But you'll need help, Lizzie.'

'Then send some. Now.' Lizzie replaced the receiver. Sometimes, she reminded herself of her father – barked commands, refusals to listen. Arrogance. She knew where his attitude came from, because he'd risen from nowhere, and many folk who climbed through life on the backs of others developed bad habits. It was as if he had to remind himself that he was a self-made man, one who had escaped the slums. But he wasn't self-made. He had reached his zenith via Mother's family name and money. Anger simmered. Yes, she was very much her father's daughter.

It was her father's daughter who filled a fleet of four large vans with antiques and other items she knew her mother would miss. It was her father's daughter who followed those vans to a secure lock-up in Manchester. She had one key, while the owners of the unit held the other. Both keys would be needed to access the storage space. She paid two months' rent in advance before going home to wait for her father to return.

Tallows looked grim. Furniture was sparse, and where paintings had hung, cleaner wallpaper and paintwork screamed, 'Look – you've been burgled again.' But Lizzie didn't care. She was her father's daughter, and she would sit on a fortune until she got the truth from whatever source. Even the attic had been emptied, because Lizzie knew how much her mother loved all that silly stuff.

The silly stuff and furniture was worth a packet – the insurance premium was high, because well over a quarter of a million pounds' worth of items had travelled to Manchester today. Her father didn't know the value of the things that had provided his environment for over twenty years. Who had said that? Was it Oscar Wilde? She couldn't look it up, because all the books were gone. But she was fairly sure that it was Wilde. A cynic was one who knew the price of everything and the value of nothing. Hey-ho. That was her beloved father to a T.

When Lucy entered the house, she knew that the phone had been ringing. It was as if it had left a sound-shadow in its wake, a trace of itself that clung to walls and furniture. She went into the kitchen, placed her purchases on the table, splashed her face with cold water, and picked up the cat.

He told her a very long story that was probably connected to confinement, homesickness and complaints about the neighbourhood.

'Shut up,' she whispered. 'I've been to Liverpool. It's brilliant. I think it's going to be City of Culture soon. The shops are marvellous, Smokey. Good clothes as cheap as chips, lovely shoes, fabulous hairdressers. And

I bought a book about its history. They're so ... lively. Mind, I might have done better with an interpreter, but what the hell? We live and we learn.'

The cat struggled until she released him. He was a spoilt brat, and she should have been a firmer mother to him. She watched while he stalked off, ramrod-straight tail twitching in anger, every hair bristling. Well, he had better get used to things, because she was going nowhere.

But she did go. She went into the pages of a book that told her about cellar dwellings, poverty beyond her ken, dockers queuing in all weather for work, Irish immigrants, Paddy's Market, ragged urchins who had survived war and gone on to become remarkable people. This was where Bolton's cotton had come in from the southern states of America, where oranges and bananas were offloaded along with pineapples, grapes and fine wines. She read about children who had drowned in vats of molasses or rotting fruit. Lucy learned in half an hour what many Liverpudlians took for granted. This was a unique and wonderful city. Its people had made it so.

The phone rang. Engrossed in a chapter concerning the development of the city's famous waterfront, Lucy was reluctant to reply, but she did. It was Glenys.

'She's what?' Lucy yelled.

'Hang on, love. I don't want my eardrum split, thank you very much. I'm sorry, Lucy, but she made sense. I tried to contact you several times before, during and after the event, but—'

'But I was in Liverpool.' In town. She had to learn that Liverpool was town. And now Lizzie was kicking up a fuss. 'Where's she put it all?'

'A place in Manchester. She filled a fleet of vans, and she did it for you, Lucy. So much for the kid who loves her daddy, eh? When I asked, she said she wanted everything kept safe in case he flogged the lot.'

Lucy swallowed.

'She misses you, sweetheart.'

'I miss her. Paul and Mike, too. But they outgrow us, Glen, and we must outgrow them. I suppose she did what she saw as the right thing. In fact, she did what I ought to have done and didn't dare.'

'Well,' Glenys sighed, 'I've done my bit. Why didn't you answer your mobile?'

'I forgot it again. I know, I know – I'm hopeless. But you must come and stay. I have to show you the shops and the restaurants – awesome. Oh, and I found—'

'Lucy?'

'What?'

'Shut up. I've a client waiting.'

Smiling to herself, Lucy replaced the receiver. After a few moments, she moved back to the kitchen, picked up her book and opened the door for the cat. 'Go on,' she urged.

He sat there, a very dramatic tail waving angrily back and forth. Used to the larger life, he was not pleased about the massive cage that kept him safe.

Lucy had another few words to say. 'We're all in prison, puss. Even our own bodies are containers. You have to deal with it. So do I. Now bugger off and chase butterflies.'

He buggered off.

Lucy sat with what she knew was a silly smile on her face. Lizzie, a daddy's girl, had grown up sensible and decisive. She saw a need, and she filled it. Elizabeth

Henshaw had come down not on the side of her mother, nor in support of her father. She had simply removed valuables to a safer place until life became slightly less confusing. 'You're a mixture of me and your Aunt Diane,' Lucy said softly. 'Pragmatic, yet creative.' Yes, Lucy had given the world a marvellous woman, and two young men who were decent, funny and industrious.

'So I can't have done it all wrong, can I?' Forcing herself to be fair, she admitted inwardly that Alan had been a good dad when the kids had been small. He'd dragged them all over the place, had taken them camping, fishing and sightseeing. There was good in everyone, and that fact should never be ignored.

There was one thing about which she would remain immovable, though. According to Glenys, Lucy owed nothing, a fact that could be proved beyond a shadow of doubt. The house was hers, and she would keep it. Alan Henshaw would have to leave Tallows. That wasn't cruelty; it was common sense. And she carried on reading about the city she intended to adopt.

Two

Margaret Livesey did not suffer fools gladly. She was known far and wide throughout the beauty profession as a hard woman, one who would threaten to sack a first-year or an improver for a badly folded towel or an untidy shelf. And she had the complete measure of her current lover, one Alan Henshaw, property developer, cheat, liar and womanizer par excellence. He was her temporary squeeze, no more than that. She enjoyed his company, but he had suddenly disappeared off the face of the earth, so he'd probably moved on to a newer model with a better chassis and automatic transmission. Which was all right by her, because she had stuff to do. He wasn't the only one who ran a business, and it was time he learned that.

Today, one of the new girls had scalded her hand and needed treatment, while a sink had started to leak halfway through the afternoon, so Mags was not in the best of moods when Alan rolled up at her house in his BMW. 'Huh,' she mumbled under her breath. 'No word for ages, and now I suppose he wants a red carpet. Tough. He can bog off, because I have had e-bleeding-nough.'

She'd been trying to reach him for several days, but

his mobile had been switched off, and she never phoned his house in case the wife answered, yet here he came marching up her path as if everything in the garden might just be perfect. He was like that. Thought he was pivotal, a fulcrum around which the rest of the world must travel in a direction dictated by him. If he was all right, everything was all right. Well . . . just let him start, because she was fit for him at present. One wrong word, and she'd probably crown him with her best Kathy Van Zeeland bag. Would he improve her day? Was her mood picking up?

It wasn't. She had to dash round all her shops and franchises this month, because she'd been offered a healthy sweetener to try out some new French products, and she never looked a gift horse in the mouth. For the sum promised, she had guaranteed that she would train her staff personally in the use of the new line, so she was packing when her lover arrived. 'Where the bloody hell have you been?' she snapped. 'Did Paul Daniels make you disappear just like that? It's been like trying to get through to Buckingham Palace.' She picked up a pair of patent leather shoes, breathed on them, and rubbed them along the front of her tabard.

Alan bit his lip. This looked like a promising start, didn't it? 'Ill,' he replied after a pause. 'I've been ill and in bed for quite a while. It's been a difficult time.'

'Too difficult to switch your phone on? Too much trouble to be bothered about me?'

He nodded. 'Rough stomach. She probably had a go at poisoning me before she buggered off.' He sighed heavily and shook his head.

Mags paused, a pile of underwear in her hands. 'What? Lucy? Did I miss an earthquake or something?

Because it would take something pretty dynamic to shift her. I thought she was part of the fixtures and fittings round at your house.'

'She's gone. And don't ask me where, because I've just been through all that with my daughter.' He watched while she placed clothing in her case. 'Going somewhere? You've still got the tan from Crete. You don't need another break yet, surely?'

Mags glared at him. 'I'm going anywhere and everywhere. Tête à Tête has sent me the Nouvelle Reine regime, and I've promised to be on site every time it's introduced. So I'll start with my franchises in the south and work my way back up country. I would have told you on the phone – if you'd ever bothered to answer it. But you didn't, so there you are. I'm off soon, and I wasn't able to give you the statutory month's notice. Sorry, boss.' Did he even notice the sarcasm?

'Oh.' He sat down. 'When will you be home from your travels?'

A jagged nail caught in the fabric of an underslip, so she stopped to do a bit of remedial work with a crystal file. 'I've been thinking,' she said. 'I need to live sort of halfway between here and the rest – Jenny can take over at this end. I thought Coventry. Because if I'm going to make a proper go of it in London, I'm living in the wrong place. There's a gap in the market just outside Coventry, and a nice little property with a flat upstairs. So I might move. It makes a lot of sense. That's why I was trying to phone you. I wanted to tell you, save you the bother of driving all the way out here.'

He opened his mouth, but no words emerged. The wife had done a disappearing act, his daughter was proving difficult, and now Mags was preparing to leave without a backward glance. He was ruined. In the blink of an eye, he had gone from riches all the way back to rags. And that had always been his greatest fear, because he'd made the steep climb, and it was a long way down to near-serfdom.

'You look like a bloody goldfish,' she remarked, painting Pearl Envy over her repaired fingernail. 'Look, Alan – we were never going to be for ever, were we? I'm not the type to settle down, and I thought I'd already made that plain. Domesticity is not my scene.'

'But I love you,' he declared. 'And I'll be free soon. I'm not letting her get away with this – not bloody likely. I'll divorce her, and she can lump it, because I'm not being messed about by anybody.'

She laughed. 'Alan, you love the one you see in the mirror every morning. That's why Lucy's upped and offed – you've never thought beyond your penis. I mean, lighten up, lad. We had good sex, and that's all it was. Come on, no need to be so down in the dumps. You'll soon find somebody else to tickle your fancy.'

He closed his eyes for a few seconds. There was a lot wrong with women these days, and he didn't know who to blame, what with the Pankhursts, Barbara Castle, Margaret Thatcher – the world had been going stark, raving bonkers for almost half a century. Yes, the lunatics had taken over the asylum. 'So this is it, then? We've come to the end of the line?'

She shrugged. 'I'll be back every six weeks or so. And there'll come a time when I won't be able to manage on my own – this is turning into a company and, while I have good people in all my units, I'll need help at top level – somebody else like me who's been trained by the best. When that happens, I can sit back a bit more. But I have to work, Alan. We both do.'

Work? He was finished. She was on her way up, while he was about to hit the basement. How much lower could he go? Back to the bottom end of Deane Road? Not likely, because he'd helped demolish those slums, hadn't he?

'I might just be able to grab a girl schooled by Herbert of Liverpool. Imagine that. She's having to move with her husband's work, but I must get in fast. She'll be good. He's the best trainer in the north. That girl might well be the sort I can use at management level, you know.'

He didn't know. He'd never heard of Herbert, but she was rattling on about hair extensions, individual false lashes, a treatment that could make nails four times stronger. Pity she hadn't used it on herself, because then she'd have more time for his problems instead of messing around with varnish and files.

She studied him. Had the news of her leaving the area hit him badly? 'What's the matter?' she asked. 'You look like you've lost a quid and found a bent penny. Straighten your face before the wind changes.'

He swallowed hard, because he was ingesting pride as well as saliva. 'She's cleaned me out, Mags. Everything was in joint names, and she emptied the accounts while we were in Crete. I've no idea where she is, and I don't know where to start when it comes to sorting out the—'

'Call the police. Have her found. She can't do that and get away with it.'

He wiped a hand across his damp forehead. 'She can. Something in the small print, something my bloody lawyer failed to see.'

'Then sue him!'

'Sue a flaming lawyer? Come on, Mags. You didn't arrive with the last shower of rain. It would be like giving a copper a black eye. Wrong target.'

Mags dropped on to the sofa. 'What about the house? Surely you own half of that?'

He gulped again. 'Technically, yes. But it's been in her family for generations, and she's mortgaged it to the hilt.'

'Bloody hell.' She leaned back and stared at him. 'You've still got Bromley Cross.'

'Have I? She's paid no bills for months, so I must owe a fortune. I'm in a trap of her making, love.'

Silence reigned for several seconds. 'If you've come here for help, Alan, there's nothing I can do. I'm still at the ploughing-everything-back-in stage. By the time I've paid rents and wages, I'm—'

'Yes, but if you sold up, you could be my new business partner. In fact, after I've gone bankrupt, the firm would have to be in your name. Then, once we're straight, we can start again with your salons.'

She laughed. 'Not on your nelly, mate. I'm a beautician to the bone, so I've no intention of burying myself in concrete and the like. Alan, I'm walking my own walk, not some man's. It's nothing personal, but I've never wanted a permanent relationship with a bloke, because I don't see the point. I hate kids, I like to live alone, and my business is my life. I aim to retire early, live on some Mediterranean island, and catch up with all the books I've never read. Sorry.'

They were all at it. Created for the purpose of nurturing human life, they were carrying on as if they were men. His daughter was promising to be the same, all career and no obstacles. Men were becoming toys, and people had a tendency to grow out of their playthings. Panic gripped his chest, and a pain shot down his arm. Bloody angina. While she went to put the kettle on, he took a pill. Between them, Lucy, Elizabeth and Mags were killing him. He didn't want to go home. Home? He had none. He didn't want sex, either. 'Is it all right if I sleep on your sofa tonight?' he asked when Mags returned. 'I can't face the drive back.' He couldn't face his daughter, either; didn't want to see anyone.

'Don't be daft. You can sleep with me, as usual.'

He shook his head. 'Stomach's still a bit gippy,' he said. 'Best if I stay in here.' He couldn't have managed sex, anyway. Sex had been one of the rewards due to a successful man. And the successful man had died.

After a sleepless night, he let himself out of the house and drove away. He crossed Mags's name off the agenda as if she had been no more than an item on a shopping list. In Bromley Cross, he parked and studied the legend on a huge hoarding – *Henshaw Developers, 20 Detached Residences.* His phone number was up there. And his metaphorical number was up, too. The office in town would have to go, as would he. My ticker won't take much more of this, he thought. He'd been ordered by the hospital to slow down, but he hadn't known how. A lad from the slums had to keep running at all costs. Filled with self-pity, he went to find something to eat, since food had always been a great comfort.

At a small café in town, he bought a forbidden breakfast, all the way from two eggs through sausages, bacon, fried bread, and right down to black pudding. He had nothing to live for, so what did it matter? Like Lucy, he needed to disappear.

Shirley Bishop, who was about fifteen years older than Lucy and on the brink of retirement, was certainly built like a battleship, if not quite on the scale of the *Titanic*. At five feet and ten inches, she towered above most women, and her girth probably matched her height. Her husband, Hal, whom she adored in her way, was at least six inches shorter than she was, and he might have disappeared had he stood sideways behind a lamp post. But he was a strong little chap, and he proved himself by working as a more than adequate gardener.

But the Bishops were about to move to a little retirement home on a site near the Lake District. Shirley had looked after Moira since her illness had worsened, and Lucy made up her mind that she would find a replacement for her, since Moira was clearly unfit to be left to her own devices for any length of time. It was a project, and Lucy looked forward to tackling it. She had something to do, something on which she could focus, and that made her existence worthwhile.

Lucy was beginning to teeter on the brink of contentment. Life was noisy, and she didn't always have vital stuff like water and electricity, but the place would come together eventually. Nipping next door became part of her routine. At first, she went to 'borrow' water whether she needed it or not, but it was clear that she required no excuses. Moira, on good-hand days, was teaching Lucy how to paint in watercolours, how to do crochet and tapestry, how to knit complicated patterns. There was so much life in Moira on her better mornings that she lifted the spirits of all who came into contact with her.

Bad times happened. She got double vision, the shakes, searing pain from top to toe and, on one occasion, had to be held by Shirley in an upright position while Lucy unscrewed a towel rail in the shower room, because Moira's grip on it could not be loosened. When she finally dropped it, she began to laugh and cry at the same time. 'See? He could have divorced me for that. I was well and truly having an affair with that bloody thing.'

Lucy held her till she was all cried out. Shirley, who was supposedly a hard case, went into the hall to blow her nose rather noisily.

Lucy followed her when Moira was safely seated. 'Don't worry,' she told the large woman. 'I'll get somebody – I promise absolutely.'

'I'm frightened for her,' Shirley whispered. 'I feel terrible about leaving, but—'

'But you have your own life, I know. Look, I haven't been here long, but I think the people in these parts have specially built huge hearts. Somewhere, there's another like you who'll care about her. And I'm here, love. As long as I'm here, she'll be all right. Cross my heart.'

'And hope to die?'

'And hope to die. Dry your face – you don't want her to see you like this, do you?'

Anyone and everyone connected to Moira was affected by her bravery. This, Lucy decided, was how Liverpool people dealt with stuff. During the second war they had been as feisty as the Cockneys, because they faced life and death head on – always say the words, don't hide away, speak your piece. They were beyond price. Somewhere, there would be another Shirley Bishop who would take over the care of Moira.

This was a bad lunch time. While Richard was out on his rounds, Moira lay stiff as a board on a three-seater sofa, every muscle tensed, fingers twisted into positions that should have been impossible. The usual nurse was away on holiday, and Shirley Bishop was in sole charge.

So Lucy did what she had done for her father towards the end of his life. For over an hour, she massaged the poor woman with cream made in part from the New Zealand green-lipped mussel. 'I know I'm hurting you,' she said. 'But bringing oxygen via blood into the area will do no harm if it does no good.' It worked up to a point. Nothing could re-sheathe an exposed nerve, but blood flow helped the pain. At the end of the session, both women were wet through and hot, but Moira was somewhat better. Gratitude shone from her face.

'You're a healer,' she said, her eyes full of tears and sweat. 'You have warm hands. Look.' She held up ten unknotted fingers. 'You'll have to work on Richard's frozen shoulder. Physician heal thyself? He couldn't cure a bloody ham in a smoke house.'

Lucy had to laugh. There seemed to be an eleventh commandment in these parts – thou shalt show love for thy partner by winding him/her up. And perhaps a twelfth ordered them to say the exact opposite of what they meant.

Shirley was doing it now. 'Oi, soft lad,' she screamed through the kitchen. Soft lad was her beloved Hal. 'Don't put it there, it'll get no sun. She's grew that from nothing, she's grew it by hand from a seed.' That was the thing about Scousers, they were full of love. It was an upside-down-ish love in the way it was expressed, but it was real none the less. There'd been nothing wrong with Bolton. The grammatical errors were different, but just as amusing, and, had Lucy lived with someone other than Alan, life might have been as good as this. But she had already begun to feel affection for this large village in Sefton, North Liverpool. Living as she did on the cusp between Crosby and Waterloo, she enjoyed a choice of shops and restaurants together with a beach, a good enough library and a cinema saved by the local people, who owned and ran the business. They had guts, and Lucy admired them greatly.

'Will you do it?' Moira asked while Lucy waited to cool down.

'Will I do what?'

'His shoulder.'

'Now? I'm exhausted, Moira. It'll take an effort to walk home.'

'Not now. Tomorrow.'

'It depends on what's happening next door, and when he has patients and visits and so forth.'

There were some things Moira couldn't say after so short an acquaintance. Had she felt able to tell Lucy that she wouldn't fear death half as much if someone might look after him ... but no, she couldn't do that. He was an adult, he was a doctor, and he would have to cope. All the same, Lucy was so right for him.

A few lost days followed Alan's encounter with Mags. He didn't want a repeat of the third degree from his daughter, so he booked himself into a small hotel on Chorley Old Road, ate infrequently, drank whisky while awake, and never changed his clothes. When the owner of the establishment had received several complaints about the smelly drunk in Room Five, she told him to go.

So he drove, in his cups, all the way up to the home he no longer had. It was a noisy journey, and a sound akin to screaming was getting on his nerves, so he was glad when he reached his destination, because he was beginning to see flashing coloured lights. Had the Martians finally invaded? He was definitely unwell, he decided, as he pulled into the driveway. He needed his bed, headache pills, a bottle of Johnnie Walker, and a bit of peace and quiet.

The noise stopped, and trouble began. Boys in blue told him he smelled like an open drain before insisting that he blew into a tube. He blew. He blew all the way to the rooftops, shouting about his wife, his daughter and somebody named Mags. 'They don't give a sodding damn for anyone, these bloody women. Sick 'n' tired,' he slurred. 'Bin a good dad. Short of nothing, my kids. And now? I'm buggered. Do you hear me? I haven't a leg to stand on.' He stumbled, thereby proving his statement to be true. 'We have to find out how to do clo . . . clon . . . cloning, then we won't need women at all.'

'Blow now, into this tube. Did you not hear our siren? Did you not see the lights on our car, Mr Henshaw? You were winding along the road like a snake escaping from a bag.'

He tried and failed to focus. 'Do I know you?' he asked, attempting a friendly smile.

'Not yet, sir. All you need to understand is he's the brains and I'm the looks. And we're both in better nick than you appear to be. You have to blow into the tube.'

46

'Why?'

'Because you're tired and emotional, and because I say so.'

'You said that without moving your lips.'

'I said nothing, sir. It was my partner.'

'Was it? Clever, that.' Alan moved in closer to his captors. 'They're taking over, you know. They are definite ... definitely taking over all the time and every bloody where. They get in when we're not looking.'

'Do they, sir?'

Alan nodded rather vigorously, lost his balance, and had to be stabilized by the officers. 'See, they're even in your lot. They've infil ... infilter ... they've got in all over the bloody shop.'

'Little green men? Pink elephants? Mr Henshaw, you are drunk, and we've followed you all the way through town.'

'Even govern-er-ment. They crept in. Like the cat in the crypt ...'

'If you say so, sir. Now blow.'

'Crapping 'n' creepering out again. All over us. We're covered in it.'

'Yes, we can smell it, Mr Henshaw. Now blow, or it's a blood test down the cop shop.'

He blew. When he'd finished blowing, he collapsed and lay in a senseless heap in the gateway of Tallows.

'Hell's bells,' said one of the officers after looking at the registered reading. 'He's got a bit of blood in his alcohol. This is beyond us, Pete. If he dies in our car or in a cell, we'll be filling in forms from now till the middle of doomsday. I'm calling it in.' He reached into a pocket, took out his radio and ordered an ambulance.

Pete stayed near the body. 'Still breathing, just about.

47

I don't know about a bender – this one looks to have been on the big dipper. Property developer, he is. My brother bought one of his houses up Breightmet way. It's crap.'

'Is it? Why, what's up with it?'

'What's right with it would be a shorter list. Like we're still waiting for the windows to fall out.'

'Really? That bad?'

'All the electrics are up the spout – the sockets fell out of the wall after a couple of months. Still under guarantee, so this fellow sent somebody round to fix things. Then the roof leaked, and they found some felt was missing. You name it, it happened. Great big crack down the gable end – my brother's still waiting for reinforced foundations.'

'Aye, so is this bugger. No visible means of support, has he?'

Alan opened one eye to find a pair of people looking down at him. Oh yes, he had gone down in the world.

'Don't move,' said one.

'I can't,' he replied. This admission was followed by a loud breaking of wind together with involuntary urination. A slight smile of relief visited Alan's face for a fraction of a second. Then he passed out again.

The ambulance arrived. 'Jesus,' gasped a paramedic. 'I've come across some smells in my time, but this takes the full beef curry plus a distillery and bad eggs. Has he peed himself?'

The officers nodded.

'Give me the reading.' He took the breathalyser. 'Dear God, he should be dead. Is this his house?'

'It is. You should see the ones he builds.'

'Try to find the relatives, will you? He's so tachycardic, he could do with a fifth gear. Neck brace and back board,' he ordered the rest of his crew. 'Get some fluids up on the hook and prepare the paddles. This fellow could have an infarction any minute. What a bloody mess.'

Pete looked at his mate. 'Just like an episode of *Casualty*, isn't it?'

'Or *The Muppet Show*,' came the reply. 'Come on, let's find this bloke's poor family.'

But there was no one in the house. While the ambulance screamed away down the road, the pair of constables pressed their noses against the windows and decided that someone had done a flit. They saw patches on walls where paintings had hung, scars where furniture had rested on carpets. 'Can't blame them, Andy,' said Pete.

Andy shrugged. 'Right. This is a job for the boys out of the blue – let's see what CID can make of it. I'm going for me dinner. That old soak's already taken up more of our time than he deserves.'

Lizzie Henshaw finally tracked down her brothers in Chester, where they were happily lazing about on the river Dee in a work-shy little boat named the *Jupiter*. Lizzie had always considered Jupiter to be a rather dynamic name, but this craft was lagging well behind when it came to dynamism. At the pointed end, it had a bit of space for a couple of chairs and a small table, which left just about enough room for someone to steer. Inside, there were padded benches on which the twins often lounged or slept, but the boat wasn't built for living on. That didn't bother them. It was summer, they were on the loose, and all they required was the company of each other and plenty of beer.

'Ahoy,' she yelled foolishly from the bank.

'Lizzie!' answered Paul. 'Stay there and we'll come and get you.'

There followed a flurry of activity that was testament to their lack of experience in the area of seamanship – or rivermanship. They were hopeless. It was their ineptitude that made Lizzie love them as much as she did, because they had failed magnificently at so many useless and pointless activities. Archery, fencing, rugby, riding, rock-climbing, football, tennis – all these hobbies had proved disastrous, because they simply weren't co-ordinated. They were brilliant, the best brothers in the world.

Lizzie scrambled aboard. 'Have you two been picking up your letters from your friend's house? Have you had anything from Mother?'

Mike shook his head. 'Nope. Bill buggered off to Paris with some big bird from Manchester, and his parents are in the States till the end of September. We've been living on the river.'

'But the *Jupiter* isn't built for living on. She's just for messing about in.'

'We've done that as well,' Paul admitted. 'The secret is not to get completely sober, then you don't care about living on shop-bought pies and chips.' He focused properly on his sister. 'What's the matter, Liz? You're not yourself.'

She perched on one of the rather unstable chairs. 'Mother's gone.'

'Gone? Where? She's not dead, is she?' Paul's face was white.

'No, no – nothing like that. She's set up bank accounts to get you two through uni and me through

RADA, then she took all the company money, all Daddy's, all her own, and mortgaged Tallows from cellars to attics.'

A long silence followed this statement.

'Never,' said Mike at last. 'You know Mums. She's too gentle and straight to do anything like that. I mean, look how he's treated her over the years. If there's a bad bugger at Tallows, it's him, not her. He's feckless, sis. And an alcoholic.'

Lizzie, her father's favourite, had always hated to hear anyone speak badly of him, yet she knew, deep down, that their mother had always been the backbone, the quiet, even-tempered core of her childhood. It was Mother who had mended broken toys, bathed sore knees, made everything right. He had seldom been there. Because his presence was infrequent, his returns to the fold had always been celebrated. Looking back, she knew that Alan Henshaw had made himself the hero of the piece, since he turned up with toys, played games, and filled the house with laughter. Yes. He did all that before buggering off yet again. 'He made himself special,' she wept. 'And made her dull. She was just there, then he'd come home, all joy, laughter and Liquorice Allsorts.'

'He never took us in,' said Paul. 'Mike and I weren't impressed. And don't blame yourself, Liz, because girls are always fastened like glue to their fathers. I think it's in the rules somewhere.' He stood at the helm of his frail little craft. 'What shall we do? Where do we live? I know we're adults, but this sudden insecurity is not comfortable, is it? We don't belong anywhere.'

She shook her head before mopping up the tears. 'Financially, we're OK as long as we get work after finishing our courses. She waited till we were old enough. That's my belief, anyway. And I've emptied the house until we manage to find out what's happening. Our father's too daft to realize that the contents are worth more than a quarter of a mill – possibly even up to a half. I didn't want him selling stuff off for peanuts. He did a disappearing act, and I came here to find you two. I just didn't know what the hell else to do.'

'Where is she?' Mike asked.

Liz shrugged. 'Everything's gone – clothes, passport, jewellery. But I believe she's got the cat, so that makes me think she's still in the UK. The police won't be interested, because she's old enough to do as she pleases. They don't bother unless foul play's suspected.'

'Where've you put the stuff from the house?'

'Somewhere called Secured4Life dot com. Manchester. I paid some rent while we try to work out what's happening. She never bad-mouthed Daddy, you see. It would have been beneath her. I can't think of her as a thief, either. So until we know the truth, I've stashed what could be moved. I couldn't work out what else to do.'

'He blames her.' This, from Paul, was not a question. 'I'd bet my honours thesis that it was the other way round. He'll be the culprit.'

Liz's phone rang. She dragged it from her pocket. 'Yes, this is Liz Henshaw. What?' She looked at her brothers. 'Right. We'll get there as soon as we can.' She closed the phone. 'He's in hospital with alcohol poisoning. The magistrates will have his driving licence if he survives. A nurse found my number in his mobile.'

They stood for a while in a quiet huddle, all sharing one thought. Mother would have dealt with this. Mums always handled everything, but her mobile phone was probably at the bottom of the Croal, and she would have bought a new one. Her old number was announced by the server as unreachable. They had lost their female parent, and her partner was probably bankrupt and definitely in hospital. Life had gone crazy, and they clung together like three lost children.

'Right,' said Paul. He was the tougher of the twins, so he would dispose of the *Jupiter*. 'Mike, you go with Liz. You're in no fit state to tie up what's left of the bloody boat. I'll follow. What a mess. Alcohol poisoning? Huh.'

In Liz's Micra, she and Mike made the journey to the Royal Bolton Hospital. There was very little conversation at the beginning of the drive, as he remained shocked, while she had said most of what she'd intended to say. Strangely, she couldn't quite manage to worry about Daddy. Mother was the bigger concern, since her behaviour was so untypical, so drastic. 'I'll bet you Glenys knows where Mother is,' she said eventually.

'And I'll wager she'll keep her mouth padlocked,' was her brother's reply. 'She's a lawyer, so she has to be trusted.'

'It could be the menopause,' she said. 'Mother, I mean – not Glenys.'

Mike stared at the road ahead. He'd watched his mother watching his father. For years, he'd caught a glimpse of something or other. Hatred? No, not quite. It was as if Dad didn't deserve any strong emotion from her, as if he'd always been a waste of space and oxygen. Contempt was the nearest he could come to describing his mother's expression. 'I think she'd been planning it for a while,' he told his sister. 'She wanted us all on our feet, you see.'

'Why would she do that, Mike?'

'Because she's wonderful. Your eyes were clouded by Dad, Lizzie. He was excellent with you, because he likes pretty things. But she was always there for all of us. Never judged us, never berated us unless we were in total breach of contract. Even then, she took care to tell us what was wrong with our behaviour and why.' He sighed. 'I feel like an orphan.'

'Dressed like that, you look like one.' This effort to lighten the atmosphere in the car failed completely. 'Mike, there's nothing we can do to mend any of it. She'll come round. She'll get in touch. Mother's not the type to let people down – far too decent for that sort of thing. I know this much – she must have been very hurt, because she loves Tallows. I find it difficult to accept the idea of her borrowing against the house. She'd have sold some of the contents if she'd needed money so badly.'

Mike nodded. 'There's more to all of this than meets the eye. I don't trust him, Lizzie.'

She didn't trust Daddy, either. But she couldn't quite manage to say that out loud, not yet, anyway. 'Here we are,' she said as she pulled into the car park. 'Let's go and look at the damage.'

The drama began at about five-thirty in the afternoon. Glenys phoned. 'Lucy, don't start panicking, but Paul sank the boat on the Dee. He was plucked out by a couple who were fishing, and he's in the Countess of Chester hospital. He wasn't too bad, because he was joking with them about weighing him in as the biggest fish ever caught in those parts. Lucy?'

Lucy's jaw seemed to have run out of oil, because it took several seconds for her to speak. 'You sure he's all right?'

'Lizzie says he is. It was she who phoned me. She's at the hospital here in Bolton, because Alan went on a giant bender, and he's suffered two minor heart attacks this afternoon. Mike's gone to be with his brother. So. What do we do now?'

Lucy's front door opened, though she scarcely heard it. 'I'll have to go to Chester. I can't leave my son like that, can I?'

'No. They're your weak spot, as I've said before, and I'm glad they're there. Paul's in no danger, but if his accident brings you to your senses I'll be glad. It's about time somebody knocked a bit of grit into you. They're your children for always, Lucy. When they're fifty, they'll still be your babies. Heart attacks aside, you should come clean and sue the bugger.'

The call ended, and Lucy burst into tears. She'd never been much of a weeper, but her little lad had almost drowned, and the shocking news had cut deeply into her maternal core. She hadn't been there for him, for any of them. Glenys was right, the three of them would be her children until the end of her life. It was nothing to do with age.

'Lucy?'

She looked up. 'Richard.'

'Whatever's the matter?' He lifted her from the chair and held her in his arms. 'Come on, love. Tell your Uncle Richard – I only came in to thank you for straightening out her indoors. What's happened?' She felt wonderful, smelled delicious. She wasn't like his other women, because she would become serious business if anything delightful were to happen.

And it all poured out, half drowned by tears. Her husband wasn't dead, though he seemed to be working

55

hard to get to the hereafter. Her son was in hospital after an accident on the Dee, while her daughter was with Alan.

'Your husband?'

She nodded against his shoulder. 'For twenty years, he— That doesn't matter now. I have to get to the Countess of Chester hospital. I meant to keep my distance during the divorce, you see. I wanted all the dirt out of the way, but—'

'But accidents happen. I'll drive you to Chester.' It was plain that he intended to take charge. He planted her back in the chair and picked up her phone. He spoke to someone and asked to be put through to Dr Beddows. 'Charlie? Yes, it's Rich. Look for a young man name of . . .' he covered the mouthpiece and waited until Lucy had given the name, 'Paul Henshaw. Went down with his ship on the Dee. Yes, yes.' He waited.

Lucy almost smiled. There was none of the captain in Paul, but there was plenty of the comedian in him, just as there was in Richard Turner.

'Thank you,' he said before placing the phone in its cradle. 'Under observation, no apparent damage except to his dignity. He says the effing boat was an effing death trap, and he wants his mother. I shall make sure he gets his mother, though I hold out no hope for the craft. It's flotsam, I'm afraid.' Richard went to talk to his wife.

Lucy wiped her face. Twice today she had heard from Glènys. As the lawyer had expected, Tallows was one hundred per cent Lucy's. So there would be no need to repurchase it, as all fault lay at the door of the building society and at Alan's feet. Or his hands. His hands had done the forging. She could go home. Did she want to go home? No. She wanted to see her son, and she mustn't think beyond that.

This second call had frightened Lucy. All three off-spring were past the cuts and abrasions that were part and parcel of childhood, yet they remained vulnerable. Now, Alan. Did she care about him? If she didn't, why was he sitting in the second row of her brain, just inches behind her waterlogged son? Why did the word 'duty' remain on her agenda where he was concerned? She would not worry about him, as he wasn't worth the energy. Heart attacks, though . . .

Richard led her to his car. 'It won't take long,' he assured her. 'And we know for a fact that he's in no immediate danger, so don't worry.'

'Thank you.' The man was the embodiment of everything her parents had wished for her, but she had rebelled, and . . . If she hadn't married Alan, she wouldn't have had Paul, Michael and Elizabeth. But if she'd married a doctor, her parents would have been pleased, might have lived longer and been a great deal happier.

'Lucy?'

'Yes?'

'Why did you escape? It was an escape, I take it?'

She sighed heavily. 'I thought they were old enough to manage without me. As for my husband, he's a fraud, and I was one of his victims. In truth, I was his main victim. He took my money, then mortgaged my family home.'

'Without permission?'

'He thought I didn't know what was going on. I kept quiet for the twins' and Lizzie's sake. Alan is an angry man. I didn't want the children to be caught in a battle. So I came here as soon as they seemed old enough. But

I know now that if it all ends up in court, none of us is old enough.'

'Why here?'

'A pin in a map. The pin stuck in the Mersey, actually, but this was the nearest land, so here I am. And it's all going terribly wrong. My bankrupt husband has got himself thoroughly drunk and is in hospital. He's had two heart attacks, and the next may be his last. If he stops working, he'll die. If he continues to work, he'll die, but he'll be happier.' She sighed heavily, her breath escaping on a sob that made her shiver.

'A mess, then.'

'Yes.'

He parked the car outside the hospital. 'Lucy, it's not your mess. It seems that you've been the peacekeeping force for long enough. Get a clear idea of what you want from life before starting to cobble together a plan for the man who hurt you, and for children who are grown. Right. I'll stay here while you visit, then I'm taking you home. It's time I had a look at your blood pressure. Go on, now. Shoo!'

He watched as she walked away. She was a lovely woman, bright, sweet-tempered and considerate. And she was built like a perfect Venus, good legs, beautiful hair, excellent teeth and … Moira was right. It was impossible to describe Lucy without reference to her magnificent bosom. Yet while he and most other men would like to bury their heads in her magnificence, she also brought out the paternal side of him. She needed looking after. But he had never been unfaithful to his wife. Small dalliances didn't count. As long as he didn't get involved, he was merely relieving himself of some tensions. This one was different.

Anyway, Lucy, too, was married. He found himself hoping almost desperately that she would not return to Bolton, that she would stay and continue her friendship with Moira, who was definitely benefiting from the new contact. It didn't matter as much for him, he repeatedly told himself. Moira enjoyed and needed Lucy's company. And that was all there was to it.

Alan Henshaw, who was a substantial figure of a man, had shrunk considerably. Or perhaps it was all the tubes, wires and machinery that made him smaller. The equipment seemed to be the size of a small symphony orchestra, while the soloist at the centre of it all was diminished by the plethora of pipes and bells with which he was surrounded. His heart was being monitored, and his blood pressure was taken automatically at set intervals. Fluid dripped into his body from above, and trickled out into a bag fastened to the side of his bed. Many of these appliances gave out beeps, alarms and ticking sounds, while the person at the centre of all the drama never so much as blinked.

Freddie Mercury singing 'I Want to Break Free' popped into Liz's head from time to time. Her dad was in there somewhere, and he needed to break free. His stomach had been pumped and, after tests and close examinations, the liver had been declared fit to be used to sole shoes. It didn't look too promising. She didn't want Daddy to die.

His nurse, a plain-spoken woman, arrived to make a routine check. 'Don't worry, love,' she said. 'I've seen worse than this walk out on its own two feet after a few days. Mind you, if he doesn't come off the sauce, he'll probably bleed to death. Get him to sign into a clinic.

He needs weaning off before he goes into a proper nose-dive. Cholesterol's in the hills, heartbeat irregular but settling, and he has a chance if he avoids booze and stress.'

'Then that's no chance,' Liz replied. 'He has a first class honours in stress, and while he's awake and breathing, he drinks. Looking back, I can scarcely remember an evening at home when he didn't have a whisky tumbler in his hand. Hopeless.'

The nurse wrote something on a chart. 'Aye. It's a bugger, isn't it, love? I married a boozer, but I soon got shut. He was more pickled than a jar of silverskin onions, and nasty with it. He came home one night, put the chip pan on, forgot, fell asleep and burned my house down. I was on nights, fortunately. They got him out. The insurance covered the mess, but I wasn't insured against him, was I? So I got rid. Of him and the chip pan.' She left the room.

Lizzie stared down at the creature on the bed. This used to be her father. This used to be the man who'd taken her and her brothers to Alton Towers, to Blackpool, Southport, the Lake District, Florida, France, Italy and Spain. Mother had just tagged along like a nanny, while he had provided all the entertainment. 'Mother read a lot,' she said to the figure and all his machines. 'She stood back and let you take the credit for all of it. But Paul and Mike weren't taken in. They knew she was head and shoulders above you. But I love you. I shall always, always love you. Silly man. You have to wake eventually. You have to face up to what's happening, Daddy.'

Being a woman wasn't easy. The first man in a girl's life was eternally forgivable, but suitors and husbands weren't. 'If a man treated me like you treated her, I'd be in jail ten times over.' She was starting to think deeply about her mother for the first time ever. How had she coped? How had she kept all that anger inside, all that frustration so well hidden? And why had she taken all the money, why had she mortgaged a house so precious to her? It was all so ... extraordinary.

'Have you been telling us lies, Daddy?' she asked.

A light came on, and a loud, continuous note sounded. Lizzie found herself out in the corridor. The crash trolley was rolled in, and staff shouted orders like 'Clear', and 'Charging to two hundred'. They were bringing him back. Well, they were trying to. The child in Lizzie sat with a bunched fist pushed against her mouth, because she would not scream. Brave little girls didn't scream when in hospital, at the dentist's, at the doctor's surgery. 'Don't leave me, Daddy. Please don't go.'

The plain-spoken nurse appeared. She looked hot, as if she had been in a Turkish bath. 'He's back, love. Go home. Get some sleep.'

'I can't,' she replied. 'I just can't do that.'

The nurse sat down next to Lizzie. 'Your brother didn't stay long.'

'No.' Liz inhaled deeply. 'He's one of a pair of identical twins. The other one fell into a river – he's in the Countess of Chester.'

'Bloody hell! More than your fair share of trouble, then. And your mam? Where's she?'

'No idea, but if she's heard about what's happened she's probably at the Countess of Chester with Paul and Mike. She ran away, you see. Just upped and offed with her clothes and every penny in the bank. No warning. It was like a magic trick but without the smoke.'

61

'I don't blame her. I told you what happened to me, eh? Women don't bolt unless they're pushed into it. You've got to start thinking about it from her point of view, love. Your dad will either live or die. He's committing slow suicide. She's probably wanting some space for thought, a break while she starts divorce proceedings.'

'Divorce?'

'Aye. She's gone to start a new life, sweetie. Some women just go – they need to get away *from* whatever. They go when they're in the middle of making dinner, ironing, washing or some such drudgery. Usually younger than your mam, though. Mid-forties, is she?'

Liz nodded.

'So she's not running *from*, she's running *towards*. But I'll bet you a pound to a penny she thinks she's run away rather than towards.'

'Towards what?'

The nurse shrugged. 'If she's thought on this for a while, and if she's taken money, she'll be after a new start. Without realizing it, she's gone for a fresh beginning. I reckon your dad's behaviour has been like water dripping on stone. It takes a while, but the stone starts to get affected. Your mam was being worn down bit by bit, you see.'

Alone once more, Liz went outside to try to reach Mike on his mobile. He answered. 'Lizzie, Paul's all right.'

'Is Mother with him?'

'Yes. She's been given a mattress to lie on, and she's taking him home tomorrow. Well, home to her new place.'

'Where?'

'Liverpool.'

'Oh. And where are you?'

'Standing right behind you.'

She turned and punched him playfully. 'So you've brought my car back, at least.'

'And how's the real invalid, Lizzie?'

'He died again, and they brought him back again.' She paused and put away her phone. 'Somewhere along the line, a huge amount of truth has gone for a walk. She's protected us, and in doing so she's protected him. Well, something like that.'

It was plain that Lizzie was coming round to her brothers' way of thinking. 'You've been aware all along,' said Mike. 'But your daddy made you into a princess, and that blinded you. I know you're not a lot younger than us, but we've been privileged, because we each had the other to talk to. We worked him out a while back. He uses cheap labour and cheap materials. When the houses start to fall down, he'll wish he had died, because there'll be a lot of people on his tail.'

'That's horrible, Mike. We don't want him to die. Do we?'

He shook his head. 'But we want Mums to survive. He's been drinking her life blood along with his Scotch for long enough. I know now, Lizzie. Mums and I went for a coffee, and she told me. Everything. She was her usual self, no anger, no resentment. The facts are plain. He stole every penny left by the Gramps. He acted exactly how they had expected him to act when they warned her not to marry him.'

Liz gulped.

'He mortgaged and remortgaged the house.'

'How?'

'Forgery. He forged Mums's signature and probably

63

some of the witnesses' too. If he lives, he has a lot to face. He has a ton of unpaid bills. The land he bought at Bromley Cross may just cover his debts, mortgages included. That was why she let him keep that project. Even then, at the end of her marriage, she looked after him.' He hugged his sister. 'There is no woman in the world like her. With the exception of you. We are fortunate. God gave us our mother's temperament.'

Lizzie sat on a bench, and her brother joined her. Both remained deep in thought for several seconds. Then Lizzie spoke. 'I wonder what she'll do with Tallows? It's a lovely place, and it shouldn't be left to rot.'

He shrugged. 'I was talking to a bloke in the car park at the Countess of Chester. He was going to take her . . . home, but she asked me to tell him she was staying the night with Paul. Richard Turner, lives next door to her, has a disabled wife. Mums gave her a massage, and it helped. He's a doctor. He told me Mums is starting a bed and breakfast business. Seems she's no intention of going home to Tallows.'

Lizzie nodded thoughtfully. 'Perhaps she'll do the same with Tallows – turn it into a hotel of some kind.'

'Who knows, sis? The only thing that's plain to me is that she won't live with Dad again. All those years she just waited and said nothing – Jeez.'

'Then she took her money back.'

'She did. And she took into account inflation, the wages he never paid her for handling paperwork, the damage he did to her standing in the community. She says he built new slums with her dad's money. There's no lack of brain in her. She just bides her time.'

'She knows he's ill?'

'Yes.'

'And she doesn't care?'

He thought about that. 'She does – that's the daft part. She phoned the Bolton hospital at least twice from the Countess of Chester. But she did say he's his own worst enemy. Very plain, she was. She said a man who drinks like that, who eats like that, and has sex all over the place can't expect to see old age.'

'Phew. That is plain for Mother.'

He stood up and opened a door. 'Come on, kid. Let's see if the lion's started to roar again.'

Three

Mike and Liz returned after a further couple of nights to a very bare-looking Tallows. Liz, who had tried hard not to think about the emptying of the family home, burst into tears when she saw the results of her hasty action. 'I shouldn't have done it,' she moaned. 'Just look at it – two chairs and a sofa. It looks like an empty barn. Poor, abandoned old house. It's as if no one loves or wants it.'

'I hope you left the beds and bedding,' he said drily, a twinkle in his eye. 'After sleeping on a mattress on the floor for two nights, we need proper beds. And, now that Dad's managed to live for forty-eight hours without the need for jump-leads, perhaps we can have a bash at getting back to normal. Come on, sis – no need for tears.'

Normal? Liz could scarcely remember what the word meant. Her father was a cheat, a fraud and a liar. He was very ill, could die at any moment and, if he did live, would be able to do next to nothing. Mother had bogged off because he'd stolen all her inheritance and mort-gaged a valuable house. How could anything ever be normal again? About one thing only she was certain. Whatever happened, she would carry on at RADA. She wanted Royal Shakespeare, and nothing less would do.

She dried her eyes and grinned. Who was she trying to kid? Anything would do as long as there was an audience. Even a TV advertisement for pile cream would—

'Beds, Lizzie? You know – the things people sleep on? Do we have some? Or have you mothballed them, too?'

'Oh, sorry. The bedrooms are exactly as they were, apart from some of Mother's French stuff and a couple of armoires and things from the guest rooms. But it looks all wrong upstairs as well. It's strange. It's not home any more, is it? You think you're grown up, then stuff like this happens, and you realize you're still a kid that needs its comfort blanket. What sad and sorry creatures we are.'

'It will be all wrong without Mums,' he said. 'OK, so my car's in Chester, as is Paul's, because Mums took him back to her other place – he says it's great, by the way. Anyway, you're the only one who's mobile. Tomorrow, we bring our mother home. We can't leave this place empty. It needs her – let's face it, Mums *is* Tallows.'

Liz sat down. 'Be careful, Mike,' she said. 'Whatever you do, try not to take her for granted, because she's changed, and that change has taken a lot of doing. She's achieved it quietly, slowly and secretly. Don't for one moment imagine that you know what's best for her. You sounded like Daddy just then. Being a man doesn't mean you know what's right. She's been walked over all her life, and I feel ashamed, because I should have noticed. Since she fled, I've been thinking about her, about the life she's led, her patience, the way she tolerated Daddy. She's a bloody good woman, Mike. Give her respect. Respect means not telling her what to do. Understood?'

67

He placed himself in the other chair. 'She can't let him live here.'

'Look, she can do exactly as she pleases. If he gets out of hospital in one piece, Mother will decide what to do – if anything. She owes him very little. It's the other way round, isn't it? He owes her. That quiet lady we lived with is still there. But behind the softness there's a brain, and she planned all this. Not the heart attacks – she wouldn't harm a flea. But the great denouement was arranged by Mother.'

Mike allowed a tight smile to visit his face for a second or two. 'Denouement? Anyone listening might think you were a drama student.'

She jumped to her feet suddenly. 'Oh, my God,' she yelled. 'I've an audition tomorrow, so I can't come with you. I'll be in Manchester – Summer Theatre in the Park, which means it will probably be a very wet affair. You see, I need it for my portfolio, real experience. Someone fell ill, and I'm trying for her part. Sorry, mate. I'll drop you off at the railway station, but I can't go to see Mother and Paul. The best thing might be for you to go to Chester by train, get your car, then drive to Liverpool. But I can't come. I have to take every chance. Mums drummed that much into me.'

'Good thing I reminded you then, airhead.'

She wagged a finger at him. 'You start telling my mother what to do with her life, and you'll have me to answer to. I'll deal with you, I promise, and I won't be kind. We may have inherited her temperament, but I think I've got his temper without the "ament".'

'Fate worse than death, being dealt with by you, little sis,' he remarked as he left the room. 'I promise I'll be good,' he called over his shoulder.

Liz stayed where she was for a while. Tallows was a house that could never have been termed cosy, because it was rather grand. Robbed of much of its furniture, it was about as welcoming as an oversized cold store in the middle of winter – what the heck was Mother going to do with it? It was becoming plain that an ideas woman had sat behind the docile wife, just waiting for the right time, the right chance. 'Tallows can't be left to rot,' Liz whispered. 'And she'll know that. She'll think of something, I know she will.'

She walked through four huge reception rooms, on to orangery, library, kitchen. By most people's standards, this was a huge house. The entrance hall alone could have accommodated a sizeable family, and the Henshaw children had taken for granted that games of hide-and-seek were special in their young lives. Paul had once spent the best part of a day in a bedding chest on a landing. He'd been discovered only when he'd come up for air.

'Wonderful house for children,' she whispered. But was it? Whenever she thought about marriage and a family, she saw herself in a more conventional place, hopefully in London and near to a park in which children could play. She liked tall, thin, London terraced properties with the kitchen in a basement below those tortuous flights of stairs, a walled rear garden, bedrooms on two upper floors above the living rooms.

After digging in her capacious bag for an elusive bit of paper, she found tomorrow's instructions. Prostitute, heroin addict. Murder victim. Act one only. Oh, well. If she didn't survive to act two, there wouldn't be a lot to do, and the script gave her just a few pages to learn. It was work, and she was determined to have it. In her game, actual employment meant more than any qualification. A curriculum vitae, along with a few photographs, carried a great deal of weight when it came to auditions.

Upstairs, she found a faded denim skirt of which her parents had never approved. Daddy called it a handkerchief, and had been heard to opine that if the skirt were any shorter, Lizzie would need to wash behind her ears. Mother labelled it a pelmet, so it was eminently suitable for the part. A once-white top that failed completely to cover her midriff was also chosen, along with shoes and boots high enough to require planning permission. She would decide about footwear in the morning.

Later, Liz lay in bed. Should she go up for the part? What if she got it and Daddy died and she needed to take time off? And shouldn't she be with him while he was so ill? Her brothers might start persuading Mother to come home. No. She mustn't worry about that, because Mother seemed to have found her backbone at last.

Track marks. What did they look like? Would the girl have them on her arms? Liz leapt up and retrieved a longish-sleeved purple jacket from her wardrobe. That should do it, because it just about covered her arms to below the elbow joints. God, this acting lark was a nuisance. But she wanted to do it. She had always wanted to do it. How far up and down an arm would track marks go? Perhaps she might draw some on her skin with one of those indelible pens. No matter how small the part, every detail must be considered, because this was her future. Acting was everything.

Mother's sister had been the same, though she'd been dead for a long time now. Mother had supported Liz's dreams, whereas Daddy had taken a very minor interest. It was time to thank the woman who had always been there for her. It was time to grow up. Daddy's little girl no longer existed. But oh, how she hoped he would live.

The flowers arrived at lunchtime the following day. An accompanying card bore the message, *Mother, thank you for all your encouragement. I got an acting job in Manchester and I send you all my love and support at this difficult time. Elizabeth.*

Lucy grinned and placed the flowers in water. The past few days had been traumatic, to say the least of it, but she had her boys with her now, and her daughter, the very person from whom Lucy had not expected forgiveness, had sent these beautiful blooms. Yet the dilemma remained. 'What am I going to do about him?' she asked the sink while catching water in a vase. The boys were easy. Noisy work had ceased for a while, and they were sleeping on sofa beds in two of her four ground-floor reception rooms. Even Lizzie seemed to be OK...

Which 'him' was the bigger problem? Alan had heart damage. If he carried on drinking, he would not live to benefit from surgery. Withdrawal from drink might cause a killer heart attack – what a bloody mess. And the other 'him' was having trouble with his shoulder. She was having trouble with his shoulder, because he was gorgeous, interesting and interested. Yet a part of her believed that he was too ... too earthy for her, too needful in the sex department. Women of forty-five didn't start playing the field, surely? Moira was her friend, too.

Should she put this house on the market and go

home? No, no, no. Tallows was her family home from way back, but it had to be . . . cleansed. The place needed to be used, but twenty-odd unhappy years meant that she could not possibly live there yet. The boys and Lizzie all preferred London, so she needed to find a purpose for the house. Left to its own devices, it would crumble its way towards death, so it needed to be used.

She looked out at the garden and caught her sons peering through holes in the fence. Oh dear. More problems loomed, because the Turner girls were home, and the twins were enthralled. It might well be easier to throw in the towel and limp back to Bolton, but she liked it here. The house contained a different history, one that was completely unconnected to hers. Richard Turner could be dealt with; the boys were young enough for dalliances, old enough to cause problems wherever they were. And, deep down inside herself, Lucy had at last found a layer of stubbornness. She was in charge. She intended to keep it that way.

Alan opened his eyes and decided that he was having a particularly nasty nightmare. Perhaps he had opened his eyes only as part of the dream – perhaps he was still asleep, because this could not possibly be real. He didn't want to look, didn't want to hear. Oh, God. Would this suffering never end?

It was real. Yes, she was gabbling on about power of attorney, banks, mortgages, plots and plans. She'd been plotting and planning for ages, but she referred on this occasion to the development in Bromley Cross. She wasn't supposed to be here. He had been expecting never to clap eyes on the bloody woman again. There was no point in closing his eyes and pretending to be asleep, since she had already seen him wide awake. There was more to this one than met the eye, and he was guilty of years of gross underestimation when it came to his not-so-beloved wife.

'Because of your illness, I thought I had better come and see you. After all, letters delivered to Tallows might lie for a while before you get them, so I told Glenys to hang fire. Right. The twenty plots and accepted plans will go some way to covering your debts,' she told him. 'When all your plant is sold, because much of the machinery is quite new, there'll be another chunk paid off. The rest of the mess you made will be dealt with by me. It's my punishment for marrying a bastard, you see.'

Bastard? She never used words of that kind. She even looked different. She looked alive, determined and quite attractive for a change.

'Sign,' she demanded.

He signed. There was no alternative. 'What about me?' he asked almost sheepishly.

She sat down in the visitor's chair. 'Once fit to travel in an ambulance, you are going from here to a private hospital outside Manchester. Easterly Grange, I think it's called. They have all the wiring you're wearing now, plus operating theatres. First, you will be dried out. If you survive that, there'll be heart surgery. If you survive the surgery, you will move to Liverpool. My family will stand a better chance of avoiding this scandal if you're out of the way. The boys may not return to Bolton after university, but we Buckleys have a long and illustrious history in these parts. You've muddied the waters, and you can't stay in the area.'

'It's a long way to fall from a horse as high as yours,'

he warned. She was carrying on like some sort of princess – who the hell did she think she was talking to? But he mustn't get angry. He'd been advised repeatedly against angry.

'Exactly. A great deal further than your recent slide off the back of a Blackpool donkey. I shall sell the plant while the company appears to be a going concern with its leader in hospital due to a temporary health problem that requires surgery. As far as purchasers are concerned, you are going for even newer, better stuff, and your company is thriving.'

He blinked rapidly. This was one clever clogs. Had he harnessed her energies properly, she might have proved a willing workhorse. But she was also an actress, very good at playing a part and hiding her true feelings. She had bided her time, and she had bested him. That was the bit that hurt most – he'd been outclassed by a female.

'Very wise,' he said drily.

'Don't patronize me, Alan. I did my best under circumstances that were never easy for me. The children were my department. I was the dragon who made them eat their greens, sit in a dentist's chair, do their homework. You did the easy bit – the spoiling. Fortunately, it hasn't affected them in the least way. They, too, have survived you.'

'Where are they?'

'The boys are with me, while Lizzie has a part in some play in Manchester. She'll go far.'

'They all will.'

'Yes.' There was no more to be said. She gathered up her power of attorney papers and placed them in a document case. Then she remembered – there was one more item to be mentioned. 'In Liverpool, you will perhaps live in my house. It's in Crosby, actually, a few miles north of the city. You will live not as my husband, but as a non-paying guest. I am turning Stoneyhurst into a bed and breakfast business.'

His eyes narrowed as he studied the compliant, domesticated female who had lived with him for how many years? Was it twenty-three? He nursed a slight suspicion that she had been the source of his children's brains, since he had never been any great shakes when it came to the realms of academia. Mike was to become a teacher of history, Paul a pharmacist, while Liz had her heart set on acting. 'You've got me exactly where you want me, eh?' he said. 'Flat on my bloody back and powerless.'

Her answer was fired back at lightning speed. 'I don't want you at all, if you're looking for an honest answer. And I am divorcing you. However, since you are the father of my children, and as your philandering, drinking and gambling days are possibly coming to an end, I am offering to house you. This isn't out of the goodness of my heart, as you destroyed years ago any goodness I might have owned. I am doing it because it will take you out of Bolton and away from the life you have wasted so far.'

'Quite the bitch, aren't you?' He thought about his socks in the bin, the pile of unpaid bills, some of which were months overdue. There was a streak of badness in her. She was far from the perfect mother she had always pretended to be.

She stood up. 'Yes, indeed. And I advise you here and now to remember that. I find myself capable of going to just about any lengths to curb your activities and to save the reputations of my children. After all, who wants a drunken gambler for a father? Or a man who sleeps around so freely that he might become diseased?' She nodded at him. 'I'll see you in a couple of months. If you're still alive, that is. Good luck – I mean that, Alan. I hope you beat the booze and do well with the surgery.'

He watched her as she walked away. For a woman with so much on her plate, she seemed quite light on her feet, almost jaunty. He had no money, no future, not unless he went cap in hand to her for every little thing. Revenge? Oh, yes. She was an expert at it. It didn't matter now whether he lived or died, because his life was over. She owned him.

Outside in the corridor, Lucy stood still, a hand to her chest. She felt as if she might be the one heading for a heart attack after such a performance. How cool she had been, how decided, how brave. Yet how much it had taken out of her. It was over. She had faced the demon and could begin now to calm down.

'Louisa?'

She felt a hand on her shoulder, turned and saw a face that rang a very distant bell in the annals of memory. For a few seconds, she simply stood and stared until she realized that she must appear rude. He looked a bit like John Lennon, but John was very dead. 'I'm so sorry,' she said. 'I've just been to visit my husband in there.' She waved her hand in the direction of the room she had just left. A name was seeping into her brain. 'Goodness,' she exclaimed. 'It's ... is it? Is it little David Vincent?'

He nodded and grinned almost as broadly as he had at ten years of age. Then he started to laugh at the surprise she was displaying. 'What?' he asked. 'What's wrong with me? Am I a disappointment? Come on, don't keep me on tenterhooks.'

There was nothing wrong with him, but ... 'But you were shorter than any of us – have you been on growth hormones? Gosh, it must be thirty-odd years – what on earth are you doing here?' He had never won a race, because his legs hadn't been long enough. Some of the gang had laughed at him, but Lucy, already showing symptoms of the domestic diplomat she would become, had tried to protect him. 'Why are you here?' she repeated. 'Are you ill?'

'No, I'm begging,' he said. 'I seem to spend half my life begging. Come on – there's a coffee shop nearby. We can't drink the hospital stuff. In my opinion, they use their beverages to finish off any surplus patients. It'll be a government plan to free up beds.'

He led her out of the building and across the road. 'Your face has changed hardly at all,' she told him. 'But I never expected little David to turn into so fine a figure of a man.'

He took her into the shop and guided her to a table near the window.

'Coffee, doc?' the girl behind the counter asked.

'Two, please. I'll spoil myself, cappuccino with sprinkles. Louisa?'

'Lucy. Skinny latte for me.'

Seated at a table with her coffee in front of her, she stared at him. Little David Vincent was a very tall doctor. 'Where did you move to?' she asked. 'One day, when we were about ten or eleven years old, you suddenly weren't there any more. I ran down to see you, and you were gone.' She remembered her sadness. 'I missed you. Everyone did, especially Diane.'

He nodded. 'Well, Dad moved on. He swapped Mum for a skeletal freak with the brains of a brick wall and all the charm of the sluice room on Women's Medical. She had money and a stud farm. So Mum and I went to Westhoughton and lived with my grandparents. It was all rather sudden.'

Lucy shook her head sadly. 'Oh, David – I'd no idea.'

He smiled, and Lucy noticed that he still had that childlike twinkle in his eye. 'Mum had no idea, either. Till she came home early from work with a headache one day and found them in an interesting position on the bathroom floor.'

'I'm sorry, David. I remember your mother. She was a nurse. It was your mother who convinced me to go into nursing.'

'She was a nurse, yes. And a damned fine mother. So. You married, then?'

'Yes. You?'

The handsome face clouded over. 'She died. So did our son. Anne was in a car accident, then Tim – well – it was leukaemia. I offloaded my general practice when Anne died, buggered off to India for a couple of years to find myself, got lost, came home and specialized as a paediatrician. Then I specialized even further and became a children's cancer doctor. Leukaemia, mostly.'

He'd been a kind, quiet child who'd often thought up interesting games. There'd been a tree house in his garden, and all the gang had met there. 'It's nice to meet someone who remembers Diane,' Lucy said. They'd done plays and concerts – all written and directed by Diane, of course. 'She was always very fond of you.'

'As I was of her. Of both of you, in fact. I always thought I'd marry one of you when I grew up. A child

78

seems to believe that everything will remain the same, that no one will ever move on.' He sighed. 'Yes, I read about her death in the paper, thought about writing to you, but what could I say? I was stuck for words. And now I'm stuck again, reduced to begging on behalf of my patients. What about you, Lucy?'

She gave him the full, unabridged version. It was as if thirty-five years had simply melted away, because she knew and trusted him immediately. She omitted no paragraph, no syllable, as it was such a relief to talk openly to someone who wasn't Glenys. 'So he's in there now.' She pointed to the large building across the road. 'And I'm not the type to sit by and watch someone die. I was tempted, mind. But at least the children were grown and at university when I did a bunk. So, nothing's changed apart from the fact that I own an extra house. If he lives, I'll have to take care of him.'

'Why?'

One little word, yet it certainly made her think.

'Why, Louisa? After all he's done?'

'He's still a human being, just about.'

He tutted. 'The same Louisa, then. You were always like that, you know.'

'Not quite the same, David. I am divorcing him. I'm by no means as sweet as I used to be. He's lying there in a terrible state, he could have another attack at any time, but I wasn't nice to him. But I can't leave him to live like a vagrant on the streets.'

'Then find him a flat and be done with him.'

She fiddled with a sugar bowl, turning it this way and that, but it looked the same from all angles, as did the problem attached to her husband. 'I want him pinned down,' she said. 'I don't want the father of Paul, Michael

79

and Elizabeth drinking himself to death in full view of the population of Bolton. Because the house will go to them when I die, and at least one of them could come back. In my will, any or all of them can live in it. Whoever lives there pays rent to the other two or buys them out – it's all arranged. I don't want them to be known as the product of the local drunk.'

'Then get him a flat in – where are you?'

'Crosby. Well, Waterloo if we want to be picky.'

He took her hand. 'Louisa?'

'What?'

'Is Tallows empty?'

She nodded. 'The cleaner and the gardener are doing their best, and Lizzie rescued any furniture of value. Why?'

'Could we go and look at it for old times' sake? Remember hide-and-seek?'

She grinned. 'I was thinking about my three just the other day, remembering them as children. I could never find them. If cabbage was on the menu, they'd go missing for a whole day. We had to use the cabbage as part of bubble and squeak in the end. By the time it was fried with mashed potatoes, any nutritional value had melted into thin air.' She watched his face, saw sadness behind his smile. 'You had no more children?'

'No. I never remarried. Annie was special.'

She noticed that a cloud seemed to pass over his face as he remembered his lost loved ones. 'Was Tim the reason why you went for childhood cancers?'

He nodded. 'And it's brilliant. I see kids like my son in remission, sometimes cured, even grown to adulthood. I want to open a respite centre, that's why I'm begging. There's a local charity, which I founded. It's the Timothy Vincent Trust, and most of the donors are people who have a child who's ill, or know one who has died. We're doing OK as far as research is concerned – that part of the money goes to London where the biggest strides are made, of course. But we need a place.' He stared into her eyes. 'An empty house with qualified staff who'll take the children and look after them while their families have a break.'

Lucy retrieved her hand and closed her bag with a snap. Now, she had two doctors to think about. 'Come with me,' she said. 'I have my car. Is yours at the hospital, too?'

'Yes. I'll walk you back to your car first, then you can wait here on the road until I catch up with you. Mine's round the back among the staff vehicles.'

During the drive to Tallows, Lucy pondered the subject of fate. If she hadn't visited Alan today, she might never have met a man who had known Diane, who had been a member of the Notorious Five – a name stolen by Diane, of course, from the celebrated Enid Blyton books. There had been Louisa, Diane, David and ... and Terri Easton, a rather tomboyish girl. The fifth? Ah yes, a red-haired lad who picked his nose, dug up worms and put them down people's clothes. Adam? Andrew? It didn't matter.

What did matter was the chance to make Tallows useful. Perhaps it would not be what was required, but it was worth a look, surely? All the time, a lump sat in her throat. But that was nothing new, because the leaving of the house in which she had been born had never been an easy move.

David found Tallows to be perfectly suitable for his needs, though others would need to look at it, of course. 'How much?' he asked.

'I'm not selling.' With the furniture gone, it looked rather derelict, she thought.

'To rent, I mean. How much?'

'I have to talk to the twins and to Lizzie first. It's their home, though I doubt they'll want to use it. But I must speak to them.'

'Of course you must. Oh, Lucy-Louisa. What brought you into my path today?'

She pondered for a few seconds. 'Tim, probably. If he's anything like his father was as a boy, he'll be charming the wings off angels. Oh, I'm sorry,' she breathed when she saw the tears in his eyes. She stepped forward with a handkerchief in her hand, and what followed was a total shock. He grabbed her and went to kiss her cheek, but she turned to wipe his face in the last split second, and the embrace landed squarely on her mouth. That was just an accident, but he clung to her. She felt his tears running down her face, yet he continued to kiss her. The shock was born when she realized she was kissing him back. There was an amateurish feel to the occasion, as if two teenagers were experimenting with their very first close encounter.

They separated reluctantly. She gave him her handkerchief before sitting on the edge of her bed. She could still taste him. 'Now, that shouldn't have happened,' she said. 'A definite mistake. Sorry.'

'Speak for yourself,' came the answer. 'I've just broken a very long duck.' He faced the window and dried his face.

'Since Anne?' she asked.

He nodded. 'You?'

'About ten years. And there would have been no response from me. I hated him using me.'

At last, he faced her. 'You were an extraordinary child, and you have become the woman you promised to be. When I was small, before the great spurts of growth began, you minded me, Louisa. This isn't the first time you've dried my tears.'

She sighed. 'David, I imagined you'd always be there. As you said earlier, we thought nothing would change.' Her parents would have been delighted. 'But perhaps we're both a bit hormonal? When my children give their answer, and I know it'll be yes, you'll have solved a massive problem, and that's exciting, so you're probably pumping adrenalin. As for me, well, I've just found freedom of a sort after years of unhappiness. It's great to be in the company of a man I don't hate.'

He wasn't answering, so she motored on. 'There are two provisos. I'd want a suite of rooms upstairs – I already have this so-called master with its own bath-room, but I'd like a small kitchen. Just a foothold, that's all I need. How many children will be here at any given time?'

At last, he opened his mouth. 'Depending on the level of care required, up to eight. We could take ten at a pinch if I find enough staff. And I hope we'll get planning permission – and yours, of course – for a temporary structure in the grounds, which would allow me to take more children in.'

'There's already a little park home down there near the woods. So there'll be room for me in the big house?'

'There will always be room for you, Louisa. And the second clause?'

'Ah, yes. Important. No alterations to the basic structure. You can divide as many rooms as you wish, but nothing solid. When I die, my children may choose to sell or to use the house differently. All that aside, there's a lovely play area in the orangery. It's all safety glass, all kite-marked. Some of them will be able to play, I hope.'

He lowered his head and stared at the floor. 'Tim played right to the end. Jigsaws, mostly – he hadn't much strength. Kids are so much better at accepting the inevitable. I've seen others die during play. It's unusual, though it happens. But the main point of focus here is the parents and their other children. Cancer rules a household, Louisa. From time to time, a family needs to be away from the sick child. Most don't go away on holiday willingly, but they go after I've bent their ears for months.'

She smiled. He was probably a very good persuader.

'Louisa?'

'What?'

'I know this seems odd, but would you consider ... going out with me?'

God. She felt as if she'd been propelled backwards through time, because he sounded so dated. Dated. He wanted to date her. She was a child of the sixties, as was he. Although her parents and other adults within her sphere hadn't joined the peace and love brigade, she was acutely aware of how manners had changed, of people's reduced respect for themselves and for each other. 'Yes,' she said. 'I'd like that. You must visit me, of course. It takes about an hour to get there, that's all. Come and look at my house.'

'And you'll be here sometimes?'

'Of course. It's my home, so I shall have to become an active member of your charity, won't I?'

'Yes. Yes, you will.' His grin was wide again.

She, too, was pleased. There were two reasons that merited celebration. She had met a man she liked and thought she could trust, while a certain doctor in Crosby might just have to accept that she was there for his frozen shoulder and no more. Richard Turner was an earthy, needful animal, while David, man and boy, had always been a sensitive creature. And the kiss had been so gentle, yet fervent. He was part of her past, as was this house. She intended to keep contact with both.

Alone, David Vincent jangled Lucy's spare keys. She trusted him enough to allow him access to her house. Something about Louisa and Diane Buckley had made them completely unforgettable. 'I haven't set you aside, Anne,' he whispered to his long-dead wife. 'Or you, Tim. But look at this. Think what can be done here.'

He lay down on Lucy's bed. It didn't smell of her perfume. There was just a faint odour of washing powder. How long had it been since he'd noticed another woman's perfume? Or another woman? In his soul, he had remained constant to Anne. Perhaps if Tim had lived, he might have sought a stepmother for him. But this was Louisa Buckley, and nothing less would do. Why? He hadn't the slightest bloody idea.

By accident, he had kissed her. She had responded. It had all been very awkward, but it had also been real. He had wept for Anne and for Tim, yet there had been another reason for that silly outburst of weeping. Yes, his duck had been broken, but it had fallen to pieces of

85

its own accord, because that misplaced kiss had been guided by someone or something. Anne? Had she decided it was time for him to find himself? He certainly hadn't found himself in India, that was plain.

'Is it to be you, Louisa?' he asked the other pillow. 'Were you sent today to visit a man you would never have seen again had he not been ill? Do you and I share karma that involves the death of your husband, my wife and my son?' From the sound of things, Alan Henshaw didn't have long to live. The guru in India had promised a second marriage, though David had remained averse to the concept. There had been one woman for him, and she was dead.

He closed his eyes and began to drift towards sleep, but found himself dreaming still of Anne.

The attendant drew back the sheet. There wasn't a mark on her face when David made the formal identification. Had she survived, it wouldn't have been easy for her, as one of her legs had been amputated at the scene. Multiple organ failure was the cause listed on the death certificate. The second thing, the real culprit, was severe trauma caused by traffic accident.

For how long had he wanted to kill the driver of that lorry? He couldn't remember. And how often had he been ear-witness to the concept that cancer was sometimes caused by shock? He had left Tim with his mother. 'So selfish,' he moaned. How on earth could a father leave his son at such a time? Did he go just to be far away from the driver of that truck?

He phoned home from Calcutta. His mother's words were few and bold. 'Get yourself home this minute, David. No more of your nonsense about meditation, please. Tim's white blood cell count is wrong. He is to go into hospital for further examination and tests.'

He came home. Tim, who had lost one parent to death and another to selfishness, lived for just a further six months. The driver of the lorry committed suicide. And it hadn't even been his fault: it had been Anne's brakes.

David had not considered his one and only child. By going abroad, he had made Tim an orphan. Letters and presents had done nothing to save him. Had the disappearance of the two people he loved most contributed to his early death? Celibacy had probably been David's penance.

He groaned and turned over, drawing up his knees until he was lying in the foetal position

Fighting for Tim, taking him all over America in search of a cure. Chemotherapy, radiotherapy, hair loss, sickness, and always a smile for Dad. The very last section of jigsaw placed correctly by Tim, a bit of blue sky. That piece was with him in the urn. Both sets of ashes were buried under a fir tree whose branches were covered every year in Christmas lights. Inside the cold, messy house – nothing. No cards, no turkey, just research.

David opened his eyes. It had been a rather odd dream, a not-quite-asleep experience. He felt strangely calm, as if a decision had been reached, as if all problems were now swept away. One accident. One kiss. Louisa Buckley.

Another doctor in another place was thinking about Lucy Henshaw, though his thoughts were more specific than David Vincent's. He needed the relief provided by close contact with a desirable woman, and Lucy seemed to grow more attractive every time he saw her. Moira understood. She remembered the avid lover, his frequent demands, and the pleasure she had shared with him. And she approved of Lucy, but Richard was getting nowhere. Lucy wasn't cold, wasn't aloof – she was simply unresponsive to him.

The massages were wonderful, but she, as a nurse, stuck rigidly to the brief – he had a frozen shoulder, and she treated just that. Sometimes he leaned his head against that remarkable bosom, but she always stepped back, or moved to one side. Was that because she wanted him and was playing it cool? Or was she displaying her intention not to become involved with her friend's husband? Perhaps she simply didn't fancy him. Whatever, he should be giving up, because he seemed to be getting nowhere. He was teetering on the brink of obsession, and it had to stop.

In the end, it was Moira who stepped metaphorically into the breach. She could no longer bear to watch his suffering, the swings from hope to despair, the pain that Lucy's perceived rejections were giving him, so she spoke to her next door neighbour one evening over a glass of wine. Having nothing to lose, she was extremely blunt, slightly drunk, and very clumsy. 'He's out. Gone to visit a dying woman,' she said. 'And he wants you,' she added. 'I expect you realize by now that he wants you.'

'Oh.' For several seconds, Lucy could not lay her tongue across another syllable. What was she supposed to say? 'Gee, thanks, I'm flattered'? Or 'I had absolutely no idea'?

Moira motored on. 'You see, we had a very active sex

life, but that's been put a stop to by this bloody MS. And I had a wonderfully romantic idea about finding him another wife – one I liked – to carry on after I'm gone. He shouldn't be alone. I feel terrified when I think of him going through life without a partner. He likes you. I think he's falling for you, and I'm glad.'

Lucy prided herself on having become used to the outgoing ways of the average Scouser. Although faster-spoken, they were very like Yorkshire folk when it came to calling a pail a bucket, yet she felt utterly stymied by Moira's bluntness. 'I'm still married,' she managed finally.

'Divorcing, though. Right from the start, I thought you were the one for him. I don't want him picking up all sorts of girls – he needs kindness, continuity, a lover. He's an extraordinary man, and a good one.' Moira reached across and patted Lucy's hand, withdrawing it immediately when she felt Lucy's automatic recoil. 'Sorry,' she said. 'I thought you were fond of Richard. I've seen you laughing and joking with him. I was sure you liked him.'

'I did.' Lucy, who had sat on anger for as long as she could remember, reined in many feelings that were suddenly threatening to overpower her. Was she expected to become an unpaid prostitute? 'But I also value myself, Moira. Your husband has sent out many signals in my direction. Had he been in possession of the slightest degree of sensitivity . . .' She paused for a moment. 'Even common sense would have helped. He should be aware by now that I have no intention of becoming close to him. Oh, and he had better see a qualified physio, as my ministrations are clearly not working, since he continues to come back for more treatment.'

'You're angry.'

'I'm furious. I know you have an incurable disease, and I've been only too pleased to help, but I draw the line at sexual favours. Would you want to supervise the proceedings?' Lucy held up a hand. 'Sorry about that last bit, but if your husband can't control his animal urges, I suggest you send him to Lime Street where the working girls hang out. He can check them for disease before jumping on board whichever train he chooses to travel on.'

'Sorry, Lucy.'

'So am I. I shall miss you.' She left the house, allowing the front door to slam in her wake. For almost a quarter of a century, Lucy Henshaw, née Buckley, had kept her temper. No, it had been longer than that: she had always been a people-pleaser. Except when it had come to marrying Alan. That single, quiet revolution against her family had produced a disaster, and she had lost confidence in her own decision-making skills. But now her hackles were up.

Laughter drifted from one of her front sitting rooms. Moira's children, Alice and Stephanie Turner, who managed to look like identical twins, were keeping company with Lucy's real identical twins. This was going to become uncomfortable, because the boys appeared to have settled here, and October was many weeks away. Anything might happen. She couldn't supervise this, didn't want to stay in the house just to protect these young adults.

The girls were studying medicine in Edinburgh, where their father had trained. Their older brother, Simon, was already working at the Royal in Liverpool. He lived in a flat near the hospital so that he would be on call to serve the master he followed, a cardio-thoracic surgeon with a double-barrelled name and the attitude of a prima donna. The son of the family was a nice lad. Lucy wondered briefly what Simon, Alice and Stephanie might say if informed that their mother was trying to hand over their father to the woman next door. She would put a stop to the nonsense right away, and she would do it in a way that might well be deemed eccentric.

She wasn't one for taking notice of whims, but she acted on one now. Opening the door without knocking, she asked her sons to come out into the hall. They disentangled themselves from their partners before joining Lucy. With a finger to her lips, she led them into the kitchen, taking care to ensure that the door was closed before speaking. 'Be careful with those two,' she whispered. 'They come from a very strange family.'

'So do we,' said Paul. 'Look, Mums, they're nice girls, good fun – there's nothing heavy going on. What on earth's the matter? You look like you've swallowed a wasp.'

'When's Elizabeth coming?'

'Sunday, possibly. Look, I asked first – what's going on?'

They were old enough to be told, so she told them. 'Moira asked me to have sex with their father. Her illness may have affected her brain, but he has become ... something of an imposition. He won't leave me alone. She says he's stressed because she can't ... well ... they don't have a full relationship on account of her sickness. I walked out of their house a few minutes ago. I'm rather angry.'

The two boys dropped into chairs at the big white

table. 'What?' Mike's eyebrows almost disappeared under his fringe. 'Mums?'

She shrugged. 'I knew he was needful, and I knew he had me printed on his bill of fare. But I thought I could sidestep him until he found somewhere else to leave a deposit.'

The twins looked at each other. Never before had their mother spoken so bluntly. 'But that's crazy,' Paul said. 'Ridiculous.'

Lucy agreed. 'If his daughters are in my house, he has an excuse to come for them. I won't be treating his shoulder, so that will cut down most of his visits. However, your friendship with Steph and Alice could make life difficult for me. I hope you understand.'

'What do we tell them?' Mike asked.

'No idea. I've found of late that the truth serves me very well. Perhaps it's almost a relief, because I lived a lie for such a long time.' She left them to discuss their problem. No, it wasn't their problem – it was hers, and she had allowed a personal difficulty to impinge on her children for the first time ever.

In her ground floor bedroom, she listened to the blackbirds as they argued about something or other. Was she being spiteful? She had no idea, but someone would have to put a stop to Moira. She couldn't go around the villages in her wheelchair interviewing prospective candidates for the post of concubine. If she wasn't careful, she'd find herself shut in a loony bin, poor woman.

The garden looked rather dry. Outside, Lucy turned on the sprinklers and listened to the screaming from next door. Moira was being given a hard time by her daughters, but better them than some stranger she might accost with her dreadful propositions. Richard, who had clearly returned from his house call, joined in. 'Who told you?' he yelled. 'This is preposterous.'

Moira added a few words to the poisonous recipe. 'You wanted her. All I did was—'

'All you did was make a bloody mess,' he roared. 'Yes, she's attractive, but you shouldn't have done this, you stupid, stupid woman.'

Doors slammed. The sound of girls arguing and weeping flooded through an open first floor window. With the blackbirds bickering on one side and the Turner girls on the other, Lucy gave up, turned off the sprinklers and went indoors. What had she done? What had she achieved? Richard would have trouble facing her, her friendship with Moira was possibly destroyed, and four young people were upset.

Her sons were waiting for her. 'You did the right thing, Mums,' Mike told her. 'Mrs Turner can't go about the place looking for a woman – at least you've put a stop to it.'

'I feel terrible,' she said. 'I don't think I can stay here.'

'You can and you shall,' said Paul. 'They're the ones at fault, not you. For long enough, you were messed about by Dad. At last you're sticking up for yourself, and it's not before time.'

'I shouldn't have involved you and their girls.'

'How else might you have ensured that the stupidity would stop? It could have been just about anyone out there – it could all have ended in court cases and all kinds of trouble. This way, we know it's over.'

Alone in her darkening kitchen, Lucy thought about Moira. Moira wasn't like other people, and that was nothing to do with multiple sclerosis. She was, well, unusual. The poor woman probably thought she was doing the best she could manage for a man she clearly adored. In her imagination, Richard would go to Lucy for sex, and return home to her for meals, surgeries, and general family life. After Moira's death, the two houses would become one, and everyone would live happily ever after.

For the second time that day, Lucy acted on a whim. She draped a cardigan over her shoulders and walked over to the next house. 'I couldn't have slept,' she told Richard, when he opened the door. 'She acted out of love for you, but I had to nip her idea in the bud, because other people might react in a different way. I understand her fear, and I appreciate your position, but she goes too far.'

'And you told your sons.'

'Of course. I have nowhere else to turn. For years, I kept my children behind a safety curtain. They're now adults, and they will protect me just as I protected them.'

He sighed heavily. 'I'm not a rapist, Lucy.'

'No. You're an attractive man with humour and wit – and a wife. I suggest you channel your surplus energies in her direction, because life isn't just about your demands and expectations. Many men have to manage life without a woman. Are you so weak? How stupid can one doctor manage to be?' She heard herself, yet scarcely believed that she was saying the words. 'Look after her, Richard. She loves you enough to go to any lengths to keep you happy. But put a stop to this behaviour, because it could land either or both of you in serious trouble.'

She found Moira weeping in the sitting room. 'Moira?'

'Lucy, I'm so sorry. I didn't—'

'Shut up for a minute, will you? The disease you have makes you vulnerable in many ways – it's not just physical. You love him enough to give him away, and that's a huge sacrifice, but you can't arrange the future – none of us can. I'm not prepared to lose you. You've helped me so much. You've given me strength and – hey – I can almost paint a tree!'

Moira dried her eyes. 'Your trees look as if they died in the Chernobyl disaster.'

'Yeah, but they're getting better.'

'Are they? I can't say I've noticed. Lucy?'

'What?'

'Be my friend.'

'I'll always be that, Moira. I shouldn't have slammed out of your house earlier. What is he, after all? Just another man. In my scheme of things, they are there, and we have to cope with them. He's no more important than the next fellow, love. You didn't get ill on purpose, did you? And you're acting like his mother, for God's sake. Leave him to his own devices. You know, sweetheart, you've done more harm than good. I was becoming fond of him until you forced the issue. So, in future, think before you speak.'

Moira managed a slight smile. 'You've always thought too much before speaking. Until now. Am I right?'

Lucy nodded. 'Spot on.'

Outside in the hall, Richard Turner trimmed the conversation he had overheard until it contained just six words. 'I was becoming fond of him,' she had said. He opened the door to his surgery, walked to his desk, and stared across at the chair in which patients sat during consultations. Should any one of them turn up and describe symptoms like his own, he would possibly make an appointment with a psychiatrist. 'You *are* obsessed,' he told himself quietly. 'And her breasts are magnificent. So, you have a magnificent obsession. And that's a film you saw with your wife.'

Moira was not stupid. He should never have used that word, because she was having trouble with memory, with acting appropriately, with life itself. But what she failed to understand was that his interest in the woman next door had deepened. Yes, it was sexual, but he was falling in love with more than a body. Lucy was a good woman, his kind of woman. Moira wouldn't mind if he slept with her, but she might create a fuss if he fell down into the unfathomable depths of real love.

So he did what he'd been doing for a fortnight. 'Just going back to check on that terminal old lady,' he called to his wife before leaving the house.

The old lady was not a patient, was neither old nor a lady, and was very much alive. She was thirty-two years old, firm of flesh and morally lax, and she was his release. This would be his second visit today, but he needed her. A brassy blonde, she had no idea of Richard's real identity, and she was excellent in the sack. She was his sanity.

Four

Days and weeks passed. Lucy Henshaw found herself to be in an interesting condition. Didn't that mean pregnant, she reflected as she made her bed. In which case, she would rename her condition fascinating. Yes, that was quite a good word. She couldn't get pregnant, anyway. It wasn't just because of her age; it was a choice she had made after the birth of Elizabeth. She feared the knife, but she'd feared pregnancy more, and had opted for tubal ligation. Yes, fascinating was definitely a better term, since her days of being in an interesting condition were long gone.

Two men were in love with her. Well, it probably wasn't real love on the part of either of them just yet, but she had apparently been reborn in the forty-sixth year of her life. She'd had a renaissance, had gone from frumpy to desirable simply by changing her address. It certainly added a slight frisson to her existence, because David was on the phone every day, while Richard was pretending to have lost interest.

A man who lost interest was interesting. She was using the word a great deal this morning, and was in danger of wearing it out, but it was apt. Richard Turner always left the house in a hurry when surgery was finished, as he needed to visit people who were confined to their homes. Until lately, he had looked for her, always giving a smile and a wave if he caught sight of her. Now he had lost interest – that word again.

He stared at the ground while he walked to his car, and though his face might not care whether or not Lucy was visible, the back of his neck betrayed him daily. It was an unusual colour, slightly north of pink, a short distance south of bright red, but it was definitely not normal. He was afraid of her. She didn't want him to be afraid. All she wanted was the respect due to her, which she'd certainly never got from the man she had married.

He scuttered round the car, bent rather too low when opening the door, and drove off at a speed that spoke volumes about his need to escape. 'Behaving like a criminal in the getaway car,' she told her image in the mirror. 'And you have changed, madam. You, Miss Proper, are advertising yourself very boldly.'

Oh, yes, she had changed, all right. Gone were the loose blouses and huge don't-look-at-me cardigans. She had invested in some top-of-the-range bras and a few pairs of Bridget Jones-style undergarments that had enjoyed, during their manufacturing days, a passing relationship with something called Spandex. They weren't belly-crunchers, so they were probably second cousins several times removed from corsetry, but they emphasized her shape. It was time to become proud of her hourglass figure. The world was full of stick insects, and Lucy had decided to stand out from the crowd. And she certainly stood out, especially at mezzanine level. Hating her own body was a thing of the past; she would embrace herself, embrace life and live it to the full.

Like a silly teenager, she was enjoying herself, preening from time to time, looking at designer clothes and bags. She'd always had a good wardrobe, but she was now investing in a capsule collection to which she added something or other almost every week. It was hardly a capsule now; it was more a complete pharmacy with a full complement of treatments, lotions and potions. Her skin was smoother and less wrinkled, as she was working with expensive creams to achieve a better appearance. If she wasn't satisfied, she knew where to go for Botox, though she did hold reservations when it came to something that sounded suspiciously akin to botulism.

She named the cause of all these symptoms the butterfly syndrome. Some people were grey, dull caterpillars for a very long time, but after a period of metamorphosis they emerged as Painted Ladies, beautiful creatures with splendid colours on their wings. 'You have hidden your light not under a bushel, but under a cardigan. From this day forth, cardigans are for cold days.'

Yet the main changes in Lucy were hidden ones. She was relaxed, positive and almost unafraid. The mouse she once was could never have been so forthright about the Richard and Moira situation. That tiny rodent would have run away, but the new Lucy caused Richard to do the running. 'In control of myself at last.' But she didn't want to control others, didn't wish to become like her soon-to-be-ex-husband. The quiet life would suit her very well. In just days, she looked better than she had in years – felt better, too. At last, she was winning. Soon, business people would sleep and eat breakfast in her house.

Work in Stoneyhurst was travelling along at speed. It

was becoming increasingly plain that she still needed to provide for her children, so her bed and breakfast accommodation had been whittled away until she could take only a handful of guests. It didn't matter any more. For the first time ever, she was enjoying a sensation named freedom. It was wonderful. But she must get cleaners. This place was far too big to be tackled by one woman, and Lucy liked company – the sort of company that went home after work. And she needed to think about Moira next door, as her long-term carer was about to disappear into Wordsworth country.

After watching Richard drive off, Lucy made the daily phone call. It was her duty to ask how her husband was faring, since she was paying all his bills. He was settling. That meant he was sedated so that he wouldn't rant and rage for a bottle of whisky. Heart surgery would be happening soon, probably tomorrow. He had lost enough weight, and his chances of survival were improved. What the hell was she going to do about him? He was a human being, and she couldn't simply eradicate him from her life.

Today, her wonderful daughter, who had been working for over a month in Manchester, was coming for lunch. She had missed an earlier planned visit, because she had been busy, but she was on her way. The subject of Tallows would be discussed, because David needed an answer. He was expected this evening. The child in Lucy hoped that Richard Turner would notice the handsome visitor. 'Behave yourself, Louisa,' she said sharply. She remembered reading somewhere that newly divorced women often went wild, sometimes performing a complete U-turn in the area of character and personality. But Lucy wasn't divorced just yet. She felt divorced, but that didn't mean a thing, because she needed the paperwork, the final decree, that passport to absolute liberty, before she was legally free.

The chrysalis had opened, and the butterfly had begun to dry out her wings. But she wasn't a Painted Lady. Neither was she a Cabbage White. The first implied a lot of make-up, and the second was the colourless character she used to be. Now she found herself able to visit Moira without running away when Richard returned. She talked to him, laughed with them both, and was becoming quite a hard case. The Hard Case butterfly? That sounded as if it had emerged from something wooden, like a coffin. Lively Lucy? No. This new butterfly would be the Coloured Courageous. But she had better keep that to herself, or people might believe she had lost the plot altogether . . .

He was in prison, and it was a jail of his wife's making. She had condemned him to this, and he didn't deserve any of it, because he'd always been a damned hard worker. It wasn't fair. He'd been a successful property developer, for God's sake. He didn't belong here. This place was for losers, failures, drug addicts and . . . and alcoholics. It was bloody boring, and he wanted to get out.

There were books, TVs, radios, DVD and video players, bars at the windows of his room, and enough staff to preclude the possibility of escape. They kept telling him he was over the worst. What they really meant was that they were over the worst, because he was sedated to the gills, and no longer had the energy to fight his way out of here. There had been a few scenes. The most memorable involved a straitjacket and a needle in his backside, so he'd been forced to calm down. They had some bloody big bouncers here, men who would not have looked out of place in the doorway of one of those seedy clubs in central Manchester.

Time didn't mean anything. He was given breakfast – fibre-intensive cushion-stuffing with skimmed milk, of course. Lunch was almost always fish with vegetables, while the evening meal was chicken or turkey with salad or more vegetables. He had no idea what day it was, and he was ceasing to care. They were killing him an inch at a time, and he seemed to have been here for ever. He remembered the other hospital, chest pains, machines, and people running about every time his heart monitor went off. There was another memory, but it was vague. Two policemen, a car, flashing lights, and some sort of siren, but it was all mixed up with impressions of Lizzie, Mags, power of attorney and bloody Lucy.

His pyjamas were loose. He could see his feet when he stood up, and that was all very good news for nurses and doctors, but he was being starved to death with malice aforethought. He wouldn't need the operation, because he'd be long gone by the time his name came up on the list. How many days or weeks had he been in here? No bloody idea. He'd probably be leaving in a wooden overcoat, but who gave a fig? Sleep was his only escape, but even that wasn't perfect. He had dreams. Most were nightmares, and the few good ones reminded him of what life might have been had he got away with his supposed misdeeds.

No visitors, either. That was, perhaps, a good thing, since even his daughter seemed to have turned against him. He hadn't seen Lucy since the day on which she'd grabbed power of attorney, while his sons had always stood by their beloved Mums. She'd been so passive and non-confrontational, and her change into a higher gear was something he would never have expected. The most annoying thing was that he had failed to guard himself, because he'd always known that she was a clever bitch underneath all that calm. 'Bloody women,' he cursed yet again.

Mr Evans-Jones walked in. So damned full of themselves, flaming surgeons. 'Go to hell,' Alan muttered under his breath.

'Mr Henshaw?'

'I think so. It was the last time I looked in the mirror, though even I had a job to recognize me. I look like a bloody scarecrow. If you think of it another way, I'm escaping this dump a pound at a time, and you're doing nothing about it. Don't bother with a coffin – a plastic bag will do.'

The surgeon sat down. 'I shall operate on your heart tomorrow, probably in the morning. You'll be glad to have it over with.'

The item nominated missed a beat or two. 'Right. So that means no breakfast. I can't tell you how much I'll miss the crap you serve in here. It's a bit like trying to eat your way through a mattress or three. And the milk's like white water.'

'The anaesthetist is satisfied with your progress, though it is my duty to tell you that there are always risks. However, those short walks and the gentle exercises have done some good. You will need time to recover, of course, but we expect a good result.'

Did these bods ever listen to anybody? Were they all deaf and ignorant? Alan fixed his eyes on the enemy.

'Does it never occur to you soft arses that some of us die in our own way? I'd sooner go as pissed as a newt and up to my eyes in fish and chips on the back of a drayman's cart.'

The doctor answered after a short pause. 'Then there's your answer. Go home. I can't force you to accept this operation.'

'What?'

'Withhold your consent for the procedure. Then go home and die. The choice is yours. You would be completely within your rights.'

'I can't go home, because I have no bloody home. And if I don't do as she says, my last weeks on earth will be spent under the arches at Turner Brew. No money, you see. She has it all.'

The surgeon decided that Mrs Henshaw was a sensible woman, though he kept the thought to himself. 'I shall need to know some time today. This may be a private facility, but I have a list to complete, and I shall have to—'

'Give it here.' Alan held out a hand. He opened a drawer and took out a monogrammed Cross fountain pen, signing the consent form with a flourish. 'Cremate me when you fail to save me,' he said. 'No service, just throw my ashes to the winds. Because I don't give a shit.'

Surgeons were not supposed to have opinions. They dealt in flesh and bone; they could not be expected to communicate with the inert, even when the inert was technically mobile. But sometimes, just sometimes … 'Mr Henshaw, your wife is paying almost three thousand pounds a month for your residence here. A further nine thousand will just about cover the operation, the anaesthetist, theatre time and medications. She is a generous woman.'

'Oh, bugger off and sharpen your cleaver. I'm past caring.'

'And you must never, ever drink again,' was the doctor's parting remark a moment before he closed the door. Yes. Sometimes, just sometimes, there was a patient who didn't actually deserve the chance to be saved.

Alan stood at his window. He'd been through one hell of a time, and it wasn't over. There would be pain, and there would be danger. But yes, it was time to take stock. He had survived a terrible withdrawal. No delirium tremens, no creatures crawling up walls, but physical torture so acute that he had railed and ranted against his wife, his family, God, Davenport Plumbers' Merchants who always overcharged, Mags for forsaking him, and the man in the next room, who cried most nights.

It was time to be sensible. Tomorrow, he would get the chance for a fresh start. If he survived the surgery, if he kept off the drink, he would go to live with Lucy in Liverpool. Once there, if he behaved himself, he might persuade her to start him up in business again. Nothing strenuous, of course, but something to keep him occupied. A shop, perhaps. No. There was no future for small retail businesses. But he would do something, and he would do it without the support of malt whisky. He had no choice. All his options had been removed, and tomorrow he might die.

Lucy loved to cook for her children. Preparing food for Alan had been no fun, because he would eat just about anything from tripe to caviar without noticing a difference. She could have served shop-bought meat pies at every meal, and he wouldn't have noticed as long as there were chips. He slurped his drinks, ate with his mouth open and, just as her mother had foretold, behaved like a pig at a trough.

Today, Lucy was preparing a feast for her prodigal daughter. She chuckled. There was nothing of the prodigal about Elizabeth, but her temporary return to the fold after an absence of weeks was certainly worth celebrating. It was a cooler day, so roast beef with Yorkshires was on the menu. Lucy's Yorkshires were reputedly so light that they needed weighing down with gravy to stop them floating up to the ceiling. Yes, it was lovely to be appreciated.

She sat down at the kitchen table for a few minutes. Not once had Alan complimented her on her culinary ability. If he survived, she would have to bring him here. She couldn't allow him a room at Tallows, not if it was going to be used for sick children. Apart from anything else, he wasn't safe when in drink. And she wanted him away from the place of her children's birth, away from all previous contacts. The man should disappear, yet she could not find it in herself to wish him dead.

Lucy closed her eyes for a few moments and pictured a long-ago scene. Ma and Pa stood over her. They didn't raise their voices, because that would have been ill-mannered to the point of indecency. They gave her all the reasons why she should not marry Alan Henshaw. He had not been educated. He was of poor stock, from a family who weren't well nourished, and she should be seeking to make a better match from within their circle. Any children would be affected by their father's paucity of learning. The man was a money-grabber, and she would suffer. He would ruin her, and she should heed their words.

Her eyes opened. How right they had been. Yet they had allowed her to marry, had given her a good wedding and a house in which she could live with her inappropriate husband. After their deaths, Lucy had inherited Tallows and a great deal of money. 'How on earth did I manage to believe that I loved him?' she asked the cruet set. 'Because he took my virginity? Anyone might think I'd been born in the wrong century. Why did I do it? Was I afraid of being left on the pantry shelf?'

No answer came from salt, pepper and French mustard, but at that moment Liz burst into the room. She flung her arms round her mother. 'You look wonderful! Sorry I've taken so long to get here, but we've been working some Sundays as well. And I am having the best time, playing a fourteen-year-old prostitute on heroin. What have you done to yourself? Isn't this house just great? And the river, too. Do you like it here? What's the news?' She released Lucy and started to examine the kitchen, the garden, the road.

Lucy watched the whirlwind she had birthed twenty years ago. Elizabeth was magnificent. Like her mother, she would never be a coat hanger, because she was shaped like a real woman. This precious girl was possessed of a very infectious joy, a need to know, a thirst for life. She was so similar to the girl who would have been her aunt ... Diane. Oh, Diane. 'Have you visited your father yet, Lizzie?'

'No. They didn't allow visitors for the first few weeks, and I really have been tied up with the theatre thing. Sorry.'

'It's all right. You have to live your life, sweetheart.'

'Where are my brothers?'

'They're with the girls next door.'

Liz stopped mid-stride. 'Paul told me about that thing with the man. Are you OK? No wonder people are falling in love with you – you look about thirty. You're an absolute stunner, Mother.'

Lucy grinned. 'He isn't people. He's just a sex-starved GP with a sick wife, and because she's unable to give him the closeness he needs she was interviewing me for the post. I hope we've engineered a stop to that. But the twins and her daughters have managed to put it all behind them. They're nice girls, both studying to be doctors. Their brother's a doctor already.'

'Very grand.' Liz flopped into an armchair.

'Your dad has his heart op tomorrow, dear. He's signed the consent form – Mr Evans-Jones phoned earlier to tell me. Once he's in surgical recovery you'll be able to see him.'

Liz sat upright suddenly. She didn't like thinking about Daddy. Theatre in the Park had occupied her to the point where she'd managed not to consider him too frequently, but here, with her family in an unfamiliar setting, she realized how drastically life had changed. 'Not sure I'll want to,' she said.

'You love your father, Lizzie. Love doesn't stop because he's done something wrong. He's still Daddy. A child's love for a parent lasts for ever. And vice versa.'

'And a wife's love for a husband?'

'Is not the same. It's not unconditional – the divorce statistics confirm that. Now. Go next door and introduce yourself while I set the table.'

Liz stayed where she was. The world was changing,

but it surely hadn't descended to the point where wives sought partners for their own husbands?

'You'll understand when you see Moira, Lizzie.'

'Do you read minds, Mother?'

'Of course I do. All mothers do – it comes with the job. Just wait till you have three children very close in age, miles apart in needs. I had a daughter who played at killing people with a poker. She used my dustbin lid as a shield, and she wouldn't wear dresses except for school. My sons were always studying something or other. They were hopeless at sports, brilliant at school. So, as a mother, you read minds and provide accordingly.'

'Right. So you want me to go and meet a woman who wanted you to deliver for her husband.'

Lucy smiled. 'Look, sweet child. Moira can hardly breathe some days. Her food is almost pureed, and she can't walk more than a few steps. Yet all she thinks about is the man she loves. She wanted a lot more from me – she was planning to leave him to me in her will. A second husband for me, a second wife for him.'

'So it wasn't as disgusting as it sounded?'

'No. I just had to make sure it stopped. Moira was playing a dangerous game, so we built a big firewall. I mean it, Lizzie – you will love her. She's an endangered species – a true eccentric rather than a manufactured one. You'll meet many would-be oddities in your game, but this lady's for real. Go on – shoo.'

When Liz had left, Lucy began to contend with another of her specialities – a real sauce anglaise. No yellow powder from a packet for her – she was a true chef, though she tended to concentrate on English food. Perhaps she would go to night school, do a bit of Italian and French stuff? It was a thought.

She worked for about ten minutes, then Paul and Mike came in. 'Mums, you'll never guess,' said the latter.

'No, I won't. Not without a clue, anyway. Go away while I thicken this sauce.'

But they weren't going anywhere. 'It happened. Just like that.' Paul clicked his fingers. 'I didn't believe in it. Did you?' he asked his brother.

'No. Never. Not until today, anyway.'

Lucy wiped her forehead. 'What?'

'Oh, so you're interested now, eh?' Paul sat in a carver. 'Head over heels,' he said. 'Hook, line, sinker, keep net and every fly in the box. Their eyes met across a crowded room—'

'Birds sang,' added Mike.

'—and she blushed,' Paul concluded, triumph in his tone.

Lucy gave up. 'If this custard's lumpy, I shall blame you pair. Start again. Paul, you're too mischievous. Mike? Come on, out with it.'

'It was like *Brief Encounter*,' the quieter twin said. 'Beautiful. But without the ashtrays and the teacups. Oh, and the trains.'

'Or *Gone With the Wind*.'

Lucy glared at Paul. 'I know you're a few minutes older than Mike, but shut up.' She turned to her other son. 'You can forget the weepy films, just tell me what happened.'

'Our little Lizzie walked in next door, introduced herself to Moira, and after a few minutes—'

'About five minutes,' Paul interjected.

She waved her wooden spoon at him. 'One more word from you, me lad, and you'll be wearing this through your nose.'

'Well, Simon walked in. He was doing all right till he fell over a chair. Staring at your daughter, Mrs Henshaw. And she was staring at him. It was electric, wasn't it, Paul?'

But Paul was standing like a first-year infant school child, a finger to his lips.

'They're in next door's garden now. Come on, Mums,' Mike begged. 'We know where the spy holes are.' He dragged his mother into the garden. Somewhere, she had a carton of Sainsbury's ready-made custard, just for emergencies. This was probably an emergency.

The three of them stood in a row, eyes pinned to knotholes in the fence. Lucy couldn't help smiling. Her daughter and Simon Turner were seated on a padded swing with a canopy. There was space between them, but it was decreasing as she watched. A centimetre at a time, they edged closer to each other.

What the hell was she doing? She pulled her twins away from the fence. 'Inside – now,' she whispered.

'What?' shouted Paul.

She pushed him towards the house while Mike followed. When the door was closed, she rounded on them. 'Why did I allow that?' she asked. 'That's not who I am any more. I don't do as I'm told.'

Mike agreed, and he said so. 'But what did you think, Mums?'

'Interesting,' she replied. 'But I shan't buy a wedding hat just yet.'

Apart from a few rather explosive laughs from the boys, lunch proceeded in an orderly fashion until the first course was over. When Liz stood up to start clearing plates, Lucy asked her to sit down again. 'About

Tallows,' she said. 'I'll come to the point right away. Someone wants to borrow it for a while. In fact, I offered, albeit provisionally, to lend it until I die, at which time the property will revert to the three of you, so I need your agreement.'

She told them about Diane and the Notorious Five, about the boy who had lived at the end of the lane, about his disappearance. 'I went to see your dad in Bolton hospital,' she explained. 'And David was there. Yes, yet another doctor – I seem unable to escape them. It all appeared to fit, because I don't want to leave Tallows empty, and I know my sister would have approved.'

They listened intently while she outlined the adult life of the friend she had mislaid over thirty years ago. 'So it's for the families,' she concluded. 'They need a break from time to time, a rest and a change of scenery.'

Liz dabbed her eyes with a corner of her napkin. 'Then we do it,' she announced. 'Boys?'

They both nodded.

'Thank you,' said Lucy. 'Now, you must change your permanent address to here – driving licences, college registration, banks and so forth. Your stuff will have to be taken out of Tallows, though I hope you'll allow me to leave all toys for the children. My contribution will be that I shall charge no rent. Bills and running costs will be paid by the Timothy Vincent Trust.'

'I took Dobbin and the dolls' house to the safe place.' Liz smiled through her tears. 'We can get them back. I just thought they were valuable, Mother. But they should be enjoyed. Children are worth more than possessions.'

'And you three are pearls. Some of the furniture can

come here, because it will fit in very well,' Lucy said. 'The rest I shall auction in London – get the better prices. And David will be here this evening.'

Paul spoke in a stage whisper. 'Is she blushing?'

'I am not blushing.'

Liz laughed. 'The lady doth protest too much, methinks.'

The twins rounded on their sister. 'Oh, yes? What about you and the fellow next door? You were practically sharing the same shirt on that swing. He fell for you, all right. Over a chair and his mother's walking frame.'

Mike chipped in. 'Reminded us of *Brief Encounter*. It could have been brief – he might have suffered concussion.'

'Leave her alone,' Lucy ordered.

'Mums, you're as bad. You went all glassy-eyed whenever you said David's name. And you're not even divorced yet.' Paul folded his arms. 'This is going to become very illuminating, Mike. It seems we have a wayward sister and a delinquent mother.'

'On top of all of which, you also have Sainsbury's custard. You can thank your brothers for that, Elizabeth.' Lucy left the table. She stood in the kitchen for a while, just listening as they quarrelled good-heartedly. 'I am a fortunate woman,' she told herself. 'Except, that is, for the ready-made custard.'

The afternoon was supposed to be quiet, but it didn't work out that way. For a start, there was Liz's phone. It rang every few minutes and, in the end, Liz left the scene and sat in the garden. Simon Turner had returned to work at the Royal, and Lucy worried about patients, since one of their doctors seemed to be permanently engaged, as was Liz's phone. She watched while her daughter giggled and blushed like a teenager. 'Love at first sight? I doubt it,' she said to an empty room. But she had never before seen her daughter in such a flap. She was like a thirteen-year-old with a crush on the head boy.

The twins had gone out to see something or other in Matthew Street, and both Turner girls had accompanied them. It wasn't time to prepare for the arrival of David, so Lucy settled down with a book. But this was destined to be a rather less than peaceful Sabbath, as she found when she answered the front door bell. She didn't get the chance to say anything, because one of the women who stood there filled the silence and the doorway immediately. She was roughly the same size as Shirley Bishop, but she was noisier.

'I know it said Wednesday. But we can't do Wednesday this week because of her and the wisdom teeth.' Next to her, the short, thin owner of said wisdom teeth looked very miserable. 'So that's why we've come today, cos we wanted to be first. I said to Dee – didn't I, Dee? – that we couldn't miss the chance.'

It had been explained to Lucy that although she was doing quite well when it came to the interpretation of the local lingo, she would eventually meet people who spoke Dinglish. They hailed from a part of Liverpool labelled 'the Dingle', and had developed a language all their own. She guessed that the big woman wasn't quite speaking Dinglish, because most of what she said was understandable.

'Didn't I say that, Dee?'

Dee nodded sombrely. 'She did. She did say that, yes.'

The big woman carried on. 'Mind, Sunday's my lucky day, isn't it, Dee?'

'It is, yeah.'

Lucy wondered whether she might have fallen asleep during chapter five of her Thomas Hardy. Or had she slipped into some parallel universe where oddly shaped people with bad wisdom teeth knocked on doors on Sunday afternoons? 'I'm sorry,' she managed while the big woman drew breath. 'Have you come to the right house?'

'We would have come on Wednesday like it said on the thing in the shop window, only Dee—'

'Yes, I got that bit. Please come in.'

When all three were seated, Lucy realized what was happening. 'The advertisement for cleaners!' she exclaimed.

The big woman looked at the lady of the house and shook her head as if in near-despair. 'Who did you think we were, queen? Jehovah's Witnesses? We're domestic and commercial operatives, me and her. Professionals, like. Dee's me daughter, and I'm Carol. We live together with her kids in my house down Stanley Road, but we can be here for breakfasts and then we can clean or whatever. Give us a try, love.'

Lucy cast her eyes over them. The big one looked as if she'd get out of breath if she made a bed, while the thinner woman was frail enough to be blown over in a light breeze. Perhaps if she rolled them together like a ball of Plasticine and cut them in half, they'd make two normal people? 'So you're experienced?' she asked.

'Very,' said big Carol. 'We've got references, and we'll work a couple of days for no money, give you chance see what we're like, like.'

'Who looks after your children, Dee?'

'Our Beryl,' replied Carol, who seemed to be the spokesperson. 'She can't talk proper,' she explained. 'Our Dee, I mean. It's her wisdom teeth.'

Lucy was trying hard not to laugh. 'What about your husbands?'

Carol chewed her lip for a moment. 'Dee's was a window cleaner what fell off his ladder and died.'

'Oh, I am so sorry.'

'It's all right – he was useless. Wasn't he, love?'

Dee inclined her head.

'Mine went to the chip shop on Thursday and never came back.'

Lucy blinked a few times. 'But that's three days. Have you told the police?'

'Thursday 1998,' came the reply. It was accompanied by a broad smile.

This was too much for Lucy. She fled into her bathroom, opened the cabinet and, once she had calmed down, brought a small bottle into the sitting room. 'Tooth tincture,' she said as she passed it to Dee. 'I don't know how much use it will be for impacted wisdom teeth, but you can give it a try.'

'Ta, queen.'

Liz came in. 'Hello,' she said.

Big Carol's mouth made a circle before she spoke. 'Ar, ay,' she said. 'You're dead fit, you are, girl.' The 'girl' arrived as 'gairl'.

Fortunately, Liz seemed to know that 'dead fit' meant pretty. 'Thank you,' she said. 'I'm going out, Mother. I shan't be too long, just popping into Liverpool to have a look round.'

'To the Royal, I take it?'

116

Liz blushed. 'He's on a split shift.'

'My husband done them splits,' Carol announced. 'Till he realized he'd had his chips.'

Lucy grinned. Chips. Thursday. 1998.

'Only with him, it wasn't work,' Carol continued. 'Against his religion, work. It was women. There was me, his wedded wife, like. Then there was a fork-lift truck driver from Speke, a girl from Formby what did people's hair in their own houses, and Barbie Bow-legs from next door.'

She turned to Lucy. 'Barbie knew I was going to kill her, like, so she buggered off to buy chips as well. Never seen her since. She's one you could recognize a mile off, because her legs have different postcodes. If she played football, she'd be useless in goal.'

Lucy howled with laughter. She curled in a ball on the seat of her large armchair, arms hugging her body against the pain. She would have to see other candidates on the stated day, but these two were a female Laurel and Hardy – the entertainment value was beyond price. She looked up and saw her daughter in hysterics, tears pouring down her face.

A twinkle in Carol's eye spoke volumes on the subject of triumph. She waited for Lucy and Liz to calm down. 'So. Will you give us a trial after this one's had them teeth dug out? She's thirty, by the way. I'm forty-nine plus VAT. I can do a day on me own, if you like. But we're a team, usually. I can lift anything, and she's like one of them Hoover attachments what can get into small spaces.'

Liz stood behind her mother's chair. 'Have either of you thought about going on the stage?' she asked.

'Only the landing stage when there's a couple of

Norwegian ships in. You can make a fortune out of them sailors. I'm kidding, love.' She spoke again to Lucy. 'We've been cutting down the jobs,' she said. 'The motor's on its last wheels, so we're trying to get a couple of clients nearer home. We've a suite of offices to clean in the evening and, if we get you, that'll be nearly enough. Won't it, Dee?'

'Yes, enough,' Dee replied.

Liz fled. Sitting in her Micra, she repaired her make-up and thanked God that Mother had come to Liverpool. Well, the fringe of Liverpool. No one should go through life without making contact with Scousers. They changed things, made stuff happen. And stuff was certainly happening, because she had seen a guy once, and was chasing him already. Liz was not a man-chaser. She had her fair share of friends in London, but there had never been anyone special. After swallowing her fear, she switched on her satnav. She didn't know Liverpool, but she would soon learn . . .

Inside the house, life was slightly calmer. Big Carol had been born in the Dingle, but she'd bettered herself by moving up to Bootle. 'They talk a bit more posher down Stanley Road,' she said. 'And the shops down Bootle is all right. Then there's the Strand – Marks and Spencers, supermarkets, shoe shops – all sorts.'

It was decided that the trial would take place the next day, but without Dee. 'She's going to look like an 'amster with its gob full,' Carol said. 'So I reckon the Monday after for her. She's in too much pain now, and she'll be rotten once they've dug the buggers out. Oh, and another thing. Never put your address in a shop window. All kinds read them notices, and they'll know you're well off if you're advertising for staff.' She grinned. 'So I took it out of the window for you.'

There would be no more applicants, then. This was a very clever woman, and Lucy was developing a fondness for her already. As for poor weedy Dee – only time would tell. 'Dab that stuff on your gums, Dee,' she advised. 'It tastes awful, but it may give you a bit of relief.'

At last, a real smile was delivered by the thin woman. 'What's your name?' she asked.

'Henshaw. Lucy Henshaw.'

'What do we call you?'

'Erm … boss? No, Lucy will do. Or Mrs Henshaw if you're more comfortable with that.'

The pair gazed at one another. 'What do you think, Dee?'

Dee shrugged. 'I can't think, can I? They're going to put a pewmatic drill in me gob and dig for bloody coal, Mam.'

Carol addressed Lucy. 'We'll use your first name, if that's OK.'

'Certainly.'

There then followed a questioning session about household equipment and brands of cleaning products. Carol and Dee would bring their own materials, which was why they were a quid an hour dearer than other so-called cleaners. 'We do inside and out, but not garden-ing or outdoor window cleaning. That's ever since her Harry fell off his perch. But we'll keep your paths nice. We do washing, ironing, cupboards, fridges, freezers, cookers and some plumbing.' Carol smiled happily. 'I done a course at night school. Dee's good at darning and mending, but we usually do that at home. I do electrics, but not gas. I'm not Corgi registered yet.'

They left Lucy with the impression that she had been interviewed. She seemed to have passed the test, anyway. As their van drew away from the front of the house, she read the legend on its side. *CAROLANDEE SERVICES UNLIMITED*. So they were registered, and they paid their taxes. They were also cutting down on work, so she would get the best out of them. And they might do for Moira as well, once Shirley Bishop had shuffled off to the Lake District. It shouldn't take much to get Carolandee to give up the evening cleaning of offices. They wanted workplaces that were close together, and Moira was just next door.

She picked up her book. This hadn't been a quiet day, but it had turned out to be successful thus far.

The Royal was huge, and it had a reception hall so vast that it felt like a railway station or an airport. In a circular booth, a small woman sat as if waiting to weigh baggage or check tickets. She looked miserable, and Liz was not surprised. Apart from anything else, this outsized barn of a room looked as if it needed a good cleaning. It was quiet today, though few would have liked the woman's job during the week. Liz imagined that poor female battling with lines of complaining patients, all certain of the urgency of their cases, all eager to get the business over and done with.

Liz wasn't quite sure why, but she knew she had to be here. Having spent no more than half an hour – not counting phone calls – in the company of Simon Turner, she was insanely keen to see him again. Had anyone asked her for reasons, she would probably have imitated a drugged goldfish, all open mouth, no sense and very few bubbles.

Simon Turner stood for a few seconds and watched Liz's confusion, which mirrored his. What the blood and sand was going on? He'd been perfectly all right until just before lunch, when this would-be actress had wandered into his life. She was a stunner, but it wasn't just that. It was probably chemical. Occasionally, he met a woman he fancied and then it was usually a case of simple science: get the sex over with, and move on.

Yet he knew already that this one was special. She was different. Life oozed out of every pore of her very comely body, and he was attracted to her immediately. It was best not to trust the term 'immediately', yet he had to see her before she returned to Manchester this evening. His mentor, Mr Garner-Hope, was not on duty today, and the only items of surgery that might occur would be emergencies. Simon's pager was turned on, he had seen his list of patients in recovery, and he was going to grab some time.

He crept up behind her. 'Boo.'

She turned. 'Ah, there you are.' She still hadn't managed to work out why she'd come, and she said so. 'My brothers have been kicking the stuffing out of me,' she told him. 'They think you and I have come from some black-and-white film that promised much, but delivered zilch. What's going on, Simon?'

'No idea. We young doctors are not as experienced in affairs of the heart as some people try to make out.'

'So should we?'

'Should we what?'

'Make out. I think it's American for sex.'

He looked round the huge hall. 'Endocrinology's quiet

on a Sunday. We could put two chairs together and work out the mechanics of the exercise. And Dermatology doesn't do weekends – should be peaceful. But there's always a chance that some lost soul might wander through. Haematology can be colourful, of course. And I have digs across the road, though other people will be in there now. My bedroom should be free, though—'

She dug him in the ribs. 'This is all wrong, isn't it? I'm not what you might term easy. My experience of sex would fit on the back of a postage stamp.'

'First class?'

'Of course.' She pondered for a moment. 'No, second. I've had some rather less than satisfactory experiences. You?'

He grinned. 'Mixed bag. Women tend to target doctors and lawyers.' He held her hand. 'Maybe it's because I'm nearly twenty-six. My clock could be telling me it's time to slow down, settle down and move down south.'

'Stop it, Simon. Don't even think of following me to London. For a start, you don't know me. I live for acting, and I exist in a total shambles. On a good day, I can find two matching shoes and jeans clean enough to wear just one more time. There are never any knickers – I've been known to go out knickerless and buy some on the way to college.'

His heart was all over the place. As a student of cardio-thoracic medicine, he might have misdiagnosed a patient with a heartbeat as dodgy as his. But was it love? And how might he find out what it was when there were two hundred miles separating him from her?

'I can transfer for a year,' he said. 'In fact, my boss would be delighted, because I might learn something new. London's the place to be when it comes to innovation. And I'd like to know you better.'

'In the biblical sense?'

He raised his shoulders. 'That as well, I suppose. Because I sure as hell want you. How long are you in Manchester?'

'The same as I am here – about five feet seven inches.'

'Obtuse. That's probably why I . . . like you.'

'All right. Another three weeks in the park, then back to Mother for a while. Do you get proper days off?'

'Yes, of course. And I have holidays due. Why?'

'Secret,' she answered. 'The thing is, I like to have the upper hand.'

'Sounds interesting, Elizabeth.' He led her outside and round a corner, because the hospital was on a busy road, and the traffic was heavy even on a Sunday. So their first kiss happened against a hospital wall while they stood among cigarette ends and crisp packets deposited by patients and visitors.

'Wow,' he said when they released each other.

'Yes,' she agreed. 'About a three, I'd say.'

'What?'

'My personal Richter scale, Simon. The earth moved a bit.'

He ran a hand through his hair. 'That would be an articulated lorry on its way to the docks.'

'So romantic.' She sighed theatrically. 'Trust a bloody doctor to find some sensible explanation.'

'Tell me about the secret,' he begged.

'No.' She raised her chin defiantly. 'The secret is for me to know, and for you to wonder and worry about.'

'Upper hand?'

'Upper hand.'

He placed a finger under the tilted chin. 'I'm buzzing,' he announced.

'Good for you.'

He explained that his pager was about to ring. 'Could be life and death,' he said.

'Then go. I'll keep in touch – that's a threat.' She watched as he ran back to his job. There was a lump in her throat, and a terrible feeling of loss. This might get worse by tomorrow, because Daddy was going into theatre, and he might die. She didn't want to go back to Manchester, didn't want to return to RADA after the holidays. But she would. Few people got the opportunity, and she wasn't going to flush her chance down the loo just because of a bloke.

She would talk to Mother. Because, after all those years spent as cook, bottle-washer, nurse, nanny and part of the furniture, Lucy Henshaw had emerged as a fully fledged human with opinions, ideas and a healthy balancing of determination and humour.

When Lucy reached the place she now termed home, Mother was nowhere to be seen, but the sound of running water could be heard from the bathroom. Ah yes – that chap was coming this evening, the doctor who wanted to use Tallows for respite. Mother had been rather coy when avoiding discussion on the subject of ... David? Was that his name? Perhaps Mother was in the same boat as her daughter?

Lucy was in her bedroom for almost an hour. When she finally entered the sitting room, Liz gasped. 'Mother! Is that cleavage? How the hell did you manage to pour yourself into that item of clothing?'

'A teaspoonful at a time,' came the response. 'It's difficult to buy dresses for someone my shape. So I had to pick a bigger size and get everything below the bust taken in. I think the girl went a centimetre too far.'

Liz shook her head. 'You look amazing. But you don't look like my mother. My mother was a bit magnolia and brown. You're wearing high heels and a little black dress. You've never owned an LBD before, have you?'

'Only for funerals, and that was from Rent-a-Tent. Now. Come on, let's have it. I know you need to talk. I can tell, because you've crossed your legs and your arms. Call yourself an actress?'

Liz grinned, then allowed it all to spill out. She'd been all right this morning. She'd been all right until a certain person – namely her mother – had forced her to go next door to introduce herself. 'This Greek god – except he was blond – walked in, saw me, and fell over a pile of stuff – nearly squashed his poor mother. And it worked both ways, though I managed to remain upright. It was as if I already knew him.'

'From the future.'

'Yes! I knew you'd understand.'

Lucy pursed her lips. 'I'm not sure about that kind of stuff, Lizzie. I've heard about it, read about it, but–'

'I drove all the way to the hospital just for a kiss, Mother. How stupid is that?'

'In my opinion, it isn't stupid at all. You'll work him out of your system, or you won't. Just keep yourself safe, and don't get pregnant.'

Liz sat back. The mother she had known for twenty years would not have spoken so openly about such a subject. 'He held you back.'

'What?'

'Daddy held you back.'

Lucy disagreed. 'Marriage did that. My attitude did it. I felt that I had to remain docile until my children were old enough to absorb the shock. He was my choice. I went against my parents' will and got my own way. It was my mistake. The person you see now was always there. And I have to admit, I wanted my money back. It was my money, the Gramps' money. But I watched and listened and waited until the time was right. Unfortunately, it has almost killed him.'

'Were there always other women?'

'Yes.'

'And drink?'

'The intake increased as the years passed. He's his own worst enemy. Your father has little self-control, so I had to invent patience of my own. And I'm worried about tomorrow. If he dies, I'll feel guilty, and if he lives, I shan't know what to do with him.'

Both women sat in silent thought for several minutes. Lucy, who didn't want to worry about Alan, was worrying about Alan. Liz wondered whether she might be going out of her mind, because no one could fall in love in a matter of hours. Even so, that was an easy concept compared to the concern she felt for her father. This might be his last day on earth. She jumped to her feet. 'I'm going to see him. If they don't let me in, I'll make a fuss.'

'You'll get in, Lizzie. I'll phone and tell them you're coming.' She paused for a moment. 'Tell him I wish him well, and that he will be housed when he gets out. That might make him try a little harder to live.'

'Thanks, Mother. You're one hell of a lady.'

'A woman, Lizzie. I'm a woman, not a lady.'

Five

The boys weren't expected back until after midnight, as they had declared their intention to visit a club or two. At least they hadn't gone silly, weren't running around telling everyone how in love they were with Steph and Alice. That, Lucy thought, would have made life completely unbearable. Her daughter was besotted with Simon Turner, and that was quite enough, thanks very much.

Paul and Mike had gone out to search for John Lennon, who had been dead for some time, but whose picture, made up of his song titles, was reputed to be available from one of the Matthew Street artists. So the twins were safe, happy and out on a manhunt. There was no need to worry about Mike or Paul and, as Lucy reminded herself, Meatloaf had declared that two out of three ain't bad.

But Lizzie, poor, lovely Lizzie, had travelled alone to visit a father who would undergo major invasive surgery tomorrow morning. On top of that, the poor girl's heart had been borrowed or stolen by the son of Richard and Moira, and the result of that happenstance could become painful. If Alan died, Lizzie might turn to Simon, might even remain in the north instead of carrying on with her course in London. She had always loved her father. Would she lean on Simon if Daddy died? Was Lizzie one of those female souls who needed the scaffolding provided by a man? Had she not yet learned that scaffolding sometimes corroded and crumbled?

Lucy could not bear the thought of her daughter suffering. She'd been such a bouncy, tomboyish child, full of life and mischief, overflowing with tales of dragons, princesses, wicked stepmothers and handsome knights who had overthrown all evil in their way. Lizzie had always been the knight, poker in one hand, dustbin lid in the other, ever the actor, so bright, imaginative and cheerful. With her eyes closed, Lucy saw her daughter leaping about, a curtain for a cloak, torn tinfoil failing to look like armour, a war cry emerging as she cut through invisible foliage to face a monster. She'd saved everything in her path. She'd definitely saved her mother's sanity. Those Lizzie moments were printed for ever on the front of Lucy's mind, where they sat alongside memories of Diane, the predecessor of Lizzie.

But the mother of Lizzie now found herself weeping. She wept for a husband she had ceased to love within months of marriage, blaming herself yet again for going ahead with the union against the wise counsel of her parents. She cried for Lizzie, who was the only person in the world willing to visit him. Moira was a further cause for sadness, because that good woman had merely sought to tidy up before the end of her life. 'I shouldn't have come here,' Lucy moaned. But she heard her own lie, and had to right this small wrong. 'It's a good place, a very good place. I can make it right.' No, she wouldn't even need to do that, because these ancient Viking villages, now modern and bustling, welcomed all comers. She was at home here. Anyone from anywhere could settle in this area.

More surprising than anything else was her need for Alan to live. Yes, Tallows had been hers, the money had been hers, and he had stolen and committed fraud. But she didn't want him to die under a surgeon's knife. She had always feared the intervention of doctors, and she now found herself concerned for a man with whom she had shared almost a quarter of a century – more than half her life. Someone should have taken better care; someone ought to have stopped him in his tracks.

She began to pace about. Yes, he ate like a pig, and yes, she had often wished he would bath more frequently, but he was a human being. He was the father of her children. And he hadn't been merely the boss of the company – he was just as likely as any labourer to come home stinking of cement. The man had never been afraid of work. He didn't deserve death, yet he needed to develop a backbone, since any life he might win after surgery would have to be alcohol-free. 'He must be strong, has to become determined. God knows what he'll need afterwards, but he must have the chance of some kind of future.'

She dried her eyes and picked up the phone. After talking to a woman at the clinic, she wrote down a number. One of the rewards Alan had earned for drying out was a private phone in his room, but she had never asked whether she might speak to him, had managed not to care. Why care now? And why was she phoning him? Guilt? She hadn't been a bad wife. She hadn't been a wife at all in recent years, since he had sought solace elsewhere.

Lizzie answered. 'Mr Henshaw's room. Liz Henshaw speaking.'

'Hello, sweetheart. Do you think your father will talk to me?'

There was a short pause before Lizzie spoke again. 'I'm sure he will. Just a moment.'

Seconds ticked by. The first thing she heard was his shallow, quick breathing. 'Calm down, Alan,' she said. 'I just wanted to say this. For tomorrow, I wish you all the very best – and I mean that. When you get out of there, we'll talk. I won't break my promise. You know I don't do broken promises.'

A worse sound came across the miles between them. 'Please don't cry,' she begged. 'I'll find you something to live for. I will, Alan.'

'Piss off,' he managed. 'Leave me alone. You've done enough damage.'

The phone clattered and banged, then Lizzie spoke. 'He's scared, Mother.'

'I know. And I haven't helped, have I?'

'You may have. I'll talk to him. Bye now.'

Lucy sat back. With Lizzie, it had always been 'Mother', never Mum or Mums, never Ma. Mother. 'Have I killed him now?' she asked the cat. 'Have I pushed him towards that final heart attack? I shouldn't have phoned. Everything I do these days seems to cause a mess. Perhaps I should keep my mouth shut.'

Smokey swept the rug with his large, bushy tail. He retained his carefully created air of superiority, and was beginning to come to terms with the fact that his mistress – well, his servant – had placed a wire lid on the back garden. The louder and more prolonged complaints were less frequent these days, though he seemed to be living with his thermostat on simmer. He missed his space, the carp, the freedom and the old kitchen. And he certainly made his feelings plain whenever addressed by Lucy.

'Shut up,' she said now. 'Sorry I asked.'

The doorbell sounded. She checked in the overmantel mirror, dabbed at wet cheeks and went to answer the door.

A large bouquet of flowers was thrust into the hall. 'Thank you,' she managed as she took the offering. 'They're lovely.'

David followed the roses through the door. She'd postponed his visit for weeks, because the house had been under repair, and her children had only today managed to be all in the same place at the same time. She had asked them about Tallows, he hoped. 'You've been crying.' The tone was accusatory. 'Louisa, what's the matter? Look at me.'

'Don't you start,' Lucy replied. 'It's bad enough when the cat tells me off. I've had a strange day. Lizzie's fallen in love. It took all of half an hour, about a dozen phone calls and a visit to the Royal in Liverpool. I expected her to have more sense.'

'She went to hospital for treatment?'

Lucy had to think about that one. 'She needed osculation and possibly minimal manipulation.'

He laughed. 'You do realize you're talking to a doctor?'

'Yes. Surrounded by the buggers, I am. I have four next door, now you in here. All right. She went for a kiss and a cuddle. Head over heels, she is. And now she's visiting Alan, who gets a several-way bypass tomorrow. There's so much wrong, the surgeon's been using

131

Spaghetti Junction as a map.' She sat down. 'He could die. There's something in me that needs him not to die. It's probably for Lizzie's sake.'

'Please don't be upset. You look wonderful, by the way.'

'And you look tall. Take a seat. I can't stop thinking about him. You see, if I'd treated him differently, it might not have come to this.'

'I suppose you could have sent him to charm school, but—'

'No, David. I should have stood up to him.'

'And I should have been there for Tim when Anne died. So many things to regret, Lucy.' He smiled at her. 'Did you dress up for me?'

'I did indeed. It's an occasion. There's champagne on ice, and I've done some nibbles. Tallows is yours for the foreseeable future. No rent, but you pay the bills. I shall become a fundraiser.'

He punched the air with a closed fist. 'Thank you, thank you, thank you.'

'No need to go overboard. And you're allowed only one glass of shampers, because you insist on driving back.'

Still laughing, he shook his head. 'Look at you. Do you remember how boyish you were, how you fell out of every tree, fell into all the puddles and streams, fell out with anyone who treated me badly? Try to think about something less depressing than Alan's condition. He got into that state all by himself. Where's the naughty Louisa we all knew and loved?'

Yes, she had been a tomboy. Diane had been more ladylike and delicate, though she'd held her own in many an argument. 'I suppose I was a bit rugged,' she admitted. 'So. When do you invade my beautiful house? Because there are still bits and pieces belonging to me and the children – shall we say a month? Six weeks? A couple of months?'

'A lot longer,' was his reply. 'We'll be scrutinized every inch of the way. These are very sick children, and we can't move them around willy-nilly like a few dozen sacks of spuds.' He paused. 'I'm so grateful to you, Louisa. You always had a generous nature, but this goes beyond the bounds of reasonable expectation.'

She noticed that he couldn't quite look her in the eyes. 'Don't be embarrassed,' she said. 'About the accidental kiss, I mean.'

David leaned forward, elbows resting on his knees. 'For me, it was a happy accident.'

He was waiting for an answer. Why did everything happen at once? Life could be monotonous to the point of tedium, then all the buses arrived at the same time. Alan was due in theatre in a few hours, Lizzie was embroiled with the boy next door, Moira lived with difficulty and in hope, Richard wanted God alone knew what, while this man ... this man was lovely. 'It started as an accident,' she said carefully. 'But it was pleasant. We're both free agents, David, though I can't get a divorce until Alan's through surgery.' She swallowed. 'If he doesn't come through, I shan't need one. If he lives, I won't abandon him completely, you know.'

He nodded. 'It would be against your nature.'

She jumped up. 'I've had a thought. This is supposed to be a bed and breakfast place, though three rooms have been commandeered by the kids. However, there are three more. I know you said you wanted to go home, but, unless you have an early start, let's drink all the champagne and to hell with it, because you can sleep here. I insist.'

He had no early start, so they began the business of enjoying themselves.

'Daddy, you have to listen to me. For once in your life, pay attention to someone who isn't talking sand, cement and timber. You've known your wife for a very long time. She will not let you down. She's not the type to let anyone down, and you know it. Mother's the kind of person who always does what she—'

'I'm not living in her house. I can't stand the bloody woman. I never could be doing with saints. She makes me feel as if I should be crawling on my belly like a snake or a slug. Too much of the lady for my liking.'

Liz thought about the attractive woman she had left in that beautiful house on the banks of the Mersey. Contained in a little black dress, Lucy had appeared to be ready for a very long night on the tiles. But Liz couldn't describe the changes, dared not tell him that Mother had blossomed once away from him. 'She's always been fair and loyal, Daddy. Let's just get through tomorrow, and we can talk again when you're better.'

'If I live. If that bloody Welshman doesn't treat me like a leg of lamb.'

She heard the sharply honed edge of fear in his tone. A man on the verge of heart surgery should not be placed under any further stress. 'Look,' she said. 'Come to London and stay with me for a few months when all this is over. I don't share, and there's just one bedroom, but I've a sofa bed in the living room. I'm near a couple of parks, and not far from museums and art galleries.

Have a break. A change. Just till you get your strength back.'

Alan almost smiled. 'That would be good for your social life, eh? When they realize you've an invalid in the house, your mates will desert you in the blink of an eye. Who wants to hang about with the bag of bones I'm turning into?' He held up an arm. 'Look at that. My granny's knitting needles had more meat on them. I'm dying a bit at a time. No. I'd be in the way, Lizzie. And I don't like London enough to stay for any length of time. It's a weekend place, not a permanent address.'

'We go out all the time. My place isn't big enough for a crowd, so we hang about in various union bars.'

'And your love life?' he asked.

'My love life isn't in London.'

He attempted another smile. 'Tell me about him.'

So she indulged her father, weaving a fantasy about a relationship that had endured the passage of time and the distance between her and the chosen one. 'Funnily enough, he's going to be a cardio-thoracic surgeon. In a few years, he'll be doing operations like yours.'

'Nothing funny about my operation, Lizzie.'

'Strangely enough, then.'

He agreed with strangely. He was being cut open by a man who came from a country where slaughter was a daily occurrence. 'Bloody sheep farmers,' he cursed. 'They're all male voice choirs and talking Welsh when there are English folk within earshot. You should see the way he looks at me. He could well let me die on purpose.'

Liz wasn't going to upset him by arguing. Normally, she would have floored him for judging a whole nation in such a negative way, but he was ill, so the Welsh would have to wait – they were more than capable of surviving the rantings of one sick old man, anyway. The main thing was to keep Daddy settled and hopeful.

She'd never before thought of him as old. But years of beer, whisky, pies and chips had walked all over a face which, since the weight loss, had started to collapse inwards along lines that were suddenly very deep. He was beginning to look like the surface of some faraway planet, peaks, valleys, and deeper crevices where tidal rivers might have flowed in the long-distant past. She wished she'd brought her camera, because this might be the last time– No. A camera would have been wrong – almost macabre if the worst happened.

'You go now, love,' he said. 'You've got that park thing again tomorrow, haven't you?'

'Yes. Tomorrow afternoon, I'm a fourteen-year-old prostitute with a heroin problem.'

'Typecast, then?'

'Definitely.' She kissed him before leaving the room rather quickly, eyes so full of tears that she almost collided with a man in the corridor. 'Sorry,' she said, a tissue to her face. 'I wasn't looking where I was going.'

He moved away, stopped mid-stride and turned to face her. 'Are you his daughter? Mr Henshaw, I mean. Look, whoever you are, come into my office until you've composed yourself. You should sit down for a while.'

Liz mopped her face again. 'Yes, he's my father.'

'I'm his surgeon. The sheep-lover, he calls me, but I'm really Evans-Jones.' He drew her into a small room on the other side of the corridor. 'I just popped in to find some notes. So glad I bumped into you. His family should be aware of what's going on here. Don't get too upset, my dear. I do the impossible several times a week, miracles slightly less frequently. But I do have a rather good track record, so try to stay calm.'

She sat down. 'Sorry,' she repeated. 'About the sheep, I mean.'

He started to dig through a pile of paperwork. 'I've been called a lot worse, I can assure you. And a lot of your father's behaviour is bravado – he's terrified of me, of tomorrow, and of life after tomorrow. The bigger personalities are often the first to crack when they see the surgeon's tools. Women, of course, are much braver. Your father's been a very sick man, my dear. Even now, he's scarcely in the best of health.'

'And he's a bit yellow. Is he going to make it, Mr Evans-Jones?'

'I assure you, Miss Henshaw, that we will do our absolute best to drag him screaming through this. But his liver is struggling, and that affects other areas of his body. One thing is certain – if he does come through, he can never drink again. His life will have to change completely, though the main factor is, of course, the alcohol. He knows that. But whether he's prepared to be sensible is another matter altogether.'

Liz thought about that. She couldn't imagine her father going a full day without a drink. He'd done it in this place, but there had been no choice. Would he carry on behaving himself when there were no bars on windows, no locks on doors? 'Tall order,' she said eventually. 'He'd have to be watched twenty-four hours a day. Even visits to the bathroom would need to be supervised. It's beyond the reach of mere humanity – none of us can provide what he requires. He isn't great when it comes to willpower. My mother is the exact opposite – very restrained and controlled. But Daddy's always been a drinker, and he's got worse in the last few years.'

'Yes, I know. And I understand – my family's had its fair share of alcohol-dependent members. Your dad's condition isn't great. But it's a darned sight better than when he was admitted.' He paused for a couple of seconds. 'Your mother has never visited. I'm assured that she phones every day to ask after him, but she hasn't been here.' He found the item he had sought. 'Bingo,' he said quietly.

'She's left him. They don't get on. Looking back, I suppose they seldom did get on.'

'Ah. But she's paying for all this?'

'And offering to get him on his feet afterwards.'

He touched her arm briefly. 'Phone at about one o'clock tomorrow. Try not to worry – I make no promise, but we've saved people in conditions worse than his. Often, it's the ones who look worst that survive, while someone with a cleaner bill of health doesn't make it. Just be aware – I'll be fighting for your father's life, as will the very good team I lead.'

'Thank you.' They left the room, and Liz watched as the man walked away. At one o'clock tomorrow, she would be painting her face with fives and nines, would be walking with the pseudo-confident gait of a teen-age whore touting for business. She believed in getting into her characters, but she wondered how professional she really was. Because a true pro would make sure the show went on, come war, weather or a dead father. But she had to make that phone call, had to find out whether her father had survived a complicated procedure that would test the strength of younger, cleaner-living people.

She sat in her car for a long time. Mother's friend would be at Stoneyhurst by now. The two of them were to have champagne and fancy nibbles to celebrate the fact that Tallows was about to be handed over to a charity. Yet Liz knew that her mother was worried about Daddy. 'God, I feel so alone,' she whispered. 'I never felt so bloody lonely in my life.'

She'd seen her father, and she'd spoken to Mother, and Mother was not available at present. There were friends, of course, but she couldn't speak about the current situation to people who were miles away, many abroad, some working. Simon? He was on call. Her brothers were out on the town with the girls next door, and Liz felt terribly isolated. She was supposed to return to her digs in Manchester, a large house lent to community players who were currently performing in the parks. But some actors never stopped acting, and she didn't want fake sympathy from anyone.

Acting was definitely in her. Blood and bone, she was a performer, but she didn't actually like many of her fellows. The 'mwah' crowd, as she termed the fussier members of her profession, were difficult to know. It was almost as if they had no true self, no core. Perhaps they had deliberately wiped the hard drive so that they could 'be' whatever was asked of them. Most of her favourite companions were studying at various colleges attached to London University, and they covered a range of subjects from sciences to politics and right through all the arts. They were the true people, but they were all part of her other life, the one that was totally unconnected with the north, with her family and all its problems.

But yes, the show had to go on. She looked at the building that contained her male parent, turned the ignition key and drove out of the car park. Sometimes, a person had to bear aloneness. Sometimes, one had to become an adult. But oh, how she wanted her mother.

Champagne loosened tongues and clothing. David removed his jacket, took off the tie, undid his cuffs and rolled his sleeves to the elbows. Lucy kicked away her shoes and threw a pearl choker on the mantelpiece. She would not be beaten at Scrabble by a visitor whose young life she had saved so many times that he should be grateful. And he was cheating. She was absolutely sure that he was pulling the wool. Well, almost absolutely sure, that was. She saw a gleam in his eyes that bragged about superiority of mind and the ability to fool his companion.

This was serious business. Locked in mortal combat, they sat on either side of the kitchen table, each glaring at the other.

'Challenge if you wish,' he said. 'But those are true medical words, I can assure you. This one's a fungus closely related to thrush—'

'Starling?' she suggested. 'Crow, blackbird?'

'You'll be sorry you mocked me, Lucy. And this other word's a surgical instrument I found very useful for unblocking my kitchen sink.'

She cursed under her breath. 'Medical bits and pieces should be banned. I mean, you're shoving Xs and Zs all over the place – how the hell am I to know whether you're cheating? It's years since I was involved in medicine – you've invented loads of illnesses since I was a slip of a nurse. But those words do not look real.'

'They're real.'

'They're not.'

He shrugged. 'Challenge, then. You are within your rights to call me out, but your forfeit will be expensive when I am proved correct.'

She stared hard at her adversary. He was not the sort of man with whom she would wish to play poker. 'I think you're a lying toad,' she pronounced. 'What sort of word is that? Look at the length of it. Another couple of letters and it would be in the fireplace.'

He rooted in a pocket and retrieved a tape measure. 'Five and a bit inches. That's not long. I mean, these tiles are quite large. In a medical dictionary, it would be just about an inch. And we all know size isn't everything.'

'What the hell are you doing with a tape measure in your pocket? What else do you have? You're ruining a perfectly decent pair of trousers.'

'Yes, Mother.' He produced a couple of fluffy Mint Imperials, a sock, some string, a small packet of Kleenex and several tangled rubber bands.

'No improvement in that department, then,' Lucy said.

He explained that the rubber bands and string were for holding together patient notes when they got bulky, the sock was a stray, but a clean one, and the Kleenex were self-explanatory. He had no idea about the sweets, but he judged them to be a decent vintage and quite edible once held under a running cold tap for a few minutes. 'What are pockets for? To keep things in, Lucy. Don't go all matriarchal – my mother failed to train me. And they're my bloody pockets.'

'No caterpillars?'

'Not on this occasion. I'll go outside and find some if you like.'

'What about the tape measure?'

'Ah.' He stood up and stretched his arms. 'Sometimes, they lose a lot of weight. I measure ankles and wrists when they're asleep. So brave, those kids. But I like to upset them as little as possible.'

Scrabble and arguments forgotten, Lucy walked into the living room and sat in an armchair. He followed, and she watched while he shoved all the detritus back inside his trouser pockets, marvelled at how the grown man had hung on to some of his childhood characteristics. He'd always been a hoarder. And now, he collected children. Sick children. Was this a penance he had imposed on himself for abandoning his own son? 'David?'

'What?'

'Do you ever get lonely?'

He shrugged. 'Yes, of course I do. So I keep busy, try to be useful, try to make a difference to children whose lives would be a damned sight shorter without people like me. I do what needs to be done. Then I go home tired enough to sleep.'

'And there's been no other woman since Anne died?'

After a short pause, he delivered an answer to the one woman for whom he had rediscovered feelings. 'No. I can't. I don't mean it would be a physical impossibility – I know I still function, but that sort of closeness is something I'd never manage to take lightly. She died. Tim's death drew a thick, black line under hers. Lucy, I couldn't go through that again. To love someone as much as I loved her, to lose another . . . No.'

142

'So you believe that anyone who gets close to you is destined to die prematurely? Do you carry some dreadful contagion?'

He laughed, though there was no joy in the sound. 'Daft, isn't it? At least I'm not afraid of my feminine side. Most men want sex and don't see beyond it, but I'm one of the few who need to be in love and who fall in love through sex. So I avoid it.'

This, Lucy decided, was role reversal at its strangest. In her heart, she was a free woman. Any contact she might have with any other man would be morally OK, as long as he was single. She found David delightful, desirable and funny, but she could make no move on him, since he was also terrified. And she wasn't truly ready, either.

'The kiss was lovely,' he said. 'Clumsy, silly, but wonderful. Afterwards, when you had left Tallows, a very fierce hope burnt inside me for all of three or four minutes.'

'Yes, David.'

'Yes what?'

'I was burnt, too. By the kiss. Look at me. Stop avoiding eye contact. Stop being afraid of me. There is a compromise, and it's staring both of us in the face.'

'Is it?'

She remembered now how he had driven her crackers as a child. He always weighed his options thoroughly, though the elements he included in the recipe were not necessarily the right ones. A deep thinker even then, he would wander along the B roads in his mind, while faster routes, the motorways, were often ignored. 'How many times a month do you come to the children's hospital and to hospices in the Liverpool area?

Take a room here. As long as you let me win at Scrabble, I'll give you a special rate.'

His jaw dropped for a few seconds.

'Close your mouth, David. There's a bus coming.'

'Live with you?'

'I mean alongside, not with as in sharing a bed. Just to give us the chance to get to know one another.' He was doing it again. He'd gone for a walk down all the unpaved alleys in his brain, was failing completely to take a quicker, more sensible route. Why did he insist on making everything so complicated? 'What are you thinking about now?' she asked.

'Samson.'

'Why? Are you planning to go for a haircut?'

'Eh?'

'I give up.' She went to make a pot of tea. David Vincent was a typical mad professor. He had gone biblical, so she had simply gone. But he had followed her. She could feel him standing behind her, could hear him breathing.

'What?' she asked, apropos of nothing.

'There's Smokey,' he said.

'And Delilah,' she replied quickly.

'What?'

'Samson and Delilah. Didn't she cut his hair and make the temple fall down or something? I tend to get her confused with the other one – dance of the seven veils.' Lucy could be obtuse if she made an effort, so she was making that effort.

'Salome,' he said. 'Wanted the head of John the Baptist on a plate.'

She shrugged. 'I'd settle for a curry, but there's no accounting for taste.'

'Louisa?'

'Yes?'

'Samson's my dog. He's a black Labrador. My neighbour usually looks after him while I'm working, though I sometimes take him with me. He's very good with ... with death. When I'm losing a patient, it's a case of bugger the germs and let Samson in. If the child wakes, the family and my dog get the last smile. And for some reason I've never completely worked out, he comforts the bereaved.'

This man was leading an almost incredibly sad life. Lucy turned away from his pain and poured hot water into the teapot. He was far too sensitive a soul for the career he had chosen, yet she understood him perfectly. The children didn't all die. Many juvenile leukaemias were stoppable, so he saw good stuff as well as bad. But the bad certainly stayed with him. She wanted to shake him, and she wanted to comfort him. But no, that would be too maternal, and she didn't need another child.

When the tea had been carried through to the living room, Lucy reclaimed her chair and waited for him to be seated. 'So you're planning to go through life without taking any kind of risk, David?'

'I stumble,' he replied. 'I muddle along trying not to think, except about my work. Set in my ways, I suppose. And I tend to keep my distance.' He lowered his tone. 'But I'm still just a man, Lucy. If I were to stay here for any length of time, I'd get fond of you. I'm already fond. And none of us has to dig very deep to find the animal in us. Two glasses of my champagne are in your rubber plant container for safe keeping. Sorry. I have to drive home. I daren't stay. And Samson's in the car. His hobby's people-watching.'

Lucy sighed. Whatever had the rubber plant done to deserve that? She stood and walked to the front window. 'It's time you let that dog out of the car. Glad you left the window down for him. Bring him in.'

'But—'

'Bring him in, David.'

He looked at the cat, who was curled peacefully in his basket. 'Smokey won't—'

'Bring him in.' She separated the three syllables as if talking to a small boy. 'For once, do something unusual. Let's take a walk on the wild side.'

She sat and waited until the beautiful black dog led his master back into the house. The canine's leathery nose lifted and sniffed the air. He could smell cat.

'Stay where you are, David,' Lucy said. 'Watch and learn. Samson's a Labrador, a breed that's non-aggressive for the most part. And Smokey had a problem, you see. His mother died, and we needed to feed him with a dropper. No sleep for nights on end. To keep him warm when he grew a bit larger, we shoved him in with the dog.' She lowered her voice to a whisper. 'My cat thinks he's a dog, so he chases other cats. Our old Butch has been dead for years, but Smokey hasn't forgotten that dogs are not his enemy. Don't tell him the truth, please. Never, ever tell my cat that he isn't a dog.'

When Samson had curled beside the cat's basket, David returned to the sofa. 'I can't hide behind the dog, then.'

'No. A few months ago, I would have been the one in hiding. I was terrified of life until I actually moved out and did something about myself. Change is sometimes required.'

Looking at her was painful. She was so beautiful, so

kind and lively and amusing. A part of him wanted to give up everything – the job, the house, the monotonous existence that was safe and predictable. But he didn't know how to let go, how to stop trying, researching, fighting for remissions and cures. 'So when Tallows is ready, you will stay there sometimes?'

'Yes. As long as you teach me enough of the medical side, I can even help – read to them, play with them. I don't want to nurse, but I'd like to know some of the rules in case there's a crisis.'

Whatever he did, Lucy was going to be in his life. She was giving him a house, for goodness' sake, was allowing the charity to use a valuable property that would make a difference in so many lives. Anne would have done the same. But she wasn't another Anne – she was Louisa, and he wanted her, and wanted not to want her.

He was too intense. Sometimes, he suspected that he hovered on the brink of obsessive-compulsive, because he worked too hard, played too seldom and was very tidy in his professional life. At home, however, he lived in a tip. Should a microbiologist stumble into David's private life, he would doubtless discover enough cultures to form a small sub-continent. It would have to be cleaned. It would have to be cleaned in case Lucy visited him.

'Where's my room?' he asked.

'First half-landing, door on the right. The door on the left is your bathroom. It isn't en suite, but it's the biggest one up there. I'll feed these animals.'

He watched while an orderly queue of two formed in the doorway. The cat was at the front, because this was his house; the dog, displaying all the gentle humour for which his breed was famous, wagged his tail hopefully. The dishes were placed together on the floor. Smokey went to his own, while Samson waited until Lucy had finished topping up his dinner with wholemeal pasta. Then he stood next to Smokey and ate.

'They could use you at the United Nations,' David told his hostess.

'No,' she replied. 'They'd be much better off with Labradors. We are the only animal that kills for recreation. Apart from minks – they're almost as unpleasant as humans. And I'm not that keen on crocodiles, though I'm sure they'd represent some of these neo-Nazis that keep springing up from time to time – Saddam Hussein and Robert Mugabe types?'

He smiled at her, leaned against the door frame and watched age-old enemies eating together. Laws were made to be broken. Why could he not alter his own stupid and meaningless manifesto? Lucy would make someone an ideal companion, a beautiful wife and, he suspected, a willing and interesting lover. What was the matter with him? If he didn't get a move on, someone would snap her up. Heat rushed to his face. He'd been thinking of her as some sort of bargain in the basement of a department store.

The front door crashed inward. 'Happy birthday, Mums,' chorused two voices. Paul and Mike drew to an abrupt halt when they saw David. 'Sorry,' said Paul. 'We forgot about you. You're the man who's going to make use of the old homestead. Yes? I'm Paul, he's Mike, and this is John Lennon.' He held up a brown paper package. 'We got him in Liverpool.' He stared at David. 'You look a bit like Lennon.'

Lucy entered from the kitchen, a dog and a cat hot

on her heels. 'This is Samson,' she told her boys. 'He works with David – Dr Vincent – helping to care for sick children. I thought you were going clubbing? And my birthday was weeks ago.'

Mike explained that they came home early because someone might have pinched John Lennon had they stayed out late. 'We had a bit of trouble finding him, and we weren't letting him go,' Mike explained.

She opened the package, her eyes riveted to the picture. 'All his songs,' she said quietly, as if she were speaking in church. 'His face – even his spectacles – made from words.'

Paul spoke to David. 'According to Mums's friend Glenys, she's been in mourning ever since he died, which was before any of us were born. Wore out two copies of "Imagine" when we were small, she did. Then we were forced to listen to *Shaved Fish* for months on end.'

'Shut up,' Lucy ordered. 'John was special. And thank you for this lovely, wonderful present. It's going in the kitchen, because I always felt he'd be happiest in a kitchen. At home, you see.' She kissed the glass that sheltered the print. 'You'll be OK with me, kid. You should never have gone to New York – I would have looked after you.'

The three men listened while she continued to talk to a dead man. Mike squatted down and stroked the dog. 'You're a grand fellow,' he said. 'She'll get no sense out of John Lennon, will she?'

David sat and watched a happy family. The twins looked like their mother, though they were by no means feminine. They seemed to have inherited her nature, too. 'My dog and your cat just had supper together.'

'Smokey likes dogs,' Mike said. 'I wish we could keep this one. He has a lovely coat.'

'Fish three times a week,' David advised. 'If you ever get a black Lab, remember the fish.'

'As long as it's not shaved,' said Paul. 'We all had our fill of that. Anyway, Mums,' he called into the kitchen, 'we're off next door for supper. See you later.' They left.

David stood again in the kitchen doorway. She was hanging her picture next to a huge Welsh dresser, but she couldn't quite reach the nail. He came up behind her, took the item and, with his arms enclosing her, placed John Lennon where he belonged. 'There. Is he straight enough for you?'

'He was always straight,' she answered. 'When he said the Beatles were more famous than Jesus, he was voicing his truth. Not many people spoke about Jesus, while everyone knew the four of them.'

David continued to hold her.

'Remember King Lear? What a fool he was? It was his jester, the court entertainer, the fool, who had all the sense. John Lennon was like that. He acted the idiot and spoke the truth. That's why I like him. Oh, and his music was a bit good, too.' She turned and faced the man in whose gentle hold she stood. 'Isn't this a bit dangerous, David?'

'Yes.'

'Then slow down. We have the rest of our lives to inject a little steel into your vertebrae.' She laughed softly. 'You'll be safe enough tonight, because my sons will be here. But you should be forewarned – I think you're gorgeous, little David Vincent.' She ducked under

150

his arm and sauntered away. It was going to take time, but Dr David Vincent was a marked man.

He lay in a bed in her house, Samson on a blanket in a cardboard box on the floor by his side. The room was spectacular, black and white with an occasional splash of red. She had style, and was clearly unafraid when it came to decoration. Metallic wallpaper stretched the breadth of the room behind his bed. Compared to his bedroom at home, this was pure, hotel luxury.

He thought about the woman downstairs. Like any other man who desired a particular woman, he wanted to breathe her in, taste her, touch her – all the ordinary things that happened daily to guarantee the future of various species. But he indulged himself, allowed himself to be different. 'Too bloody precious to be normal, David,' he whispered. 'Too bloody precious to step on unknown soil. You're a coward.'

It was a warm night, so David had settled on top of the covers, just a couple of throws over his body. She was downstairs, and sleep seemed to be a million miles beyond his reach. 'I'm not right in the head,' he told the dog. He'd undergone bereavement counselling, psychotherapy, acupressure and hypnosis. Nothing worked. That wasn't true, because work worked, but it was a distraction, something that engrossed him to the point where he didn't have time to think about his pathetic self. She made him think. By God, she presented a challenge.

Lucy had been talking about a new cleaner who was starting tomorrow. She was half of a pair, and the other half was attached to rotten wisdom teeth that needed surgical removal. 'When did I stop cleaning?' he asked.

Samson delivered a quiet, polite woof before going back to sleep.

Mrs Moss had been the cleaner – Anne's cleaner. He'd let her go when he'd buggered off to India, and the house had scarcely been touched since then. He was a disgrace to his colleagues. Although people in the medical profession had a reputation for living in dirt, he didn't know anyone who existed as carelessly as he did. It had to stop. No. It had to start. Life must begin again, because he was on the verge of thinking that he might just—

The front door slammed. It wasn't the twins, because they'd been back for an hour or more and were asleep in an area referred to as 'the gods', because it was built into the roof at the rear of the house. David sat up and listened. He heard movement, then two female voices. One was raised until the words stopped and the crying began. He pulled on a towelling robe he'd discovered in the bathroom. It made him hot, but that couldn't be helped. 'Stay,' he said to Samson. 'I won't be long.'

He crept downstairs and listened guiltily at the door, which was too thick to allow sound to pass clearly through its panels. After a few moments, he knocked and entered. 'Sorry,' he said. 'I heard a noise and thought I'd better . . . Is this Lizzie?'

Lucy nodded and motioned him to sit in an armchair. 'What's the matter?' he mouthed.

Liz dragged herself out of her mother's arms. 'Sorry,' she sobbed.

'Don't apologize on my account,' he said. 'I was having difficulty sleeping among all this splendour. Brilliant wallpaper,' he told Lucy. 'Bold and brave. It works. Now, why is this beautiful girl crying?'

Liz, slightly calmer, focused on the stranger. 'Dr Vincent? Glad to meet you, though I'd have preferred to be in a better state. I think I've run away. I'm supposed to be in Manchester.'

'I know I've run away,' Lucy said.

'I used a car to get here.' David smiled at the weeping girl. 'I gave up running when I stopped playing cricket.'

'He was rubbish at cricket, anyway.' Lucy stood up and walked into the kitchen. She knew that David would make her daughter feel better; she remembered the kindness he had displayed in childhood.

Behind her, David addressed her daughter gently. 'Is this about your dad, Lizzie? Because if it is, that's perfectly reasonable. You say you've run away?'

She nodded, too upset for speech.

'Sometimes, life's too hard to face.'

She blurted it all out to this stranger. The words were crippled by emotion, but she managed to make herself understood. She had to be a trouper, had to go on stage tomorrow no matter what. Except that it was already tomorrow, and she was going to be exhausted. If she phoned the hospital at one and learned that her father was dead, she would be unable to perform, and that would be unprofessional. Even if he didn't die, he'd be on the edge, fastened down in some high dependency unit – so was she really an actor? The show had to go on, no matter what.

David listened intently to every word. 'Your mother has a cleaner starting tomorrow, I believe. To be honest, I find the prospect of this particular woman terrifying, but Louisa will need to be on hand. I'll go with you to Manchester. I'll be there in whatever you call the wings when you're out in the open. You don't know me, but I knew your mother thirty-five years ago.'

Lucy entered with mugs of hot chocolate on a tray. 'Carol Makin can manage without me, David. In fact, if I stayed, she'd be organizing me as if I were an untidy wardrobe. We'll both come, Lizzie. I'll make the phone call, and we'll talk about it after the play.'

Liz shook her head. 'No. I have to know right away. Stuff happens all the time to people in the theatre, but they carry on. Because a real performer can march ahead, and—'

'And you're still a student.'

'The will to continue no matter what – that sort of thing isn't learned, Mother. It's either in you or it isn't. It's all part of being an actor. An actor wouldn't need his mother tonight, because he'd be completely wrapped up in tomorrow. I'm too engrossed in my selfishness. It's not even the idea of his death that's frightening me – it's my own pathetic reaction to it. I shouldn't be so worried about me, should I?'

'And a doctor whose wife has just died shouldn't be coming over all hare krishna on top of a mountain in India while his son develops leukaemia,' David said.

This statement put a stop to Liz's tears. 'No,' she whispered.

'Yes,' he replied. 'We all have failings. The secret is to learn from them. Hare krishna might have helped me reach a purer state of inner consciousness, but it did nothing for my boy. Might he have been saved? I'll never know. So. Did you drive here after a panic attack?'

Liz mopped her eyes with a tissue. 'I visited my dad.

I've no illusions about him, but he's still my father, part of my family. Even when Mother divorces him, he'll be a huge portion of my history. I don't want to lose him. He's shrunk in the past few weeks. He looked ancient. He's not fifty yet, but he looks about eighty.'

It took both of them the better part of an hour to calm Liz to the point where she fell asleep on a sofa. Lucy pulled a car rug over her child, then left the room with David. 'Thank you,' she said. 'And I mean that. I'm glad you were there. She needed me for the love, you for the sense. Will you drive tomorrow? I'm a bit jittery, too.'

'Of course I'll drive. I'll need to make a couple of calls to get my patients diverted to other doctors, but it's all doable.'

She put her arms round his shoulders. 'You're a good man, David Vincent. I'm not ready for you yet, but I promise you that when I am I'll show no mercy. You're lovely, you are. I managed you when you were a child, and I can manage you now.'

'I would question that,' he said before attempting a change of subject. 'Doesn't she look like Diane? Lizzie, I mean.'

'Yes. I think my sister came back to me in my youngest child. She's talented, lively and afraid. Whereas you are talented and afraid without the lively bit.'

'And you're going to be my lively bit?'

She smiled. 'I'll poke a stick through the bars of your cage and see what happens.'

'And if I bite?'

'You'd better.' She abandoned him and returned to the main job. She was still a mother, and David would keep.

*

155

Sleep eluded Alan. They'd given him something, but it wasn't going to work. Perhaps the dose was low, as he was to be anaesthetized in the morning. It was two o'clock. In a few hours, he would be a piece of meat on a slab with that bloody Welsh butcher standing over him. Meat. 'Will I ever taste steak again, will I ever have another cup of tea?'

Starvation was now total, something to do with the operation. Easterly Grange had always skimped on food, supposedly for his own good, but this was ridiculous. He had no appetite, and he reckoned that was because they had shrunk his stomach to the size of a walnut. He wasn't afraid, he told himself repeatedly. But he was lying, and he knew he was lying. Death was not a pleasant prospect, but neither was life if he could never have another drink, a smoke, or a decent plate of northern fare.

The chap next door was moaning again. Night after night he did this, but the staff had been unable to move him. Alan's room was no longer locked, because he was supposedly through withdrawal, and this was one of his small rewards. He walked into the corridor and listened, an ear against the door behind which the wailing man was parked. Very quietly, he turned the knob and let himself into the room.

A woman sat next to the bed. 'Sorry,' she said. 'He's being shifted upstairs tomorrow, because the rest of you need some peace. You can come in. He won't know you're here. Sometimes, he doesn't know I'm here.'

Alan closed the door. 'What's up with him?' he asked.

'Brain tumour,' the woman whispered. 'They did what they could, but there's damage and that's why we've

had all the crying. He went a bit childlike, and now ...
What about you?'

'Heart op, nine o'clock. I can't sleep. Nothing to do with your husband – I think I've got used to him, and I have a thing that plays music through headphones. It's not him. I'm nervous.'

'You must be. I'm Trish, by the way.'

'Alan.'

They sat and stared at the frail, sick man in the bed. He looked a lot older than his wife, Alan thought. Just a shell, he was curled and twisted as if left out in the weather for months on end, no shelter, no care. 'How long's he been like this, Trish?'

'Months. It started with headaches and a bit of double vision, some dizziness – could have been anything, but it wasn't anything, it was something, something big. They had a go – took away about eighty per cent of it, but they damaged some of the good cells as well. We managed. Till it kicked off again for its second bloody half. Too late for chemo. So we just sit and wait. I sit and wait, that is. Howie lies there moaning while I try to keep the business going.'

'Howie? That's never Howie Styles.'

She turned slowly and looked at Alan. 'The same. Biggest builder in Manchester, and now look at him. You knew about him?'

'I did. I'm Alan Henshaw. Had to give up work because of my health. The wife and kids are gone – I made sure they had all the money. Because after tomorrow, I'll be dead or an invalid.'

'Henshaw the developer from Bolton?'

'Yes, that's me.'

'So – where's your missus?'

He shrugged. 'Buggered off somewhere or other, pastures new, I reckon. The kids are all at university, so I've done my bit.'

Trish Styles stood up and took Alan's hand. 'Good luck, lad. I'm going home now, but I'll ask after you tomorrow.'

He sat for a while with his neighbour after Mrs Styles had left. This man in the bed wasn't much older than Alan, but he looked about the same age as Adam. His wife was a nice little body, ordinary, decent and probably very rich. She would soon be a rich widow, but she'd be able to pick and choose. Trish Styles wouldn't want anything to do with a knackered builder from Bolton, would she?

Anyway, he'd probably be dead, so what was the point of speculation? In this cheerful frame of mind, he left Mr Styles and went to try again to fall asleep. Or should he stay awake for his last few hours on earth? What did it matter? This was a holding bay for the undertaker's parlour anyway. This dump was already dead.

Six

Carol Makin in her fighting gear was a sight to behold – easily as impressive as the average galleon in full sail. She slammed the door of her van and kicked a rear wheel with one of her Doc Martens, and had Lucy been able to lip-read she might have been privy to some good, old-fashioned Anglo-Saxon curses. Wearing leggings stretched to within an inch of their lives and a tabard that was clearly home-made, Carol looked like a modern-day Valkyrie, armed to the teeth with buckets, mops and a box of implements that would not have seemed out of place in a torture chamber, or on a field of battle. She stepped into the living room. 'You off out?' was her greeting to Lucy, who explained that she was bound for Manchester.

'Bloody hell, that's a shame. Wouldn't go there if you paid me. Still, I suppose someone has to do it.' She sniffed and gave David the once-over. 'Who's this one, then?'

'A long-standing friend,' Lucy replied.

'Then he'd best sit down, eh? You can get very-close veins from being stood up all the while. Me mam was a martyr to them. Worked at the biscuit factory all her life, God love her, ended up with legs like blue ropes twisted all over the place. At the end, she couldn't look a custard cream in the eye.' She stared hard at David. 'Have you got very-close veins?'

'Close enough,' he said.

Disdain coloured her expression. 'I do know the right words. I just like to keep folk on their toes, that's all. Unless they've got varicose doodahs, in which case they should be sat with one or both legs in an elevated position supported by whatever. Now, I don't need no help from nobody, Lucy, but have you anything particular wants doing?'

'Just find your feet.' Lucy tried not to grin, because the enormous woman had probably not seen her feet in a decade at least. 'And leave the boys in bed – in my experience, they're less trouble when asleep.'

'And how long have we had a dog? I seen the cat yesterday, but—'

'My dog,' said David. 'And he's coming to Manchester.'

'Bloody cruel,' Carol said under her breath as she walked away. 'RSPCA wants telling.'

'What's wrong with Manchester?' David whispered when Carol had left the scene.

'Nothing.' Lucy grinned. 'This, in case you hadn't noticed, is Liverpool. There's been a war on for the better part of fifty years, but Manchester's nearly twice the size of Liverpool, so Scousers depend on their wits. I'm on their side, actually. They need a bigger airport and a huge conference centre, then they could pinch some of the Manks' business. But I'm not proud, so Lizzie and I will shop at the Trafford Centre while you take Samson home. Ah – here's Lizzie now.'

The girl entered the room. She looked rather wan,

but at least she wasn't weeping. 'Sorry to keep you waiting, Mums,' she said.

Lucy's face lit up. 'That's the first time you've ever called me Mums.'

'Is it? When I talk about you with the twins, you're Mums sometimes. But Mother suited the old you. You were too dignified and patient for any baby names. Seeing you with your top shelf hanging out of that little black number last night, I thought – yes, the boys are right. She's a Mums, and she's sexy. Mind, having a sexy mother can be a bit unnerving.'

David agreed, though he said nothing.

Carol walked in. She had now added a pair of orange Marigolds to her delightful ensemble. 'Well,' she said, a rubber-gloved hand on each bulging hip. 'Sight for sore eyes, or what? You're a stunner, girl.' The 'girl' emerged as 'gairl' again, but no one was counting. 'I seen you last time, but you look bloody great today. Sort of pale and perfect. Tell you what, love. Yer mam says you're an actress, and if you don't get snapped up in the blink of me eye, I'll eat me golden retriever.'

The room stopped for a beat of time. 'You have a dog, then?' Lucy managed eventually.

The cleaner shook her head mournfully in the face of such stupidity, returned to the kitchen and came back with a brass-coloured rod in an orange hand. 'See? It goes down the back of radiators and retrieves stuff. You click it and it grabs hold of socks and knickers what have fell down the back, like. Some people don't know nothing.' She laughed. 'It was me dad's. He couldn't walk proper at the end, and this was his golden retriever.'

Lucy glanced at the clock. 'We have to go, Carol. Just one thing – don't let the cat out through the front door and make sure any front room he's in has all the windows closed. I know it's a nuisance, but he's precious, and he knows it. There's food in the fridge if you're here through lunch, and I'll see you soon.' She turned to go. 'Oh, and if you do eat, stay with your food, or he'll pinch it. He thinks everything here is his, and we're allowed his leftovers.'

The three of them went out to the car. With the dog lead in her hand, Lizzie asked her mother, 'Where do you find these wonderful people? You had a collection of oddities at Tallows over the years, didn't you?'

'It's my magnetic personality,' she replied. 'And I love folk who're just that little bit different.'

'She's a big bit different,' David whispered.

Lucy dug him in the ribs. 'Sizeist,' she accused.

Lizzie said nothing. But she took it all in. David was made for Mums. And Mums was made for him.

She looked good. Richard Turner peered through a gap in the blind and watched while she got into that bloody man's car. Her daughter followed. Lizzie must have decided to leave her car here, because she was now sitting with a large black dog in the rear seat of the visitor's Audi. The visitor was a pocket-patter, one of those who seemed to look vague most of the time. He was also a leukaemia specialist and an old friend of Lucy's, someone she had known for most of her child-hood.

Paul and Mike had been full of news last night. Apparently this Dr Vincent was going to occupy Lucy's pile, a grand house of whose existence Richard had not been fully aware. So. She was sexy, clever, beautiful and loaded. She was also a benefactor, since she intended to allow the doctor to use the house free of charge as a respite care centre. She had volunteered as a fundraiser, so she would be seeing a lot of Dr Vincent.

Lucy was in a dark suit today, one of those cleverly cut things that probably cost an arm and both legs. She had good legs. She had good everything, but Moira had muddied the waters so badly that Richard could scarcely look Lucy in the face these days. He'd been forced to settle for a pale imitation, one Lexi Phillips, supermarket worker, bleached blonde, owner of two large breasts and three or four brain cells. When in her bed, he closed his eyes and thought of Lucy. Lucy, Lexi, the same initial, but miles apart. There was no after-talk with Lex. Why couldn't Moira learn to keep her trap shut?

Alexandra Phillips had no idea of Richard's place in society. As far as she was concerned, he was a businessman, one who dealt in this and that. Liverpool had many this-and-that-ers, so she probably thought he was a crook. He didn't care. Moira was out of bounds, as was Lucy, so he had to take what he could get, because a man had needs. An educated man had many needs.

Dr Vincent had stayed the night in Stoneyhurst. 'It's none of my business,' Richard whispered. 'But oh, God, how I wish she'd never come here, because she's turned me upside down.' She was ruining his life – no, he was doing that himself. But the sight of her, the sound of her – these were pleasure and pain, and he'd be better off if she moved back to Bolton, or wherever she'd come from.

It was almost time for surgery, and the car was disappearing at the end of the road. Never before had he desired a woman this strongly. No, that wasn't true.

The poor, wonderful, crazy creature he had married had been perfection, but a disease had stolen her, and he would never find her like again. Without informing himself fully, he had fallen in love with the woman next door. A song bumbled about in his head, words and music colliding before arranging themselves until the whole thing began to make sense. Phil Collins? 'The First Cut is the Deepest'. Was it? Moira had been ill for so long that he could scarcely recall how he had felt when the diagnosis first arrived. Was it Phil Collins or Genesis?

But this second cut felt like major surgery without pain management. He hated a man he hadn't met, a man Lucy had known for many years. What chance did Richard have? His wife was alive. According to Lucy's twins, David Vincent was a widower, an expert at Scrabble and a good sort. He had arrived with no attachments, no dependants apart from a large black dog. The man was an exact template of the sort of partner Lucy might want.

Richard would never manage to wish his wife dead. The character he had loved for half his life was still there, and he enjoyed her company. When she wasn't begging Lucy to give sex to her husband, or to marry him in the fullness of time, that was. Oh, the shame of it.

Patients were arriving. They all sat together in the waiting room, and he didn't like to leave them for too long. Which was silly, because germs transferred in seconds, and hung around long after their carriers had disappeared. Whatever, he went to do the job that many thought less worthy than work performed by surgeons and hospital medics. They were wrong. Because here was the hub of medicine; here was where a decent diagnostician performed the most awesome of all tasks. Without a good GP, there would be no chance for anybody.

They came and gave him his pre-med. He was already dressed in the hospital's best off-the-peg frock, open all the way down the back, pretty bows at neck and waist, to hell with any danger of modesty.

The sheep-lover entered. 'How are we today then?'

'I've no idea how you are, but I don't care if you cut my head off. Whatever was in that needle's made me happy as a pig in muck.'

'OK. Good. Just thought I'd pop in before I scrub. I was very careful this morning – killed only two sheep. But I'll get their blood from under my nails before starting on you. When it comes to the sewing up, what is your preference? Blanket stitch, chain stitch, cross stitch? And would you like a particular colour of sewing thread?'

Alan found himself laughing. 'Oh, how glad I am to have a mad Welshman as my doctor. Go on, Taff, owld lad. Get ready to do your worst. You've got me in stitches already, and we've not kicked off. Just make sure the referee's fair. I don't want a red card before I've even dribbled.'

He was placed on a trolley and wheeled out to the corridor. It was very *Holby City*, all ceiling lights and pinging lift doors, but without the urgency displayed on TV. Someone called his name. 'Alan? Is that Alan from room seven? Hang on a minute, you lot.'

Too tired to raise his head, he tried to place the voice. Last night. Remember. Styles – her first name was Trish, and she was standing over him. 'All the best, love,' she said. 'I'll be here later on when you come back.'

Would he be here later on? He couldn't manage to care. One of the porters explained to the woman that the patient had been given an injection, and wasn't fully responsive. 'It'll be a longish job,' the man said. 'We'll be sure to let you know when he's back, Mrs Styles.'

'Thanks. Look after him.'

Well, somebody cared, then. He was pushed into a lift that travelled very slowly because it was for sick people, and the porters were talking about runners in the three-thirty at Haydock. Life went on, it seemed. Whether he lived or died, nothing would change, and only his daughter and the wife of a man with a brain tumour would give a toss. Anyway, he had a chance, didn't he? Taffy the sheep man thought there was a chance. He had quite a decent sense of humour for a Welshman, did old Taff. And if Alan could only get his hands on the drug they'd given him, he'd never need another drink.

Lucy and Lizzie went on a huge shopathon at the Trafford Centre while David made phone calls and took the dog to the neighbour in Bolton. Samson liked going next door, because there were children who rolled in mud, water and any other forbidden substance that happened to be available, and the dog shared their enthusiasm for such naughtiness.

Phone calls were made, and David returned to the scene of the crime when he had sorted out ward rounds and outpatients. He knew it was a crime when he picked up the two women, since they had between them enough packages and parcels to justify the hire of a removal van. 'Anything left in there?' he asked, pointing to the enormous shopping centre. 'Because if there is, you may as well go back and pick it up, get the full set.'

Lucy awarded him a withering glance. 'The trouble with men,' she said, 'is that they have no concept of the joy that comes with shopping. Take a man into a department store, and he shrivels and starts sulking and looking at price tags. No imagination.' She handed him a small paper bag. 'That's for you. Don't say we don't care about you.'

'Thanks. I think.' It was a navy-blue tie with matching socks. The problem lay in the picture of Bart Simpson lowering his shorts to display a bare backside. Bart was on the tie just once, but was repeated many times on the socks.

Lizzie completed the set when she handed him the underpants. 'Children like these things,' she told him. 'They won't see the underpants, but you'll know they're there.'

They were right, of course. About the tie and the socks, anyway. He worked with sick kids, and all children loved cartoons.

'They had the Tellytubbies, but I thought Bart's bare bum was the clear winner,' Lucy said. 'Madam here bought four pairs of jeans, and they all look the same to me. She says jeans freaks will know what's what. Four pairs of shoes as well, David. Anyone would think my daughter had more than her fair share of feet. She's an octopus.' She wished her daughter would stop looking at her watch. It was eleven-thirty, and Alan would be in theatre.

A glance passed between Lucy and David. 'Do you know how to get to Heaton Park from here?' he asked. 'Or am I going to need satnav?'

'Satnav,' Lizzie replied. 'I've never gone to the park from Trafford before.'

When the shopping had been squashed into the boot, two spent-out women and one exhausted doctor climbed into the Audi. David had not been in close company with women for a very long time. They had busy minds and hurrying bodies. They were always up to something and, in spite of tiredness, he was enjoying himself. But the problem remained. Lizzie's dad was probably on bypass and, at any moment now, a team would be concentrating on his repaired heart and trying to shock it back to life.

The drive round the edge of the city was quiet. When asked how she was feeling, Liz answered in broad Lancashire dialect, so she was clearly busy getting inside her part. They left her alone with her demons, yet they knew she was glad to have their company.

After snacks in a small café, they repaired to Heaton Park and abandoned Lizzie to the make-up department, which was a large tent behind the arena in which the play would take place. Now it was Lucy's turn to start checking her watch. 'Stop it,' David told her several times. 'We can't phone until Lizzie gets here, anyway.'

She arrived at ten minutes to one. Lucy's gasp was audible. 'Where's my daughter?' she cried. 'What have you done with her, and who the heck are you?'

Lizzie shook her head, then lifted her face to the heavens. 'I think I look great. Just pray the skirt doesn't ride up, because I'm wearing a thong.'

David hid a smile. She looked every inch the tart,

make-up thick and colourful, hair backcombed and piled all over her head with little wisps escaping here and there. 'You look great,' he said. 'Here.' He handed her his phone. 'I've programmed in the Easterly Grange number – have this call on the National Health, because God knows you'll get very little else.'

'I'm scared, David.'

'Do you want me to do it?'

She nodded. 'My hands are shaking. You get the hospital, I'll do the talking.'

But before David got through, Lizzie's own phone rang. For a moment, she didn't know what to do, but she decided to get rid of the caller first. 'Hello? Sorry, I have to go and— Oh, it's you.' She paused. 'Yes? And you're pleased with him? How did you get my— Oh, I see. I don't know how to thank you. But ... well ... thank you so much.' She closed the phone.

'Well?' Lucy took a step towards her daughter.

'Mr Evans-Jones found my number on Dad's phone. He knew I was worried, so he wanted to put me out of my misery. Dad's doing well. They have to keep an eye on him, but they're pleased. Only close family allowed for the next few days, but he survived it, Mums.'

'Good, I'm so glad, love.' And Lucy was glad. He hadn't been much of a husband, but this girl wanted her daddy to live, and he would live. He had to live. 'Go and do your bit, Lizzie. I bet you'll be wonderful – can't wait to see you in action.' She looked again at the clothes. 'Mind, the sort of action you're ready for shouldn't really have an audience.'

'Mums, you are so ... old-fashioned.' The young hooker walked away, hips swaying in an exaggerated fashion. David offered his arm. 'Shall we?'

Like a pair stealing a day off work, they wandered round one of the biggest parks in Europe, buying ice creams and cups of tea, watching children running about, waiting for the summons to attend Lizzie's play. They were easy in each other's company, and might have been mistaken by onlookers for a married couple because they looked so right together.

The awaited summons arrived, a great bell booming across the grass. They had reserved seats in the front row, which placed them almost on top of the action, though there was none for at least ten minutes, as audience members were still arriving. All they could see was a row of four vertical boards, like plain flats on the stage of a theatre. Yet there was electricity in the air, as there always is before a performance. David whispered to his companion. 'She'll get through it, Lucy. There's a lot of you in her. I dare say she'll always finish what she starts.'

There were no curtains; there was no stage. Six men in overalls walked on with lamp posts and billboards advertising foodstuffs and designer gear. They stood and clicked their fingers in rhythms that became quite intricate and skilful. Through a sound system arrived Dave Brubeck's 'Take Five', a piece from the sixties that was reputedly almost impossible to conduct, since it had an unusual number of beats to the bar. The clicking kept several tempos, all of them perfect, all in keeping with the complicated music. Brubeck faded, and the clickers left.

They were replaced by beat-boxers, five lads whose mouths were the only instruments required to produce amazing sounds. One started a stopwatch, and the graffiti artists entered. They sprayed the flats, producing pictures that made the word STREETS across the boards.

All round the lettering, pictures appeared as if by magic, so quick were the movements of these gifted craftsmen. When the stopwatch marked the end of the time allotted, the painters disappeared, and the applause was tumultuous.

A wooden floor was carried on to the stage by all the players, Lizzie included. As she was required to bend, lift and shift, Lucy's daughter had exchanged the brief skirt for jogging bottoms, which was just as well. Once placed and judged steady, the large board was used by four black street-dancers whose abilities defied description. 'Now, *that's* testosterone,' David whispered to Lucy.

'Beautiful,' she answered.

The scene was set. Drug-dealers, pimps and prostitutes arrived. A fight broke out because a dealer was on someone else's patch. The language was plain, direct and peppered with swear words. Lucy watched while her daughter was beaten up by her pimp before walking to join other girls by the side of a park pathway that was clearly a road. Real cars kerb-crawled and occupants took their pick of the girls. Lizzie was the first to be driven away in a newish Mercedes.

A wonderful rivalry between remaining girls led to more fights involving pimps and their human property. Dancing resumed. Large packages of white powder were taken into a corner, then smaller wraps were brought out. When Lizzie returned, her reward was contained in a hypodermic. She 'died' about eight feet away from her real life mother.

It was back to the clicking. 'Pure, pure, too pure,' was the chant. 'Dead, dead, too dead.' A siren sounded, and the cast disappeared, leaving just one deceased child prostitute centre-stage. The ambulance, complete with sound and blue light, had been made from an old Bedford van. Lizzie was placed on a stretcher, a red blanket covering her completely. She was pushed into the vehicle, then the driver and paramedics stopped for a smoke. The girl was dead, so there was no hurry. Someone scratched a record through the speakers, and the two smokers delivered what Lucy recognized as rap. The speeches contained statistics relating to runaways, drug deaths and child prostitution. It was all rather grim.

When whistles sounded, cigarettes were ground underfoot, and the ambulance pulled away. Four policemen clog-danced on the wooden floor, each man leaving after his cut of the profits had been handed over by members of the cast, who came on singly, furtively and in motorbike helmets employed to make them anonymous.

Act one was over. 'She made a lovely corpse,' David said beneath applause.

'It's a bit gross, though.' Lucy clapped and stared ahead. 'Is that really life as some child sees it?' The writer was an eighteen-year-old from Wythenshawe. He was also one of the graffiti artists. 'Is it like that?'

'For some, yes. Are we staying for the rest? I'd like to see it, but I'd bet a pound to a penny that Lizzie wants to get to Easterly Grange. She did well. And she has guts. Wonderful girl.'

'Her language was . . . interesting.'

'She didn't write it, Louisa. She's an actor – she does as she's told. When a kid wants someone to move out of the way, there's no excuse me – it's eff off all the way.'

Lucy grinned. 'She did make a lovely corpse. She seemed not to breathe. It was quite terrifying to see my daughter dead. Ah, here she comes.'

The corpse walked. 'I'll just change and get the slap off my face,' she said. 'Then will you take me to the hospital, please?'

'Of course we will,' Lucy replied.

David just smiled. No one had asked him, and he was the driver. And he was pleased about that, because it seemed to give him a position in the household, one that might even be taken for granted. He was in loco parentis. Just on the male side, of course.

It had turned out nice again. George Formby used to say that, didn't he? Alan was in a small ward, and he had a nurse all to himself. She wasn't great to look at, but he wasn't going to complain, because he was alive and almost pain-free. They had some brilliant drugs in this place. A heart operation? Give him a couple of days, and he'd be fit to go six rounds with Mike Tyson.

She was talking to him. 'You're supposed to be family only, but I imagine she's a bit like family, you being next to her husband all these weeks.'

What the hell was she on about?

'Mrs Styles,' she said, 'Husband cries a lot, brain tumour, poor soul.'

Trish. She was talking about Trish. 'Wheel her in,' he ordered.

Now, this was his kind of woman. Thin as a reed, smartly dressed, quiet, knew her place. She wouldn't be buggering off with all her family's assets, wouldn't leave her dying husband to the tender mercies of some BUPA hospital in the middle of nowhere. He greeted her carefully. 'How is he?'

'That's a nice thing to do, Alan. Asking about my husband, I mean. You're only just out of surgery yourself, and you're thinking about somebody else's problems – and he kept you awake for nights on end, bless you both.'

Even now, with the remnants of anaesthetics in his blood, Alan Henshaw knew what he was doing. Butter them up was his second commandment. Avoid big boobs was the first. Women who travelled through life behind a pair of large secondary sexual characteristics had some kind of power. Neat little women seemed grateful, could never do enough for a man. Lucy had seemed docile, but he had caught occasional glimpses of something in her face, an emotion that was possibly on kissing terms with contempt. He should have known, should have put the money back a bit at a time, could have been cleverer when it came to using her signature. Scheming bloody cow she had been—

'Alan?'

'Sorry, love. I keep drifting.'

She sat down. 'You thought you were dying, didn't you?'

'I did.'

'So will she give you your money back?'

He thought about this for a few seconds. 'We parted on bad terms, Trish. There'll be a divorce, and I'll be on my uppers. To be honest with you, I'm homeless. My daughter tells me the house is going to a charity for the rest of Lucy's life.'

'Can she do that?'

He swallowed. 'I've nothing against charity myself, Trish. And there's no fight left in me. All I want is an easy life, a bit of a roof over my head and something to keep me interested.'

'Right.'

He closed his eyes. The seed was planted. Styles in room eight was on his way out with a brain tumour, poor sod. The biggest disappointment in Trish's life had been her inability to have children. There was no son sitting in the wings, no daughter with a husband ready and willing to take over. Trish would be lonely. Trish would need someone to oversee the business. By pretending to be asleep, he needed to answer no questions. He'd laid the foundations; she should be left to think about things for a while. When the end came, when her husband died, she might just turn to Alan.

The next patient came in and sat down.

Richard, busy writing notes relating to someone who needed blood tests, did not look up immediately. 'I'll be with you in a second,' he said.

'Hello.'

A chill ran the full length of his body, right from the top of his head all the way into his toes. It couldn't be. It was. 'Lexi? What the hell are you doing here? Are you ill?'

She crossed her legs, the upper one swinging in clear demonstration of anger and impatience. 'Miss Phillips to you, Dr Turner. This job of yours – a bit of this and a bit of that – have I been your bit of the other? Like this, that and the other? Entrepreneur, my backside. You're just a dirty old man with a crippled wife, aren't you?'

'But . . . what are you doing here?' he asked again.

She smiled. 'Been on your books for over a month, babe. There was a queue, but I'm a patient patient, and I live right on the edge of your catchment area. The nurse done my blood pressure and all that when you were out on your rounds. I hung about outside till you went.'

'But why—'

'Never trust a woman, sweetheart. When you fall asleep, they go through your pockets. Letters, notes, driving licence. I got your real name and address, started hanging about outside, saw your brass plaque, watched you with your little black bag.'

'I see.'

'Oh, do you? Have you got some kind of permission from the Pope or the boss of the National Health Service? Because as far as I know, you're not supposed to bed your patients unless they're down the ozzy after an operation, or in their own house with flu or something. Even then, they're supposed to lie down by themselves. You've had me seven times since I joined your practice. I made a DVD. It could go anywhere, could that. On the Internet, to the cops, to all the people down the NHS. See? I'm not as thick as you thought I was. Dead interesting, the DVD is, because we got up to some fancy shenanigans that night. You'd be out of a job faster than shit sliding off a shiny shovel.'

For several moments, he knew how Moira must feel on a good day. There was no pain in him, but he didn't trust his arms and legs to take any orders he might try to deliver. This little tart had his life in her steadier hands. Purple nail polish, yellow hair, skin that looked a great deal worse in the clarity of daylight. 'Right,' he managed. 'What do you want of me?'

'I told you – I'm a patient patient. I don't want nothing. Yet. Well, not much, anyway.'

He stared hard at her. She had discovered his rather

substantial Achilles heel and was enjoying herself thoroughly. 'What do you want?' he repeated.

'All this.' She swept both purple-tipped hands outwards. 'A ton a week will do for now, but only for now. I'm not quite as patient as I'd like to be.'

'And?'

'When she dies, I fancy being a doctor's wife. I asked your nurse, like. About what sort of man you were, about your family and all that. So she told me about the MS and said Mrs Turner's not a bit well. Shame.'

He felt as if someone had hit him with a house brick. This cheap little tart could never fill that role.

'We're good in bed,' she announced.

'Keep your voice down – the waiting room's just–'

'Empty,' she snapped. 'And you'd better keep an eye out in future, see if you've any new patients, like, because if I can do this, any of your past bits on the side could have a similar idea. I want you. I want your life. If you'd looked on your computer, or in the filing cabinet, you'd have known I was on your list. But you can't be bothered, can you?'

Richard pulled himself together. He took out his wallet and passed its contents across the desk. 'I'll give you the rest tonight,' he said. 'There's about seventy here.'

Lexi snatched up the notes and rose to her feet. 'Oh. And don't be getting any ideas about insulin – I seen it on the telly where people what's not diabetic gets murdered that way. And I am diabetic, so no overdoses, right? My friend'll blow your cover if anything happens to me. And remember the flavoured condoms, hon. We have to make sure you get your money's worth. I'll buy the squirty cream and the chocolate spread, because I get a discount.'

She left, then came back. 'I'll bet you that's what happened to Marilyn Monroe,' she said thoughtfully. 'Insulin, needle shoved up her back passage where it wouldn't show.' She sighed. 'I've always felt close to her spirit – know what I mean?' The door closed behind her, and he heard the stiletto heels ruining the parquet as she stepped through the hall.

Richard Turner went to the window and watched Alexandra Phillips tottering down the street. The shoes, like the nail polish, were a lurid shade of purple. No way could she be considered wife material. She was clever in a streetwise sense, but she would never manage to carry herself as Moira had before the illness had started to– Moira. There were now two reasons for keeping Moira alive. He loved her, and he didn't want to be lumbered with a pathetic imitation of womanhood whose main concerns in life seemed to be visible panty line and dark roots in her hair.

'I'm stupid,' he said to himself. Lexi was smarter than he had been led to believe. DVD? Internet? She could have him ruined by the end of the week. 'Stupid, stupid, stupid.' Moira had been right, as usual. He should confine his adventures to the level of society that understood; he should have chosen someone like Lucy to turn to in times of great need.

But he had a recovering pneumonia on Tithebarn Road and a baby with croup on Rosedale Avenue. Life, as they said, had to go on. He needed time, needed to pretend to cooperate with Lexi Phillips. There had to be a way. There was always a way.

Carol Makin was swilling Lucy's steps when Litherland Lexi staggered out of the doctor's surgery. Bloody hell.

Some folk were hard to leave behind – like bad smells and warfare, they spread too far for anyone's good. What the hell was she doing up here, anyway? Ideas above her station, or what? Perhaps she'd moved again. Perhaps another set of neighbours had got fed up with her carryings-on. Anyway, didn't she work on the checkout in a Waterloo supermarket these days? Or was she still servicing Scandinavian sailors whenever their ships docked?

The woman was reputed to have suffered from every sexually transmitted problem from crabs right through to gonorrhoea. 'Could be something worse these days,' Carol muttered under her breath. 'Walking bloody disaster, that one.' Well, she was nearly walking. She'd have made a better stab if she'd worn shoes that didn't come with an oxygen mask and a government health warning. Who did she think she was? A blinking teenager? And if she wore that skirt a fraction shorter, the daft tart would get stopped for behaviour likely to cause a breach of the peace.

It was always sad to see mutton dressed as lamb, but it was also hard to feel sorry for Lexi. In her early thirties, she looked a lot older than she was. If she'd owned even a grain of sense, the woman would have dressed herself better, because she shouldn't be classed as mutton, not at her age. Oh well, there were steps to finish.

Dr Richard Turner came out, and he looked harassed and angry. The cleaner wasn't surprised, because most folk who came in contact with Litherland Lexi looked a bit the worse for wear after the encounter. 'Morning,' she called cheerily. 'I'll pop in and see your missus later. Lucy says she likes visitors.'

'Thank you,' he answered rather curtly.

Carol watched as he drove away. She wondered anew whether his less than happy countenance might be connected in any way with Lexi. If he'd read her notes, he would have plenty to think about. There'd been talk about abortions, and a few beatings when she'd wound up her clients to the point of abuse, but some of it was hearsay. The Legend of Litherland Lexi was a tale that had been much embellished while travelling through the area, but it was based in a great deal of truth.

She emptied her bucket and walked back into the house. There had been no sound from the top storey, so she guessed that Lucy's boys, along with most of their generation, were gifted when it came to sleeping. The girl wasn't like that, but females tended to be faster off the mark than mere men. They had to keep moving to get the males on their toes – perhaps women were created for that purpose.

After a small lunch of tinned salmon and salad, Carol made her way to the doctor's house. She would take her full lunch hour, but she intended to dedicate it to the poor soul next door who had MS. Carol knew all about MS, because her sister was a sufferer. Beryl ruled with a rod of iron, and she did it from a wheelchair. No one could work out how or why, but Beryl could freeze an escaping teenager from forty paces. She was brilliant with kids, and should have been a teacher or a proba-tion officer, since she was far more effective than an ASBO.

Having made sure that Lucy's sulky cat was safe, Carol went to visit Moira. She'd been told to walk in and shout, so she did.

'I'm stuck,' came the answer.

'Where?'

'In here,' Moira yelled.

'But which here, love? There's a lot of heres and theres and everywheres in these houses.'

'I'm on the loo in the downstairs bathroom, back of the house.'

Carol entered the bathroom. 'Bloody hell, girl. You're in a state worse than Russia – you're not on the lav, you're halfway down it.'

'I know. It's a talent I've developed over the years – I'm just refining it until I get it right.'

Carol heaved the woman up, fastened the nappy, pulled up pants and trousers, then pushed her into the wheelchair.

'You've done that before,' Moira accused her.

'I have. Sister. Our Beryl. MS. Looks after me daughter's kids and rules the whole flaming street like the Queen of Sheba. I'm telling you now, love, if they found a cure, she'd be bloody dangerous. She had a burglar once – just the once. Wheeled herself up behind him and inflicted grievous bodily harm with the Sacred Heart.'

'With what?'

'A statue of our Lord with his heart on the outside of his frock. Have you never been in a Catholic church?'

'No.'

'There you go, then. You've had some luck in your life. You get the Immaculate Conception – that's Mary in a white frock and a blue shawl. Then there's the Sacred Heart bleeding down his white nightshirt. Stations of the Cross with Christ struggling his way up the hill of Calvary all round the walls, and always a little fellow with a collection plate. You've missed nothing.'

When Moira was settled, her visitor bustled off to

make cups of tea. Then she sat down and proceeded to regale Moira with the terrible tale of Litherland Lexi. 'I nearly fell down the steps when I seen her tottering out of your husband's surgery. She looked like the last one off the Liverpool night bus on a Sunday morning, all spindly heels, smudged make-up and a hangover bigger than Birkenhead. What's she doing round here?'

'No idea.' Moira was enjoying herself. Collecting people was so much easier when they came to her. Getting out, even in the scooter she named 'my trolley-along', wasn't as easy as it had been. 'Perhaps she's had a disagreement with her doctor and needed a new one.'

But Carol was motoring on. Information tumbled from her in huge blocks of words, some colliding with others, vernacular mixed with unexpectedly perceptive statements, all delivered with wit and humour from a brain that had never been adequately utilized. Carol was a clever woman. She spoke about the bouncer who got done for cocaine possession, and it was all Lexi's fault. A senior policeman's wife had created a stir about Lexi's relationship with her husband, the inspector. 'Mind, she looked better in them days. Almost human, you might say. That cop nearly lost his job over her.'

'Was she a prostitute?' Moira asked with feigned innocence.

'Was she a prozzie? Give over, Moira. She's the human equivalent of the Mersey tunnels – both of them. On top of that, there's her shoplifting, handling – and not just men – drugs, fights with neighbours, or blokes she brought home, or cops, or her family – the list goes on.'

'Quite a character, then.'

Carol nodded vigorously. 'Just wait till your feller

comes in from surgery one day all white-faced and shaky. When he reads her notes, he'll have a fit with his leg up.'

Moira smiled. 'A fit with his leg up' was definitely Dinglish. 'Well, someone's got to look after her, Carol.'

'She's had all them diseases what nobody can spell. When we lived by her, we counted ten different men on one day. I was ill in bed, so I saw the buggers. It's a wonder she didn't go bandy-legged after spreading herself out that many times in a few hours. Thank God she's had no kids so far. Mind, she's only in her thirties.'

Moira was thrilled to bits. Gems like Carol Makin were few and far between. She imagined that this woman had appealed to Lucy because she, too, liked quirky characters and oddities. 'Your daughter's working with you, isn't she?'

Carol delivered her daughter for the umpteenth time. 'Thin as a bloody rake, but it was a terrible birth. They kept telling me to push, and I kept telling him to push off. Me husband, I mean. Not that he was there, like, but I decided during labour that unless he tied a knot in it, he could bog off. He was always pissed, anyway. I sold him on to a woman from Seffy Park. He thought it was his idea, but that's the only way to handle men. Let them think they run the world, and they're happy. Five more kids, he had with her.' She grinned. Every time she gave an account of her husband's disappearance the tale altered. 'Or he could be with Barbie Bow-legs from next door. Who knows?'

Moira developed a photograph in her mind. She saw a harassed mother from Sefton Park, five children clinging to her skirts, a man trying to escape the noise and trouble that were his own creation.

'So there she is, our Dee – Deirdre's her proper name. I tell you now, there's more flesh on a wire coat hanger than there is on her. And she popped out her kids like bullets from a well-oiled revolver. Mind, she didn't empty every chamber in her six-shooter, because Harry fell off his ladder after number four. Died on the spot, like.'

Moira lost control and started laughing. Again, Carol knew exactly what to do. She separated her hostess from the teacup, mopped up the spillages and carried on as if nothing had happened.

'Thanks,' said Moira, feeling lucky to have got a word in.

Carol continued. 'She's having her wisdom teeth done, and she looks like a hamster collecting for its larder. Been a martyr to her teeth, has my Dee. The number of times I've told her to get them out and have a nice set of falsies, but will she listen? Will she buggery. I suppose she's old enough to please herself, like, but they never stop being your baby, do they? Especially when there's just the one. Anyway, our Beryl's looking after her, so it's all warm salt water, rinse and spit. Great believer in salt water, our Beryl. If the kids get a graze, she's there with her Saxa and jug, no mercy. The screams are heart-breaking.' She grinned. 'But it makes them more careful, because they can put up with cuts, but not with our Beryl and the salt water.'

Moira wondered, not for the first time, why women like Carol didn't have great careers. Here she was, cleaning houses for a living, yet she had brains to spare, enough life in her for ten or more people, and a sense of humour that spoke volumes about talents she had failed to hide.

When Carol had left, the room seemed bare. It wasn't just the size of her body that had filled the space; it was also her personality, the humour, the innate generosity of a woman whose heart embraced life totally in good times and in bad. Moira had met Carol just once, yet she missed her as she might miss a lifelong friend. Being alive was certainly worthwhile. And she had every intention of meeting Our Beryl.

Lizzie looked through the glass panel in the door. Her father was once more attached to several items that were plugged into the mains, and he had fluids dripping into him from a bag on a stand. He was very thin, which was possibly a good thing, since he had been a big man for as long as Lizzie could remember. But he didn't look like Daddy, didn't look right.

She swallowed. If this was a man 'doing well', what about those who weren't? Were they in the morgue, all lined up in a queue for the undertakers? A nurse tapped her on the shoulder. 'Are you Mr Henshaw's daughter?'

'Yes. I'm Elizabeth – usually Liz, or Lizzie.'

The nurse smiled. 'He's been upgraded already, you know. He had a nurse to himself, now he shares one with the next fellow. Your dad might just be about to surprise us all. He's doing brilliantly.'

Lizzie continued to stare at 'brilliantly'. He was as white as the sheet on which he lay, as motionless as a statue in some museum. The only signs of life were in the machines that surrounded him, television screens with green lines whose shapes altered with every beat of his repaired heart. 'He looks terrible,' she managed finally.

'So would you if you'd been a couple of hours on an

operating table. I mean, we're not pretending he's not ill, and we're not saying he'll definitely make it. What we can tell you is that he's as well as possible at this moment.'

Lizzie placed her heated forehead against the glass. 'I bet you think I'm daft, but I'm scared to go in.'

'Not daft, love. Just human. Don't expect a lot from him, because he's still full of rubbish from the anaesthetics. Come on, I'll hold your hand.'

They entered and stood beside his bed.

One eye opened. 'Oh yes?' was the greeting. 'Am I some kind of exhibit at the bloody fair? The thinnest man alive, the chap with more tubes than the London Underground? I could murder a chip butty.'

Lizzie found herself grinning.

'See?' said the nurse. 'Now, that's unusual. He should be drifting around like a balsa boat in a bath, but no. He's asking for toast, tea, eggs and anything else he can think of.'

'Not whisky?'

The nurse squeezed Lizzie's hand. 'Not yet, love. One day at a time, eh? He needs to go to what my old mother used to call Alcoholics Magnanimous. But that has to be his decision. He has to do it for himself, not for you or anyone else. There's a chance, just a small one, that he won't die of liver disease if he steers clear of booze. He's drifted off again. Come on, let's leave him to it.'

On a landing, Lizzie stopped and placed a hand on her companion's arm. 'See that car there? It's full of UST.'

The nurse grinned. 'What's that? Some kind of pasteurized milk?'

186

'Unresolved sexual tension,' Lizzie replied. 'That's my mother.'

'Nice-looking,' the nurse said.

'Yes. And with her's the man she should have married. She'd have been happy with somebody like David, but she rebelled when her parents put their foot down about him in there.' She jerked a thumb in the direction of the ward they had just left. 'That teaches us two things. We should listen to our mums and dads, and when we are mums ourselves we should learn to keep our traps shut.'

Lizzie's companion chuckled before excusing herself in order to continue with her duties. Alone, the daughter of Alan and Lucy Henshaw stood for some time staring at the couple in the car. They shared history from a time when life had been fairly safe and predictable, and now they had come together in the wake of tragedies and disappointments. Lizzie's father was the greatest of his wife's regrets. Greedy for power and hungry for money, he had stolen from her, had greatly underestimated her, yet had made her stronger in the long run.

David had lost a wife who, according to Mums, had been the great love of his life. Weaker than his current companion, he had run away to a guru on top of some hill in India, had sought solace in meditation and newfangled prayer to gods who didn't exist. Were they gods, or were they elements in nature? 'I'll ask some time,' she said quietly. His son, a virtual orphan, had died of a nasty disease, and that poor kid's father had been absent at the beginning of the illness. David had not grown stronger. He remained fidgety, unsure and almost childlike in some respects. Lizzie and her mother had discussed him at length, and it was clear that Mums was interested, yet hesitant, as he often seemed to be frozen and set in stone, rather like a fossil at the North Pole.

As an outsider, Lizzie could see what was required. Mums wanted someone to care for, because her children were beyond the age where they needed close vigilance. She needed to take him into her bed and into her heart, because she was a generous woman who was also capable of showering tremendous love on all who travelled within her sphere.

David was different, more complicated. Emotionally, he lived in the past, body and soul still welded to the ghosts of his wife and child. An overwhelming guilt forbade him to move on, so he was afraid of commitment. But Lizzie had watched, had taken in the expression on his face every time he looked at Lucy. His elemental self clearly desired this wonderful woman, but he was afraid. Mums had spoken about his deep uncertainties, but Lizzie had been too worried about Dad and everything else to take everything on board. Now, she watched David and tried to work him out for herself.

His fear stemmed, Lizzie suspected, from two sources. One was that the size of his love might suffocate Lucy, since he could give himself only completely. He was rather close to the hero in some age-old romance, the perfect man – created by a female writer, of course – who fixed on one woman only. Dad was like a splinter group in a single body, because he could give bits of himself to any woman who would have him. Dad and David were poles apart.

The other fear in Lucy's potential suitor was the terrifying concept of loving and losing yet again. If they came together, he would, perhaps, depend on her too much, might have insufficient self-confidence to expect her to stay with him. If the unthinkable happened, if she died, he would probably never recover.

'I should have studied psychology,' Lizzie said.

Something had to be done. Life was becoming rather full, what with Dad ill and still naughty, Mums head-over-heels yet determined to appear unaffected, David Vincent not knowing whether he was coming or going, Theatre in the Park taking up time. And Simon. Lizzie was a rare animal, since she was a twenty-year-old virgin. She hadn't expected to fall in love, because that wasn't to be allowed on the agenda until she was working, famous, and able to identify a suitable man who might tolerate her potentially nomadic existence.

It had happened quickly, and was not to be trusted. Yet she did trust him. Whereas Mother – Mums – was with a man she had known before, a decent, trustworthy if rather absent-minded doctor, and Lizzie needed to find a way of getting them together. She wondered briefly whether Carol Makin might be experienced with a soldering iron, and giggled when she imagined her mother and Dr Vincent glued together for life. One thing she could do. There was a coffee machine downstairs, and she would take her time over a cup of Kenya blend. That might leave them in a car full of UST for another ten minutes.

Lizzie was wasting her time, because the couple in the car were ignoring any unresolved sexual tension to discuss what might become of Alan. Lucy thought he would return to drink at the earliest opportunity, while David believed that the man currently recovering from open heart surgery might have learned his lesson at last.

'He's through the worst. He was through that before they wheeled him into theatre. Withdrawal from any drug is a nightmare, and he'll know he can't endure that again.'

Lucy didn't agree. 'Drink is all he has. Even Lizzie's seen through him, and he'll have nowhere to turn. No job, no home, no family – unless I can find some very clever way of handling him, he'll be dependent on alcohol within a week.'

'What makes you so sure?'

'Half a lifetime of living with him. I think he sweats booze. When he comes into a room, it immediately adopts all the elegance of a distillery-cum-brewery, especially when he belches. His clothes reek of it. Until I moved into my own room, I smelt of it – from the bed covers. He's too far gone, David. You think a few weeks in here is a cure?'

'No. I think the surgery is the final cure. He'll be terrified. After weeks of enforced alcohol-free living and painful withdrawal, he had the line drawn by a surgeon. It wasn't just drawn, Lucy – it was cut into his flesh. The operation is the full stop at the end of this paragraph.'

He pointed to the building. 'This place is Nemesis for him. I know Rhys Evans-Jones. He's operated on kids whose hearts have needed attention after chemo. That man is one tough bastard who instructs parents like a disappointed sergeant major dressing down the ranks. I shouldn't like to be on the receiving end of his scalpel. And I don't mean a hand-held instrument – it's his pep talks, his threats, his dogged determination to scare the living shit out of sinners. Mark my words, Lucy. He will have made a lasting impression on your husband.'

Lizzie opened a rear door and climbed into the car. 'He's fine,' she told them. 'Except he wants a chip butty.'

'Good. Shall we go home, David?'

He turned on the engine.

'How are we for UST?' Lizzie asked.

'Is that some kind of treated milk?' Lucy enquired.

Lizzie groaned. 'Home, James. And don't spare the Audi.'

Seven

Lexi must have been waiting just inside the door like a crouching cat, because she opened it and pounced as soon as he began to push the envelope through the flap. He stepped back automatically until he saw the triumph in her face as she leapt from the hall and on to the front step. For the first time in his life, he felt near to murder. He had experienced strong dislikes before, but never hatred. So this was how easy it could be, then. A quick loss of temper, a step too far, a corpse on the floor, and years in prison. During those years, though, Moira would die, and since he could never leave her he would never succumb to the impulse to kill.

'Here comes the man in black once more,' Lexi proclaimed. 'With his car parked at least three streets away, because I'm not good enough.' Her voice rose slightly. 'Good enough for a quick shag, like, but not for anything more perma–' She gasped. His hand was at her throat, and it was a very strong grip that interfered with voice and breathing. He moved quickly, pushed her into the house, and kicked home the door when they were both inside the stuffy, ill-decorated hall. Another ounce of pressure, and she would drop like a stone, but he was not a taker of lives.

Richard saw and enjoyed the fear in her eyes. 'Listen, you stupid bitch,' he whispered. 'If you are going to ruin my life and, far more important, the little piece of agonizing time that's left to my irreplaceable wife, you can do that just as easily from beyond the grave. Alive or dead, it makes no difference, because you're a burden on society, and you wouldn't be missed. Don't play games with me, because you're not in my league. You're just a dirty, stinking whore.'

He threw her on to a sofa. 'Where's the film? Come on – where is the blasted thing? I thought I might send it to Hollywood, see what Spielberg thinks of it. I shall insist on Richard Gere and Julia Roberts to play our parts, of course. Lost your tongue? Oh, dear – did I hurt you? So sorry. It was completely intentional, I assure you.'

Lexi was clutching her neck, while her eyes darted from side to side. She was terrified, and she didn't frighten easily. Situations like this one had been part and parcel of her adult life, but this was an educated man, and she feared him.

'There'll be no bruising to spoil your delightful appearance – I know what I'm doing. Trust me – I'm a doctor. Where's this DVD?' He folded his arms and towered over her. 'Where?' She was bluffing, wasn't she?

'Not here,' she managed. 'You don't think I'd be daft enough to keep it where you could find it, eh?'

'Get me a copy. Moira knows I have other women, because she sanctioned the idea, since she is way beyond the point where sex is even possible for her. I'd like to show her what I've been up to – she takes a great interest in everything I do, even insists that I find release somewhere. She may be disappointed to know that I've sunk to your level, but she'll get a good laugh out of it. God knows she has little enough to laugh at. Well?'

Lexi shook her head.

'Then where's the camera?'

'I lent it off somebody.' Her tone was weak and husky. 'What have you done to my neck? Will my voice get back to normal?'

'Just be grateful that I didn't break your bloody neck. But I promise you now – the day that little film of yours makes its international, red-carpet debut, you die.' He watched while she swallowed painfully. 'Right. Are we being filmed now? Where did you hide the camera? I can be very persistent, Alexandra. My wife knows I have adventures, but she'll be upset when she finds I've been lying down with a prostitute, so I'd rather she didn't know this particular truth. However, I'll show her the evidence if you insist. Well? Camera?'

'It was upstairs. But it's not here now. I've give it back to my friend, and she's gone on her holidays. I only lent it off her.'

'Borrowed,' he said automatically. 'Now, hear this. No matter what, when Moira dies, I won't marry you. She's one in a million, and there's every chance I'll stay single. But, from a practical point of view, the way you speak, the way you dress, you could never play the part of doctor's wife. So let's talk business, shall we? For a one-off payment, will you sell me all copies of that film?' This was the test he'd decided to set. Her reply might tell him all he needed to know. A film? She couldn't even use the camera on her mobile phone, so she was hardly likely to attempt a hidden camcorder job.

'No. I won't.'

He sat in an armchair next to a 1950s fireplace, all

beige mottled tiles and lacquered brass ornaments. An ironing board, its cover stained and peeling, stood to one side of the chimney breast. This was not an organized woman.

There was no DVD. Anyone in a strong position would have asked how much he intended to offer. After all, she could have taken a few grand, given him a couple of copies and kept the master. 'There'll be no more payments of a hundred pounds a week,' he advised her. 'The filming is a lie – I'd stake my life on that. You're a tramp, Lexi. Remember, I've got your notes. Now that I've read them I shall need to check my own health, because you're a tart. You've been to prison, haven't you?'

She shifted uncomfortably on the sofa. The trouble was, she hadn't thought it all through properly. Having laughed at him for not noticing that she was on his list, she'd forgotten that he would have access to her full medical history, which was colourful. It was difficult to keep up with him, because he had a brain that travelled faster than the speed of sound, and she simply wasn't clever enough. But she would get to him. Oh yes, there was more than one way to skin a cat. Why should he get away with abusing her? He lived the grand life, posh house, nice car, good clothes. And she spent several hours a day pushing bar codes over a check-out light. It wasn't fair. But she was still afraid.

'I'm going home now,' he said. 'Back to a wife I love beyond the reach of ordinary words. Love's a little bit more than a roll in the hay. And you'd better find yourself another doctor, because I'm too far away for you, really. I know you're in the catchment area, but I'd rather you went elsewhere. Stay away from the surgery, away from my family, and definitely out of my reach, you tramp.'

She simply stared at him. It wasn't over. This time she'd gone off half-cocked, but she wasn't finished, not by a long chalk. For most of her adult life, she'd been walked on by men. All she'd tried was to better herself, and this article had told her he loved her, albeit only in the throes of passion. He was another user. Fear turned to fury, because the creature represented all who had hurt her, all who had failed to pay, men who had left her diseased, or pregnant, or stranded somewhere with no fare to get home.

Richard Turner jumped to his feet. He retrieved the envelope containing thirty pounds, opened her handbag, took out her purse and counted the other seventy. 'I don't pay scum,' he snapped. 'This is my money, and I'm keeping it.' He pushed the squashed notes into a trouser pocket. 'Shall I give the money to a charity that looks after fallen women? Or perhaps I could spend it on my wife.'

She cleared a clogged throat and found her voice. 'Get out of my house. Go on. You're the scum, using women because your wife's ill. Call yourself a doctor, and you can't even help your own dying wife? There's still things I can do about you, Turner. You've had sex with a patient, and that's a fact you'd best not ignore.'

He laughed mirthlessly. 'And you'll be believed? Remember, I've seen your notes. I don't even need to read between the lines – your history's as plain as a pikestaff. Just try it. Just you try it. Because believe me, I'll be ready for you no matter what. Blow me up to my employers if you wish, because any man would refuse to trust a trollop.'

'And the neighbours might have seen you coming and going.'

'Doctor on call?' he suggested. 'Come on, you can't have it all your own way. I found you ill in the street, brought you home, and have been keeping a check on you out of the goodness of my heart.'

'For an hour and a bloody half?'

'Like I said, Lexi. Try it.' He walked out and slammed the front door.

Outside, he found himself shivering like an autumn leaf in the wind. What if there was a DVD? She wouldn't publish and be damned, because she was already damned, had very probably been rejected by decent society many years ago. If she couldn't make money out of it, she wouldn't use it. Even if it did exist. Which it didn't. How many times had he berated patients for getting into stressful situations? Wasn't this a case where the motto 'Physician, heal thyself,' might be applied? He was a fool, a damned fool, and his heart was beating too fast.

However, he almost ran to his car, sitting for some time in the driver's seat because he didn't trust himself on the road. It was as if he had yet again developed some neurological condition that wasn't a million miles removed from his wife's MS, because his limbs weren't steady, and his breathing was uneven. Life was bloody grim, and he couldn't quite work out how to improve it. Poor Moira. Bloody Lexi hadn't finished, he was sure of that. Even without her imaginary DVD, she could do damage to Richard and to his family. He had to talk to his wife immediately. If Lexi did go to the authorities, Moira should be warned first.

A shadow on the pavement caught his peripheral

197

attention, then the view from his windscreen disappeared. Yes, here she was with her famous squirty cream and chocolate spread – she wasn't taking anything lying down, not at the moment, anyway. The road on which he was parked was near the docks and flanked by commercial premises, but people still walked through here. He turned on the engine, flicked the windscreen wiper switch and stared at her when a fan-shaped hole appeared in the mess she was creating. He leaned on the horn, engaged first gear, and leapt forward. For a split second, he didn't care if he hit her. Anger rushed through his system, and a headache threatened.

Lexi jumped out of the way and folded in an untidy heap on the pavement. He stopped and stared into his rear-view mirror until she stood and walked away. Unused to red-hot temper, he stayed where he was for a few more seconds before driving off in the direction of home. She was alive. 'You haven't killed her. Yet,' he told himself aloud. He had to deal with this, and he couldn't do it alone. Windscreen washers failed to shift the mess, and he was driving half blind. He needed water and detergent.

On Crosby Road South, he parked and knocked on a door. Explaining that he was a visiting doctor whose parked car had been decorated by delinquent children, he elicited the sympathy of a whole family. Father, mother and two boys came out with buckets and sponges to wash the mess from the screen. They didn't stop there; after cleaning the glass, the sons mopped and polished the whole vehicle while he sat and drank tea in their living room. There were good people in the world, and he wasn't one of them at the moment. Being in this place was balm to his wounded soul, because it represented real humanity.

This was proper family life; this was how it had been for him, Moira, Simon, Alice and Stephanie. He left some money for the boys and a business card for the parents. 'Anything I can do, just phone. I truly appreciate your help.' He stood up and looked at the gardens. This was a very ordinary, neat council-built house with a through room, but the gardens front and back saved it from the norm. 'Is that all your work?' he asked the husband.

'Yes.'

'Splendid. You garden for a living?'

'I do.'

Richard smiled. Something good had come out of something terrible today. 'In a week or so, telephone me if you need clients. We are about to lose a very good gardener to retirement. He does most of the houses on Mersey View, and some of the parks on the marina side of our road. There should be work for you then.'

Every face in the room lit up. Richard blinked some moisture from his eyes and made a hasty exit. He was, he reassured himself, a decent man. Deep down where it mattered, he knew that he wasn't a bastard, though many would think badly of him if they knew how he 'cheated' on his sick wife. He had never cheated. And now he would turn to her again, because she was his cushion, his soul mate, his best friend.

Having had Velux windows put in the roof at the back of the house, Lucy had created two new rooms for her twins, so she could let five for bed and breakfast. The sixth needed to be kept for Lizzie, who was expected soon, because the park season was over and she wanted to spend time with the beautiful Simon next door. Soon, though, all three would be back at college, and Lucy would be able to concentrate on herself and the business.

Motherhood never ended. That had always been the case, but she had allowed their final years at university to act as a punctuation mark, or even as the end of a chapter. There was no end. She would always be their mother. As for their dad, well ... Paul and Mike had refused point-blank to visit him. Their excuse was that they didn't want to upset a man who was recovering from surgery. They were angry; Alan was still their father, but they would always be on Lucy's side. And although Lucy maintained her status as mother, she could not force them to do her will, since they were adults.

These were adults? God help the world! She tidied up after her boys and checked the small shower room that had been installed between the two bedrooms. Picking up underpants, shirts, jeans and socks, she wondered yet again whether she had raised her children properly. Lizzie lived like the creator of whirlwinds, while the boys were clearly used to having servants pick up after them. Not at college, though. They probably lived as untidily as most students.

The roof space at the front had been boarded and lit so that it could be used as storage for her children's property. No Velux windows here, because the house had come with a set of rules that precluded such adventures. But she had to provide for her children, probably until they found full-time work after finishing their education, so she had to store their possessions. And she was pleased, was glad of their company. If only they could be a bit tidier, they'd be almost perfect.

Never mind, she told her inner self as she descended flights of stairs. She had started off with seven bedrooms to let, one of which had turned out to be big enough just for linens, and now she had five. And then there was David. Yes, she needed to keep one for him. So that left only four.

Why was she smiling? What was happening in the grey cells behind the eyes? No, much further back than that, and in muddy waters, because she wasn't sure, couldn't quite see. Yes, she could. No, she couldn't. She stopped on a landing to straighten curtains. Yes, no, yes, no – she had a pantomime script running in her head. Downstairs, where she lived, there was a king-size bed in a very grand room. Everywhere looked rather splendid since she and Lizzie had released from prison items that had once graced Tallows. She would do it. She would. One person could never fill a king-size bed, even when said person had a tendency to lie diagonally . . .

'Stop it,' she whispered. 'Bloody well behave, Lucy-Lou.' Pa had given her that nickname aeons ago. From Lucy-Lou, Lucy had evolved, and her rather upmarket given name had been left for years to rest on its laurels.

Some little devil that had dozed for ages in her soul had come to life of late. Occasionally, she listened to it; sometimes, she told it to bugger off, but she couldn't kill it. Like Superman, it survived all attacks, all attempts at demolition, because it was . . . it was her youth. She continued down the stairs. Did anyone ever grow up completely?

Lucy Henshaw, really Buckley, looked at herself in a mirror. At forty-five, a woman was wiser than she had been, but some splinters of those teenage years remained. The need for adventure, for closeness with another human, for a real future – all these requirements and hopes lived on behind an older face, beneath a heart whose beat was still capable of altering at the sight of a certain man. Or men.

David would not need a room for very long, because—

The phone rang. It was a fancy item that delivered several ringtones, and this was his. 'Hello, David.' He was doing two things at once again. She could tell when he was multi-tasking, because he became quieter and even more vague than usual. Men were like that. Women, who were used to simultaneous demands, had evolved differently. 'Put the book down, or the pen, or whatever it is you're fiddling with.'

'Sorry, ma'am. How are you?'

'About the same as I was when you last spoke to me. Three-quarters of an hour ago.' She looked at her watch. 'Sorry. It was fifty minutes.'

'Ah.'

She waited. 'How's Samson?' she asked after counting past ten.

'Fine.'

Lucy sighed. She remembered the 'Would you consider going out with me?', the bungled kiss, the holding of her hand while Lizzie had died so brilliantly in the park. He was a beautiful soul, kind to the core, almost as messy as a small boy, serious to the point of obsession when it came to his work. David was not perfect, yet his imperfections were the very qualities that made him lovable. Lovable. 'Why did you call?' she asked.

'To hear your voice.'

OK. That was a fairly good answer. Obvious, but acceptable. He missed her. 'You miss me,' she accused him.

'Well, of course I do.'

It was like pulling teeth. He was as much use as a grilled kipper when it came to small talk. It was hard enough to pin him down when he was here in the flesh, but on the phone there was no chance of eye contact, no opportunity to skewer him to a chair and make him talk. 'Hopeless,' she said. 'Absolutely hopeless.'

'Am I?'

'Yes.' This could work in her favour, too, she decided. If he wanted to hide behind the phone, she would play the same game. 'Your room is still ready. Any time you have to work at this end of the East Lancashire Road, you and Samson can stay here.' She paused and bit her lip before continuing. 'But what do we do with the dog when you claim your rightful place?'

'What?'

Doctors were not as bright as they used to be. They seemed to need a picture painting every time something different or new was suggested. Unless it was medical, she supposed. Even then, they wanted diagrams. She crossed her fingers and closed her eyes. 'When you move into my room.'

'He can stay with your cat who thinks he's a dog.'

Lucy almost punched the air in triumph, though she managed to contain herself. How quickly the answer had come. It was clear that he, too, had a little devil resident in his psyche. 'You just put more than six words together, David. Are you less afraid of me these days?'

'I was never afraid of you.'

'Really? Were you afraid of yourself?'

203

'Of us,' he said calmly. 'Strong chemistry. If it doesn't work, we'll lose a good friendship. You see, Louisa, chemistry isn't always stable. It can burn brightly and briefly, it can maintain its own life, turn to poison, or disappear into the ozone. It can also explode.'

Lucy found herself smiling again. 'You're still an all-or-nothing boy, still the little lad who tried to clear the brook on a rope that was too short and almost drowned.'

'Ah, but I knew you'd save me.'

'Hang on to that thought, man.'

'And let go of the rope?'

'Of course. But not until the twins and Lizzie are out of the way. There's still a little of the prude in me.' She lowered her tone until she was almost whispering. 'We began, you and I, at Tallows. We were children there. Perhaps we need a tryst, an afternoon in my room in the old house. The place needs decontaminating, anyway.'

He laughed. 'And what am I? A bloody anti-bacterial detergent?'

'I'll let you know the answer to that when I've wiped the floor with you.'

'You're too quick for me, Louisa Buckley.'

'I always was.'

A few seconds passed. 'Louisa?'

'Yes?'

'Is it real?'

'That's what we have to find out. You can't bungee without jumping. Oh, but that's a rope you can't let go, because they harness you to it. Worthwhile things always involve risk. Anyway, I'm going now to visit Moira for cocoa. What an exciting life I lead.'

'Is she the one whose husband is after you?'

'Richard has no ticket to ride.'

This time, his laugh was louder. 'Are you being vulgar?'

'I am.'

'Thank goodness for that. Go and drink cocoa and give my best to your wonderful neighbour. Moira, I mean.'

'Bye, David.'

'Bye.'

Lucy replaced the receiver and sat back, a hand to her mouth. She had no idea why she was covering the broad grin, because there was no one else in the house. The twins were at a barbecue in the next garden with the Turner girls, and Lizzie was still in Manchester. Or was she? Simon Turner had taken a few days off, and he was missing, too . . .

Lucy walked into the hall and glanced through a small pane of glass in her front door. Richard, who had driven away earlier, had returned and was tidying the interior of his car. She opened the door, went out, ignored him and walked up the ramp that covered the Turners' steps. His face looked thunderous, and she was in no mood for storm.

Moira looked up when Lucy entered the room. 'Hiya, babe. He's in a mood. It's one of those very black ones – he won't talk to me. Sometimes it's like living with a delinquent teenager on crack cocaine.'

'Will he want cocoa?'

Moira shrugged. 'Make some, take it out to him and if he doesn't want it he can have a bath in it for all I care.' She went on to explain that he'd come home in a strange state, and that he wouldn't talk to her. It wasn't her fault – she'd done nothing wrong, and he was being a pig.

Lucy wasn't making cocoa for pigs. She provided a mug for herself, and half a mug for Moira, who didn't want to be scalded by hot liquid. 'Talk to him, Lucy,' she begged.

'Moira, I don't do bad moods. I'm having enough trouble as it is with David's reticence.'

'No progress, then?'

'I wouldn't say that, exactly. It was something Carol said. She's the one I'm hoping will take over from your Shirley. You've met her. I can tell by the grin on your physog that you've met her. She has a sister with MS and she's looking for jobs in houses that are close together, because her van's a candidate for euthanasia, so it'll be the bus for her and Dee. I'm hoping they'll look after both of us.'

'Oh? And what pearls of wisdom did she deliver?'

'She said the secret is to let men think they rule, but to do the steering for them. Something like that. So I'm steering him gently, and I think he's beginning to warm to the idea of having a partner after so many years. But I can't deal with Richard in a bad mood, love. He's tossing things around in his car. Bits of paper, books, maps – even the floor mats are out on the pavement.'

'Yup. That's a bad mood, right enough. You just wait till he has a really bad one. He sets fire to things, goes round the house looking for rubbish, has a bonfire, bugger the neighbours.' She paused. 'He's a good man, though.'

'I do know that. Now, put your cup down, I'll take your top off and we'll tackle those knots in your shoulders.' First, she put Beethoven's Moonlight Sonata on the sound system. Moira often responded well to music.

206

She started at the base of the skull, smoothing gently over vertebrae that felt as if they were forming extra bone. As Lucy worked down the spine and across the rigid shoulders she applied more pressure, while Moira's hands and arms jerked about in reaction. After a while, confused and exposed nerves settled to the point where limbs quietened down, and the patient was relaxed and on the brink of sleep. Lucy wouldn't cry. She covered Moira with a throw, as she wanted not to disturb her by dressing her again. Sometimes, when she tried to help this woman, her heart seemed stretched to breaking point, but she never wept until she got home.

Later, after walking past Richard's car in which he continued to thrash about like a stranded fish, Lucy entered her own house and indulged the need to cry. It was anger, for the most part. After cancer, diseases such as Parkinson's, muscular dystrophy and multiple sclerosis were among the cruellest she had ever come across.

He phoned yet again, and he was different this time, on her case right from the start. 'You're crying. Why are you crying? Has he touched you? That GP from next door, has he tried anything?'

'No. I'm all right, David.'

'Like hell you are.'

She placed the phone on the table and dried her eyes. When she picked up the instrument, it was dead. Her mobile sent out the text signal. *On my way. Love you. David.*

That damned fool of a lovely, wonderful man was driving just short of forty miles to reach the woman he ... loved. He had listened to her crying, and he was travelling miles out of his way. She should stop him. She didn't want him to act like a father; she planned for him to be her—

'Lucy?'

Her husband?

She turned. It was time she started locking her door, because Richard Turner was standing there. 'What?' People should knock. People should not come in without invitation when a householder was having a soul-clearing weep. Crying, like going to the loo, should be done in private. She was almost furious, and she didn't quite understand why. 'Don't bring your bad mood in here, because I've enough on without your banging about and lighting bonfires. Go away. Tidy your car, or something. I thought you were keeping your distance from me, anyway.'

'Why are you crying?'

She exploded for the first time in her adult life. 'Why? Because she's in the house, stuck there, day in and day out. Because I try to help her with massage, and I know it brings just temporary relief. Because all she thinks about is you, you being settled after she dies, you having some kind of partner who won't make your life a misery. She is the most selfless person I've ever met, and you stay outside rattling about in your car, having a paddy. The kids have been burning burgers out there – why don't you go and throw a can of petrol on the barbie.' Tears streamed, and her words were broken by sobs.

'Lucy, what on earth got you into this state?'

'You. Your selfishness, your needs, your bloody importance. She's so ill and so lovely. She deserves better than you, because she is magical and special and all the things you'll never be. She asked me ... you know what she asked me, because I heard you tearing her apart afterwards. I put a stop to you, Dr Turner.'

He was becoming angry. First Lexi, now this one, and all he had come for was an *A–Z* of Liverpool so that he might find his way to a chap who used to be a private detective. Lexi would be stopped. But now he was distracted. 'By telling your children?'

'They are all I have. Go home. You are getting on my bloody nerves.'

It was clear that she had snapped, and he did the same. It was all suddenly too much for him, and he needed contact. He grabbed her, held her close and kissed her hard on the mouth. 'I love my wife,' he said. 'And you are bloody wonderful, especially when you're angry.' Lexi? Who the bloody hell was she? Cod roe, while there was caviar to be tasted?

Lucy blinked stupidly. It occurred to her that this had been her first ever real kiss, that she had enjoyed it, that she wished she hadn't enjoyed it, and that the curtains were open. Perhaps the children had seen what had just happened. 'My boys and your girls are out at the back in your garden. Let me go.'

He obeyed and mumbled an apology. She busied herself with stupid things like cushions, newspapers and seed catalogues. 'You'd better go. Moira isn't happy, because you're in a filthy mood, so you'd better talk to her. And I'm expecting David.'

'Ah.' He shuffled about uncomfortably. 'I've searched the car, but some kleptomaniac has buggered off with my *A–Z*, and I have to find a street I never heard of. Do you have a copy? Someone I know has moved to West Derby, and I need to find the route to his office.' He noticed that she was blushing. The embrace had affected her, then, but perhaps she was simply embarrassed. 'I came home to talk to Moira, and found her too ill, Lucy. I lost my rag with the illness, just as you did.'

Lucy said nothing. He had come home because he needed to talk. *He* needed. It was all about him, just as it had always been about Alan. Alan the developer, Alan the good-for-a-round-down-the-local-pub chap, the hail-fellow-well-met builder, the big man. And here stood his shadow, the best diagnostician in Crosby and Waterloo, a saint with a crippled wife, oh what a shame and isn't he handsome?

Yet desire still burnt. Two men. She had possibly waited all her adult life for a train to arrive, and now she had a pair. One was the non-stop express, and it was standing here, fully fuelled, lit up and ready to move. The other was on its way. It was a slower train, but its reliability was undeniable. Richard was dangerous. All fast-moving things were hazardous, but therein lay the attraction. The devil in her soul was alive and well, so she threw her neighbour out of the house. The *A–Z* was nonsense, because he could have got directions to wher-ever by looking in the phone book and finding the name and number of the man he sought. One telephone call, and he could have the bloody route described to him. And what about the Internet? He wasn't thinking straight. Something had happened, and he needed to talk. Whatever the reason for his wish to confide, Moira was too ill to be upset.

'I won't be used,' she muttered. 'Not any more. If anyone's going to be a user, it's my turn. Oh, and Moira's, too.'

She wouldn't phone or text David when he was driving, because he was a one-thing-at-a-time person, and he shouldn't be distracted while on the road. It was too late to stop him now, she decided. But he could help. Yes, yes, he could. She dashed next door and pushed Richard out of the way. His wife was awake once more. 'Moira?'

'Yes?'

'Any hospital appointments this week? Dentist, therapist for breathing and swallowing, chiropodist, prayer meeting, or, perhaps, another sordid afternoon with your lover in Blundellsands?'

Moira pretended to think. 'No. I'm clear now until the next wife-swapping evening. I'm giving line-dancing, bell-ringing and aerobics a miss this week.'

'Then come to Tallows. The house itself is scarcely furnished, but there's a terrific orangery and a summerhouse complete with every mod con. Loads of land, woods, brooks – let's see the good weather out together. He can have his paddies and his bonfires without bothering you.'

'He is still in the room,' Richard announced.

'Did someone speak?' Lucy turned and winked at him. 'Hello, honey,' she purred with exaggerated bonhomie.

He blushed to the roots of his hair and left the scene. In the surgery, he sat and swivelled in his chair. They were laughing at him, and he was trying hard not to be bothered. Two things helped. If he thought carefully, he could swear he remembered seeing pleasure in her eyes for a moment after that spontaneous embrace. And the 'Hello, honey' had been double-edged, half mockery, half come-on. He would bed her by Christmas. But first, Lexi must be dealt with.

*

They were pleased with him. He had survived the surgery, his weight was down, and the cholesterol reading had been halved. No more butter, no more cheese, no more beer. And Howie Styles was dead, God rest him. The funeral was out of the way, but Trish wasn't. She visited Alan almost every day, and was turning out to be eminently suitable for him. Because her husband had been dead long before his actual demise, she didn't grieve as much as some might have expected. And she had a friend; she had Alan.

But he needed to be clever. To get what he wanted, it would be necessary for him to absent himself completely from his past life. He didn't want Lizzie turning up to put both feet in it. The decree nisi was through and, in a matter of weeks, the divorce would be final. While the boys had never visited, Alan's daughter came from time to time, and she even had the address of the private convalescent home to which he should be moving. So it was now or never.

Trish was twittering on about low-fat cheese and bacon that was treated so that most of the fat was removed. He liked her twittering. Lucy had never done that. Latterly, his soon-to-be-ex-wife had delivered very few words, though she had spoken often enough on the phone to their sons and daughter. 'Trish?'

'Yes, love?'

'Do you have a spare room?'

Her face lit up. 'Only about ten or eleven. Howie built us a grand house, because the builder's place has to be an advertisement, yes?'

He nodded. 'I've been straight with you, Trish. Lucy's got everything, because I really did think I was going to die. And who am I to take property from kids with leukaemia?'

'What do you want to do, Alan?' Anticipation and excitement burgeoned in her heart. She didn't want to be alone, had never been alone. With no children and few family members to turn to, she had been dreaming of living with Alan, and he was making it so easy, bless him.

He breathed deeply. 'I've been in here so long that I'm becoming institutionalized. Can I stay with you for a while? And can you sneak me out of here today? I don't want all the questions and the lies I'd have to tell. Will you help me?'

Too emotional for words, Trish nodded her consent. It was settled. She and Alan would disappear to Alderley Edge, and they would live happily ever after. It might be all skimmed milk and sugar substitutes, but she would get recipes, special omega spreads and porridge. It would be a life. She would have a life, and so would he.

A very different David arrived just before half past ten. He was led in by a pleased dog, who made a beeline for the cat. The animals circled one another, the usual sniffing, licking and paw-tapping forming the larger part of their happy greeting.

'Why were you crying?' demanded the human guest. 'Come on – you'd better tell me.'

Lucy looked at him with new eyes. His hair stuck up all over the place, lending him the air of a startled hedgehog frozen in someone's headlights on full beam. There was something very wrong with his shirt, since one of the buttons was fastened into the hole above, thereby forming a bubbled effect which left the hem out of line. Baggy corduroys meant that even if he stood to attention, the trousers would probably remain at ease. But his shabby appearance was not what made the difference. She went for the light, humorous touch while she worked out what had changed in the man. 'Who got you ready?' she asked. 'Because they didn't even tuck your shirt in.'

He marched right up to her, and she refused to laugh. He marched, but his trousers strolled. 'Lucy, will you stop being flippant? I'm sick to death of your clever repartee and half-answers. Stop messing me about, or I'll get angry. And even if I don't go green and split my clothes, you wouldn't like me when I'm angry.'

In spite of his rather decrepit appearance, the man was splendid. 'You shouldn't have come, David. I was crying because Moira's so ill and so brave. By the time I'd wiped my face, the phone was dead, the text arrived and—'

'And what?'

'Someone came to the door.' It wasn't his outer appearance that made him different; it was the look in his eyes, the way he held his head, the tighter mouth. This was the decided man and yes, she was falling in love with him. She hoped he'd never lose the string and the rubber bands, but at this moment a fully-grown scarecrow was wrapping her in his arms as if to shield her from all slings and arrows. He smelled terrible. 'Have you been playing in the bins again, David?'

'Sorry,' he mumbled. 'Sugar soap and stuff.'

'Ah. Cleaning?'

'Trying to. Nothing's been touched in over a decade. I seem to be having a fresh start. But I had to come and hold you. Your voice on the phone isn't enough any more.'

Lucy closed her eyes. Diane was standing in the doorway of David's tree house, and she was being mother. She wore a black hat with feathers hanging over her face, and she blew at them continually. With arms folded over a yellow apron, she upbraided her children. 'David? Louisa? Come here at once, because supper is served.' The two of them hid behind a bush, parting its branches just to have a view of their angry little parent.

And here they were again, holding on to each other. But this time it wasn't a game, wasn't funny. She touched his face. 'You're lovely, you are. Even with sugar soap and grease, you're special. Thank you for caring. Thanks for coming all this way.'

'I'd go to the ends of the earth, and you know that.'

'Ditto,' she said, biting back a silly remark about Demi Moore in *Ghost.* This time, the kiss was no accident. It was a different day, a different man, one who had made some decisions about himself. No longer clinging solely to a desperately sad past, he hung on to his future until his future was breathless.

He used a finger to tilt her chin. 'Who's managing whom now, baby?'

He was a big man, a powerful man; he knew it, and she needed to acknowledge the fact that he had made huge strides, and that he had made them for her. 'You'll have to excuse my daftness. I've never had real love before, you see. So if I get a bit stupid and say the wrong thing, it's because I'm wearing L-plates. You're the grown-up now. By gum, tha's changed, lad.'

He smiled. 'OK, Mrs L-plates. I'll talk you through the

theory, but the mechanical side of the operation will probably take care of itself. Do you have automatic transmission?'

'Do you have a van with one of those lift things in the back?'

He burst out laughing. 'You should probably see a psychiatrist, darling. Why would you need a van with a lift? Am I missing some strange sexual connotation here?'

'No, no. I want it for Moira, of course, for her wheelchair. I'm going to bring her to Tallows for a week or so. He's in a bad mood. I think she should leave him to stew for a while. There's something afoot, and she could do with a break from it.'

David, who didn't like the sound of Richard Turner, concentrated on Lucy's request. Yes, he had access to a suitable vehicle, yes, he would borrow it, and yes, he would pick them up and drive them to Bolton. He would plug in the summerhouse fridge and buy basic foodstuffs; he would also visit the two women every day at Tallows.

'Promise?' she asked.

'It's a threat. I have to keep an eye on you and, more particularly, on Moira. Now I'm going to talk to your boys through the fence – I need to borrow clothes.'

'Kiss me first. I want to remember the heady perfume you wore when you finally declared yourself.'

He kissed her chastely on the cheek before going out to beg clean clothing from her sons. She wasn't going to have everything her own way – oh, no. Sometimes she needed her bottom slapping. With that delicious thought in mind, he carried out his mission, was told where to look for what the twins termed gear, walked back to the house, and was met at the back door by the second love of his life. For a moment, he paused and looked at her. No. This was the love of his second life, a life he had denied himself for too long. Then he noticed the expression on her face. She was clearly perturbed. It seemed he couldn't leave her for five minutes. 'Lucy?'

'He's gone missing, David.'

'Who has?' He walked to her side and placed an arm round her shoulders.

'Alan. Lizzie just phoned me. Mr Evans-Jones told her they'd found his room empty. They think they might know where he is, but there's something about patient confidentiality and me ceasing shortly to be next of kin. He needs tablets. He needs diet sheets and help not to drink. It seems he took with him a prescription for enough drugs for a week, but after that he'll need a GP.'

'He's not your responsibility.'

Lucy sighed deeply. 'I know. But what people tend not to realize is that a husband is a woman's first child. I don't love him, and I probably never did. But he's ill, David.'

'Right,' he said. 'Come in and let's get all our ducks in a row,'

In spite of unease, she grinned. She hadn't heard that expression in years, but she remembered it now. Little David Vincent's ducks in a row were plans written in proper order on paper. This time he used no writing implements, because the list wasn't long. 'OK. Tomorrow morning, I go to work. You?'

'Glenys is briefing silk in Liverpool tomorrow morning, so I'm meeting her at the Crown Court, then we're going to lunch. She likes window-shopping, but I'll keep it as short as I can.'

'Fair enough. When I finish work, I'll get the van and

drive you and Moira over to Tallows.' He picked up her hand and kissed it.

'You forgot one of the ducks. Fridge in the summer-house, basic foods.' There was no lack of confidence in David; he had simply wanted love to make sense and, as it never would, he was accepting it for what it was – exciting, uncertain and good for the soul.

'Right. Missing duck replaced and in my sights. Meanwhile, I'll get what I can out of Evans-Jones. You talk to Lizzie again. We'll find him. I promise you, we'll find Alan.' He dropped another kiss on her head before leaving the room to steal clothes and have a shower.

The twins came in. Dr Turner was lighting a bonfire, and the air was tainted by whatever he was cremating. 'He's gone berserk out there. Steph says he lights fires when he's in a bad mood – shall we tell the fire station we have a potential arsonist in our midst? Oh, and your boyfriend is borrowing clothes from us. What's going on?' Paul asked.

'Your father's missing.'

'Is that all? We thought it was something serious.'

Lucy stood up and wagged a finger at her elder son. 'You have a too-clever mouth, Paul, and until you start tidying up after yourselves – both of you – you're far from perfect. Whatever Alan's done, he's your dad. Whatever I might do, I'll still be your mum. He gave you many good times when you were young, but he has failings like everybody else. The man's had some nasty surgery, and he probably isn't well. So shut up.'

He shut up, and they both retreated to the gods.

She shouldn't have spoken to Paul like that. Although she was his mother, she was no longer in charge. Everyone else in the world seemed to make the adjustment – why couldn't she? Because she wasn't perfect. No one was perfect. Then she looked at the dog and the cat curled together, a mixture of black and blue-grey fur in a heap near the window. Where there was no free will, there could be no sin. God had made some good stuff, but He'd given mankind too free a rein.

Mankind entered. It sported jogging bottoms and a T-shirt bearing the legend *EMERGENCY SUPPLIES* above a plastic bubble containing a condom. 'Your children have some very strange clothes, and few of them fit me. Intelligent boys, though. Humorous. They say you're in a paddy. Are you in a paddy?'

Lucy shrugged. 'It's men,' she told him. 'My sons won't make an effort with their father, while their father cares for no one but himself, yet he is one half of their parents. Then there's Richard the Lionheart next door. Came home disgruntled and started throwing things around in his car. I gave Moira a massage, and she explained to me that he gets like that, and not to worry till he starts lighting fires.'

'He's lighting fires, Lucy. Shall I dial the emergency services?'

She shrugged lightly. 'Well, there are toxic fumes. He's probably burning plastics among other stuff. But he's the only one breathing the air in the garden, so leave him to it.' She paused for a moment. 'I think he's in some kind of trouble. He said he needed to talk to Moira, but that she's too ill.'

'So he spoke to you?'

'Yes, but only to ask for a map.' Sometimes, confession was self-indulgent, and David didn't need to

219

know she'd been kissed by a man he perceived as a threat. He certainly didn't need to be told that she'd enjoyed the encounter.

'Perhaps he's emigrating?'

She laughed. 'To West Derby? No, something's happened. He's like a cross between a bear with a sore head and a baby who's thrown the dummy out of the pram. Come on, misery-guts – give me a cuddle. We've a hard day tomorrow.'

He sat and held her, whispering in her ear, 'Much as I'd love to spend the night with you – and I am equipped, as you can see from the T-shirt – we had probably better postpone while your boys are here.'

'OK,' she whispered in reply. 'We'll pretend that's your idea, even though I made the rule first.' She smiled broadly. 'And I've been doctored. Got myself done when the vet had a special offer going. Now, tell me about some of these children who need my house.' If her parents were looking down on her now, they would be pleased about Tallows.

He was on ground he understood, and he amazed her. Not only did he know the patients, but he could recite a list of siblings, parents and their jobs, the areas where they lived, and his opinion about clusters. 'But the truth is, we don't know why. Pylons, nuclear plants, crop-sprays, electrical sub-stations – all investigated, all blamed. Remove those factors, and we still get occurrences.'

'Genetics?'

'Again, nothing proved, nothing predictable. And there are so many different types. Broadly speaking, we've made huge progress, but none of us will be satisfied until we've beaten the bugger. As with other cancers, we move forward all the time. Then we hit a wall and start again. But every time we hit a wall, we're more knowledgeable.'

He was buried in his work, and no man, woman or beast would ever excavate him. But he didn't need digging out; what he required was someone who would listen and distract him, who would be there at the end of days good, bad and indifferent. Living in two or three different places might help, as might new friends, a woman who gave more than a damn, her children and all who accompanied them on the start of their journey into adulthood.

'What are you thinking about?' he asked.

'You, mostly. There's a missing ex-husband skulking at the back of my head, and a daughter who, I suspect, is shacked up with Simon Turner. His mother let slip that he has a week off, and Lizzie has been less than forthcoming about her return to the fold. Says she's coming back to see me, her brothers, and the boy next door, but I think Simon's jumped the queue.'

'Oh dear.'

But Lucy had decided not to do 'oh dears' any more. She'd made a few mistakes of late, and she was learning that she had to be there for her offspring, but only in the background. Imagining that she could simply exit from the scene while they were at university had been a faulty idea. She couldn't walk, but they could.

However, if they encroached on her life, she would put them straight. They were on the cusp betwixt and between, and she could reclaim her own existence as long as she didn't push them away.

Lizzie had already gone. There was something very real between her and the Turner boy, and age didn't come into it. 'They're in love,' she told David now. 'And it will work, or it won't. It's nothing to do with age. Except it is, because Lizzie's my child, yet she's a woman. When they're tiny, that's the easy bit. Getting it right now is harder. But I'm trying.'

They talked well into the night. Subjects covered included Anne and Tim, Lucy's brief career as a nurse, Alan and his women, and some of the crazier behaviour of Lucy's three children. It was as if the intervening years were being eaten away along with all the anecdotes.

'So you did have some fun with Alan, then?'

'Yes. One of the best was when his cap went in the cement mixer. It was a disgraceful piece of headgear, but he loved it. So he brought it home and left it to set, then bought a water feature and stuck his concrete cap on the angel. He called it Northern Sprite and was going to enter it in competitions. Well, if folk can get away with piles of bricks, unmade beds and animals cut in half, why not?'

David yawned. It was three o'clock. 'I'd better go to bed, Lucy.'

She stood up and held out a hand. 'My bed. It's all right, I've thought about it. We're too shattered for adventures, but won't it be lovely to wake up together? Come on. Just children hand in hand. My boys never surface before ten, anyway. Look at Samson and Smokey – it would be a pity to disturb them.'

'Your cleaners?'

'Oh, sod it, David. We live once.'

There was a bit of giggling on her part, because the condom container in the T-shirt made a noise every time he moved until he discarded the garment. Then they lay in their tree house, which structure had been transformed as if by magic into a large, grown-up bed. Time meant nothing; it was as if they had never been apart.

Eight

Alan, realizing that he was doing a fair imitation of a goldfish out of water, closed his mouth with a deliberate snap. He stepped out of Trish's Mercedes and stood on a path as wide as many B roads. Behind them, ornate gates hummed their way back towards the closed position. Gardens at the front of the property were formal, with massive lawns, shrubberies, fountains and flower beds. There was even a maze, and the rockery was the biggest he had ever seen.

It was an amazing sight, one that left Tallows a mere understudy standing in the wings, because Styles was the brainchild of a man who had died only recently. It was real, it was new and it was now. Young trees lined the private road, and the acreage beyond the building appeared to go on for ever. Alan knew that even had he worked for a hundred years, he could never have matched Howie Styles, because the man had been an artist. 'How many acres back there?' he asked. 'You could build a whole estate of semis and still have room to spare.'

'I don't know how much land there is. It'll be on the deeds, I suppose,' Trish replied. 'Let's just say I've never walked that far, and Howie mowed the grass on one of those sit-and-ride mowers. We have three, because it takes three men to do the lot. It's like looking after something the size of Jersey, I can tell you that.'

It was an awesome house in a fairytale setting. They entered the mansion through double doors and stood in a hall that rose the full height of the building with a domed and glazed roof at its centre. Two staircases swept away, one at each side of the entrance area. It was flamboyant, yet understated because of carefully chosen colour combinations. 'Bloody magnificent, Trish,' he said. 'A great credit to a great man, God rest his soul.' Trish smiled and led him through the rest of the house. She appeared to be bored, putting Alan in mind of the curator of an art gallery who had seen it all before, and too many times to count.

Everyone in the trade knew that Howard Styles had left his mark on Manchester and surrounding towns, but this place was almost unbelievable. Trish, also, was hard to understand, since she seemed too trusting, especially when she opened a safe inside which she stashed her pearls. The double row of baubles around her throat had meant little to Alan, but she pronounced their value to be over two thousand pounds when she put them away. 'Howie was very security conscious,' she said. 'Keen as mustard when it came down to that sort of thing.'

Alan offered no reply. If she dumped him and he had the combination to this lock, there was probably enough in the safe to keep him for a few years. Yes, there were several possibilities here, but he'd have to clear off pretty damned sharpish if reduced to thieving. Anyway, he liked her too well, didn't he? She was a gradely little woman, just his type – no nonsense, no frills, and with a boyish figure. Most of all, she was needful, so there was a chance that he might be appreciated at last.

Alderley Edge was probably the most expensive place in the north. In the county of Cheshire, it housed business tycoons, lottery millionaires and footballers by the score. The area in which Styles stood boasted estates whose price tags were beyond the reach of mere mortals. Trish had been happy to tell Alan the estimated value of her property, though it clearly meant little or nothing to her. She would have been content in a three-bed semi, yet she told him in matter-of-fact terms that Styles was worth more than six million, and that most of the 'daft' houses out there were owned by footballers and their WAGS. 'My Howie built two or three of them, and he did his best to persuade the clients to have a bit of sense. But the rest? Wear dark glasses and a false smile. It's like being on some Hollywood set – the houses aren't real.'

'Not in the same class as this, any of them I saw as we drove through,' Alan said. 'Talented bloke, your old man.'

Trish giggled. 'Did you see the one like a miniature castle?' she asked. 'There's another one a couple of miles away that looks like a wedding cake. Howie had a good laugh at that one, I can tell you. He used to say Cheshire is visible proof that their brains are in their feet. Mind, he was a great Manchester United supporter, hardly ever missed a home game. I couldn't even tell him how they were doing towards the end, though. All that crying was just a symptom – he didn't know who I was for well over three months. I lost him long before I buried him, Alan.'

There was an indoor swimming pool next to a huge

bar with two full-sized snooker tables and a dance floor. The push of a button produced a second dancing area over the pool. Every bedroom had its own en suite, while the main living rooms were vast. 'Just the two of you lived here?'

'We lived in an advert, love. The swimming pool we never used – it was there to show what he could do. Ninety per cent of this house is what Howie called salad dressing – here just to prove that he was good at his work. A health farm type of business is interested in making another of those places where people can come to relax and detoxify. They've made an offer. I'm selling it and Howie's business, because I don't need either of them. Then I'll move to the seaside, I think. The countryside round here's gorgeous, but I'd sooner live by the sea. All my life, I've wanted to look after retired Blackpool donkeys. I love animals, me.'

A dart of pure fear pierced his chest. Pain in that area still managed to scare the daylights out of him. 'So you don't like this house?' How could anyone with a full set of marbles take against a place such as this?

Trish shrugged. 'Neither of us ever really cared for it. We threw a big party at least three times a year, and he got business that way. You see, people who live in houses as big as this are trying to prove something. Howie was showing that he could build a decent mausoleum, because you can't live in a mansion like this. It's for what he called rich zombies, all money but no life in them. No, we were happiest in Blackpool. Can you imagine two people rattling about in here? We had to phone each other on our mobiles – it was the quickest way of making contact, and I suppose it saved on shoe leather. This isn't for me, you know.'

'No, no. I can see that. It's not my idea of comfort, either.' But the six million quid could be a great solace, he mused. This was an uncomplicated, good-hearted woman, yet she wasn't stupid. She had come from the slums and had married into the slums, but Howard Styles had built up a magnificent company known for its quality and efficiency. For every month added on to a stated date of completion, the customer got a huge five per cent reduction. Each substandard result within a project meant a free replacement, while the craftsmen attached to Styles had to remain alert and obedient, or they'd be gone with the wind.

Alan was a bit worried. She seemed to like him and to want to help him, and she knew he was penniless, but would she get rid of him when she returned to Blackpool? He couldn't just ask, not yet. If he jumped in carelessly, he might muddy the waters. He must keep himself in check for these first few days or weeks, leave her to make all the decisions, since he was hardly in a position of strength.

'Your bedroom's the fourth on the left,' she advised him. 'And Howie's dressing room's next to it. Use his clothes – you're about the same size now you've lost that weight. Shoes, too. We'll get you back to normal in no time, just wait and see. There's a little gym next to the pool, and we have a fitness trainer who comes twice a week.'

He couldn't drink. Because she knew that, there would be no table wines, no visible bottles of whisky or brandy. The bar near the pool had been stripped, its optics denuded, shelves bared, spaces under the counter stacked with soft drinks and squashes. Trish was quiet, but thorough. Something else that had occurred recently to Alan was the knowledge that he was no longer fit for work. His main anxiety had been related to the thought of being idle, but idleness suddenly suited, especially if this lady might just carry him through an interesting retirement. 'So. What do you do in Blackpool?' he asked.

Trish beamed. 'Bingo, tea dances, line-dancing and whist club. We were just starting to learn contract bridge when Howie got ill, so that was a non-starter. Then there's bowling – they've some lovely crown greens up there. We're members of a health club – keep fit classes and yoga. And we visited our donkey sanctuary a couple of times a week when we were there. We saved a couple of horses as well that were due to become dog meat. He was fond of horses, my Howie. In fact, he liked all animals – even rescued a llama.'

Alan hoped the horror didn't show in his expression. There was always a price to pay, and he was in no position from which he might bargain. She held all the cards, all the money, the only chance of a future for him. Apart from anything else, he might go to prison unless someone hid him. And the last thing he needed was Lucy. Even bingo and bridge might be better than living with a hand held out for the crumbs from his ex-wife's table. 'And you have a house there? In Blackpool, I mean.'

She picked some photographs out of a drawer and almost ran to him. 'It's gorgeous, and you can see the sea from the upstairs front windows. I've always liked Blackpool. I used to go on day trips with Mam and Dad when I was a kid. They couldn't afford a boarding house, so it was there and back in a day, on a charabanc. And now I look at all this and wish they'd lived longer, because me and Howie could have done so much for them. I miss him. Not the poor Howie I had at the end, but the man I married. He was such a lovely, kind, gentle man.'

He took the pictures and looked through them. The Blackpool house was detached, between the wars, and quite attractive. She was right, of course. Who wanted to live in Alderley Edge when Blackpool plus six million was an option? 'Have you ever thought about a yacht?' he asked casually.

Trish laughed. 'You must be joking – I can't even swim. But we were considering – Howie and me – getting a place in France. Somewhere near the Loire, I think he said. He liked fishing. We were doing an evening class in conversational French, but ... Well, it wasn't to be.'

'Aye, it was a damned shame, him dying like that before his time. The only good thing was he didn't know anything at the end, once he'd stopped crying.'

She grabbed his hand. 'I'll not forget how you asked about him when you came round. Never a thought for yourself, just for my Howie. But I have to make one thing clear, love. I can't stand drunks. I'll look after you as long as you stay off the booze, but if you let me down, you'll have to go, because I'd never cope.'

He decided to ask. 'Do I go to Blackpool?'

She laughed. 'If you can keep up with me, pet. And if we get on. Properly, I mean.'

He understood. She was lonely, and she didn't want him to sleep for ever behind the fourth door on the left. 'Right.' He gave her a peck on the cheek. 'I'm bloody starving, Trish. Me belly thinks me throat's cut.'

'And you even talk like he did. He was always bloody

starving. Till he went off food altogether, I mean. That was when I knew he'd lost the fight, because nothing came between him and his food – ever.'

'So where are the servants?'

Trish's laughter echoed round the enormous house. 'Why do you think there's a sofa and a telly in the kitchen? We lived in there, me and Howie. Staff come in during the week and clean the rest of the whited sepulchre. Apart from sleeping upstairs, we spent most of our time in the kitchen, and I do all my own cooking. He loved gardening, and he used to help a lot out there. I enjoy cooking, so we jogged along nicely, and the help stayed out of our way. It works.'

'Do you want me to give you a hand with the dinner, then?'

'Not if you want to live. Sit. Turn the telly on, and find something you like to watch. After our meal's settled, we'll go for a constitutional in the grounds. You can meet Damien.'

'Who?'

'The llama. Howie reckoned Damien has the three sixes tattooed somewhere under the matted wool. He spits. Then there are peacocks, geese – they can get nasty – ducks on a pond, and some horses. They're used by special schools for children who'd never get to ride otherwise. People come and look after them, but they have their own entrance at the back of the estate – we never see the horse people.'

Alan switched off as she prattled on about her bloody animals. 'I've found the horses a home: another house where the owner will carry on letting the kiddies ride. As for Damien, he's going to a Yorkshire sheep farmer who already keeps llamas, because they frighten away anything that might try to damage the flock. So it's all arranged. As long as I manage to offload the house, that is.'

She prepared vegetables, baked potatoes and chicken stuffed with olives and tomatoes. They watched the news, and were halfway through the meal when the doorbell sounded.

'Oh, bugger,' Trish said. 'I forgot. It's the health farm people with some of their staff – they want to look round. The really big bosses are French, you know. So they might just throw in a nice little farmhouse near the Loire if I play my cards right. See? If you think about things, life can dovetail very nicely.' In this happy frame of mind, she set off across the vast hall to open the door.

Alan followed cautiously. It might be his daughter. Easterly Grange could have put two and two together and— He stopped in his tracks. It wasn't his daughter, but it was someone who could muck up his life good and proper.

'Come in,' Trish said, widening the doorway. 'So good of you to travel all the way from London. If you'd like to start upstairs, that's fine. You don't want me dogging your heels every inch of the way. And if you need to spend the night, we've adequate accommodation for all of you.'

A man explained in broken English that they had a hotel nearby before thanking her for giving them free rein.

Alan heard the man, but did not see him. His eyes remained locked into the gaze of the woman who stood by his side. No. It couldn't be. He backed away into the kitchen and sat down at the table. Never in a million years would he have expected to see her again. And his appetite had gone.

Trish returned. 'I've left them to it. If they're willing to give me a good price, then I'm out of here.' She paused. 'You're not eating.'

He explained that he was full, that the quantity and quality of food to which he had become inured had reduced his appetite, and that her cooking was superb. 'I'll get some air,' he said. 'You catch up with me when the visitors have gone.'

'But should you be on your own?'

'I'm used to it. And I won't go far.'

'Promise?'

'I promise.'

He sat in a gazebo for a while, hands trembling, a headache threatening to become more powerful by the minute. Was there no escaping the past? He raked through the ashes of memory in an attempt to assess whether the arrival knew enough to damage his chances with Trish. Was his luck running out again?

He walked away from the house, because the visitors might want to look round the grounds. Damien spat at him, and the geese chased him. So he put himself away in a large shed and hid behind stored timber. 'Don't talk to her, Trish,' he whispered. 'Please, don't talk to her.'

Waking in the arms of a man was wonderful; waking in the embrace of Dr David Vincent was special beyond words. Lucy imagined that many folk would laugh if they knew how chaste they had remained, but she knew differently. The magnetism was there to the point where it all but crackled in the air, yet they had managed to sleep without indulging the need to be closer. Separately, they were strong people; together, they were almost unbreakable.

'No jokes today, missus?' he asked. 'Nothing about unfinished business, unstarted business and my ability to lie unmoved next to a red-hot woman? No digs at my manhood? Hairy legs? Snoring?'

She awarded him a pseudo-disdainful glance. 'Later.'

'So you aren't cured? Will I still have to cope with all your sillinesses?'

'Yup. You use the bathroom first, because you're in Bolton today, am I right?'

'You are.' He stayed where he was. 'It wasn't easy, Louisa. And it can't be maintained. Tallows, then?'

'Tallows. After we've found my beloved ex, and preferably when Moira isn't there. I suppose I could leave her for an hour, but—'

'It's not enough. I want longer than an hour, my darling. A lot longer.'

She managed not to shiver. 'I agree. There's more to us than the merely physical. I feel as if I've come home after emigrating to some strange place. The thing is, where is that strange place? He can't have gone far, not after being in hospital for so long.'

David rolled away and picked up the phone. 'I'll talk to Rhys, see what I can get out of him.'

'At half past seven?'

'He's like me, babe. He takes the whole thing very seriously. I have to catch him before he goes into theatre at one of the hospitals. Alan was lucky to get him, because he's definitely the best in the north when it comes to dicky tickers. For all I know, he could already be standing on a helipad waiting for a picnic box with a heart in it.'

'Even I know that's not his job.'

'All right, all right.' He dialled. Lucy listened to the banter. It was medical, vulgar and very witty. Then the questioning began. Feeling like an eavesdropper, she left him to it and went for a quick shower. When she returned, he was sitting on the edge of her bed. 'Well?' she asked, towelling her hair.

'He's possibly with the childless widow of some millionaire from Cheshire.'

Lucy dropped the hair-drying towel. 'Possibly? And do we know the name and address of this possible person?'

'No. Rhys said she's had enough shocks lately. Her other half died recently in Easterly Grange – brain tumour.'

'Isn't she in mourning?'

'Rhys also says she's a good little soul who did her grieving before he died, because she lost him an inch at a time. Then she started to visit your old man. She was seen in one of the corridors just before Alan did his disappearing act. So, taking into account your husband's need for money and his preference for stick-thin females, well, it's not rocket science, is it? He's with her. And you know very well what he's capable of. But you'd be better to leave him to it.'

'No.' She sat next to him. 'She has to be warned.'

'How?'

'Listen, sunshine. You're the brains of this outfit – I'm here just as decoration and landlady. We need to find out who died in that place. I'd never forgive myself if I didn't talk to her.' She was tempted, though. It would be so easy to walk away and let the world get on without her help.

He thought for several moments. 'Let me search for a way, please. If you barge in, she'll think you have an axe to grind.'

'I have! And his head's the bloody grindstone. Look – he has a date at Bolton Magistrates' Court in a few days, because he's going to lose his driving licence. We could hang about there.'

'With an axe?'

Lucy dug her companion in the ribs. 'Don't get clever with me, son.'

He pushed her into a prone position, climbed on top of her and tickled her until she screamed. 'That's a deposit,' he said. 'Returnable if we don't reach completion.'

'Caveat emptor,' she replied, trying to cover her near-nakedness. 'Buyer beware, because you don't know what you're taking on.'

'I've just seen most of it.' He stood up and announced his intention to go for a shower.

'David?'

'What?'

'I love you.' There, it was said. He was adorable, intellectually sound, amusing, handsome and imperfect. She couldn't remember when she'd last said those three precious words to Alan. Poor Alan. Poor Alan? What about the widow who'd landed herself with him? She was the one who deserved pity, surely?

David turned in the doorway. 'I was thinking last night. Pondering the mysteries and all that stuff. And I decided that you were the second love of my life, but that's not the truth.'

'Oh? What am I, then?'

He smiled, and nodded knowingly. 'You're my second life. You're the love of that second life and the core of it. I remember you not just from childhood, but also from the future. I read Einstein on the fabric of time – oh, years ago. I don't know how or whether he managed to prove it, but he saw the fourth dimension as one – past, present and future all together.'

'So there's no such thing as time?'

'Apparently, we made it up to give the Swiss something to do with all those wooden cuckoos. Oh, and for calendar makers, of course.' He left the room, then popped his head back round the door. 'Mind you, try telling that to a child waiting for Christmas. Tim used to open those doors on the Advent calendar at the crack of dawn before counting how many days he had to wait.' He disappeared again.

Lucy sighed contentedly. He had just let Tim go, and she had been both witness and an element in the cause. Children were never replaceable, while his love for Anne had clearly been absolute. But surely it was easier to start another adult relationship than it was to say good-bye to a child? He was making strides, was more relaxed and easy in her company. Lucy quickly threw on some jeans and a blouse in order to go and help Moira finish packing.

Carol and Dee were in the main sitting room. The large woman looked up from her task of changing a cushion cover. 'Hiya, Lucy. We heard you screaming. Is that him of long-standing what I heard talking in yonder?' She inclined her head towards the bedroom. 'The clue was his bloody dog shedding hairs all over me floors.'

'It is David, yes.'

Dee giggled. 'Has he managed to sit down yet? Because various veins and piles go hand in hand, you know.'

Lucy was learning fast that Liverpudlians had a way of abusing words and throwing them together that was deliberately double-edged and, on occasion, confusing. She raised an eyebrow at Dee. 'I've got him a rubber ring,' she said seriously. 'We blow it up with a bike pump.'

They both studied her for a few seconds. Was she keeping up, or was she serious? 'She's learning,' Dee pronounced.

Carol shook her head. 'Ooh, I don't know. I mean, she's only a Woolly. They can be a bit slow. But a rubber ring? Can you see a doctor like him sat on a rubber ring?'

Dee thought about that. She still looked as if she had mumps, though a more accurate description would be a mump, since just one side of her face remained distorted. 'No. A doctor wouldn't sit on a rubber ring.'

Lucy tutted. 'I'm going away with Moira for a few days. Will you come back and feed the cat in the evenings? He'll be sulky, though I doubt he'll commit suicide by starvation.'

Carol announced that she would stay at Stoneyhurst until Lucy returned, and that she would, if necessary, force-feed the two reprobates in the roof. 'And if you'll throw in that long-stood-up feller, I'll have the time of me life.'

Lucy punched the big woman playfully. 'He's spoken for.'

Dee's face lit up. 'Told you,' she said. 'You owe me a fiver and a fish supper, Mam.'

'Shoo,' Lucy ordered. 'Both of you. Bugger off upstairs and clean a couple of bathrooms.'

When they had gone, Lucy watched Richard retrieving something from the car against which he had committed GBH the night before. He still had a face like thunder, so she remained thoroughly determined to get Moira to Tallows for a while. What on earth was the matter with him?

David came in and followed the line of her gaze. 'Acting like he's lost a quid and found a penny. It's perhaps as well you're getting Moira away from there tonight. He looks as if he could use the services of the bomb disposal unit. Mind you, they'd need a few sandbags – he seems to be packing a fair amount of dynamite. What the hell's up with him, Louisa?'

'Something specific,' she replied thoughtfully. 'And something he can't tell her while she's so ill.'

'Any ideas?'

'A woman, I'd say. He misses sex.'

'So do I, but I don't make a career of it.'

Lucy grinned. 'I noticed.'

At last, David was on his favourite horse. 'See? I knew you'd say something. I knew that clever mouth of yours wouldn't stay shut for more than a few minutes.' He was trying hard not to laugh. Years of misery, childcare and introspection had fallen away from the shoulders of this capable woman, and her humour was the factor that had kept her sane. 'And I wouldn't change a hair of your head. You carry on putting me in my place, honey, because you are my sense of proportion.'

'Oh, get in that kitchen, pour coffee and eat your toast.'

He went into the kitchen, poured coffee, and ate his toast. She was a bossy-boots, but he would deal with her later and in another place. Einstein was wrong, because the future was going to be a very wonderful story. 'The future is real,' he said aloud.

'What?'

'Shut up and eat your toast.'

Glenys and Lucy walked for miles. The shops were nowhere near the Crown Court, though they found a decent lunch in a poshed-up cellar not too far away from where Glenys had handed over her brief. But they went for a post-prandial stroll and did some serious window-shopping in the centre of the city, finally turning back to face the Mersey as they sauntered in the direction of their parked cars.

On Hanover Street, Lucy ground to a halt. 'There it is!' she cried. 'Supposed to be the best hairdresser for miles, and you need a mortgage to walk in. Do you think they'll charge us for looking through the windows?' But the windows were not seeable through. Clients who paid hundreds of pounds for hand-knotted extensions didn't want the world and his wife staring at them.

As the pair turned to walk away, the door opened and a figure stepped out of the salon. Once again, Lucy ground to a halt.

'You keep putting your brakes on,' her companion complained. 'Or are you running out of fuel?'

'I know her.' The woman was never out of the newspapers, since she ran a prize-winning business.

'Really?'

'Glen, go back to my house. Tell your satnav 32, Mersey View, Waterloo. Poetic, what? Go on. All you need is to follow your nose up the dock road. I have to do this by myself. Go on, shoo. I'll be OK.'

While Glenys walked away towards her car, Lucy watched the woman who had emerged from the hallowed portals of Liverpool's third cathedral, a building dedicated to the cause of female beauty. It was Herbert's place. A fabulously flamboyant perfectionist, he ruled this corner of the city with a rod of iron that failed completely to conceal a heart of finer metal.

The woman outside Herbert's of Liverpool was pushing items into the back of a van when Lucy joined her and asked if she might help.

'Oh, ta.' The woman did a quick double-take. 'Erm . . . do I know you?'

'You know my husband.'

A long pause was followed by, 'Oh. Yes. Well. Look, if there's going to be a fuss, can we sit in the van? Only I've just handed over to one of Mr Herbert's staff, and she might be watching, and if she tells Mr Hedouin, my new boss, I could be ruined. Please? Your husband was ill, and he needed someone to talk to, and I've not seen him in ages, honestly . . .'

They climbed into the van. 'Right, Miss Livesey,' Lucy began. 'There'll be no row and no fuss, because I am getting a divorce from him, so calm yourself. And you're right – he was seriously ill and might easily have died. He's been in hospital for weeks.'

Mags Livesey nodded rapidly. 'I know. He fell off the

face of the earth again, and I went to his office in Bolton and they told me where he was. So I bought some flowers and grapes and clogged it halfway across Manchester, and they wouldn't let me see him.' Blushing bright pink, she looked Lucy in the face. 'I never loved him, you know. But he looked so bloody awful when I last saw him – I could tell he was getting sicker, even though he pretended to be all right. You see, I told him to bog off, then I felt all guilty in case I'd made him worse.'

'He's disappeared yet again,' said Lucy. 'And none of it's your fault, Miss Livesey.'

Mags smiled tentatively. 'Just call me Mags. You're making me sound like some godawful headmistress.'

'All right, Mags.'

The self-made woman relaxed slightly. 'Good job it's a small world, eh? See, I got the franchise for this Nouvelle Reine stuff from Tête à Tête in Paris, and a right bloody mouthful that is for somebody who doesn't know French.'

'Go on.'

'Well, they were right pleased with me, because I worked damned hard, and they've made me an offer no bugger would refuse. To cut everything short, I'm selling my shops, handing over the franchises, and going to work at a health spa called Styles in Alderley Edge, all marble columns and swimming pools.' She paused for effect. 'Had a look round yesterday. And guess who was lurking in the hall? Yes, it was the man himself.'

Lucy shivered slightly. No one should have to put up with Alan. 'Tell me, is the householder recently widowed?'

Mags bit her lip. 'She is. That's why she's selling, and the price tag's over five million.'

Lucy whistled.

'Look,' continued Mags. 'You never got this from me.' She rooted in the depths of her vast handbag. 'Your Alan is at this address.' She passed over a card. 'That's the name of the man who died. All kinds of folk will have his business card – you could have picked it up anywhere. You should see where they live, it's all foot-ballers and big business folk. She's Trish, and she's nice. Dead normal.' Mags stopped and ran her eyes over the woman next to her. 'It was all lies, wasn't it?'

'What was?'

'You nicking his money and bogging off with it.'

'Yes.'

'I'm sorry. He was wanting to cadge off me, trying to get me to sell my business to shore his up. I told him where to go, and he went. But I've been in your house in the past and seen your photo – that's why I recog-nized you. In my line of work, we never forget a face.'

They prepared to part on good terms, and Lucy was about to step out of the van when a thought occurred. 'Any chance of a favour? I'll pay you.'

Mags nodded. 'Ask away.'

'Here's my mobile number.' Lucy passed a card to the beautician. 'If you're in Bolton this coming week, give me a call. If you can spare a couple of hours, I've a lovely friend who'd enjoy a bit of a makeover. And so should I.'

'Right. You're on, mate.'

They shook hands. 'I like you,' Lucy said.

'Yes, I like you and all. I'll do what I can for you and

your friend before I go back to London for all these meetings. Then if you ever want a weekend break at Styles, I'll try to do you a special price. You've good bones. I could do a lot with you.'

'Thank you.' Lucy waved as the van drew away. Leaning against the tinted windows of a monumentally expensive beauty emporium, she sent a text to David. *Didn't want to disturb u. Have found Alan. Lucy xxx.*

So. She knew where Alan was, but she didn't know what he was up to. Did she need to know? Shouldn't it now be every woman for herself? If she could just leave well alone, he would be out of her hair for ever. In which case, why had she bothered at all? Sometimes, she came perilously near to losing patience with herself. Yes, no, yes, no . . .

'Hello, Lucy.'

Oh, bloody hell. She arranged her features in a fashion intended to be neutral. 'Richard. I'm just on my way back home. You?'

'I had to see . . . someone.'

'This isn't West Derby.'

'Someone else.'

'Ah.' This kind of thing happened to men all the time, she supposed. They managed to love one woman, but to make love to many. Her attraction to Richard Turner was animal – well, it certainly wasn't vegetable or mineral – yet she loved David. Richard was probably a toy, something disposable, an item to be thrown away after use. Because she was female, she wasn't supposed to speculate in this manner. But she did, though nothing would persuade her to endanger her relationship with David. 'I must get my car. Glenys has gone ahead – she's my lawyer, from Bolton.'

'I've been to see a lawyer,' he said.

Lucy stared hard at him. He put her in mind of a deer that was failing to outrun a lioness. Yes, serious hunting was executed by the females of most species . . . 'What's the matter with you? All that banging around in the car last night, then the funeral pyre in the garden – your behaviour isn't doing Moira any good. She told me about the moods. She predicted the fire-starting and the refusal to talk. Why make her worse?'

'That was not my intention.'

'Then straighten yourself out before I bring her back from Tallows.'

'Yes, ma'am.' He delivered a mock salute before walking away. As he moved, he found himself smiling in spite of everything. Lucy could order him around any day of the week – he relished the idea of being subservient to so magnificent a specimen of womanhood.

She watched him. He was attractive and overtly available. But he wasn't for her, and she berated herself inwardly. After years devoid of all physical contact with a man, years during which she had scarcely contemplated sex, here she stood eyeing up the talent like a sixth-former on her way home from school. She marked it down as emotional regression and went to find her car.

Lexi was livid. The bloody nurse/receptionist at Richard Turner's surgery had sent a letter to a Liverpool lawyer, copy to her. It stated that Miss Alexandra Phillips had joined the practice, had visited Dr Turner only once, and that the author believed the visit had been made with a view to entrapment.

She came at an earlier date (see enclosed records) for a medical examination, which I performed, as the doctor was out on calls. Thereafter, she had one appointment, and Dr Turner struck her from his list immediately after the consultation. I have no knowledge of their relationship, but I can assure you that any close contact between these two adults must have occurred before she joined this surgery. Our part-time doctor, Celia Cooper, will verify under separate cover that she never treated Miss Phillips.

They were all bastards. They would stick together no matter what, while she would be left like rubbish in a wheelie bin waiting for the council to dispose of her. It wasn't fair. He'd had his roll in the hay, and now he wanted rid of her. Doctors, lawyers, police – they were all in cahoots, and her reputation would no doubt precede her if she put up a fight.

Laurel and Hardy were probably in on it, too. They worked for that well-stacked woman next door to the Turners, but they were in and out of the Turner house like rats in a sewer. Carol Makin, who was built like a tank, and her daughter, Dee Baxendale, were seasoned adversaries of Lexi's. Dee, the opposite of her mother, did a fair imitation of a pipe cleaner, but she had a gob that could clear a drain from forty paces. Their Beryl suffered with MS, so they probably considered themselves experts in that area. Richard's wife had the same disease.

Lexi would have to play very dirty. They would have trouble pinning anything on her, because she intended to play anonymously. Doc Turner would know who was waging the war, but he'd keep it to himself, since he was a coward. All men were cowards. Women, on the other hand, made things happen. And boy, was she about to make things happen! But she had to go home first and think about it.

As she turned towards the marina, she noticed Carol Makin on the top step of the house next door to the Turners'. Lexi lifted her chin and put her hands on her hips. 'Was Weightwatchers shut, then, love?'

Carol raised two hefty fingers in a V-sign. She wasn't going to start shouting her mouth off on Mersey View. But Litherland Lexi was here again, God save the Queen and may the best man win. 'Dee?' she stage-whispered. 'Come here.'

Dee arrived, armed with a feather duster and one of the plastic pipes belonging to Lucy's Kirby vacuum cleaner. 'What?'

Carol pointed down the street. 'Fetch,' she ordered.

Dee shot down the road like greased lightning. Lexi, who seemed mesmerized, allowed herself to be prodded, pushed and steered like a cow on its way to market. In her high-heeled shoes, she was no match for Dee in the speed department, while shock accounted for her lack of reaction to this unusual form of persuasion.

In the hall of Lucy's house, she was placed on a monk's bench and ordered to stay. Dee muttered something about Mam having missed her way: she should have been a dog-trainer with all this fetching and staying. 'I'm sorting me cupboards,' she announced, before leaving the enemies to their own devices.

'What are you doing round here?' Carol began.

'None of your business.'

'I can make it my business if I want. I'm housekeeper

here, and Dee's my deputy. It's our job to keep the place nice, and nothing can be nice if you're part of the picture.'

'I don't have to tell you nothing,'

'Then you can stay sat there like cheese at fourpence till Mrs Henshaw gets back with her lawyer. And the doc next door won't be long.'

Lexi swallowed. 'I left me bag in a taxi, and I was told the driver lived down here. I've been looking for him for weeks.'

Carol leaned forward. 'Listen, you. There's no taxi drivers along this stretch. They're all doctors and law-yers and stuff like that – professionals. So bugger off and stay away if you know what's good for you. Don't go shouting on Mersey View, or they'll be sending for the busies. We aren't used to your sort in these parts.'

As soon as Carol stepped back, Lexi shot out of the house. She had to be at her till in half an hour, and she didn't want to be late again. There were computers and printers in the office at the back of the shop. If she could force herself to be nice to Greasy Bleasdale, he might let her have a lend of his equipment for half an hour.

She staggered up to the main road, flagged down a black cab, and continued on her way to work. Mrs Turner was going to receive some very revealing letters. He said his wife knew he played away – did he think Lexi Phillips came down in the last shower of rain? It was time he learned never to kid a kidder. It was time he grew up. It was also time he learned a bit of sense, because he'd been let off lightly so far.

In the back of the cab, she removed the crippling shoes and tried to rub some life into her feet. Thank goodness she kept a pair of flatties in her locker at work, because she might be on shelf-stacking. She didn't know which was worse – filling shelves or sitting on her arse for hours on end. But she did know that life wasn't fair, and Richard Turner was having it too easy. Well, easy would be a thing of the past. She'd make damned well sure of that.

On his way back from Liverpool, Richard stopped at the house where his car had been cleaned. Shirley and Hal were leaving in just over a month, and Richard posted through the letter box an invitation for interview for the gardening jobs on Mersey View.

On his way back to the car, he saw Lexi passing in a black cab. Where had she been? What the hell was she doing in these parts? Didn't she know there was nothing she could do? Witnesses at the practice would back him up, and as long as that was the case no medical council would turn a hair. But was his local reputation about to take a battering?

He went home immediately. Celia was taking surgery, so there was time for him to nip back and see if anything untoward had occurred. Two cars stood outside Lucy's house – hers, and another that was presumably the property of her lawyer. The boyfriend, Dr Vincent, was to come back this afternoon to collect Lucy and Moira. He was suddenly glad that Moira was leaving. If Lexi was going to kick off, it would be easier without Moira in situ.

He entered his own house quietly. The dulcet tones of Carol Makin bounced off walls throughout the whole ground floor. 'So I says to her, "What the bleeding hell are you doing round here, like?" And I shoved her on to

Lucy's monk's bench, and I says, "They don't have taxi drivers on Mersey View, because we're all professionals." And she went a right funny colour, because I've seen her round here before, and she knows I have. Are you taking both these skirts with you, love?'

'I'll have to, Carol. You don't think Lucy'll mind my accidents?'

Shirley chipped in. 'No. She's as sound as a pound, is Lucy. She's managed you and your problems before. And if she can't cope, she's not daft. That David'll get you some help.'

That David. Richard was sick to the wisdom teeth of that David. David Vincent had the best woman Richard had come across since meeting Moira, yet he seemed an airy-fairy sort of chap, always engrossed in thought, always here with his bloody dog and his bunches of flowers.

But Richard had other fish to fry. He walked into the sitting room. 'Hi,' he said with forced brightness. 'Who's been looking for taxis, then?'

Carol stared at him for a few seconds. She had her own theories about this fellow, but she had better keep her gob shut. Well, not shut, but on a low light. 'Litherland Lexi. Expert in sailors, sex, shoplifting and supermarket check-outs. She's a bother-causer.'

'Ah. So you chased her?'

'Dee did. With a feather duster and a bit of vacuum cleaner. My Dee might be thin, but she's feisty.'

Richard smiled at his wife, and she returned the compliment. 'You all right now, babe?' she asked.

'Yes, fine. I've come back for notes, then I'm off to visit the sick and the imaginative.'

'The imaginative?' Carol raised an eyebrow,

'They imagine they're too ill to work ever again,' Moira replied for him. 'Usually a bad back, till Richard finds them heaving furniture or climbing ladders. He copped one enjoying himself on a bouncy castle the other week. He's supposed to walk with a stick, but he got caught out. Richard always finds them out in the end.'

'And what do you do then?' Carol asked. 'Dob them in to the soshe?'

He smiled. 'I have never in my life dobbed in anyone to the financial arm of the social services. I praise them to the hills, tell them how proud I am of them for having overcome such a terrible illness, and remind them to visit the job centre. In the end, they do. Most of them, anyway.'

This one was a right clever clogs. Carol had met his type before in posh houses she had cleaned: a gob full of marbles, always saying the right thing, then mucking about behind the wife's back. And this wife deserved better, because she'd enough to cope with without a fancy-talking whoring fool for a husband. Lexi was looking for him. If he'd been with Lexi, he deserved a red card, bugger the yellow warning.

Carol made her excuses and left the house. She didn't like him, didn't like the way he looked at Lucy. Men took little notice of fat, shapeless women, but fat women noticed everything. As did Dee, who ate like a horse and managed to look like someone in the final stages of some eating disorder. No men looked at her, either. Carol and Dee were just essential items of furniture, but they missed nothing.

She found Lucy in the kitchen. Her friend, Glenys, was outside in the back garden. 'I don't like him,' Carol announced. 'He's slimy, sly, and full of himself.'

'Who is?'

'That pie-can of a doctor next door. He looks at you, Lucy, as if he wants to rip your clothes off your back.'

'He's just sex-starved, Carol.'

'I don't think so. There's been a well-known knicker-dropper hanging round. What are you laughing at? Have you never heard of a knicker-dropper?'

'I have now.'

'Well, if he can't have you, he'll take what he can get. And what he can get from Litherland Lexi is a damned sight more than he might have bargained for. She's trouble. She's had a row with just about everybody apart from next door's goldfish – she could start a war in an empty room. And she's hanging about like a bad smell on a hot day.'

Glenys came in. Carol summed her up as yet another dumpy little female who could pass through life without being noticed. A lawyer was a good thing for Glenys to be, because she could study people without fear of interruption. The invisibles were the ones who came nearest the truth, since few bothered to address them, yet it was the unaddressed who saw through all the talking, all the excuses. 'Hiya,' said Carol. 'I'm the housekeeper, and I'll be making breakfasts for guests when Lucy's having a break. I'll live here while she's away.'

Glenys shook Carol's hand. 'Hello, Carol. I'm her lawyer, and she's told me all about you and your daughter. A couple of gems, by all accounts.'

The big woman blushed. 'Well, if we're gems, we're

still uncut and definitely not polished. Rough diamonds, you might say.'

'You'll do for me,' Lucy said. 'But do try to tolerate my neighbours. You don't have to like them, but please try not to let it show.'

Carol muttered a few words about doctors thinking they knew everything, some of them knowing nothing, and herself having bathrooms to see to.

Glenys burst out laughing when Carol had made her exit. 'Where do you find them, honey? Can't you collect stamps or Victoriana or something normal?'

When the hilarity had subsided, Lucy told her friend about the encounter in town. 'So,' she concluded. 'He's with some other woman who's come into money. According to his card, Howard Styles was a developer in the Manchester area. Mags Livesey says there's a massive house – big enough to be made into a Champneys style health spa and worth over five mill.'

'Bugger,' muttered Glenys. 'So I guess we have what Houston might describe as a problem.'

They sat in companionable silence for a few minutes. 'I'm copying this address,' Glenys said finally. 'Then at least he'll know when the divorce is final. As for the rest of it – well, if she's recently lost her husband, she's vulnerable. Let me look into it. I need to know about her family, about who's going to prop her up in the next year or so. Because if it's Alan, she's in trouble. What do you think?'

Lucy raised her arms and shrugged. Part of her insisted that she'd done her bit and that this new women should be left to get on with it. Yet knowing what he was, and what he was capable of ... 'I'm confused,' she admitted.

'Millions, Lucy.'

'I know.'

'If his health improves, he'll steal from her.'

'I know.'

'What can we do?'

Lucy stood up. 'Well, I'm going to the summerhouse with Moira, and having salad, salmon and wine when we get there. We're travelling in a wheelchair-friendly van, and I'll use Alan's car while I'm in Bolton. And I'll keep in touch with you, because I want you with me when I go to Styles.'

'So you've decided?'

'It seems so. She has to be warned, and in case she thinks I'm lying just to upset their applecart, you will bring the paperwork.'

'You sure?'

'Not completely. But the woman – whoever she is – deserves a chance. Look what he did, not to me, but to his own children. Paul, Mike and Elizabeth are all he has, yet he mortgaged their property, stole their legacies. If he's capable of that, he might well clean out this Mrs Styles.'

When Glenys had left, Lucy went next door to see how Moira was faring. She found her quiet, unsmiling and twitchy. 'Moira? Whatever's the matter?'

Moira lowered her head. 'I knew it would happen. That's why I wanted to find somebody decent for him, somebody who'll be here after I've gone.' She lifted her chin and looked into Lucy's eyes. 'I hoped you'd be the one. That was why I did that stupid thing. Somebody's looking for him now, you see. Carol and Dee know her, and they chased her. He's got himself involved with the type he thinks of as safe, because he can't love her and it's just sex. But I know he needs love, you see, and I also know he's well on his way to being in love with you. So I took a chance and, well, you know the rest of it.'

Lucy sat down. 'I'm going to marry David, Moira. Don't say anything, because I haven't told him yet. I find Richard very annoying and very attractive, but it's never going to happen.' She waited for a reply, but none was forthcoming. 'Are we going to Tallows?'

'Yes. Oh, yes. Lucy, I've tried to help him and he won't listen, won't even speak to me about the creature that's hurting him. The cleaning of the car, the fire, the silence – it's all down to the whore Dee and Carol shifted. I can't do anything until he talks. Let him have some space. We're going.'

So they went.

Nine

Moira looked forward happily to her journey inland towards the foothills of the Pennines, because David had promised to travel via the prettiest route. A lift took her up from the pavement into the van, where her wheelchair was bolted to the floor after safety belts fastened her to the seat. When the luggage had been similarly pinned down, Lucy and David climbed into the front seats. The drive took just under an hour and, during that time, the passenger in the rear had the opportunity to appreciate the advent of beautiful scenery, and also to view at close quarters the relationship between David and Lucy.

They laughed a lot, though she was louder than he was. At every opportunity, at junctions, traffic lights and pedestrian crossings, he turned to look at Lucy. Feeling something of a gooseberry, Moira watched while pretending not to. She was in the company of a magic she remembered, though she experienced no jealousy or resentment. These two deserved some happiness, and she hoped that they would live long and enjoy it. There were many valuable people in the world, and she was in the presence of two of the best.

Perhaps it was because they shared history, however

ancient, that they seemed perfect together. They were completely in tune, head over heels in love, and delightful to study. She was for him, he was for her, and that was an end to it. In some place beyond vision, in heaven or within the deepest roots of nature, a decision had been taken. The couple were bound together, their co-existence inevitable from the hour of birth.

They stopped at the bottom of a hill. 'You're in Lancashire now, Moira,' David told her. 'No dark, satanic mills any more, no slave-drivers to hang a lad for stealing a fent of cotton.'

'Fent?' Moira asked.

'It was usually the end of a weaver's bolt, and it often had flaws in it.' He pointed to the hills. 'There was snow in summer up there, yards and yards of calico left out to bleach in the sun, because they had no chemicals. If you took a bit of that summer snow, you hanged. The cotton came from America to Liverpool, then was brought here by drays or barges. We were all Lancastrians then.'

'Liverpool's always been Lancashire to me,' was Moira's answer. 'And so has Bolton, come to that. All this Merseyside and Greater Manchester rubbish – we're Lankies, every last one of us. Except for the accents, of course.'

'Boundaries,' David said. 'Created and moved in the interest of politicians. It did them little good.'

Moira sat back and thought about her husband. Richard, an exciting man who had moods, was definitely not the type for Lucy. In fact, when she looked over her shoulder into her own past life, Moira realized that the give and take in her marriage had been, for the most part, a one-way street, since she had done most of the giving. And the forgiving. She continued to adore a man whose selfishness was becoming legend. Lucy, newly released from domestic servitude, would have flattened Richard, while he would never have appreciated this woman's wit and humour. He had been with a whore. Moira had no proof, yet she knew it . . .

She looked out at the bowl that contained Bolton, gazed at pleated moors rising and dipping in gentle folds towards Yorkshire. It was a fabulous place. They drove through villages filled with weavers' cottages, stone-built and with proud little aprons of garden laid out towards the pavements. There were ancient churches, old pubs with exterior beams and string courses that had stood the test of centuries.

Lucy turned. 'Here we are, love. On your left, the big house. It's been in my family for generations.'

'Impressive,' Moira said. It wasn't a house – this was a mansion, and Lucy, God bless her, was about to turn it over to the Timothy Vincent Trust.

'It's devoid of furniture,' Lucy said, 'so you and I are living in the dolls' house. We bought the shed when the kids were in their mid-teens – somewhere for them to have adventures without parents breathing down their necks. They brewed their own beer in it, rolled joints and grew out of all that by themselves. Sometimes I thought I was too lenient, but they turned out OK, I think.'

'It's hardly a shed.' Moira looked at the pretty little wooden house.

Lucy agreed. 'It's a park home. Two bedrooms, dining kitchen, shower room and a nice big living room. Lots of trees behind, and a large garden leading up to Tallows. It's peaceful.'

Moira muttered something about Bedlam being peaceful after him and his fires. It was lovely here. She was brought down to earth via the lift, and David scooped her up from the chair and carried her into the house. 'Back in a minute,' he said as he left the room, muttering to himself about finishing something or other. Lucy went to check the food in the fridge. He had remembered – salmon, wine, salad and potatoes. He was a good lad.

'How could you leave all this?' Moira asked. 'The woods, the garden, that wonderful house and this little fairytale cottage? I'm sure I couldn't have given it up. It's absolutely glorious.'

'It was, and it will be again.' Lucy put the kettle to boil. 'I'll just make sure the beds are—' She stopped in her tracks for a few seconds. What the heck was he doing? She ran through the living room and opened the front door, then leaned against the jamb while she looked at him. He was a star. He was a one-off. He was a long way past merely wonderful.

David stopped hammering. 'Sorry. I meant to finish it, but work claimed me, and my own house has been invaded by industrial cleaners who haven't the slightest idea about how to save research. Fortunately, most of it's on my laptop, and the stuff in boxes is easy to find, but I tend to scribble on bits of paper and—' He stood up. 'What's funny?' She seemed to be near to hysteria.

'You are.'

'I'm doing my bloody best, madam. No one can do better than his best.'

Lucy's eyes filled with tears, but she continued to laugh. Only David would take the trouble to build a ramp that would be needed for just a few days. Only

David would roll out a long wooden track to make the pushing of a wheelchair over lawn easier for both pusher and pushee. He was vague, brilliant, talented and daft. But mainly, he was almost selfless, because he saw a need and did his utmost to fill it.

'Louisa? Say what you have to say. I need to get on with this.'

'I told Moira I'm going to marry you.'

His mouth twitched. He sniffed, nodded, and resumed the hammering.

'David!'

'What?' He stopped banging. 'Bloody what?'

'Did you hear me?'

He nodded again while hammering home another nail.

She turned to go back inside, and he leapt to his feet. 'When did you decide?' he asked.

'Oh, about forty years ago.'

'OK. Thanks for letting me know.'

Inside, Lucy stood near the window and watched him. He was having fun with hammer and nails. He was laughing. After a few seconds, he pulled out a disgraceful handkerchief and wiped his eyes. He was hers.

Moira fell asleep on the sofa. David, who had finished his ramp, led the woman he loved outside. 'To the woods?' he asked. 'Remember how it was all those years ago?'

Lucy remembered. 'To the woods' had been her sister's war cry, delivered with monotonous frequency throughout the long, hot summers of childhood school holidays. Diane's idea of hide and seek had been eccentric, since the rules had changed daily, and Lucy had never quite managed to keep up. David had experienced some difficulty, though he had always managed not to care. 'You collected creepy-crawlies,' she said. 'In matchboxes and old tins.'

'I did. Especially those that had committed insecticide. I was looking at ways of preserving the dead, but my chemistry set seemed to dissolve everything, which was a source of great annoyance. I love you.'

'I know. You loved spiders, too.'

'Useful creatures, arachnids. They dispose of flies. Why did you tell her before you told me?'

Lucy loved these mixed-up conversations. As owner of a butterfly mind, she understood his quickness of thought only too well. Something came into his head, and he dealt with it immediately. 'I was afraid that she might still want to bequeath Richard to me. So I hid behind you. Let's face it, you're tall enough.'

'Oh.'

'But I intended to marry you anyway. After my divorce, naturally.'

'And if I'd said no?'

They stopped walking. Standing at the edge of Diane's forest, she took his face in her hands and kissed him. 'I feel close enough to read your mind. I knew you wouldn't refuse me.'

'You can manage me.'

'Yes.'

'We shall see about that,' he said. 'There are more cards up my sleeve than you'd find in three packs, plus jokers. You won't manage me, Louisa Buckley. We shall be equal partners in the crime named marriage. However, as pointed out by the eminent Jeffrey Archer, some are more equal than others.'

'And?'

'And I am stubborn enough to train you in the arts of wifedom. I shall undo the kitchen chains when I come in from work and, after our meal, I shall fasten you upstairs. It will not be an easy life for you, slave.'

Lucy laughed. She could not think of the past quarter-century as wasted time, as she had been endowed with three wonderful children, but how she longed to be settled with this precious man. From the pocket of her trousers, she took her mobile phone. 'Interesting messages today,' she said. 'About love and stealing moments – shall I read them out? Some are rather risqué – body parts and so forth . . .'

'Why bother? I sent them.'

'I thought we needed more than stolen moments.'

He stopped and stared hard at her. 'My condition has deteriorated of late. There's little hope of recovery, and no remedial treatment, because at this point I'd probably sell my soul for five minutes with you. And you know that. So why don't you shut up for once?' No longer nervous or hesitant, he kissed her and held her firmly.

Lucy relaxed and allowed herself to fall into the moment. He was strong, gentle and in charge. She knew with blinding certainty that he would never hurt her physically or emotionally, that she must never hurt him. They were both vulnerable, both damaged and needful. 'Where have you been?' she cried when he released her. 'Where the hell have you been, little David Vincent, with your spiders and your woodlice?'

'Alone and in grief,' he answered. 'But now I've come home.'

'So have I.' She pulled herself together and dried her eyes. 'Right, come on. I have to go to the house for more blankets – I don't want Moira to be cold in the night. We need to be quick, as I'd like her not to wake alone in a place she doesn't know well.'

'And I don't want to sleep alone,' he grumbled.

She looked him up and down. He had come a long way in recent weeks. 'When we get round to exchanging contracts – me, you and caveat emptor – you won't sleep at all. You'll be very much awake, sunshine. Unless I decide to spike your cocoa.' She stalked off ahead of him.

David chuckled. He seemed to be engaged to an extremely lively woman, but she wasn't going to win every battle. Four decades, he had known her. The in-between years didn't count, because he and Louisa had never completely lost each other. He closed his eyes and remembered a very tall girl holding the hand of an undersized boy. She had stood between him and bigger lads, had known even then where and how hard to kick the bullies to make them collapse.

He followed her to Tallows. The same female who had dealt with the rough and ready had been stayed by motherhood. Only her offspring had stood between her and Alan. Had she been childless, the killer blow would have been delivered much earlier, and with compound interest. And now she had tracked him down. David grinned. God help the man, because he'd probably finish up filleted, roasted, and served up with an apple in his gob.

She was calling to him. He picked up speed and joined her at the door to the laundry room, which was open. 'Has anyone been here? From the charity?' she asked.

'Just me,' he answered. 'And I brought my own tools

to make the ramp. I haven't been inside for days – not since I showed the last lot of committee round.' He examined the lock. 'It's not a break-in.' Perhaps her husband was inside. 'Stay here,' he ordered. 'I'll go in.'

But she followed him. In the kitchen, the central table was scattered with the remnants of a meal, and Lucy recognized a scarf flung over the back of a chair. 'Elizabeth's here,' she said happily. 'She could fill the Albert Hall with her clutter. I'll go and find her – she may not be decent.'

'She was hardly that the last time I saw her, Louisa. Theatre in the Park? She wore very little, but she wore it well. You could take some tips from her – she's you all over again.'

'David? Do you want me to walk round half naked?'

'Sometimes. And with an audience of only one.'

She tutted, wagged a finger and left him to his own devices.

Ten minutes later, she returned to the kitchen.

'Louisa?' He could see immediately that all was far from well. He got up from his chair, and led her to it. 'Water?' he asked when she was seated. 'Or something stronger?'

'No. Nothing.' She cleared her throat and breathed deeply. 'Get Moira. Bring her here. Please. I can't say anything until she's here.'

'But—'

'Please, David. Trust me. Just do as I ask.'

He left the house.

Lucy sat alone in a kitchen where she had toiled for years to feed her family. But she didn't see the dressers, the freezer, her much-loved Aga, failed to notice the lovely Belfast sink she'd had installed last year. Because a picture was printed on the front of her mind, a vision of beauty so perfect that it would have been difficult to describe in mere words. No, it had been a sculpture rather than a painting, something dimensional and recognizable – not one of those great, ugly lumps of stone with two heads and a hole in its belly.

She lowered her eyelids and, in her mind, opened the door to Lizzie's bedroom again. They were nude and intertwined, limbs threaded loosely through limbs, heads together on a white pillow, her hair spread across fairly good Egyptian cotton, his paler curls masking half her face. Fast asleep, they seemed to breathe in unison, and didn't stir when the door opened. Lizzie. How often she had explained about her virginity, how loudly she had proclaimed her status! And now she had given herself away to Moira's son.

But that wasn't all. Lizzie's hand, weighed down by one of his arms, rested loosely on the tanned skin of his back. Curled like some exotic flower, it gave out splinters of light, prisms bouncing from a raindrop on a petal. Almost as naked as the day of her birth, Elizabeth Turner wore just two items. In white gold or platinum, a solitaire diamond nestled against a plain circle of similar metal. They were married. Oh, Lizzie, Lizzie . . .

Lucy closed the door and opened her eyes. Simon was a decent man. But Lizzie's chosen path promised to be fractured and unsettled ... 'Now I know how my parents felt,' she told the empty room. But no, that wasn't the case, because Simon Turner was not Alan Henshaw. It had been so quick, though. They had known each other for just a few weeks – love at first sight? Would Moira be upset, would Richard rant and rage?

At last, David returned. He entered the house backwards, lifting Moira's wheelchair carefully over the step. As they came through from the laundry, Lucy smiled hesitantly at her next door neighbour. She would probably deal with the news; her husband was a different fish kettle altogether.

'Have you got a ghost?' Moira asked cheerfully while David wheeled her in. 'I've always wanted to be in a haunted house. Are you haunted?'

'No. But there's been a development.'

Moira looked round. 'Lovely kitchen. When did you have it un-fitted?'

'Last year.' Lucy glanced at David. 'I apologize for throwing you out earlier, but I must tell Moira first. No – stay. She had to be here, but you'll hear about it soon enough, so it might as well be now.'

'What?' Moira stared hard at Lucy. 'He said you were as white as a sheet. You frightened the poor man.'

Lucy squatted in front of the wheelchair and took Moira's hands in hers. 'Right. Simon and Lucy are upstairs in bed. Together.'

Moira remained quiet for several seconds. 'Randy little sod,' she declared eventually. 'Sorry.'

Lucy inhaled deeply. 'She's wearing a wedding ring. And a rather decent little diamond. They must have booked the registry or wherever practically as soon as they met. I suppose they realized we'd all say it was too early, too quick, so they kept us in the dark.'

Because of her condition, it was quite normal for Moira to tremble and shake in the face of shock. But not one muscle moved involuntarily. With a hand to her mouth, she looked into Lucy's eyes. 'I shouldn't have called him a randy little sod,' she said quietly. 'He told me. Not about marriage, but he spoke endlessly on the subject of your daughter. Eliza, he calls her, as he believes she'd be perfect in *Pygmalion*. I warned him. "You'll be courting a minstrel," I said, "and heaven only knows what's in front of her – even Hollywood, God forbid." He adores her, Lucy.'

Lucy bowed her head. 'I'm not angry,' she said. 'It's always been difficult to lose my rag with Lizzie, even though she turns my house into a Steptoe and Son yard. But I'm hurt. She's always been so open with me.'

David pulled Lucy into a standing position, folding her in his arms where she rested for a while. 'It's all right,' he told her. 'Sometimes, young love is so over-powering that it eats away at reason. Their decision to present you with a fait accompli is understandable, because they're both of age and they might just as well take all the flak in one sitting. We're going back to the summerhouse. I won't take no for an answer, because this is the right thing to do. When they notice us, they'll come to the shed. We must bugger off and leave them their dignity. They're adults.'

Yes, he was definitely in charge. In lighter, brighter moments, she might steal his thunder, but there was no point in arguing now. David was vague, adorable, intelligent and daft. At times like this, the intelligence won.

Blackpool was OK if you were five years old with a bucket and spade and a burning affection for donkeys. Alan had been dragged to the sanctuary, to a tea dance, and to five sessions of bingo. Trish had to do the driving, because his licence, wherever it was, probably wasn't worth the paper it was printed on, so he was trapped. He'd been honest with her about the drink driving, and now she had him where she wanted him twenty-four hours a day. It had to be like this, because if he showed his face the mortgage company would have him sliding into court faster than sugar pouring off a shiny shovel. He was a man in hiding.

'It's just as well you're with me,' she told him sweetly and with monotonous regularity. 'I'll make sure you don't drink.'

It was like being behind bars again. Six million was a hell of a lot of money, but he wasn't seeing a penny of it. The Blackpool house was nice enough, and Trish looked after him. She looked after him rather too well, and the only time he grabbed for himself was spent in the bathroom. If he went for a walk, she accompanied him; if he wandered into the garden, she was at the window waving and smiling and being so bloody pleasant that he wished ... wished what? That he was living with Lucy?

'Coo-ee!'

Here she came again, Trish the kind, Trish the saintly, Trish who wouldn't leave him alone because she was his guardian. He walked into the house and sat in the dining room, a child summoned from the playground to have his lunch. The self-appointed dinner lady would stay with him and make sure he ate all his greens, all the omega-oil-soaked fish, the special margarine, the bloody garlic, the bloody parsley, skimmed milk in his coffee, an apple and an orange, two fifths of his daily five allotted portions. He was sick to death, and he needed to go somewhere.

'Is that all right for you, love?'

Love? They were sleeping in the same bed now, but nothing was happening. How many times had he shared a beer and a laugh with the lads at work? How often had they scorned the childless, those without lead in their pencils? And here he was, a flaming eunuch, no desires, no needs, just an eating machine, and he mustn't forget to take that low dose of aspirin. 'Very nice, Trish.' He paused for thought. 'Erm ... I was just wondering if you'd drive me to Tallows some time soon.'

'Your old house in Bolton?'

'That's right. She's not there. I don't think there's anybody there, but just in case, I'd like you to stay on the top road. Don't come near the house, because it might cause trouble.' He hoped the locks hadn't been changed. 'There's stuff I need – like my dad's watch and an old brooch that belonged to my grandma.' His dad had never owned a watch, but there might be a brooch somewhere. What he really needed was cash, and there could well be some of that in the floor safe Lucy didn't know about. The fact was that he couldn't remember how much or how little, but he had to give it a go.

'All right,' she chirruped. 'We'll go this after.'

She was sweet. She was too sweet, like an overdose of powdered saccharine on his morning Weetabix. 'Thank you,' he said. 'You've been very good to me.'

'I've been good?' she cried. 'That sounds as if you think it's over.'

Over? Where the heck could he go with no car, next to no money, and nowhere to live? 'It's not over. I just need some stuff, and I can't drive. I know I haven't been to court, but they'll have given me a ban because I was well out of it for days, so I must have been miles over the limit. Just in case there's somebody in the house, I need you to stay out of the way for half an hour, that's all.'

'OK,' she answered brightly. She didn't feel bright inside, though. There was something wrong with him, and she believed it not to be physical. He was cheesed off, possibly depressed. Deep inside her chest, a bubble of terror threatened to rise to the surface. She managed to quell it, but only just. If he left her ... If he left her, she might as well be dead.

Alan plodded his way through lunch. She wasn't stupid. She didn't need Styles, so she was selling it. Thrown into the deal by Charles Hedouin was a nice farmhouse in the Loire valley, and she'd mithered for that until she'd got her own way, so she was clearly a long way from daft. But on a day-to-day basis, she was boring.

'Eat your fish,' she suggested.

He ate some of his fish. He wanted to stand up, throw the plate at her and walk out of the house, but he couldn't. How the blood and guts had Howie Styles tolerated this woman? Childless and sad, she obviously turned the man in her life into a baby, something to lavish care on, something she could control. He wasn't used to this. At least Lucy had left him alone to get on with his life. At least she hadn't watched him swallow every forkful of food.

There must have been two sides to Howie. There was the genius who worked with architects and did as good a job as any of them, then there was the simple man. He'd loved all kinds of dancing, bingo and donkeys. But Alan wasn't a Howie. And Howie had never retired, hadn't spent every waking moment with his wife. During his illness, he probably noticed little. But Alan noticed, by God he did. Like a rat in a trap, he could find no way out. Maybe this was his penance, the price he had to pay for treating his wife so appallingly.

'You're not happy, are you?'

He swallowed yet more fish. 'I'm fine,' he lied. 'Sorry I can't ... you know what I can't do in bed just yet, but it's not that. I think I need a bit of a job, something to get me out and about a bit more. An income of my own, some pride, a bit of dignity. I've no money in my pocket, Trish. All I do is take, take, take. That's no good for a bloke.'

She folded her arms 'Out and about, you'd find drink. I understand, really I do. When we gave up smoking, Howie and myself, it was murder. Then I went to a site one day and there he was, bold as brass, smoking a roll-up in one of the sheds. I already knew, because I could smell the smoke on his clothes. He blamed that on other folk smoking near him, but I knew better. So I made sure I caught him at it.'

She was a good jailer. Alan didn't know how many years he had left, but the thought of spending the rest of his life in prison was hardly attractive. 'I need my own money,' he repeated.

'Then I'll employ you. As soon as you're properly better, you can keep this house in good condition – decorating, putting in a new kitchen and bathroom, keeping up the gardens and helping at the sanctuary. I'll pay well '

She wanted to own him, body and soul. He wasn't too sure about the body, because she showed no sign of wanting sex, but he was her reason for living, her mission, her foundling. Something had to give. Dying of a bad heart and alcohol was a possibility he understood.

He had fought it and, with the help of the Welsh sheep-lover, he had won. What had he won? The chance of dying from boredom, that was all.

'I'll go and get ready, then,' she said.

Alan, carrying the remains of his meal, crept into the kitchen and wrapped fish and greens in a paper towel. He buried his guilt under debris in the bin, washed his hands and stared out at the rear garden. She would be at him all the time, helping with the flower beds, supervising his painting, making suggestions, turning his life into a total bloody nightmare. He wasn't a kid, and he hated Blackpool.

She didn't even have a cheque book, had no need of one. The accountant paid all household bills, and she took cash from machines in the bank or in the street. He needed her pin. She had it in her personal address book, but it was disguised as a phone number. 'Howie told me to do that,' she had told Alan gleefully. 'I've a memory like a sieve, so it was a good idea.'

So. How could he get his hands on that little book? And when would he get the chance to dial every single number until he got the false one? What if it wasn't a false one? She might have chosen an arrangement of numbers that happened to belong to a phone somewhere on the planet. And the pin would be just part of the number. On top of all that, how long might it take her accountant to realize that she was withdrawing her limit of a thousand every day?

'Are you ready, love?' she called from upstairs.

'Love' again. She didn't love him. He was a male version of one of those horrible, scary, pot-faced dolls some women collected; he was something to dress, to pamper, something to display in the passenger seat so that she didn't look like a woman on her own. His misery was beginning to show, and he knew it. But what could he say? 'Give us a couple of hundred grand and I'll bugger off'? He didn't own even the train fare to get out of Blackpool, and he wasn't going to steal from her purse, oh no. He needed a lot more than she carried in her handbag.

'I'm ready now,' she shouted.

They sat in the car. 'You're going to leave me, aren't you?'

He sighed. 'All right, I may as well say it, Trish. I like you a lot.' That was almost a lie, for a kick-off. 'But I hate Blackpool. It was OK when I was a kid on the sands with Mam and Dad, but I'm not one for dancing and bingo. Why don't you go to bingo with that Maisie next door?'

Trish frowned. 'I always went with Howie.' There was a catch in her throat, and she swallowed hard. 'We did everything together, went everywhere together. We didn't need many friends, because we had each other.'

'But he also worked till he got ill, Trish. It's different if a man goes to work. Lucy and I made space for each other, and—'

'And where did that get you? In hospital with alcohol poisoning and a bad heart, while she buggers off with all the money. I'm doing my best. All I care about is keeping you well and off the booze.'

'I need space,' he said. 'I'm not used to being looked after so well. Yes, I was married, but there was no contact. She cooked, saw to the kids, and that was about it. When we spoke it was usually on the phone – I'd ring to say what time I'd be home for a meal. I'm used to the company of men, and I wasn't afraid of getting dirty.

Mixing concrete, fixing windows, guttering, tiling – I'd turn my hand to anything. When I came out of Easterly Grange, I thought I'd never be strong again, but I am. In the house, I'm getting claustrophobia.' He looked at her. 'Don't cry. I won't leave you, but we have to work something out, because I feel as if I'm going mad.'

Trish nodded and dried her eyes. 'I can't be on my own, Alan.'

At last, she had said it. She clung to Alan because she feared isolation. He understood that, appreciated it, because Trish was a frightened little woman, and he, too, had known real fear within the recent past. He remembered only too well lying in the room with barred windows, the pain of withdrawal from his drug of choice, the inability to want to remain in a world that had no place for him. 'I don't want to be by myself either, Trish. I just want some space, a job to go to – even if it's just part time.'

'All right,' she said. 'We'll have to sit down and make a plan. You can't work while we're in France, but there must be builders round here that could do with an experienced man for a few months every year. Or we could buy you a partnership.'

'OK.' Relief flooded his veins. 'Thanks, Trish. You're a little gem.'

On that note, Alan and his gem set off for Tallows.

They had been stark naked for days. The robes they had worn after showers had been used while they were eating in the kitchen, but apart from those occasions they had romped about like a couple of maniacs who had escaped from a naturist club. He was her Adonis, she his Aphrodite, and nothing would spoil this honeymoon.

'I had a dream,' Lizzie said. 'Mums opened the door, stood and looked at us with tears in her eyes, then she just smiled and went away.'

Simon chortled and dug her none too gently in the ribs. 'Hey, your mother's gorgeous. My dad fancies her rotten, but she's hooked herself up to Dr Vincent. We aren't the only ones following instinct. I look at Lucy, and I understand Dustin Hoffman having it away with Mrs Robinson.'

She hit him with a pillow. 'Just because you've landed a job at Guy's, don't start thinking you can have everything you want. You can have me, just me and only me. One foot wrong, and I shall be arranging your funeral.'

Smiling broadly, he tried to look at her dispassionately, but it was no easy task. She was built like her mother, slender, but well-endowed in the upper storey. Lizzie was also intelligent, inventive, funny and uninhibited. And she was his wife. Had any of his friends at the Royal told him he would be married by the middle of September, he would have laughed them out of the building. 'You're beautiful,' he said for the hundredth time.

'I know. How lucky are you?'

'Very.' He dropped back on to the pillow. 'Come here.'

'No.'

He laughed. A modern man in his own estimation, he had truly believed that virginity was not significant, yet he had wept alone in a bathroom after their first time. She was passionate. Nothing short of the greatest love would have persuaded her to give herself so freely. As for himself – he had known that first evening when he had tripped over Mum's Zimmer, a chair and a rug. He had literally fallen for her on sight.

They had eloped half a mile to Waterloo register office, had dragged in a couple of mates from the hospital, and sealed their fate. 'I didn't know it would feel like this, Liz. Surrounded by pretty nurses and young female doctors, I thought I knew it all. I knew nothing.'

'Nor did I. For me, love was something that would grow. I thought it didn't just happen like it did with us. Are we crackers? Shall we live to regret it? And will you like London?'

'Whither thou goest, I will go.'

'Book of Ruth.'

'Yes. We both know we've taken a huge leap, yet people in their thirties and forties do the same and still end up in the divorce courts. It's a gamble, and nothing to do with age. But I don't want to live without you. Ever.'

Lizzie blew him a kiss, gathered up her robe and went towards the large bathroom, the one with a power shower big enough for two people. Something stopped her. Through a landing window, she saw the newly laid wooden path that spread all the way down to the distant shed. Was that a ramp leading up to the door of Mums's little park home?

'Simon?'

'Boo.' He was behind her. 'What?'

'We are not alone,' she whispered. 'And whoever's living in the shed may have seen our car.' The family always parked on the west side. She and Simon had used the east. 'That's a ramp, probably for a wheelchair. Who do we know with a wheelchair?'

He inhaled deeply. 'Quite. OK. What do we do?'

Lizzie pondered. 'We get clean, then we come clean.'

'They'll kill us.'

'So we die together, martyrs to the cause. Come on, let's have our shower. And don't get frisky this time, because I'm not in the mood.'

'First time for everything,' he sighed. 'Is this the beginning of the slippery slope?'

'Shut up and fetch the shampoo. You'll find your slippery slope when you stand on Mums's Imperial Leather soap.' She shook a fist at him. 'You know, I can't tell you how happy I am to have married a total idiot. Heart surgeon? They're scraping the barrel.'

He turned on the shower, checked the temperature and dragged her in. 'You're so easy,' he whispered between shower-dampened kisses. 'Not in the mood . . ?'

Carol Makin was in her element. She was staying in a posh gaff overlooking a series of perfectly manicured little parks with a good view of the marina behind those well-kept lawns and beds across the road. The huge Georgian houses had been erected to contain the families and servants of successful merchants who had lived in Liverpool's glory years. And those years were coming back, because this great, ebullient, brave seaport was soon to be the City of Culture, and things were looking up.

So was she. Well, she wasn't looking exactly up, but she had her eye pinned to a character who kept to-ing and fro-ing on paths through the neat gardens at the other side of Mersey View. He was a funny-looking bloke with a limp. And he was too casual, as if he had set out not to be noticed. But if he thought he was blending in with the landscape, he was definitely wrong. Who the hell was he? Was he casing the joint? Scarcely fit to be a burglar, he upped and downed from good leg to bad like a marionette with a string missing. No way could he shin up a drainpipe without breaking the other leg and his mother's heart.

Then she saw Lexi. So did Hopalong Cassidy, because he hit the deck quicker than a bale of cotton dropping from a crane at one of the cargo-landing stages. 'Blood and guts – he's a private dickhead,' she muttered. 'What the hell is–' Carol ran to the door, opened it, folded her arms and leaned casually against the jamb. 'Hiya, Lex,' she called. 'Fancy a cuppa?'

Lexi ground to a halt. She couldn't work out what the hell Carol Makin was doing here at this time of day. As for a cup of tea, she would sooner drink arsenic with the devil. 'Bog off, you fat cow. I'm looking for me purse and me handbag.' She turned away and walked off.

As soon as Lexi disappeared, Limpy Dickhead jumped up and followed her. He stood out like a boil on the face of a baby as he lurched along in pursuit of the Litherland whore. Carol went back into the house. This was all the fault of him next door. It needed dealing with.

Lexi was thoroughly cheesed off. Having various kinds of sex with Greasy Bleasdale had been horrible. She'd been with some mingers in her time, but dealing with Greasy in a storeroom between bog rolls and Harpic had definitely been a low point in her career. However, she'd been granted a couple of hours on the computer, and she was ready to start putting Richard's wife in the picture.

A kerb-crawler stopped and wound down his window. 'Would you like a lift, love?'

He didn't look too bad, and the car seemed decent, so she got in beside him. 'Thanks,' she said. 'I'm Lexi.' He wasn't pretty. He had what might be termed a face only a mother could love, but he was offering to take the weight off her feet, and she wasn't one for refusing favours.

'Tom Rice. I'll take you home, shall I?'

She gave him the address. He looked vaguely familiar, but she couldn't place him. Perhaps she'd checked him out at her till in the shop, or maybe he lived somewhere close to her.

'I've been for a walk down Mersey View,' he told her. 'Lovely, those gardens across from the houses. They own that land, you know. The people on that stretch have to keep the parks in good condition.'

'Oh.' That must be where she'd seen him, then.

When they reached her home, she invited him in. He looked clean, at least, and that was more than could be said for Greasy Bleasdale, who was always sweating like a pig, especially when standing near a woman.

'Give me your number.' He passed her a pen and a small notebook. 'We'll go for a drink one night, eh? Only I've sprained my ankle, and I've learned my lesson just now pottering about near the marina. Driving's bad enough. But I'd like to take you out.' So would Richard Turner, but he'd want to take her out in a different sense . . . He retrieved his notebook. 'Thanks. I'll sit here till you're safely inside. And I'll phone you when my foot's better.'

She got out of the car. He would sit and make sure

she was safe. Nobody had ever cared enough to think about her wellbeing. Had she met a decent man tonight? Perhaps, at long, long last, she could be with a bloke without money changing hands. He was no beauty, no spring chicken, but he'd treated her like a lady.

He picked up his phone as soon as he was out of her street. As always, he said as little as possible when communicating with a client. 'Dr Turner? Tom here. Contact has been established.' He severed the connection immediately. As an ex-policeman, he was only too aware of the level of surveillance that could be achieved these days.

Tom Rice had always approved of working girls, because they saved other women from bother. As long as they kept themselves clean and checked by a doctor, they did more good than harm. He'd served alongside officers who had seemed not too keen to solve a crime when a prostitute had been the victim. It was as if they didn't matter, as if they were less than human. Poor Lexi. He quite liked her. If he wasn't being well paid by Richard Turner, he would definitely have been on her side. He'd never liked bloody doctors.

As they neared Bolton, Alan began to feel nervous. He didn't know why. All he wanted was to enter the house in which he had lived since the death of Lucy's mother, and there would be nobody at home, since his so-called wife, soon to be ex, had buggered off to bloody Liverpool, and the kids could be just about anywhere in the world. All the same, he imagined pain in his chest, but he told himself that the pain was just a memory, and that he was not about to enter a nest of vipers.

They stopped on Darwen Road. 'So you want me to

wait here, then?' Trish asked, her voice high and unsteady. She was afraid that he might never come back. She was just the taxi driver, and he was going to make up with his wife and disappear for ever. Panic closed in on her, and her rate of breathing increased. She had never lived alone, couldn't cope alone, and her terror might frighten Alan off if she let him see the true extent of it.

'Trish?'

'Yes?'

'I'll be back. There's no way I'll be stopping here. My business has gone, she's sold the plant right down to the last cement mixer, and the project I'd planned is down the pan to pay all the debts she never cleared. As for the house, well, it's mortgaged from footings to chimney pots.' The mortgage company would be looking for him. They couldn't get their money back from Lucy, because she'd never borrowed it in the first place. 'Oh, and if you do buy me a partnership, it'll be in your name,' he said. It would have to be. Any assets he obtained would be taken to repay the money he had borrowed by forging Lucy's signature. He could very well go to jail for fraud . . .

'It doesn't seem right to be just in my name, love. You'll be doing all the hard work.'

'I'm bankrupt,' he said. 'Anything I earn will have to be cash in hand, or in an account with your name on it.'

'How much do you owe, Alan? If that wife of yours won't pay the debts, let me make a clean start for you.'

He swallowed hard. 'It's a lot. She cleaned me out by over two mill, but that was company money. The mortgage on the house is for just under half a million. If that was paid, I'd be in the clear. They couldn't take any more from me, and I wouldn't go to prison. The two million's gone for good, but I need the mortgage money to put me right.'

Trish lifted her chin. 'Prison? No man of mine goes inside. Look, I'll pay the building society and wipe your name off the bad books. You'll no longer be bankrupt, and you can start again in our joint names. You'll be able to hold your head up high again, and all I want is to be Mrs Henshaw. How about that?'

She was buying him. In return, he would have to pay via bingo, tea dances, whist and line-dancing. But she could make everything OK. If she did pay off the loan on Tallows, he'd become visible and viable again, but he'd still be trapped in Trish's simple, childish idea of life. He couldn't run and wouldn't run, because whatever else Trish might be, she was loyal. And he was tired.

He took her hand. 'Trish Styles, will you do me the honour of becoming my wife?'

She blushed and giggled like a girl. 'That sounded so old-fashioned.'

'Then give us an old-fashioned answer, girl.'

'Yes. Yes, I will marry you.'

Every man had his price, he mused as he sealed the deal with a kiss. And now, with his heart filled with gratitude, he needed to get into the house for a new reason. If he could find enough cash, he would take this good woman to Preston's of Bolton and buy her the best ring he could afford. Like him, she had known poverty; like him, she had dug her way out of it with the help of her marriage partner. He would take the bingo, the dancing, and even the bloody donkeys, because he was sick of running around, tired of being a wanted man, and fed up with women. This one would be enough. He'd make damned sure she was enough.

She was asking him a question. 'Sorry,' he said. 'Say that again.'

'Your mortgage company. I'll start sorting out the payment tomorrow. Find out how much, and I'll put an end to all your misery.'

It was as if heavy chains had been removed from his limbs. He was still tied – tied to her – but with silk or velvet rather than with base metal. It would be all right. He would make blinking sure of that.

'Can you just park here for a minute, please?'

David applied the anchors, and the van stopped. 'What now, missus?' he asked. 'I'm doing my best to stop a drama becoming a crisis worthy of discussion at the next G8 conference. Also, poor Moira can't see back there, and she can scarcely breathe. If any one of those bloody things bursts, we'll all be talking like Donald Duck – that's helium, you know.'

Lucy turned and caught a glimpse of Moira, who was giggling like a child. She was holding on to the strings attached to thirty heart-shaped balloons. 'Good job this wheelchair's pinned down, or I'd be flying back to the shed. And I'm starving. I'd just about kill for a ham sarnie.'

David tapped his fingers on the steering wheel. 'Look here. If they find out we're there, and we're not there, that'll make them worry, and they're already worried. But if they find out we're there and we are there, they'll cope better.'

Lucy turned to look at her festooned friend. 'Didn't Shakespeare have a wonderful way with words?' Then she awarded full attention to the man she loved. 'Listen, buster. We've stopped because here, on our right, we have a cake shop. I know I can't get a proper wedding cake at this point, but Sally in there specializes, so she'll have a little bride and a little groom, and we can stick 'em in any cake.' She left the van and crossed the road.

Moira cleared her throat. 'She's lovely, David.'

'She's beyond that,' he answered. 'For me, she's a life-saver. I was buried in work, and she dug me out. She's beautiful, and she has a heart the size of Brazil. But I can tell you this, Moira. If and when she ever loses her temper, we'd do better if we all moved to a different planet. There are years of anger bottled up, and whoever takes the lid off gets splashed.'

'It won't be you. She thinks the sun shines out of your stethoscope. It'll be my Richard. He's like a dog after a bitch on heat, and she's already clobbered him once. Nothing physical. She just stopped him in his tracks when I did my stupid bit of matchmaking.'

'Good. She's spoken for.'

Moira was only too happy to hear that. She had realized of late that her other half was not really fit for marriage. He needed too much of his own way, and she had been lenient with him. Lucy believed that her children had been allowed leeway, but that was nothing compared to the way Richard had developed. Was it all the result of MS? She looked through the window. 'Blood and guts, David – what the hell has she got? Just look at the state of her.'

He looked. His beloved Louisa was staggering across the opposite pavement with a three-tier wedding cake. Was there no end to the woman's powers of persuasion? He leapt out of the vehicle and ran to offer help. After relieving her of the burden, he chased her back to the van.

'It's cardboard,' he told Moira. 'Madam was pretending it was heavy.'

Lucy climbed into the passenger seat. 'I just wanted the sympathy vote,' she said sweetly. 'The cake is some kind of plastic, but the icing's real. And the bottom tier holds a dozen small fancies, so job done.'

There followed a discussion on the subject of concealment. The cake might be covered by a car rug, but Moira's balloons were a different matter.

'We'll just have to ruin the lawn again,' was Lucy's decision. 'Drive round to the back of the shed, and take everything in through the kitchen door. I have no other ideas except, perhaps, we might plead insanity.'

'I am quite sane, thanks,' David said, a laugh breaking his words.

'And I've no desire to be so,' added Moira.

Lucy looked at her other half. He had put his foot down again. The hastily arranged party was his idea, since he believed that Simon and Lizzie needed support rather than criticism. 'If you seem to be against the marriage, you both seem to be against your children,' he had advised. 'Don't push them away. No fuss, just a few fairy lights and a couple of bottles of champagne.'

It had grown from that. They now carried with them half of Marks & Spencer's food hall, six bottles of Sainsbury's on-special-offer pink champagne, the crazy cake with bride and groom on top, and thirty uncontrollable balloons. Short of hiring the Dagenham Girl Pipers and the Luton Boys' Choir, they had done a thorough job.

Once back in the little wooden bungalow, Moira ate her longed-for sandwich while the other two idiots ran round with plates, fairy lights, silver horseshoes, ice buckets, a false wedding cake and a ghetto blaster. They couldn't find a wedding march in the small collection of CDs, and Lucy expressed the opinion that neither Floyd Cramer's 'On the Rebound', which was hers, nor her sons' collection of rappers would be suitable. So she settled for Robbie Williams singing 'Angels', because it was beautiful.

Once more, she found herself overruled. 'Play that one second,' David told Moira, who was to be in charge of music. 'But first, I think Ronan Keating's "When You Say Nothing At All" is more suitable. Here it is. There's a beautiful sadness in 'Angels', and the message in the other one is spot on. It's about love that needs no words.'

'You're special,' announced Moira. He'd left her with Aerosmith's 'I Don't Wanna Miss A Thing' and 'How Do I Live' by LeAnn Rimes. 'My Richard would have chosen differently, I'm sure.'

'David's perfect.' Lucy took his hand in hers. 'Not ashamed of his feminine side, are you, darling? He likes Westlife. Few men would admit to that. I never met a more thoughtful and loony human being. And you're staying, David. You're in loco parentis on the male side. I can be stubborn, too.'

'OK. Now. Where are they?'

'In bed, if I know anything about my son.' Moira swallowed the last of her sandwich while the other two pretended not to worry. Her choking fits were dramatic and life-threatening, yet she soldiered on. Only days ago, she had been on a diet that was almost liquid, but she was loth to give up her real grub.

When the swallowing was over, Lucy told her that her son would need to educate Lizzie.

'No!' Moira's eyes were wide. 'In this day and age? Oh well, never mind. He researched the subject when he was about seventeen. Other boys had mucky mags, but he chose the medical route. I bet he could write his own book about female orgasm. They'll be all right. They'd better be all right, else I'll kill him myself.'

'They're coming. They look great together.' David backed away from the window. 'Get your finger on the button, Moira.'

'Are we still on about female parts?' she asked innocently.

Lucy heard their footfalls on the ramp. 'Cue music,' she whispered. Then the door opened, she saw her daughter and her son-in-law, and she burst into tears. They were beautiful people.

Ten

There was hardly any furniture. Apart from a couple of rugs and a few chairs, the lower storey of Tallows had been stripped of its identity. Lucy wasn't coming back, then. But someone was living here, and that someone was his daughter, because bits of her were scattered through kitchen and living rooms and even on the staircase. Alan experienced a couple of pangs, as Lizzie was just about the best thing to have happened in this barn of a place. His sons were good lads, but his daughter was special.

For ten or more minutes, he waited and listened. When no one appeared, he returned to the laundry, took a crowbar from behind the dryer, and began to work on the stone-flagged floor. This was where he had kept his stash, emergency money for drinking, gambling, and all other just-in-case occasions that cropped up in the normal run of life. Nowhere near as fit as he had thought, he had difficulty in lifting the slab, but he managed, just about. He dialled the number, opened the floor safe, grabbed what was left, and replaced the flagstone in the nick of time.

'Who the hell are you?'

Alan clapped a hand to his chest, turned, and saw a tall, blond man in the doorway. 'I could ask you the same question, because I've lived here for over twenty years.' He shouldn't have said that. This bloke could be a detective, and Alan needed to stay hidden until Trish had cleared his debts.

'So you're Mr Henshaw?'

Alan offered no reply.

'Simon Turner,' the young man said. 'Your daughter's husband.'

'What?'

'Liz and I were married last Wednesday. We told no one, so you're not the only person left out of the loop.'

Alan staggered and righted himself by leaning against the washing machine. 'My Lizzie? My little girl?' The true nature of paternity hit him in that moment. Someone was touching his daughter. Someone had inveigled his way into her heart and into her bed. Had it been one of his lads married, that would have been different. But not his beautiful Lizzie. Her whole life flashed before Alan's eyes – the child on a beach, running in these gardens, looking at animals in the zoo and at the safari park, spilling ice cream down her clothes, playing Mary in the school nativity at Christmas. 'You do right by her, or I'll find you and bloody well kill you.'

Simon nodded thoughtfully. 'I shan't steal from her, won't forge her signature or abuse her in any way. As for you, take care. I'm training in cardio-thoracic surgery, and I can tell you here and now that you need to look after yourself. Open heart procedures are costly and time-consuming, so start respecting your body. For now, just try to calm down. Watch your blood pressure and eat very little saturated fat. Stress is to be avoided, too, so don't make a rod for your own back by committing any further crimes of fraud.'

Alan gulped audibly. 'Does my Lizzie know all my sins?'

'Most of them. But don't worry, because she's her mother all over again. They both seem capable of endless forgiveness, though I dare say either or both could be pushed to the edge by lunacy such as yours if it continues. What the bollocks were you thinking of, man?'

It had to be said. 'I'm an alky. Some days, I didn't know whether I was coming, going, alive or dead. It's no excuse, but booze is my master. I still live from one drink to the next, but the difference is that I'm not taking any alcohol. Inside, I'm screaming. But I'm living with somebody who holds me back. And that's the God's honest truth.'

They walked into the kitchen and sat one each side of the table.

'Well, I believe you.' Simon stared at the vision before him. Alan looked older than his years. Too-rapid weight loss had left him looking rather like a balloon from which half the air had escaped. A man in his forties should have retained some elasticity in his skin, but this one had lived too hard, and he was wrinkled. 'How's your liver?' he asked.

'Thanks for asking. Some of it's shoe leather, but some of it works.'

'It can regenerate up to a point.'

'I know. Where is she? Did you say your name's Simon?'

'Yes.'

'Where's my Lizzie?'

'In the shed with both our mothers. Lucy found out about the wedding, and she and . . .' he decided not to mention David, 'she and my mother decided to give us a little celebration. In fact, I've come to collect some CDs from upstairs, so I'd better be quick.'

Alan lowered his head. 'I can't come and see her. It wouldn't be right. But when the party's over, tell Lizzie I love her.' He gulped. The word love had scarcely visited his vocabulary for a long time. 'And tell Lucy ... Just tell her I'm sorry.'

'OK.' Simon dashed off in search of music while Alan walked into the hall and let himself out through the front door.

He crossed the lane and stared at Tallows for a while. He had been a selfish bastard and was a selfish bastard to this day. He wouldn't change, because it was too late, and the life he had lived had been too full of resentment. But clouds formed by alcohol had blurred his judgement. At least he was beginning to see himself for what he was. The old maxim about giving and taking was starting to make sense. If Trish Styles paid off his huge debt, the one for which he should be serving time, he would moderate his behaviour.

It was an elegant house. He heard his boys screaming in the woods, saw Lizzie in a mud-spattered party frock, watched them playing, quarrelling, enjoying a game of cricket, scarpering when a window shattered as a ball entered the house. All gone now. Line-dancing was to be the price, together with bingo and cards. He would probably moan about life, but he had to pay Trish back. There was no way in which he might recompense Lucy, but she'd taken her pound of flesh, hadn't she?

Hiding behind a hedge, he sat down and counted what remained of his fortune. Give or take, it was about two grand. Trish had blue eyes. They were frightened blue eyes. This money would be used to take away a bit of that terror. In some strange way, the caring for and protecting of Trish was also a repayment to Lucy. It wasn't going to be easy, but he could only do his best. He might rail against donkeys and tea dances, but by God, he would stick to her. Trish wanted stability, but so did he. The fool he had been needed to be left in the past, because he required predictability, a timetable of sorts and freedom from debts and worries.

When he reached Darwen Road, he saw her and waved. Her little face lit up like a child's at Christmas. He got into the passenger seat. 'Hiya, kid,' he said. 'Well, here I am. Told you I'd be back, what? Come on, let's have a smile.'

'Hello, love. Are we going home now?'

He shook his head. 'No. We're off to look at sapphires.'

'Are we?'

'You can't be engaged without a ring. Don't start blubbering, I'm not in the mood. Right. Town. It's thataway.'

Trish composed herself. 'Did you find them?'

'What?'

'The brooch and the watch.'

Alan slapped his head with the flat of his hand. 'Doh,' he uttered in the style of Homer Simpson. 'See, if I'd been pissed, I would have remembered. Tanked up on whisky, I never forgot a thing. I was daft in other ways, like judgement in the broad sense, but I never forgot little details. My body's not used yet to being without booze.' He turned and looked at her. 'Don't let me drink, love.'

'You join AA and I'll join Al-Anon. We can do it. I know we can.'

'We can and we will,' he said. 'Now, I've got a bit of money, and we're off to the greatest jeweller in the north. Sapphires and diamonds. Then if we're quick, we'll be back in Blackpool for your blessed bingo.' Yes, it was time to pay his dues in full.

There were only five of them at the party, but they managed to produce enough noise to make the place seem full. To be fair, it was full, because thirty large, heart-shaped balloons took up a great deal of space. When the helium-filled intruders became too great a nuisance, the inevitable happened. David was the first to inhale, and the Queen would probably have laughed herself sick had she been privy to his rendition of the national anthem.

Lizzie delivered an ultra-falsetto 'Amazing Grace', Moira blessed the company with 'You'll Never Walk Alone', while Lucy chose to murder 'Morning Has Broken'. 'That was bloody awful,' David announced. 'I'm not sure I can live with that.'

A silence followed. Lizzie approached her mother. 'Mums?'

'It's not my fault,' David said. 'I'm only following orders. She told the world I was going to marry her, and she filled me in only yesterday. Sorry, Louisa.'

Lucy held her head high. 'I love him,' she told her daughter. 'I loved him when I was ten, but he was like a brother. Diane and I used to pray for a little brother, you see. But David's not a brother any longer. Actually, he is longer, because he was a shrimp of a kid.'

'So, you were as quick as we were, then.' Liz grinned and waved a finger. 'Mother, you can't possibly be sure in so short a time. I'll bet that was what you wanted to say to me and Simon.'

Lucy shrugged.

'Did you open my bedroom door? Did you see us together with no clothes on?'

'Yes.'

'Ah, it wasn't a dream.' Liz turned her attention to David. 'You'd better look after her, young man. I have raised my mother to a very high standard, and she doesn't mix with riff-raff. Can you feed and house her? Can you keep her in the manner to which I have allowed her to become accustomed?'

He nodded and mumbled something about industrial cleaners and an oven with a missing door.

'She's used to ovens with a full complement of doors. Why industrial cleaners?'

David laughed. 'Because even the dog was complaining about the squalor.'

'Where is he?' Liz asked.

'Playing with the children next door. He loves kids, but he's never eaten a whole one.'

Lucy stepped in. She warned her new son-in-law to hide all his clothes, because Liz would wear them when her own were dirty. She told him to employ a cleaner, since Liz's idea of domestic hygiene was a square foot of visible carpet and a pair of matching socks.

Simon sighed. 'I know. She already put me in the shabby picture. We'll be fine. What can I say? Someone has to take her off your hands. You don't want to be lumbered until she has to be auctioned off on eBay, one previous owner, buyer to collect. You wouldn't get much unless you threw in a set of pans and a food mixer.'

Moira was happy. She was in the company of family and friends, was pleasantly drunk and, if she could hang about for a few more years, might become a grandma. Liz had declared her intention to live in London, to work only in Britain, probably as a waitress or an office temp, since good actors were ten a penny, and it was time she became minimally domesticated. They were hoping to live in London, since Lizzie's dream had always been a tall, thin house with a long, narrow walled garden. For the time being, they would use her one-bedroom flat, and yes, she would have to be tidy.

'My mother's grinning like an ape,' commented Simon.

'She's expecting.' Lucy sat next to Moira. 'She's expecting a grandchild.'

Lizzie made an explosive sound. 'Give us a few minutes, Moira.'

Lucy, too, was strangely happy. The young couple looked right together, sounded right, probably were right. There was a kindness in Simon that shone from his eyes – he must have inherited that quality from his mother.

The other reason for Lucy's contentment sat at the opposite side of the room, confectioner's custard spilled on his shirt, a silver horseshoe dangling from a ribbon round his neck, while a party hat folded from a page of the *Financial Times* sat at a rakish angle on his head. He was counting his famous rubber bands. Lucy smiled. He had not grown up. Please God, he never would.

*

Richard was having trouble coming to terms with isolation on the family front. He was in contact with patients and medics on a daily basis, did his house calls, and spoke to reps from pharmaceutical companies, but he remained a needful man. A house without Moira in it was a ship abandoned. His girls were never in, his son had disappeared, and a terrible picture of the future was developing before his eyes.

It didn't look good. He missed Lucy. The thought of her sleeping next door, with or without David Vincent, was torture. The knowledge that she wasn't within reach was worse. He loved two women. One had been in his life since the 1970s, the other for a couple of months. Moira was the one who kept his feet within touching distance of the ground, while Lucy had now become a torment who haunted his dreams both day and night. His wife was dying, and the gorgeous female who had bought Stoneyhurst would never be his.

He stepped out of the shower and pulled on a robe. Sometimes he was ashamed of himself; on other occasions, he told himself he was normal, marginally oversexed and very lonely. Moira had always been happy to listen and advise, but her health was deteriorating, and he didn't want to hurt her any more. Lexi was threatening to do just that, to break the heart of a wife who remained loved at a level that could not be understood by someone Richard thought of as a mere tart. So Tom Rice was trying to keep tabs on her, but he was temporarily out of action due to an ankle injury. Richard trusted Rice and only Rice, so he had to wait for the man's health to improve.

He dried his hair. Moira had accepted his dalliances with women of sense and social acceptability, but she would never forgive him for Lexi. Had she met the working girl in other circumstances, Moira would have been polite, even supportive, but street women were for other men, those who didn't give a damn for their own health or for their families' peace of mind. 'I bet Moira knows anyway,' he told the towel. 'I can't go on like this. Something in me is going to give.' Never before had he felt so angry and inadequate. Lexi had to be frightened off. She couldn't destroy his career, but she might well hasten the death of a woman who deserved a more tranquil life, however short that span might turn out to be.

'I want to kill the bloody woman,' he said as he shaved. 'I'd love to break her scrawny neck. Hurry up, Tom Rice. I need to be told what she's up to.' One thing was certain. He wanted to stop the Lexi business before Moira came home. He had only days.

The smell hit him as he descended the stairs to the ground floor. On the doormat, *The Times*, Moira's *Daily Mail* and assorted items of post failed to cover completely the stuff from which the stench emerged. It was dog excrement. Loosely wrapped in the pages of some gaudy magazine, it had spilled across an area of several square feet, and Richard felt his gorge rising. A doctor was used to unpleasant odours – they were part of life, and certainly an element in death – but this was different. It was deliberate, foul and sickening. Had Moira been here, she might have fallen in it. And the stairlift people were coming today, as were patients.

Should anyone trouble to ask in times to come when he had actually snapped, he would surely nominate this moment. A woman of absolutely no significance had done this to upset him, and to damage Moira. Temper rose, underlining his need to vomit. He ran to the downstairs bathroom and relieved himself of bile, since his stomach contained no food. The bitterness of gall was a clear reminder of his hatred for Lexi. All sense of proportion was deserting him as he cleaned up the dog mess in order to open up for morning surgery. It had seemed so small a thing, that brief dalliance with a shop girl. But she was evil. Like many cancers, she needed to be excised for the greater good.

He used almost a full bottle of Domestos, and the area near the door stank of it, but it was an acceptable stench. The bloody woman had even deprived him of his crossword, and he could only hope that nothing of significance had arrived in the mail, most of which was now on fire in the back garden. He scrubbed his hands until the skin glowed before rubbing in an anti-bacterial gel. There would be patients soon, and life had to go on. Up to a point, that was.

Shirley arrived. She mentioned the smell, and he told her he had spilled a sample taken from a patient. 'Can't be too careful,' he said as he walked into his area of work. A secretary entered the scene, the phone began to ring, and Richard stepped into his role. Doctors Shipman and Crippen visited his mind, but he sent them on their way when notes and coffee were delivered to his desk.

He dealt with pregnancy, an irritable bowel, two cases of chronic depression, asthma, and a plethora of coughs and colds. But in his mind he was punishing Lexi, and many patients were surprised because for once he issued sick notes as if they were confetti.

Last of all, he gave an audience to a female who was not on his books.

Carol Makin sat, and the chair groaned in protest. 'I seen it,' she announced.

'You seen – I mean you saw what?'

'That Litherland Lexi putting something through your door.'

The silence that followed was deafening and long. 'Oh,' he managed at last.

'Listen, doc. You know how people tell you stuff what you can't tell nobody?'

He processed the sentence before nodding.

'Me and our Dee has to be like that, because we've looked after some famous people, and professionals like yourself. Now, all I know is this – where there's Litherland Lexi, there's trouble. If you need me and my daughter to give you a hand, say the word.'

'Right.'

Carol leaned forward, and the chair complained again. 'Even her own family doesn't want nothing to do with her.' Carol didn't like Richard much, but he helped the sick, and Lexi helped nobody but herself. 'So think on,' she added. 'We're next door, and we'll be looking after your house and Moira when Shirley leaves.' She stood up.

He imagined that the chair breathed a sigh of relief. 'Thank you,' he said carefully. 'But there's nothing for you to worry about. She's mentally ill and beginning to imagine things. They have it on the medical grapevine that she may well be suicidal due to repeated infections of a sexual nature. Even royalty's had its mad members as a result of syphilis. Now, I haven't told you any of that. Miss Phillips joined my list, and I sent her to someone better qualified to deal with her particular ailment.

She took the rejection badly, because in her head she's had a close relationship with me. I shall telephone her doctor as soon as you go. Do not approach her. And I am trusting you, Carol.'

'Right.'

'I'm supposed to say nothing about people's illnesses and confidences.'

'I understand.' At the door, she turned. 'What did she put through your door, doc?'

'Dog dirt.'

'Filthy bitch.'

He sighed. 'Remember, Carol. Sick people don't always know what they're doing. And I don't want my wife to know what's happened while she's been away. Her heath is precarious enough without any further pressure.'

Outside, Carol stood for a while on the pavement. She looked left, right, to the front and to the rear, but Lexi was nowhere to be seen. Richard Turner was a sly bugger, but Carol would believe him before she'd believe anything out of the mouth of Lexi Phillips. Something had gone on between him and Lexi, and his tongue hung out whenever he saw Lucy, so he wasn't to be trusted completely, but he was only a bloke, and they understood nothing beyond sex and car maintenance. Yes, this one was a doctor, but he still kept his brains behind his fly and under the bonnet of his precious motor.

She re-entered Lucy's house. Dee was having five minutes with *Heat* magazine and a cup of coffee. 'What's up?' she asked her mother.

Carol delivered her tale. 'There's something wrong,'

she concluded. 'That private dickhead was following Lexi – him with the limp what I told you about. Maybe the doc's telling the truth and she's away with the mixer, but he's one of them men you can never be sure of.'

Dee agreed. 'He's after sex, Mam. Poor Moira can't do nothing no more. She's like our Beryl, all tablets and nappies, but he still wants his oats, eh? Well, he'll get nothing off Lucy, however hard he sniffs. She'll be wed by Christmas, I reckon. And depending on where she lives, you could be here running the bed and breakfast. So you can chase Lexi in your spare time if you live here. I couldn't be bothered with her, to be honest.'

Carol got her cup and sat down. She was glad Moira had gone away, because this Lexi business was pressing. Anybody who posted dog muck through the door of a posh house had to be mad, evil, or both. If this wasn't nipped in the bud, it could make Moira a lot worse. 'Shall we go and see her, Dee?'

'Litherland Lexi?'

'No, Princess Anne, you daft bat. Of course I mean Lexi. What do you think?'

Dee pondered for a few moments. 'No,' she said at last. 'This is our livelihood – you, me, my kids and our Beryl will soon depend on this house and next door. If we get involved and the shit hits the fan, you and me'll be covered in it. Not him, though. Not Dr Fancypants and his rambunctious hormones. Stay well out of it. I mean that, Mam.'

Carol drained her cup. Dee spoke a lot of sense. She was right: if something untoward got uncovered, it would be best to stay away from any resulting flak. 'OK, missus. Finish your bathrooms and get home to Beryl.

I have to stop here, but I'll keep wmeself to meself. He knows where I am if he needs me.'

Moira was having the time of her life. She loved the shed, and declared on several occasions that she'd be happy to spend the rest of her life in it. Further confidences forced on Lucy were less pleasant. Moira was sure that Richard was up to no good, that he had overstepped a mark, and she said that she was enjoying being away from him. 'Simon and the girls were easy to raise. He's bloody impossible, and I didn't realize that until lately. So bloody selfish. He needs a good hiding.'

At first, Lucy didn't say much on the subject. The me-too speech would not have been suitable, since Moira already knew the extent of Alan's sins. Lucy was aware also that there was a deep and abiding love between Moira and Richard, and that no amount of sexual straying on his part would diminish that love. 'Well, we have to go back soon,' she said after one of Moira's longer tirades.

'Not yet. Please, not yet. Just because I'm sometimes in a wheelchair doesn't mean I have to stay with him. I can liquidate some of my share in the house – equity release, I think it's called – and put myself away where I don't have to put up with prostitutes looking for him.'

'You're not sure that she was looking for him.'

'I flaming well am sure.'

Lucy sat down. 'There are many kinds of love, Moira. And no, I'm not going to deliver a lecture, but I want to remind you. There's the silly, romantic kind where you stop eating, drift through a dream and wake up either still in love, or decidedly out of it. Then there's the merely physical that has no roots. Lastly, there's the one that abides. It's almost spiritual, and it contains elements of the first two, while being a meeting of minds. You and Richard have that.'

'Do we?'

'Absolutely. How many women care enough to look for a second wife? You know none of us lives for ever, so you tried to ... well, you know what you did. If he fell for someone, he wouldn't abandon you. In fact, it's more positive than that, because I'm damned sure he'd do anything and everything to make your life better. He's having a stairlift fitted, isn't he? A small thing in a way, but just for you.'

Moira sniffed. 'He's been with a prostitute.'

'He made a mistake. We are all victims of our own frailty.'

'Are you? Have you slept with him yet?'

Lucy smiled. 'I have, and we slept. David and I are lucky, because we seem to have what you and Richard have. We rag one another mercilessly, we need each other, and we're getting him out of his doldrums before starting to jump around like a couple of kids. It's real.'

'And the wedding?'

'Christmas, but I haven't told him. Then we get the big house done up for sick kids and we have a honeymoon next summer.'

'But he doesn't know.'

'Of course he doesn't know. He's too busy curing people and counting rubber bands.'

'What?'

'Never mind. I'll tell you when you're old enough. For now, I am going to chase your son and my daughter. They can't leave it to us, love. Richard needs telling, and they are going to do it.'

She left Moira to her own devices and went to the big house. In the kitchen doorway, she ground to a halt. Her daughter, white-faced and clearly tense, was washing dishes. 'Hell's bells,' Lucy exclaimed. 'Housework? Are you ill?'

Lizzie stuck out her tongue. 'I have many talents, Mums. It's just that I have chosen not to employ them until absolutely necessary.' Her hands slowed. 'I'm terrified of Simon's dad.'

Lucy grinned. 'He's just a man. Men are tall little boys. Do you want me to come with you? David has the week off, and we're meant to be out for the day, but he'll sit with Moira if I ask him to.'

Lizzie shook her head emphatically. 'No. Richard wants to get into your knickers, so his reaction would be a false one if you're there. Simon can deal with him. We won't come back. Is it OK if we use my bedroom at Stoneyhurst? I don't think I'm up to sharing living space with Dr Turner.'

Lucy stayed to wave them off. Of course they'd be welcome on Mersey View. Who could resist two such beautiful creatures? Simon had to work some notice at the Royal, after which they would travel to London so that he could take up his new post, while Lizzie would return to RADA.

She went upstairs and found that Lizzie's room had been left in pristine condition. An effort had been made, and that was good enough. 'I spoiled all three of you,' she whispered. A thought struck. What if Mike and Paul got serious about Alice and Steph? 'My life would become hyper-medical,' Lucy told herself. David, Richard, Simon, Steph and Alice – they could staff their own private hospital.

The mobile rang. At first, she didn't recognize the sound, until she remembered that David, while in his cups under the famous *Financial Times* hat, had loaded 'Amarillo' as her ring tone. 'Hello?'

'Lucy?' It was Glenys.

'Yes, Glen. How are you doing?'

'OK. I finally got hold of Howard Styles's widow. She wasn't in Cheshire – she has a second house in Blackpool. I got her on her dead husband's mobile.'

'And?'

'He's with her. She asked him to put the kettle on, and she used his name. I know Alan's not an uncommon forename, but I'm guessing it has to be him. They're going back to Alderley Edge on Thursday. I've arranged to meet her in a coffee shop on Friday morning. When she asked why, I told her it was personal and connected to the death of her husband. She knows I'm a lawyer, and she has all my phone numbers.'

'Thanks, Glen.'

'Are you up for it? It could get nasty, Lucy.'

'I have to warn her. It would be subhuman not to. Let's face it, you should really have got the police, because Alan stole money from a building society. We're not being cruel.'

'OK.'

Lucy turned off her phone. Sitting on a chaise, she looked through the landing window. David had arrived with what Moira termed the fasten-me-down van. Dressed in his version of casual clothes, he looked as if he'd been dragged through a hedge backwards. Like many Englishmen, he managed to confuse casual with disgraceful. Yet it was in these moments that she loved him most. He was the other half of her, and she wished she'd met him again years ago, wished she'd been there to help when Anne and Tim died. It was time to buy him some decent leisure clothes – if she could get him into a shop, if she could force him to try things on.

Today, they were taking Moira over the Pennines to visit Yorkshire. She had never seen it and, in Lucy's opinion, no one should go through life without looking at what she called God's temper tantrum, the wild and wonderful area that she always thought of as unfinished, as if the manufacturer had run out of steam and decided to leave it half done. Tomorrow, Mags Livesey was coming to give them both a new hairdo and a facial. That would cheer Moira no end, because she hadn't seen a beautician in years.

'Louisa?' The cry drifted upstairs.

She laughed quietly. David often used her full handle, the name she had been given, the one her parents insisted on until Father and Grandfather had started the Lucy-Lou game.

'Coming,' she called.

They met halfway down the stairs.

'When?' he asked.

'When what?'

'Bed. Together. You and I.'

He was coming along nicely if she could just ignore the clothes. 'Soon,' she promised. 'Now, what if we decide to take Moira somewhere nice for lunch? They won't let you in.'

'Ah.' He looked down at himself. 'I forgot. Had some trouble with the van, did a bit of engine-tweaking, and should have changed afterwards.' He smiled at her. 'How soon is soon?'

'Soon. We'll call at your house on the way and find

something decent for you to wear. When Moira's settled back on Mersey View, I'll come and stay in your very clean home if you'd prefer there to here.'

'Next week?'

'Probably the week after.'

'Good. That gives me time.'

'Time? You said there was no time. Didn't Einstein—'

'Shut up, Louisa.'

'OK.'

They walked downstairs together.

'Why do you need time?' she asked again.

'I'm not going to tell you. It's meant to be a surprise, and I need to get . . .'

'Get what?'

'Stuff.' He turned on her and pulled her roughly into his arms. 'Not all your own way, Louisa. Never, never all your own way. I love you far, far too much to let you get away with mayhem.'

Yes, she was doing a good job. In warning him that she could manage him, she had thrown down a gauntlet, and he refused to be managed. Underneath the academic, the man survived, and within that man a child endured. Behind the dreadful grief, a flicker of hope had been lit, and it burgeoned now into a flame that warmed him and allowed him to consider coming back to life. He could love again, and she was to be the happy recipient of his affections.

They travelled to his house, and Lucy stayed in the van with Moira while he changed. The place was smart, detached and at the better end of Chorley New Road, within spitting distance of golf club and crematorium.

'What are you laughing at?' asked the passenger in the back.

'Well, he can play golf there in the winter, and warm his hands across the road afterwards.'

'Lucy?'

'What?'

'Did anyone ever tell you your sense of humour's warped?'

'Not until recently. I led a very quiet married life.'

'And now you're making up for it.'

Lucy turned in her seat. 'Watch this space, Moira. I'm still warming up. You ain't seen nothing yet, babe.'

He came out of the house in suit and tie. It was becoming plainer by the minute that he did consultant or mechanic, with no stations in between. 'I've got a catalogue at home,' Moira said. 'Get his measurements, and we'll see what we can do. He's hopeless, isn't he?'

'Delightfully so. Don't way a word.'

They drove to Yorkshire and had a wonderful day.

Alan knew how Atlas might have felt had someone lifted the world from his shoulders. The sun shone more brightly, sand and sea suddenly became colourful, while even bingo improved, especially when he won a national prize of a hundred grand. His cheque remained in a drawer, as he was still an undischarged bankrupt with a possible prison sentence hanging over his head. 'I could have bought you a better ring,' he told Trish. She didn't know he was a criminal, did she? With luck and a strong following wind, she would never know.

'I don't want one.' She looked at her Ceylon sapphire and diamonds. 'This is beautiful, we chose it together, and I'm not parting with it. Anyway, come Friday afternoon, you'll not be bankrupt. The payment will be on its way to the Halifax, and I hope that ex-wife of yours is proud of herself.'

In an untypically honest mood, he was feeling proud of Lucy. She could have sent the cops to the hospital, could have had him locked up by now. The fact that she hadn't made sure he was in jail meant a great deal to him. She was straight, honest and generous. He couldn't remember his last real conversation with her, and that fact made him feel terrible. It was a bit late in the day to start developing a conscience, but guilt pursued him every inch of his new life.

Then Trish's second mobile rang. He watched as her eyes filled with tears, because she hadn't heard Howie's ringtone in weeks. She answered it. 'Hello?'

While listening to the party at the other end, she asked Alan to brew some tea. He stood just inside the kitchen, and his heart sank. She was making arrangements to meet a lawyer on Friday. They were going for coffee at the Boule Miche, a pretentious and overpriced joint in Cheshire named after some famous street in Paris. Napoleon bloody Bonaparte had a lot to answer for, he mused irrelevantly. Friday. The very day on which the money would begin to walk from her account into the Halifax.

He put the kettle on. 'Who was that?' he asked when she joined him in the kitchen.

'A Gloria Benson,' she answered. 'Something to do with Howie. She wouldn't say, not on the phone. Lawyers are like that, aren't they?'

People who gave false names almost always clung to their real initials. Gloria Benson was Glenys Barlow. Lucy would probably be there. Easterly Grange had given him away, and doctors were supposed not to do that kind of thing. There was no point in asking Trish not to go, because if Glenys had Howie's phone number, she probably had the address of Styles.

In that moment, the longest three days of Alan's life began their slow, torturous countdown. There was one option, yet he couldn't face it. Were he to pre-empt Lucy and her lawyer by telling Trish the full truth, he'd be out on his ear and foraging with the seagulls. And there was always the small chance that Gloria Benson might be the real name of the caller.

'You've gone white,' Trish told him.

'Just a headache. I'll take a couple of painkillers.' But the real pain would not be shifted, since it was rooted in terror.

A doctor was privy to all kinds of information. No one had sent for Lexi's notes, though she would need them soon, since she was a type one diabetic. Like most who were condemned to become pincushions twice daily, the woman had seldom mentioned the fact. His practice nurse had noted the condition, and Richard must have signed a repeat prescription, though he had no memory of the occasion. Ah, yes – it was one of those automatics that went to her pharmacist. Even without a prescription, Lexi could obtain insulin from the chemist with whom she was registered.

He read and reread her bulky file, found occasions on which she had been treated for depression, thanked God that her history was in hard copy rather than on a computer. He added his own comments, dating them to accord with the day on which he had struck her from his list. *There are some symptoms of depression again, and*

I feel she should attend a surgery closer to her home.
Should she fail to improve mentally, she may become ...
He paused.

If he wrote the word 'suicidal', that might be a step
too far, and it could attract attention. Yesterday had
been dog dirt; today's gift was a letter printed from a
computer and addressed to Moira. It informed her that
her husband was sleeping with whores, many of whom
were being treated for STIs. She wasn't giving up, and
Moira would be back in a few days.

He stood at the window and looked at the little parks
across the way. Footpaths allowed members of the public to walk through the gardens, though they were
owned by householders on this side of Mersey View.
His patch was a simple lawn with rose beds in it. Moira
loved roses. He would have to do something, because
anything addressed to Moira was given to her by Shirley.
And he wasn't always available when the post came,
since employees of the Royal Mail seemed to adhere to
no strict timetable these days.

Murder was a subject about which he had seldom
thought. He'd treated a killer, a pleasant man who had
eventually been arrested and found guilty of shooting
his wife and her lover. On the day of the crime, Richard
had sedated the distraught culprit, just an ordinary
bloke who had snapped after pretending to find his wife
covered in blood.

'And I snapped over a bit of dog muck.' No. He had
snapped because his poor, sick wife had become a
target. She could have just months left. If she got pneumonia again, it could well be weeks. And he would not
allow those weeks to become infected by a disorder
named Lexi Phillips.

He finished his task, stating that in his opinion she needed a doctor on her doorstep in case the depression grew worse. In his bag, he often carried insulin against the odd occasion on which one of his patients forgot to take the dose. Hyperglycaemia was dangerous, and a doctor needed to be prepared. For the same reason, he carried chocolate and glucose, since a hypo was no fun either, and elderly patients sometimes had nothing sweet in the cupboards. Insulin could be a killer. For a depressive diabetic, it offered an easy enough exit from life.

He phoned Tom Rice. 'How's the ankle? Is it? Good, good. Look, things have gone quiet, so send a bill and I'll give you a bit extra to compensate for loss of business. What? Yes, I'll let you know if and when I need you again. Bye.' There. That was another job done. Richard hadn't wanted a witness appointed by himself to be at the scene of the crime. What crime? Did he have the stomach for it?

Since taking the oath, he had saved many lives. The acutely ill who could not be made safe by him had been passed on to hospitals, but Richard was an excellent diagnostician. He was also human, and he didn't like all his patients, but he did his best no matter what the circumstances. There had been a handful of mistakes, and he sometimes kicked himself inwardly after managing not quite well enough. This was a different kettle altogether. To kill, to stop someone taking in oxygen, to look into eyes from which all light had been taken deliberately – that was a horrible idea.

A few years earlier, Richard had attended a teenager who had chosen to die at home in the company of his loved ones. After three runs of chemo, there was little hope, and the brave young man had parked himself and his bed in the dining room of a clean but shabby terraced house. The courage of that intelligent, gentle boy had left a mark on Richard's heart. His ambition had been to join the RAF as a pilot. But, as those blue eyes had closed for the last time, the doctor had become a third parent, and he had wept with the family. They were believers, and the real father had said, 'Enjoy your flight to heaven, son.'

Was one life more valuable than another? And who was he to preside as judge? A strong opponent of the death penalty, he often decried southern states in America where locals bayed for blood whenever a murder occurred. In his opinion, they were mad Bible-thumpers who carried on as if they were still in wagon trains surrounded by the indigenous population whose land they planned to steal. They were backward, stupid, ill-educated, and he was thinking of joining their ranks.

Did Lexi have a better side to her nature, one to which he might appeal successfully? Could she be bribed? He knew she wanted to own her house and to furnish it better. But if he were to provide her with the means of achieving that, she might very well continue her campaign, because she was obsessed. He had dealt with obsessive behaviours and had passed them along to specialists who had achieved some degree of success, but Lexi was particularly tenacious and disillusioned. She wanted to be a doctor's wife, and imagined herself living a different life, one to which she felt she was entitled.

He wasn't a murderer. He couldn't do it, could he?

Williamson Square was its usual busy self. Children played in a fountain whose jets rose at unpredictable intervals from the ground, and shrieks of delight turned the place into a playground. Pigeons quarrelled over scraps deposited by humanity's careless lunch hour, and a couple of attractive young people sat on a bench opposite Liverpool's Playhouse Theatre.

'Your name could be up there soon,' Simon suggested.

'Yes, and you'll be in London taking advantage of some poor young nurse while I'm at a safe distance.'

'No I won't.'

'Yes, you will.'

'See?' he said. 'We're already practising for pantomime.' He looked at his watch. 'We have to do it. We have to go and tell Dad. We've had a lovely tapas lunch, enough coffee to give us both strokes, and now you want to go to the Albert Dock.'

'I've never seen the Albert Dock.'

He shrugged. 'Just think water, old bricks, and new shops selling silk scarves and prints of both cathedrals. It'll still be there tomorrow. As for the ferry across to Birkenhead, we can take that any time. You're procrastinating in a public place. You could get arrested for breach of the peace or behaviour likely to result in a disturbance.'

She delivered a withering glance. 'He's your father.'

'And your father-in-law. We're in this together, Rocko.'

'Who the hell's Rocko?'

Simon sighed. 'I was being a Chicago gangster.'

'Don't give up the day job. Come on, then.' She looked down at herself. 'I should have worn something more . . . demure.'

'Wrong.' He pulled her to her feet. 'He appreciates a fit maud.'

Lizzie didn't need an explanation. Fortunately, nobody had been lumbered with Maud as a forename for about a hundred years. 'I know he fancies my mother, and he frightens me to death. He's almost lecherous.'

He squeezed her hand. 'Do you love me?'

'Absolutely, unquestionably and for always.'

'Do you trust me?'

'See above – same answer. You're not just my lover, sweetie, you're my best friend in the world. I just can't stand your dad. Your mum I could eat on toast – I love her to bits.'

So he set out to explain his father. He asked how Lizzie would feel if sex just stopped, how she might react if she had to change nappies on an adult, the very man to whom she was married. 'It was never a fragile marriage, darling. He's not young, but not old enough to give up on life. We're animals, Eliza. The saintly man who's with your mother is unusual, but Dad isn't. He adores Mum, yet he's staring down a long, dark corridor called loneliness. Sex helps to switch on the lights for a brief period. My mother understands that.'

Lizzie sat down again and looked at a man with a little stall. He was selling tea towels, tablecloths and other items of linen. Behind him, a woman berated her child, while two teenage girls giggled, heads together, as they shared a private joke. A drunk sat on the ground, a precious bottle clutched to his chest.

Two policemen dashed across the square in pursuit of nothing at all. They ground to a halt, spoke to the mother of the naughty child, then to the man selling household fabrics. Heads shook, and the cops gave up chasing the invisible, settling instead for the drunk, as he was the only piece of culpable humanity on the scene. 'The whole of life in one little square,' Lizzie commented. 'Come on, then. Into the lions' den.'

They drove up the dock road, Lizzie exclaiming over the beauty of stone walls punctuated by little turrets. Narrow-gauge railway lines crossed their route, and Simon tried to illustrate the history of the area. 'Men queued ten deep for jobs. Starving kids chased wagons for a handful of molasses, and more than a few were run over and killed. It's been a cruel place, yet it managed to be glorious. It will be again, once the big liners start to dock here. Liverpool's coming back to life.'

'Built on the blood of slaves,' Lizzie said.

'Yes. I think the first ship sailed in 1699. The *Liverpool Merchant* picked up over two hundred Africans and deposited them in Barbados. It's regrettable, yet it happened and carried on happening. But we can't always pay for the sins of our forebears.'

'Slaves picked the cotton we spun in Bolton. We're all guilty.'

'Yes, we are. Just blame London – I always do. The money men invented the system, while we poor, ragged northerners endured the industrial revolution on their behalf.'

Lizzie looked at him. 'Are you sure?'

'Not at all. Although if in doubt blame London is a pretty sound principle.'

'But you love London.'

'I love you, and you aren't all good. If I told your mother what you did last night while I was sitting so innocently . . .'

They both started to laugh. Lizzie could hear the edge of hysteria in the noise she was making, and she hoped that her new husband wasn't noticing. She knew that he, too, was afraid, but for a different reason. His father was a one hundred per cent northerner. In his mind, Simon had grown up in the north, had been educated by tax-payers in the north, and should practise in the north.

'He'll hit the roof,' she said.

'Let him. He can probably fly, anyway. Worshipped by so many, he has to be superhuman.'

The rest of the journey was made in silence. Lizzie wished with all her heart that Mums could have been here. She'd always been the anchorman, the roots of the family, the one to whom everyone turned when things looked grim. Except for Dad, of course. He'd never turned to anyone. And where was he, anyway? Another bloody disappearing act by the famous Alan Henshaw. Was he alive, dead, or somewhere in between? Fathers were a damned nuisance.

Simon parked the car. Lizzie, holding on to the thought that fathers were pests, leapt from the vehicle, across the pavement, up steps and into the house. He was reading a newspaper. 'Hello,' he said, eyes travelling from her face to her bosom.

'We're married,' she gabbled. 'We married at Waterloo register office last Wednesday, and I love him. I'll always love him. And he loves me, and he's coming to London and working at Guy's.'

Richard laughed. He was still laughing when his son entered the room.

'Dad?'

'She's a character, son,' Richard pronounced. 'How old are you, Lizzie?'

'Twenty-one in January.'

'Moira was about that age when we married.' He folded the newspaper. 'Hang on, this calls for a toast.' He left the scene.

'How did you manage that?' Simon whispered.

'I didn't. My boobs convinced him.'

'I told you they were a bit good. Mind you, there'll have to be some improvements if you want to catch up with your mum.'

The cushion fight was still ongoing when Richard returned with champagne in an ice bucket. 'How long has this marital strife been happening?' he asked.

Liz stopped long enough to ask whether Richard knew a good lawyer.

'It's her,' shouted Simon. 'Last night, I was sitting there minding my own business when this woman here, who is a complete stranger to me, crawled across the floor and—'

He had no chance. Lizzie clouted him in the face with a brown suede cushion. 'Don't you dare,' she screamed. 'Don't you bloody dare.'

Richard felt tears pricking. He turned to fetch glasses. 'Give up, Simon,' he advised. 'There's only ever one winner, and its gender isn't male.' He poured the bubbly, raised his flute and drank to bride and groom. Then he passed each of them a full glass, sat down and told them about Moira, how they had met, how beautiful she had been, how wonderfully naughty. 'She was mad,' he concluded.

Simon offered his sympathies, saying he knew how that felt.

'You have no idea, son. Picture the scene. We're in Scotland, and I'm doing a Queen Mother – waders, rod, walking into the water. So I've a keep net with beautiful wild salmon thrashing about in it, and your mother puts them back in the river.'

'Why?'

'Because she felt sorry for them. Then we went back to the guest house, and she ordered local salmon for dinner. I could have sold them my catch. I could have been a classic hunter-gatherer getting food for my bride. But no. She thought they were too pretty, so she put them back.' He shook his head. 'Never expect sense, Simon.'

'I'm sensible,' Lizzie protested.

'You?' Simon threw up his hands. 'The washing up was there for two days till I explained about E. coli.'

'Are you incapable of doing dishes?' Richard asked his son. 'Don't take her for granted. Don't assume that there are jobs for men and jobs for women. Now, tell me about Guy's.'

Lizzie breathed a sigh of relief. When the conversation turned medical, she went next door to visit Smokey. Cats were easier than doctors.

Eleven

Ian Wray, the new gardener, was serving his apprentice-ship alongside Hal in four gardens attached to the terrace, and in several of the park gardens on the opposite side of the road. He was happy. Hal was Ian's preferred kind of old-time gardener, the pay was good, his employers seemed OK, and life was beginning to look up after a long spell without sufficient employment. He registered as a working man, paid his dues, and was no longer dependent on the state, which was fine by him.

But there was something wrong with the doctor whose car he had helped to clean. He seemed edgy, and he was giving shorter than normal shrift to anyone who addressed him. His wife was away with the woman next door, and both houses were being run by a pair of strange creatures named Carol and Dee, because Hal's wife was busy packing in preparation for the retirement move.

When Ian and Hal went into Lucy's kitchen to eat sandwiches and drink tea, the subject under discussion was the evil nature of Litherland Lexi, which topic sounded rather Agatha Christie to the new man. So the two gardeners ate lunch and made a hasty exit, because listening to the pair of cleaners was a confusing business, whilst flowers were easy, since they didn't have a lot to say. 'Come on,' Hal whispered. 'Before we get dragged into whatever this is.'

'Are they always like that?' Ian asked after their escape. 'Those two women, I mean.'

'No,' came the swift reply. 'Sometimes they're worse, because my Shirley's with them. When she's part of the mix, it can get a bit like the three witches at the start of *Macbeth*. Toil and trouble? You've seen nothing so far, lad. Give me a plague of greenfly any day.'

Inside the house, Dee and her mother had reached somewhat of an impasse. Dee was all for keeping her head well below the parapet if and when the bullets began to fly, but her mother wanted to wade in, Marigolds, Doc Martens, drain rods and the lot. 'She was here again last night,' the big woman said. 'Another letter through his door. She doesn't bother with stamps no more. Hard-faced bugger, she is. And Moira's coming back any minute. I won't be here to keep an eye on things during the night. Dog dirt and horrible messages? Whatever next? She's got to be stopped before she does somebody a real mischief.'

'Moira comes back Friday.' Dee was fed up to the back teeth, which were not yet accustomed to their new role, the rearmost four having recently been removed. 'Sorry, Mam, but I'm having nothing to do with it. I love Moira and Lucy, I do, I really do, but you're going about this all cack-handed, and you'll do more harm than good if you're not careful. It's none of our business, and that's the top and bottom.'

Carol remained on track, though her words indicated a diversion. 'But our Beryl's in a wheelchair.'

Dee's jaw dropped for a split second. 'What's that got to do with the price of fish?' Dee rephrased the question, because Beryl loved her salmon and trout when they could be afforded. 'Mother, listen to me. What's our Beryl being chairbound got to do with him next door, Litherland Lexi and letters? Eh?'

Carol was thoughtful for a few seconds. 'Look. If he gets one of them letters in his hand, right?'

'Right.'

'And if he has his window wide open, right?'

'Right.'

'And if he reads that letter aloud to his wife while Lexi's outside listening, right?'

'Wrong, Mam. Because Moira's with Lucy.'

Carol wiped her forehead with the back of her hand. 'We don't need Moira, because we've got our Beryl. Lexi'll see a woman in a wheelchair with its back facing the window. She doesn't know what Moira looks like, does she?'

'I don't know,' Dee sighed.

'Well, even if she does know what Moira looks like, the wheelchair will be the wrong way round, and she'll think it's Moira. So if Moira – I mean Beryl – laughs out loud at the letter, Lexi likely won't send no more.'

Dee sat down and lit a hand-rolled cigarette. In her opinion, Lexi would carry on doing this that and the other until the cows came home, or until she found a new victim. If the letters stopped, worse might happen. The woman was crazy, and she could get dafter if she thought her letters were the subject of mockery. 'Leave it, Mam. For a kick-off, Lexi doesn't come every night. On top of that, the doctor won't want our whole family knowing what he's been up to. And you could drive

Lexi all the way to mayhem and murder. You know she's a bad bugger. So stop it. Learn to keep your nose out. I mean it, Mam.'

Carol stared hard at her daughter. Dee was thin, frail-looking, and as strong as a horse. She was also clever and streetwise. 'I suppose you're right,' she admitted with reluctance. 'But I even feel a bit sorry for him, and you know he's not my flavour of the month. I mean, we know Lexi, so we expect her to be bad. He's not used to her type of carryings-on. I know he's done wrong, but she's wronger. She's wronger than anyone I know.'

'But we're leaving it, Mother.'

'Poor Moira.'

'Mother!'

Mother. That word was a sure sign that Dee was serious. They had to carry on working here, because the van was at death's door, and these two houses together would be convenient. Also, Lucy wanted someone to run the business from time to time, so the fortunes of the Makin/Baxendale clan looked promising, as long as they kept their noses clean. It was tempting, though. Carol would have dearly loved to get Lexi's face and push it through the old mangle in the back yard. Along with dolly tub and zinc bath, the geriatric wringer served now as decoration, its top and base covered by greenery and flowers. Lexi wasn't worth the spoiling of so beloved an article. 'She wants killing. We should get the health department in to shift her, because she's vermin.'

Dee stood up and grabbed her tickling stick. She waved it under her mother's nose. 'See this? We clean houses, Mam. Let priests, doctors and police deal with the rest, because it's none of our business. Who do you think we are? MI5? Sometimes, we just have to accept that we can't do nothing, and this is one of them times.'

'And they passed by on the other side? Remember that one, Dee?'

'I do. Good Samaritan. If somebody was lying here battered and bleeding we'd do something about it, because we're decent people. But this lot's different. You can make it worse by wading in. So stop paddling and piddle off.'

Carol laughed. Dee was definitely her daughter. 'All right, babe. But I'll not stop worrying over that poor Moira.'

That poor Moira was having the time of her life. It all felt like a fairytale: a tiny house, woods, country lanes and rides out in the van. She'd been to Lancashire markets, to the moors, to Yorkshire, but today the world was coming to her. 'So this woman who's giving us a bit of glamour was your husband's girlfriend?'

'That's right. He even took her away to Crete not too long ago. She was just the latest in a long string of mistresses.'

'And you're not bothered?'

'Not in the least bit. In fact, she's been extremely helpful, because she found the disappearing man for me. And now she's going to make us beautiful.'

Moira looked into a hand-held mirror. 'Does she do remoulds? Because my tyres seem to have lost a fair bit of their original tread. In fact, I could do with a whole new body. Does she bring a selection? I kid you not, Lucy, if I were a car, you'd keep the number plate and fasten a new vehicle behind it.'

Lucy had learned to laugh at her companion. Some

of the statements from Moira might appear to elicit sympathy, but now that Lucy knew her neighbour better, she realized that Moira was just being Moira. 'We've a ramp in the main garage,' she said helpfully. 'Mags could jack you up on it, and she could have a good look at your undercarriage. New exhaust, better suspension – who knows?'

'I'd do better with a catalytic converter and without my husband. I think I've gone off him for good this time. He's getting on my bloody nerves, and I don't know what to do about him.'

Lucy refused to rise to that one. Having phoned Carol on several occasions, she had endured an earful of Litherland Lexi, dog muck and nasty letters, but she hadn't said a word to Moira. Richard would have to do the honours. His wife already suspected that he'd used the services of a prostitute, but Richard had to say the words. Until he unburdened himself, Moira would probably remain angry with him. But there was one thing Lucy could say, and she said it. 'Just before we came here, he told me he wanted to tell you something, but that you were too ill. Remember? You came over all shake, rattle and roll. That was when he started attacking the car and setting fire to rubbish in the back garden. Has he phoned you recently?'

'Yes.'

'And did he discuss anything apart from Simon and Lizzie's marriage?'

'No.'

It was hopeless. Lucy would have to wait until they were back in Liverpool. But it was all building up inside her, and she needed to stay calm. The urge to batter Richard and to put a stop to the poster of packages and letters made her angry, and anger was an emotion she had sat on for some considerable time. Tomorrow she was to face the widow of Howard Styles, because a parasitic plant had fastened itself to the woman, and Lucy knew how hungry that creeper could get.

Meanwhile, David was getting ... not exactly desperate, but keen. He was doing things to his house, and Lucy knew that he was doing those things for her. But she had to be one hundred per cent sure of his readiness. The man could employ cleaners, buy new furniture, get his gardens landscaped, but that was all mayonnaise. For almost a decade, he had mourned a wife and a son; for less than three months, he had moved in the direction of Louisa Buckley, a child he remembered and looked back at through rose-tinted lenses. He was a big, strong, beautiful man, but he was vulnerable. 'As am I,' she whispered.

'What?' Moira was still looking in the mirror and was clearly displeased with what she saw.

'Nothing. I was just trying to remember the lyrics of a song.'

Moira studied her friend. 'You worry too much. And you've nothing to worry about. Look in the mirror – you don't need a facelift. I need an everything lift. When are you going to put poor David out of his misery?'

'Don't you start. It's complicated.'

Moira clicked her tongue. 'Rubbish. Unless you intend to work your way through the Kama Sutra, it's simple. You just—'

'Stop being obtuse, love. You know what I mean. He's still a bit up and down, and—'

'There you go, then.'

Both women burst out laughing. This was almost a

repetition of last night's discussion, the body of which had been embedded in the vulgarity of women when no men were present. Lucy pulled herself together. 'He blames himself for not getting Anne's car checked – he carries a huge weight of guilt.'

'And for the boy,' Moira added. 'Going to India like he did, he's bound to feel awful. But Lucy, he's so happy in your company. His love for you will save him, so just get on with it. You are the cure. He needs you, babe. Also, he's one of the best men I ever met in my whole life.'

'I know. He's so special that I can't believe my luck. I could well turn out to be a disappointment, Moira. I'm no seasoned athlete when it comes to sex.'

Moira shook her head slowly.

'Well I'm not!'

'Neither is he,' Moira declared. 'Just love him. Just get into bed and hold him and let things happen. Whatever you do, don't let him slip through your fingers.' Once again, both women dissolved into laughter that was near-hysterical.

Moira's turn of phrase might be accidental. On the other hand . . . Lucy doubled over. Even thinking 'on the other hand' was torture, since she knew that if she repeated those words, last night's conversation would begin all over again, and at full volume. Moira Turner had clearly led an interesting and full life before multiple sclerosis had claimed her. She stuck rigidly to her opinion that men were amateurs in the field of vulgarity, and that a roomful of women left to itself became a hotbed of sexual allusions. 'The men tell the jokes,' Moira had said. 'The women live the bloody jokes, because they invented them in the first place. We're the ones who see the opposite sex in baggy Y-fronts and socks . . .'

'Straighten your face,' Moira ordered now. 'You want to think less and act more before he gets fed up with waiting.' She sniffed. 'Daft cow.'

Mags arrived. She 'coo-eed' before opening the door. 'Are we decent? Oh, and I've driven my car all over your lawn, Lucy.' She hauled in some bags. 'Instruments of torture. And you must be Moira. MS, isn't it?'

Moira nodded.

'My Auntie Jessie had that,' Mags said. 'Went to Lourdes with some nuns in a big bus.'

'Cured?' Moira asked.

Mags shook her head. 'No, but when they got her out of the water, her wheelchair had come up lovely – new tyres and a complete respray.'

Moira laughed. 'She'll do,' she told Lucy. 'Mad as a box of frogs, and the old jokes remain the best.'

They were both subjected to facials, Indian head massage, manicures and pedicures, and new hairstyles were to be next on the agenda. Mags was merciless. Lucy found herself staring at the floor on which her tresses were spread. 'But I'm not sure—'

'Shut up and be grateful,' said Mags with mock severity. 'I'm taking ten years off you.'

'Oh, she is,' Moira agreed. 'When you see it, you'll drop dead ten years before your time.' She turned her attention to the beautician. 'What style do you call that?' she asked.

'My own. It's called Cause Célèbre, though I can't say it properly. Every applicant for the Styles job had to invent a hairdo. It was a bit scary, because I was in Paris, and they were all jabbering away, but there were a few other English stylists there and they helped me out a bit with the language. I won. I got the cordon rouge et blanc – striped like an old-time barber's pole – a trip down the Seine with Monsieur Charles, lovely dinner on the boat with champagne and all that, and a visit to somewhere called Versales.'

'Versailles?' suggested Lucy.

'That's the chap. Dead boring, just a load of old furniture and beds. But best of all, I won a week observing at Tête à Tête. And now, I get Styles.'

'What's it like?' Lucy asked.

Mags, who certainly proved herself to have an eye for detail, launched into her current favourite subject. She described marble columns, sweeping staircases, minstrels' gallery, swimming pool, rooms for treatments, grounds into which Monsieur intended to extend. 'It's massive,' she concluded.

'And Mrs Styles?' Lucy asked.

'Lovely woman. Mind, she sounds a tough cookie when it comes down to business. The firm paid top whack, and I believe she got a house in France as part of the deal. And yes, Lucy. Before you ask, I think he's still with her. Blackpool, I believe.'

Lucy said nothing. Tomorrow, she and Glenys Barlow were to meet Trish Styles in a coffee shop. Tomorrow, the woman of Alan's choice would learn the truth, since Lucy's conscience refused to allow her to let sleeping dogs lie.

'You're done, missus.'

'Am I bald?'

'Not quite.'

Lucy stood at the mirror and gasped. 'I love it,' she cried after close scrutiny. 'I look – oh, I don't know how

I look, but the hair's brilliant. You are one talented woman.'

Moira chuckled. 'Dr David Vincent's going to get arrested as a paedophile. Isn't it a bit like the urchin cut, Mags?'

The beautician agreed. 'But you need a lot of hair to get the height at the crown and the depth at the back. Now, Lucy.'

'What?'

'To keep it like that, go to Herbert every three weeks – four at the outside. He's the only man with staff who'll be able to keep up with it. Then watch out all over Liverpool, because Cause Célèbre will be popping up just about everywhere.' She sighed. 'I'm famous, Moira.'

'Oooh! Give us your autograph.'

'I'll do better than that. See the black bag over there? It's full of products, and they all come with instructions. Use them regularly, and you'll both slow down the ageing process.' She began to tackle Moira's hair. 'Bloody hell. I thought Lucy's was thick, but you could weave a hearthrug out of this lot. What have you been using? Fertilizer?'

'Yup. I stand in a bucket of horse poo every night.'

While Moira's hair was work in progress, Lucy went to make tea and put together a few tasty morsels. Mags was a decent woman who seemed to have escaped unscathed after contact with Alan. Would Trish Styles be as lucky? Or would Alan learn her signature and start emptying her bank accounts? The woman had just lost her husband, for goodness' sake. Yet the other part of Lucy continued to raise its ugly head. She could simply turn away, walk away and stay away. But she wouldn't. She knew full well that she was unable to leave the recently widowed Trish to the untender mercies of Alan Henshaw.

The back door opened. 'Louisa?'

Ah, here came the beloved. 'Hello, sweetheart. I thought you were off to buy clothes.'

He stood and stared. 'You look terrific.'

'Ah, the hair.' She'd forgotten it. 'Mags is still here. She's cutting Moira's hair now. Then she'll do our make-up.'

'You don't need it.'

'And you're very sweet.' All his reticence was leaving him. The fear of getting involved and losing loved ones was drifting away into the past, and Lucy was delighted with him. But there was always something happening. Tomorrow loomed. There was going to be trouble in Moira's life, too, because some bit of stuff had fallen off Richard's plate, and it was rotting all over Mersey View.

'Why do I need clothes? I found loads when the house was being cleaned.'

'David.' Lucy sighed. 'Costume drama is out, dearest. You need decent, casual clothing. Not shabby junk for odd job work, and not a consultant's pinstripe with tie and white shirt. Moira will sort you out tomorrow while Glenys and I are in the lions' den. You need a couple of jumpers, long-sleeved tops, T-shirts and trousers – two or three pairs. And no baggy Y-fronts. Don't ask why,' she said when he opened his mouth to speak. 'It's a joke. One of Moira's.'

David continued to look at her. Looking at her was one of his greatest pleasures, but he was having a bit of hormonal trouble, the sort of difficulty he had not endured since his teenage years. Louisa Buckley was driving him mad. She was always busy, was usually surrounded by people, and he was getting just a little tired of waiting. 'I cannot continue like this,' he said bluntly.

'Neither can I. But please, don't expect too much of me. I may not be any good at it. I'm a bit afraid of doing it badly.'

He raised his hands and shrugged. 'That makes two of us, then. I'm not exactly versed in the art, am I? So. Tomorrow we go to Alderley Edge, and I buy clothes under the instruction of Moira while you try to warn Trish whatever-her-name-is that your husband's a bad bugger.'

Lucy sighed. 'Yes, that's about the size of it.'

'I could make a vulgar remark at this point, Louisa.'

'Too late – I already heard it. Moira and I spent yesterday expressing our basest thoughts. She's one terrible woman. Come here, lover.'

The way he held her was different, as the fear had gone. His hands roamed, and the kisses were hungry. Lucy was no longer walking on eggshells, because this lovely man had finally put away thoughts of loss.

'I'm the love of your second life. It will be soon, I promise. And it doesn't have to be at Tallows, or at your house, or in Liverpool. It'll happen wherever it happens.'

'Louisa?'

'Yes?'

'How did we spend that night together without making love?'

'I shall never know the answer to that. Probably because my boys were in the house, and possibly because we weren't quite ready.' She returned to the task of making tea. His eyes were boring into her back. Whatever, wherever, it had to be soon. And why should anyone else matter? Why should she continue prim and proper because her sons and her daughter were in the house? 'Stay with me tomorrow night,' she suggested.

'But aren't Lizzie and Simon there?'

'Yes. As are Mike and Paul. In a couple of weeks, there will be bed-and-breakfasters, but so what? We're beyond the age of consent, we're free people – well, I suppose I am technically married, but to hell with it. Hal put a bolt on my bedroom door, so while people can get from the hall into the kitchen, and from there into the body of my flat, they can't enter our room.'

Our room. He liked the sound of that. 'Carol and Dee?' he asked.

'Are adults. They are also employees, and they've been running a book.'

'A book on us?'

She laughed at him. 'They're now taking bets on the month of our marriage. I got Moira to put fifty quid of my money on December. That should pay for a short honeymoon, then we can have a proper one next summer.'

His grin widened. 'Is this you managing me again?'

'Of course.' She picked up her tray. 'I make all the minor decisions, but I'll leave the more important ones to you. Like opening this door for me now so that I can carry the food through.'

He opened the door. She was a minx, and she would continue in the same vein. His Louisa was adorable. But he was determined to smack that bottom, because she deserved chastisement.

Sometimes, Alan felt as if he'd never had the surgery, because the pain in his heart had returned. He was unable to treat it, since his drug of choice was no longer available to him. The resulting introspection was not pleasant, as he was becoming only too well aware of his sins, and depression began to hang over him like a black, rain-bearing cloud. The pain in his heart was not physical; it was the weight of past misdemeanours for which he could never atone and, on top of all that, he seemed to be experiencing genuine affection for Trish.

Did he love her because she was the right woman for him? Or did he love her for volunteering to get him out of severe financial trouble? Tomorrow, the money would begin its travels. Tomorrow, Trish would meet Glenys, who had disguised her name. He dared not ask whether the transfer of funds was going to be swift and electronic, or slowed to a near-stop by the advent of the weekend. Nor did he dare to beg Trish not to go tomorrow, as she would want to know why, and he couldn't tell her. Had he been able or willing to drink, none of this would have bothered him. The small, niggling details of life had never been obscured by alcohol, but the bigger picture had been for ever rosy or forgettable.

Strangely, after a brief period of impatience, he had grown used to Trish, to dancing, to crown green bowling, donkeys and bingo. She was a good cook, a gentle soul, and she twittered on happily all day like a budgie in a cage. There was comfort in her endless chatter, encouragement in her sunny optimism, security in the certainty that in Blackpool, at least, the days had a pattern.

But they weren't in Blackpool any more. No longer impressed by the sheer size of Styles, he heard the electronic gates closing behind him and felt that he was imprisoned. Trish was no longer his jailer. This was confinement of his own making. He could blame no one for his situation, because he was its sole architect. There was only one option open to him, but the thought of laying bare his soul, and seeing the disappointment in Trish's face, horrified him. He was a coward. On top of everything else, he was a yellow-belly.

'You get to the doctor in the morning. He was pleased with you last time, but I think you're getting a bit of post-operative depression. I found it on the inter-web. It says you're always excited when the surgery's over with, but that a descent into negativism is not uncommon. You've descended.'

He had. She was right enough, but this had nothing to do with his open-heart procedure. He was going to be alone, homeless and, as there was nowhere else to go, dependent on Lucy. And on the prison service . . . 'I'm not a good man,' he announced quietly.

Trish stood at the kitchen island, rolling pin held aloft. 'There's none of us perfect.'

'I've been dishonest in my time.'

She placed her weapon on the work surface. 'Alan, do you think my Howie got as far as he did by telling all the truth all the time? I mean, he never stole directly, but he didn't drop his prices when he bought in bulk. To win, he had to be wise, and to be wise, he was forced to be cunning.'

Alan dropped on to the kitchen sofa. 'I feel better in Blackpool, love.'

'Aye, well, I dare say we both do. I just have to see this lawyer woman tomorrow, then we'll go back. Glad

335

you're settled there, because this place is all but sold. The main thing is to stop you going to jail. You owe money to the biggest building society in the country.'

This was torture. Trish had been nurse, cook, friend and supporter since the day he had escaped from Easterly Grange – she had even organized his exit from the place. After so many weeks in his own room, he had become slightly stir-crazy, and had not appreciated her attempts to help him on the road to recovery. She had fussed and mothered like a clucky hen until he had been tempted to throw food at her, but ... but she was a good woman, and she meant to save him from real prison, from a long sentence for fraud. Would Glenys prevent Trish from carrying out her promise? 'I wronged my family,' he said hesitantly. 'My wife I treated with contempt. I have two sons I don't know, and a daughter I loved until she outgrew me. They'll be getting on with life, glad to be rid of me, all of them.'

'Alan?' She stood still, hands covered in flour, pastry spread before her waiting to line a dish. 'Alan?'

He smiled at her. She was what his father might have termed a grand lass, since she was loyal and faithful. 'You've been a treasure,' he told her. 'I'm going for a bit of a walk. They told me to get plenty of gentle exercise.' He left her standing there, hands floury, pastry still waiting to line the same dish.

Alan had developed a strangely comforting relationship with Damien, the llama from hell. Damien no longer spat at him, which was just as well, since llama spit was more than spit – it was stomach contents. He hand-fed the animal with kitchen scraps before stroking the woolly neck. 'I'd be better off dead. They'd all do very well without me.'

Damien continued to chew in that strange, side-to-side way, grinding the food for minutes before attempting to swallow.

'I've got the rope, and I've found a strong enough tree. You see, Damien, I could be locked up by this time tomorrow. They'll tell her everything I've done, and Trish will leave me to it. Hiding away won't be easy, because I've nowhere to go.' He swallowed. 'Except to Lucy. And the Halifax will soon find her. I'm finished, lad.' Could he use that rope? Could he hell.

He walked back to the house. Trish was twittering, but he explained that he was tired and going up to bed. She berated him for not eating, but he simply switched off and didn't hear any more. There was nothing he could do, because his number was finally up. No matter what Trish said now, she probably wouldn't speak to him at all tomorrow.

His dreams were populated by loud men, slamming doors and the quiet voice of Lucy. 'Guilty,' she whispered again and again.

'Wake up!' Trish was shaking him. 'You must be having some terrible dreams, Alan.'

'Yes, I was.'

'It'll be this post-operative depression again,' she said. 'Stop worrying. Tomorrow, you won't be a bankrupt any more, and we'll find a business to buy into. It's nearly over now, love.'

She was right, of course. It was all over bar the shouting.

Lexi had been a bit hacked off. All the drama had gone out of her life, and she was fed up with Mersey View and its crackpot residents. Just one more thing to be done, and she'd be out of there. It was going to be bright, colourful and difficult to forget, so it would suffice as her swan song. Purple. Yes, that was her signature colour, and it should do very nicely.

Greasy Bleasdale had found out what she'd been doing on the work computer. Because of that, he wanted her to make herself available as and when he needed something to rub up against. But Lexi had her standards, and servicing a sweaty bastard across his desk or in the men's loo after the shop had closed was definitely outside the terms of her contract with the supermarket chain. And things were getting worse. When she was shelf-stacking, he often crept up behind her to cop a feel. Again, she found this behaviour unacceptable.

She'd been stuck in the back room yesterday cutting cooked and cured meats, and he'd had a go. If she'd been quick enough, she might have grabbed his member and introduced it to the bacon slicer. It would have been a brief acquaintance, but she would have enjoyed every second of it. However, prison for separating a filthy swine from his closest friend was not a good idea. But she had to get out of the job.

And she might just do that, because Tom Rice, the guy with the limp, was interested in her. She'd had to come clean about her past, because he was after her street-wisdom, her knowledge of working girls and their clients. It was something to do with his job, but she wasn't sure what he did. He'd told her she needed to dress more quietly, and she'd be answering phones for some of the time.

Finally, he phoned and told her the truth. He was a private detective, had been a policeman, knew her history, and wanted a bright, intelligent woman in her thirties to help him. 'I can only be in one place at a time,' he said. 'So whoever gets the job will be split between office and overspill.'

'Overspill?'

'When I've trained an assistant, he or she will get the cases I've no time for.' He gave her his address. 'Wednesday, four o'clock, interview. OK?'

OK? It was bloody marvellous. 'Shall I give my notice in at work?' she asked.

'Not yet. I've three others to see. Pretend to have a dental appointment on Wednesday, and we'll take it from there.'

She was excited. She'd be able to disguise herself, buy wigs and posher clothes. Would she get an allowance for clothing? Should she phone him and ask? No. He liked her. He knew all about her past, and he still liked her. And, when it came to finding out stuff about folk, she was A1. Greasy Bleasdale would soon become history.

Richard turned off his mobile phone, since he needed no noisy interruptions. Concentration was necessary. Tonight, he had to focus totally on his dilemma, and on his plan to remedy it.

Without Moira, the house had no soul. Without Moira, he had no soul. The creature from Litherland was continuing in her efforts to discredit him, and his wife would be back tomorrow. He'd promised that he would never use a prostitute, but he had failed to keep his word. Yes, he'd taken up with a supermarket check-out girl and yes, he had been careless, but he hadn't been aware of Lexi's past. 'Someone with a bit of education,' Moira had always said. 'Someone who knows about my

339

condition.' Latterly, she had even sought a life companion who might take the job of wife after Moira's ... He couldn't bear to think the word.

He patted his pockets, thereby reminding himself of Dr David Vincent, saint, protector of sick children, creator of a famous charity, lover of the only other woman Richard truly wanted. The phone was on vibrate only, the stuff he needed was distributed evenly throughout coat and trouser pockets, and it was now or never.

Murder was not to be undertaken lightly. Murder dressed as suicide was even more difficult. Self-disposal was something Moira contemplated almost daily, and he didn't want the woman he had married to be pushed over the edge by a tart. Lexi's behaviour was not improving. She didn't know that Moira was away, so she would believe by now that her letters had resulted in no reaction from either of the Turners, and her campaign might well intensify. Why hadn't he come clean? Why hadn't he explained to Moira that he had made a huge mistake?

And why, why, why was he even contemplating this dreadful deed? Wasn't it rather like taking a neutron bomb to finish off a bluebottle? He could tell Moira – albeit rather late in the day – what she probably knew already, then everything would slowly get back to normal. Except ... he swallowed. No. Not normal.

The notes. He had photocopied the lot before passing them on to Lexi's latest doctor, and he had read them all. The woman had been treated for minor burns in 1978. Her scars had healed, but people in the next house had perished. Diabetes type one had been diagnosed within months, and an endocrinologist had commented in writing that the shock of the fire might have contributed to the child's worsening health. She had gone for counselling, but had been unable to speak about the fire. Had a five-year-old child killed her neighbours? Would she kill him and Moira?

He walked to the window. The girls had returned to Edinburgh for some daft half-marathon involving hospital beds, an old ambulance and a dozen or so off-duty fire fighters. According to Alice, the proceeds were to go towards putting the prof of Anatomy and Physiology out of everyone's misery once they could find a vet willing to do it. In spite of his misery, Richard smiled as he remembered some of the giddiness displayed by himself and Moira while cavorting with a crowd along the Royal Mile on rag days.

Simon, currently resident next door with his stunning bride, would be deserting the north. Richard was alone. This was how it would be when Moira was no longer attached to the mortal coil. His daughters, both beautiful women, would go wherever their chosen specialty took them, though he had hopes for Steph, since she seemed to be veering towards neurology, and Liverpool was the centre of excellence for that discipline. The centre of excellence could not yet cure Moira, but Steph was determined to work in the field that might, one day, come up with decent remedies for multiple sclerosis, Parkinson's, muscular dystrophy and all the other merciless evils that killed people an inch at a time. 'I can't do it,' he told the window.

Looked at in the cold light of day, the situation seemed ridiculous. He had indulged in sexual activity with a woman of ill repute, though she was no longer working as a prostitute. The idiot woman had demanded marriage, and he had lost his temper with her. Dog excrement and letters were no big deal, and he would probably have taken a chance had he not read the notes. Now, he lived in fear of arson, and this was not the cold light of day. This was the dimming light of a September evening, the harbinger of winter. In weeks, clocks would skip back one hour, and out of the safety of shadows might arrive those whose activities required the blackness of night. Muggers, burglars, car thieves and ... arsonists.

Perhaps Lexi had played with matches. Perhaps one of her siblings had set fire to the house next door, but he could not erase the notes from his mind. She had been traumatized and reduced to silence. There again, she could have been riding close to hyperglycaemia, but he could not be sure.

The suicide note was written, and he had handled it only with surgical gloves. In his pockets sat more gloves, a syringe, a sharp in a closed plastic carton. The insulin was of the type she used, and he just had to give her an overdose, plant her prints on paper and syringe, and leave the scene. Moira would be safe. 'Will I be safe? Will I be able to live with this?' he whispered.

All doctors did a module on psychology. It was useful, as it provided some insight into the workings of the mind, and such knowledge was necessary for a practitioner who dealt with a broad spectrum of human behaviours. Even now, he remembered the lectures on psychopathic disorders. Murderers were special. They had an extra bit of wiring, a circuit that bypassed the usual path along which thought and emotion travelled. Serial killers were amazing, because they had no fuse box, no safety valve that might cut off when the brain went into overdrive. They felt nothing, had no sympathy, no empathy, no love in them.

'I'm no killer. I have love.' He also had a package from the local DIY store.

After replacing the insulin in the surgery refrigerator, he put away gloves and sharp, placed the suicide note in the shredder and found a screwdriver. In every room and on every landing he fixed a smoke alarm. If anyone asked why he had bought so many, the reply sat in readiness on the tip of his tongue. His wife could no longer walk any distance, so the household needed to be guarded properly against the danger of fire.

He rolled up his sleeves and finished off work he had started earlier. Outside, he fixed a light that made night into day if and when anyone approached the front door. Let her come. Moira would forgive him. Moira always forgave him.

During their last evening together in the shed, Moira opened up. She talked about early symptoms, double vision, knees that became disobedient, face pain misdiagnosed as neuralgia, total exhaustion, scans and other tests that finally told the truth. 'He was in a state worse than mine. He closed the surgery on Liverpool Road, moved his work into the house, and started reading. There's not much he doesn't know about MS. Underneath the terrible jokes and the manufactured courage, there's a dreadful fury. He's angry not with me, but with my illness and with God. The fact that he can do little or nothing to help makes matters worse.'

Lucy stared down into her glass of burgundy. 'What's the big deal at the moment, Moira? Because I think he's on track for some kind of nervous collapse.'

'Do you?'

Lucy raised her head. 'I feel as if I know him, you see.

There is an attraction between us, and he's one of the men I might have loved. Not like David, not a meeting of minds and all the other rubbish that goes with true love. And Richard gets on my nerves, annoys me a lot. But he's in trouble.'

'It's of his own making,'

'He goes elsewhere for sex.'

'Yes.'

'And he confesses his sins to you, because that's your role in his life now. You're his mother confessor. You're his counsellor, psychologist, whatever. The fact is that you have been complicit in his misdeeds.'

'That's right.'

'You even briefed him to choose from the intelligentsia, the better educated, the cream.' She would say it now. 'Because you're a snob, Moira.' That should do it; that should release some of the anger.

'Bollocks.' Two spots of colour appeared on pale cheeks. 'I want him to find a wife or a good partner, someone who'll look after him. My illness is life-limiting, and I—'

'Why?'

'Why what?'

'Why control him? He's old enough to make his own choices.'

'And daft enough to make the wrong ones.'

'So? Let him pay the price. It's his problem and his privilege.'

'That ... article hanging round Mersey View is a well-known prostitute.'

'She's supermarket staff. Once upon a time, she worked the streets, and she's a bit of an Amazon when it comes to war. Like Carol, Dee and Shirley, she stands her ground.' Lucy made no mention of dog dirt and letters. But she had a plan.

When Moira was in bed and all dishes were washed, Lucy took herself and her phone outside. For about half an hour, she sat on a swing and wondered whether she was doing the right thing. Then she decided that she didn't want to get anyone out of bed to answer the phone, and she pressed the buttons before it got too late. 'Richard? Yes, 'tis I.'

'Is Moira all right?' were his first words. No matter what, no matter who, where or why, he would always love his wife, and Lucy knew that.

'She's not bad. Eating solids, walking to the bathroom, needs a bit of help when she gets there. Oh, and she's speaking English – none of that mixed up stuff. She's happy here.'

'Away from me.'

'Not at all Richard, can you get cover for a few days?'

He blustered for several seconds before asking for her reasons.

'She's happy here. I'd like her to be happy with you here. Just for a few days. Talk to her in an unfamiliar but pleasant setting. As you well know, this illness of hers affects her emotions, her immune system, and all bodily functions. Sometimes, a new environment can make a difference.'

And it poured from him. Although Lucy knew some of it courtesy of Carol and Dec, she made no attempt to interrupt. As she heard the increasing desperation in his voice, she wanted to offer comfort, but she held herself in check. The bloody woman was possibly capable of arson, though he wasn't sure, and he was breaking the rule of patient confidentiality by passing on information he had gained from notes. There were now fourteen smoke alarms in the house, while the outside had been fitted with a single light that used enough electricity to power Blackpool during the illuminations season.

'Richard, why didn't you tell me before?' No reply came. 'Richard?'

'Because I love you, damn it all.'

'And you love Moira.'

'Yes.'

'Then get a locum. She needs you. She needs you enough to want to hear from your lips all you have just said to me.'

'It'll make her ill, Lucy.'

'And this silence, this distance between you will make her well?'

He delivered the rest of it, serving up a recipe whose components included surgical gloves, insulin, syringe and needle. 'I can't do it.'

'Of course you couldn't do it. Richard, I'm not a medic. I'm just a nurse who hasn't practised for years. But I can tell you're en route for a breakdown, because you'd never have considered murder if you were well. Get a locum, get the hell out of there, and come to Tallows by four tomorrow afternoon.'

'But—'

'No buts. Leave butting to the goats. If you love this wonderful woman, do as I ask.'

'And if Lexi comes here while I'm away?'

'I'll be there. Set a thief to catch a thief, and a woman to catch a woman. If I need muscle, I'll have my sons and David.' She thought about what she had just said. 'I'll have Mike and Paul. David can be the referee.'

He cleared his throat. 'If David hadn't come along, you and I—'

'If's a big word, Richard. If only's the story of my life. I'll see you tomorrow. Four o'clock, behind the house called Tallows.'

Lucy sat for a while after the call had ended. She fastened her cardigan, because the evening air was cool. All around her, leaves were curling and crisping in accordance with the rules of Mother Nature. Soon, they would fall in soft whispers all over the grass, geese would skein their way across the sky, and the earth would lie dormant for five months. The price of beauty was the yearly sight of its death. But it wasn't death. It was sleep.

Her own winter had lasted for almost twenty years. Marriage to Alan had meant silence, shadows, the loss of self. Even in sunshine, she had felt the chill, and she had stopped looking for rainbows. She remembered that first sight of the river when she had bought the Liverpool house on the spot for cash. It was home. Well, it was one of her homes. Because she and David would have three between them, and that was good. But there had been a rainbow over the Mersey on the day she had taken Stoneyhurst. She had bought a rainbow.

Poor Richard. He was probably right. Had David not happened along, she would probably have become one of his sacrifices. Moira had endured because she filled one of his many needs – she was his mother. But he was mercurial, and sexual partners were dispensable, replaceable. David was a for ever man; he was also the other half of her.

As if on cue, her phone rang. He wanted to say good

night from his lonely bed. He was absolutely bogged off about sleeping on his own. Why couldn't he come to the shed, because he knew how to be quiet, and what time did she need him in the morning for Alderley Edge, and was Glenys going in her own car? And why was Louisa laughing at him?

'You're lovely,' she said. 'I worked out that we'll have three homes when we marry – mine, yours and Tallows.'

He snorted. 'And I'll lay odds that we'll never be in the same place at the same time. You are avoiding me.'

'I'm not. It's just that stuff keeps happening.'

He sighed in an exaggerated fashion. 'And will stuff happen tomorrow?'

She thought about that. 'Possibly. We're setting a trap. I'll tell you about it after you've bought some decent clothes – bring a fortune, because it's Alderley Edge – and after I've sorted out my husband.'

A pause ensued. 'Are you creating these circumstances, madam?'

'No. I just seem to get dragged in.'

'You will be bloody dragged in when I get hold of you, lady. This is getting ridiculous now. Am I using the wrong deodorant? Would you like me to book myself in for a facelift and body waxing?'

'No. Come as you are.' She doubled over with laughter when he decided to go vulgar. Bodily fluids, body parts and ancient curses were thrown into the arena. Then he got silly. He had never been kept in suspenders for so long, nor had he been so consulted. This was the one. This was the lunatic she'd always needed.

Life without drink was different. Until recently, it had been pleasurable, as if some deity had tested Alan's eyes and given him a pair of good spectacles. Trish was an excellent woman, and even line-dancing was almost fun. He had been in danger of becoming content, and contentment was worth more than happiness, which was a fleeting emotion that was incapable of enduring.

But at this moment in time, Alan needed whisky. He would have sold his soul for a double, his body for a full bottle. And that was the price, of course. If he drank again, he'd be in a box within months. After tomorrow, he could well be in a jail cell, a prisoner of his own past misdemeanours. He couldn't wipe the slate clean, couldn't stop tomorrow happening. But he could absent himself . . .

Darkness threatened. The nights were drawing in, and this one might be his last. He threw the rope over a thick bough. Albert Pierrepoint was never around when he was needed, was he? The famous hangman had been renowned for his attention to detail, the carefully planned quick deaths he had provided. Alan would strangle, and it would be slow.

The old garden chair was in place, the rope was ready, and no gardeners came on Friday. Now, he had to go in for cocoa. Tomorrow he could choose between death and jail. In truth, he had already made his decision.

Sleep eluded Moira. Lucy had gone outside and was probably talking to David. They had an excellent relationship and a good chance of enduring the trials of marriage. Marriage could be hard work. Richard was high maintenance, and poor Lucy had already been through one difficult partnership, so it was perhaps as well that she had met someone she could trust.

These few days spent in the company of her friend

and neighbour had taught Moira that life without a male partner could be fun. She had missed Richard, of course, had felt the lack of his cutting wit and his physical elegance. He was, she supposed, better looking than David, but perhaps she was prejudiced.

This happy little interlude would end tomorrow. She was going home to a damned fool. She loved a damned fool. She, too, was a damned fool. With this pleasing thought in mind, she finally drifted into sleep.

David lay in splendour, and in splendid isolation. The bedroom was the best of all the beautifully decorated rooms. It was the bridal suite, with its own newly installed bathroom, a four-poster bed and amazing furniture. She would love it when she eventually got round to seeing it. He grinned. Louisa, at forty-five, was reliving the thirties she had missed. She was fun. She was naughty, and he adored her silliness.

Money had been no problem, since his income had sat around gaining interest since . . . yes, he could allow that thought. Since the death of his only child, David had needed little. He ate, paid his bills, and studied his way through every spare moment. But he could see his money now, as he had spent a great deal of it to make a home fit for his beloved.

He clasped his hands on the pillow behind his head. Louisa had been wise. Behind the daftness, she housed a very fine brain. She couldn't compete with the dead, so she had slowed everything down for his sake. Had he been divorced, she might not have hesitated for this length of time. But Anne, a much-loved ghost, had needed to be laid carefully away, and that had taken over a decade.

'Thank you, Louisa,' he whispered. 'Though I still intend to deal with you.'

Richard Turner packed a bag. Having called in a couple of favours, he was now able to travel to Lancashire in order to ... Lucy was right: he had to tell Moira everything, up to and including his plan to commit murder. She would understand, because she always did. Lucy did, too. Between the two of them, they formed one perfect female companion. Moira spoiled him and made him laugh, while Lucy could have been, should have been...

He shivered. Some thoughts were too delicious to merit more than a few seconds. She would be wasted on that medical equivalent of an anorak, the goodly nerd who did a fair imitation of a train-spotter or a devotee of real ale. He was vague, untidy, dull and very annoying. What on earth was she doing with a rollmop herring when there was caviar to be had?

Caviar? She'd been plain enough, had called him selfish, and she was probably right. And he had been out of order lately. Otherwise, how on earth had he managed to contemplate murder? It was time to open his mouth and let the truth out. Lucy was right. That was her one failing – she was usually right.

Trish was feeling unhappy, and he wouldn't talk to her. Having tried to pinpoint the start of the awkwardness, she suspected that it had begun when she had announced her intention to meet a lawyer in the Boule Miche coffee shop. She had phoned the lawyer, and had got nowhere. Business was best discussed face to face, Trish had been advised. 'You're not drinking your cocoa, love.'

Automatically obedient, he took a sip.

'What's the matter with you, Alan?'

He shrugged. 'Post-op depression, as you say. I'll take this upstairs and get an early night.' He left the scene, mug in hand.

No good night kiss, then. Trish took a mouthful of her own cocoa. It didn't taste right. Nothing tasted, sounded or looked as good as it once had. She loved Alan, but he seemed to be going off her. Even though she was prepared to discharge his bankruptcy, he seemed cold and distant.

What had she done wrong? And look at the size of this kitchen. She couldn't wait to be out of here and settled somewhere normal. But not alone. Life alone was bigger than this damned house. She was afraid. He was afraid. His fear was almost certainly tied to the woman she was going to meet tomorrow. Well, Trish would wear her five-hundred-pound suit and some good shoes. Power dressing was essential, because she had no idea what she would be facing in that coffee shop.

When she got to bed, he was pretending to be asleep. He'd poured away the cocoa – she could tell from the shape of the stain in his mug. She undressed and lay as stiff as a board beside him. Tomorrow was a big day. She couldn't work out why, but it was going to be momentous.

Lucy almost jumped out of her skin when her mobile rang. How did she get rid of bloody 'Amarillo'? Children understood these things, but there was seldom a child to hand when you needed one. By the time she located the offending article, it was well into *Sha la la lala lalala*, and she was well into desperation. The shed was not soundproof, and Moira could be well awake by now and trying to dance.

It was Richard. 'Sorry,' he said. 'I'm here.'

'Where, you soft lad?'

'Here. Look through the window – I'm outside.'

She opened the door, and he almost fell in. 'Where is she?'

'Asleep in there.' She pointed to the door behind which poor Moira was trying to rest. 'Try not to wake her – she was a bit wobbly tonight.'

He disappeared. Lucy sat on the sofa and wondered how much dafter the world could get. Her beautiful daughter had married the boy next door after knowing him for five minutes. David was turning into a sex-starved teenager, while Richard had been planning murder. A woman named Lexi was attempting to hasten Moira's death, Alan had disappeared, and tomorrow a posse was to be formed in order to hunt him down in Alderley Edge, home of the rich, the famous and the stupid. Oh, bugger.

Right. This was it – she'd had enough. Shower cap – don't spoil the hair – quick swill, towel dry, dress, pick up the keys to Alan's BMW, write a note for Moira. *Stay as long as you like. I'll call in when I get back from Cheshire tomorrow. Love to both, Lucy xx*

It was eleven o'clock. She sat in her husband's car and saw a half-empty bottle of Johnnie Walker peeping shyly from beneath the passenger seat. 'Oh, Alan,' she sighed. 'If you'd stayed off the sauce and made me a proper partner, I would have found you the bloody money.'

There was a full moon low in the sky, but it was no longer red, because the sun, its partner in crime, was long gone. Ancients had feared the harvest moon, believing it to be bewitched and bleeding. 'I'm going to Chorley New Road,' she advised Earth's single natural satellite. 'Come with me if you like.'

After crossing through town, she pulled into David's drive. Someone had done the garden, since the front window, once hidden completely by very tall grass, was fully visible. She took a key from her purse and let herself in, her breathing slowing while she waited for the alarm to sound. Nothing. The red eye in a top corner of the hall winked at her, but no siren followed. He'd forgotten. He was forgetful, and she adored him. Samson pushed a cold, wet nose into her hand before returning to his basket, a lavish, padded item chosen by a master who clearly loved his dog.

She entered the kitchen and switched on the lights. It was all new: bright white units, stainless steel splashbacks, Belfast sink, cooker with seven burners. Lights on kick-boards poured changing colours on to a metallic floor. It was fabulous. The living rooms were also stunning, and he had done all this for her.

Lucy crept up the stairs. Every time a tread creaked, she flinched, but she held on to the hope that his sleeping, like everything else, was done thoroughly.

Oh, God. He had bought her a four-poster and, if her eye was as good as she suspected it to be, it was French and a restored antique. He knew she loved château furniture. She felt like weeping. He was asleep, bedside lamp still burning, a book drooping from his hands. After removing his skew-whiff reading glasses, she relieved him of his book. It was Anne Robinson's autobiography, so at least he had managed to put down the medical tomes.

In the en suite, which had clearly been a large bed-room in an earlier life, she found a double bath, plus a double shower. He was living in hope, then. Twin wash-basins perched boldly on a granite surface above storage cupboards, and the mirror was surrounded by lights so bright that they were judgemental. Naked, she stared at herself, noting every crease, every bulge, oversized breasts that seemed to be moving south for the winter.

'You have to be brave,' she mouthed. David was going to be a lights-on man, so he might as well see what he was getting, warts and all. She shivered, pulled on a robe that was still damp from his shower or bath, switched off the bathroom lights and returned to the bedroom.

He was still asleep. She threw off the robe and, with excruciating slowness, peeled back the duvet and slid in beside him.

'You're late.'

She almost jumped out of her skin. 'You sod. I thought you were fast asleep.'

'Nope.' He turned towards her. 'Thank you for fitting me into your busy schedule. Who's looking after Moira?'

'Richard. I told him to come.'

'Excellent. Now, be a good girl and think of England. You can leave the rest to me.'

Twelve

Lucy sat at the kitchen island in David's suddenly spotless house. She was wearing one of his shirts, plus a pair of sunglasses she'd discovered in the depths of her Tignanello handbag, and she felt stunned. She hadn't expected him to be so ... so what? Competent scarcely covered it. Amazing was, perhaps, nearer the mark. But she was absolutely exhausted, and a busy day lay ahead.

She also nursed a vague suspicion that she was sitting outside the head teacher's office after receiving punishment, and it wasn't fair, since she'd done nothing wrong. Or maybe last night had been some sort of competition, in which case he'd taken gold. Stamina? The word had been invented for Dr David Vincent. There'd been champagne, too. But champagne didn't create hangovers, did it? The world was too bright, and he was too flaming cheerful for such an early hour. And, in spite of all the above, she was deliriously happy. She wasn't going to tell him that, though. Not yet, anyway. Because he, too, was learning how to play the game, and he was cleverer than she was.

'Why the shades, Louisa?'

'Flashing bloody lights under your cupboards. And

356

my head's become a holding cell for the Jerry Springer Show. Please, please, try not to clatter.'

He shrugged, stamped on a black button in a corner, and returned to the task of making breakfast. 'Lights gone,' he said, amusement colouring the words. 'And my kick-board illuminations don't flash, they come and go. Slowly. Very slowly.'

Samson sat between them, head moving in the direction of each speaker, so that he was doing a fair imitation of a Wimbledon audience.

She knew all about very slowly. 'You sod,' she said, not for the first time in recent hours. 'Are you related to Tchaikovsky? That 1812 thing?'

'No idea.'

Tchaikovsky had experienced difficulty when it came to endings. The 1812 Overture had about fourteen finales all stitched together like the pieces of some patchwork quilt he'd made out of odds and ends. 'Any Russians in the family, David? And do you realize what I have to do this morning?' She patted the dog. The dog was the only sensible person in the room.

'Erm. Probably no to the first question, then yes to the second.' He turned. 'Eggs over-easy or sunny side up, hon?'

'I don't do eggs.'

'Right.' He went back to the job in hand.

There was a surreal quality to the morning. Here she sat in a blue-and-white striped shirt with a size sixteen collar, and there he stood in a plastic apron with NOTHING TO DECLARE printed across its front. And he had nothing to declare, because he was naked apart from the apron. For a man in his forties, he retained quite pert buttocks. In fact he retained ... What was he up to now? He seemed to be placing in a basket everything he had prepared. 'What the f— flipping heck are you doing, David?' He was holding out one hand in her direction, while the other picked up the basket.

'Picnic. Come. Come along, do as you are told for a change.'

'But ... we're not dressed for a picnic. We're not dressed at all.'

'Come. My house, my garden, my woman. Git yo ass outta here, baby.' He then addressed his pet. 'Stay. You can come to Cheshire later. Or you can go next door. I'll leave you to think about it.'

'How will you know what he wants?' Lucy asked.

'He'll stand near the car, or he'll go next door. He's easy. Which is more than can be said for some extraordinarily difficult people.'

It was very cold in the garden, especially for two people with no shoes, no socks and very little clothing. And it was only seven-thirty, and— Then she saw what he had done for her. It was an almost faithful copy of the tree house from thirty-odd years ago, from those Diane-David-Louisa days when the sun had been brighter, clouds fewer, life fuller of joy. He had rebuilt their childhood.

'Oh, David.' She was truly moved, because he had done this himself – she knew he had. 'What a wonderful surprise this is. The care you must have taken to make it look so much like ... Oh, bless you, but I can't climb that ladder. I'm forty-five, darling.'

'I can climb it. There again, I'm only forty-four. There are blankets in the tree house. It's worth the effort just to get warm.'

She climbed, reached down to take the basket, sat

down and waited for him. It was the same inside, too. Crude seats made from rough wood were topped with old cushions and pillows. On the wall were pinned drawings and paintings of hated teachers, beloved teachers, trees, flowers and houses. Diane's drawings. 'You saved everything,' she said when he was seated beside her. 'Everything.'

'Yes – even our cricket scores and a couple of school reports. And the photograph – those two tall girls with a shrimp of a lad – you, me and Di. Take this blanket and wrap up. Don't be sad. We're home now, Louisa.'

Lucy imagined him coming back from school on the fateful day when his mother had decided to move out. He had run off to collect his life from the tree house; he had taken Diane and Louisa with him. 'You're the last of the great romantics, aren't you, sweetheart?'

'I hope not. There must be more of us somewhere.' He poured coffee and placed a plate of toast on an upturned plastic box. 'Eat. You'll feel better.'

She pretended to glare at him. 'Will I? Three hours' sleep, I had.'

'Are you complaining about the quality of my work? And I did overtime for which there'll be no extra charge. Well? Did I disappoint?'

'No.'

'What, then?'

'I'm bloody knackered.'

A self-satisfied expression appeared on David's face as he leaned forward and planted a kiss on her nose. For a rusty, middle-aged man, he seemed to have done quite well. The champagne had perhaps been rather too much gilt on the lily ... Yes, she had a hangover. But there was mischief in her eyes – she was playing a part.

359

'It's a wonder I can walk at all,' she said.

'Louisa?'

'What?'

'Shut up.'

She shut up for a few moments. In the corner, a pile of *Beano* and *Dandy* comics stood alongside exercise books and a tin with a photograph of Buckingham Palace on its lid. Their sweetie box. 'Is it all real? Are those Diane's brushes and paints? Is that my copy of *Black Beauty*?'

'Yes. Now, tell me about Tchaikovsky. You were indicating that I went on too long last night?'

She said nothing.

'You were given adequate warning. I said you'd be dealt with. I've lost count of the number of times I threatened to stop you in your tracks, lady.'

Wrapped in a rough blanket, she started to laugh. 'You're trying to tame me, aren't you?'

He sniffed meaningfully. 'Trying, yes. But the anger needs to come out first. You held on to your temper for so long in that moribund marriage – the magma has to escape at some point.'

She thought about that for a few moments.

'Am I right?' he asked.

'I don't know. Richard's been my target so far. You won't ever be that. I know they say you always hurt the one you love, but I can't imagine that I'd ever really lose it with you.'

'And Tchaikovsky?'

'Oh, just confiscate his baton.'

He paused, a fried egg sandwich held just south of his chin.

Lucy, seeing the devilment in his eyes, clouted him

and his sandwich with a grubby pillow. 'You were punishing me, punishing me, punishing me.' With every 'punishing', she delivered a blow. The bloody man was laughing. 'You're wicked.' She screamed. 'You made me wait and wait, and I'm still aching. Oh, you think you're so clever, David Vincent.'

And they were children again. It was another of their pillow-and-cushion fights, and they were no longer middle-aged. For a split second, Lucy heard the terrible, high-pitched scream that had been the property of her dead sister. Both out of steam, they sat down again. The whole area was covered in egg, toast and coffee. Now it really did look like the scene of childhood crimes. 'It will have to be cleaned,' Lucy said.

'I can't do it now,' he admitted. 'Meting out your punishment was very hard work. What was his first name?'

'Who?'

'Bloody Tchaikovsky.'

'Fred.'

'Ah.'

'Came from Pontefract. His mam and dad invented Pontefract cakes. He ran a chip shop and composed in his spare time.'

David nodded sagely. 'I thought he worked in Russia?'

'He did. He was in possession of a very long baton. He could fry cod with one hand, and crack nuts with the other.'

'Eh?'

'Nutcracker Suite. Very talented man. Sugar plum fairy.'

'Was he?'

'Oh, yes. Great disappointment to his parents. It was illegal in those days, and he could have ended up on that treadmill with poor old Oscar Wilde. "To whom might we bequeath us Pontefract cakes?" his father and mother asked. Simple folk – hence the poor grammar.'

'Very sad.'

'Yes, I thought so, too.'

They sat for a while contemplating the tragic fate of the grandchildless makers of liquorice circles. 'Chopin was Fred.' David smiled. 'He was a Pole.'

'So he wouldn't need a baton?'

He shrugged. 'No, but I was concentrating on his Minute Waltz. I think I could manage that one. I mean, why should I hang about making life good for you? A minute sounds just about right to me.'

The fight resumed. Throughout all the silliness, Lucy came to understand what real happiness was. While complaining of tiredness, she felt more alive than she had in years. And it was all because of this wonderful man who had built a tree house for her and in loving memory of Diane.

He ironed the skirt she had worn last night. He was a good ironer. Then he brushed dried egg from her hair, snipping out just one strand where the mess had set like concrete. This precious piece was placed inside his grandfather's hunter, an item he always carried in a pocket because it kept good time and didn't need a battery. 'You'll do,' was his expressed final judgement.

She had no intention of sallying in the direction of Alderley Edge with a man in a plastic apron, and she said so. He took her upstairs, flung open a wardrobe door and shouted, 'Ta-dah.'

'Heavens above,' Lucy declared.

'And I needed no help. But no way was I going to pay Alderley Edge prices. This is my casual and oil-free collection courtesy of Marks and Spencer, Debenham, and a catalogue entitled *Man of the Moment*.' He showed her the magazine. 'This is the underwear section, and please note that I bought no Y-fronts, baggy or otherwise. You may also agree with me that every one of those models has at least one pair of socks stuffed into the underwear.'

'Jealous?'

'Do I need to be? Hey! You're blushing.'

'Did you take Viagra?'

'No. And you are still pink.'

'Get dressed,' she commanded before leaving the room. Downstairs, she sat grinning like the Cheshire cat. Bugger. They were going to Cheshire. But she continued to smile, because she had done the right thing. Keeping him at arms' length – well, not quite, but waiting until now – had been a necessity. David could love one hundred per cent, and nothing less would do for him. At last, he had allowed poor Anne to rest.

He entered the room wearing dark trousers, a polo-necked white sweater and a collarless jacket. Circular glasses tinted blue completed the illusion. All right, he did look a bit like John Lennon. Holding a tennis racquet as substitute for a guitar, he began to murder 'Sergeant Pepper'.

'Cease immediately.'

He stopped and shrugged. 'Well, I thought I'd remind you that you've come as close as possible to sleeping with John Lennon.'

'For three hours.'

'Whatever. Many people have told me I look like him.'

'They're right. But that has nothing to do with why I love you. Now, naff off and find something sensible to wear. Dressed like that, you'd be mugged by WAGS in Cheshire, because they're too daft to remember that John's dead. Stop messing about.'

'But I enjoy messing— OK, I'm going.'

Lucy closed her eyes. If this man became any more lovable, she would surely die. She could scarcely bear to think about his wilderness years. She'd had her children, but David had depended for sanity on his work. He was loving life again, because he was loving her.

He came back, this time dressed sensibly but casually in shades of brown.

'I can't go on like this,' she told him. 'I'm sorry, but I really can't.'

'Why?'

'Because I have to live with you, David. I can manage Tchaikovsky or Chopin – I love classical music and the tree house and the fights and all of it. But I can't manage being away from you.'

He ignored the urge to hug her, because he didn't want to crush her white blouse. Today, she needed to be crisp. 'A solution will be found, madam. Now, we have to go. The dog's gone next door. He has abandoned us to our fate.'

'Sensible animal.'

'Dreading it?'

'Oh, hell. I wish I could just leave it alone, because it's none of my business, but Trish Styles is on her own, no kids, just Alan and her money to keep her warm. Glenys will meet us there. She's going to Manchester

Crown Court with an affidavit or something.' She puffed out her cheeks and blew. 'That's supposed to get rid of tension.'

'I wish you'd told me that last night. I was bloody terrified when you turned up. That's why I pretended to be asleep. You thought I was confident, huh? Well, I wasn't.' He led the way out. 'I could have puffed and blown into your ear all night instead. We could have been very relaxed by now.'

He opened the door for her. 'I'll be outside the café in my car. Any trouble from Mrs Styles, come and get me. I'll blow in *her* ear instead.'

Mrs Styles was in a bad way. He'd gone. And she was running, sweating, screaming in a five hundred-pound suit. This house was a ridiculous size. She'd checked every room upstairs, but he could be in any of a dozen wardrobes. Or in the roof. His things were still here, but he wasn't. No note. She removed the good shoes and pulled on her wellies. Howie had bought them for her – they were yellow and covered in red flowers.

For the first time in months, she walked across the land at the rear of Styles. Alan had taken a liking to the llama, but he wasn't with Damien. In the sheds, she moved wood and boxes, called his name, wept a million tears. Then, on her way back to the house, she saw what he had done. A primitive noose dangled from the bough of a tree. Beneath it, an old garden seat waited to be used as a launching pad by a man who clearly intended to take his own life. And hers. Why? She pulled down the rope and carried it with her back to the house.

She didn't want to live without Alan. He was more than just a partner, he was a piece of continuity, a man who had cared about Howie, who had been there for Trish in her darkest hour. 'Why?' she screamed. He wasn't drinking. He'd been all right until lately, but he'd gone miserable and quiet, and he wanted to die.

She sat on the kitchen sofa and tried to collect her thoughts. Her head was a mess, as was her hair. Mascara stung her eyes, and mud clung to the skirt of a suit that had been a treasured outfit. That woman would be waiting for her down at the Boule Miche. She was a lawyer. Perhaps she'd have some idea of what needed doing in this impossible situation.

But she didn't want to talk to anyone. He would come back, even if it was just to hang himself. So lawyers could go to hell in a handcart, because she loved Alan, and she would look after him just as she'd looked after Howie. God, she hated this bloody house. She was alone in a blinking mausoleum. A thought struck. Had Alan gone to get drunk before killing himself? Was he intending to die because he couldn't carry on without his whisky? He knew she wouldn't live with a drunk, because she'd been very clear on that score.

The phone rang, and she ignored it. When it stopped the screeching, its echo bounced off walls for several seconds. Oh, God. That might have been Alan. She was going to do a 1471 when it rang again, and she snatched it up immediately. It was her accountant. 'Did you ring a minute ago?' she asked.

He hadn't rung earlier, but he wanted to know what was wrong.

And she let it all out, because Eric had been Howie's pal, and she trusted him. When she'd delivered the tale, he announced his intention to come round within the hour. 'Thanks, Eric,' she said. At least she wouldn't be on her own. She hated being alone, even in Blackpool, and that was a proper house.

Meanwhile, she set out to search the place thoroughly. She looked in every bathroom, in every cupboard and under all the beds. This time, she kept very quiet so that she might hear any movement. He wasn't here; he had abandoned her because she was ordinary, because she liked ordinary, boring things like bingo and dancing. But would any man kill himself because he hated line-dancing? It was a mystery. She changed her clothes and went downstairs. The woman in the Boule Miche could sod off.

The woman in the Boule Miche was chomping her way through a second Danish. Glenys loved her food, and it showed, as she was one of the unfortunates whose measurements fluctuated in accordance with the status of her willpower. 'I had no breakfast,' she told her companion.

Lucy grinned. Her breakfast was all over the tree house, but she didn't want to complain.

'You look very smug,' Glenys remarked.

'Yes.'

'Yes? What the bloody hell does yes mean?'

'Yes, I slept with him, and yes, I didn't get much sleep.'

The lawyer drained her coffee mug. 'You little devil. Any good?'

'Unnervingly so. I thought he'd be tentative, but ...' She raised her shoulders. 'I was wrong. He's spent thousands on the house, even bought an eighteenth-century four-poster. French. It has a new mattress, of course. We don't want any foreign bugs.'

Glenys shook her head morosely. 'I'm going to advertise. Virginity, free to good home, taker collects. What do you think?'

'You don't love yourself, Glen. That's a pretty face, so use it. Go to a gym, eat a bit less, lose thirty pounds and practise on your trainer. Many of those young men who train women offer their services. Then, when you've practised, find a husband.'

Glenys thought about that before announcing that she didn't want anything that lived in. She'd much prefer something that served its purpose before going back to its own flat, house, mother, wife, whatever. Kids she could manage without. They brought with them washing, ironing, cooking and homework, and were not commensurate with a lifestyle that included theatre, restaurant meals and a very good brandy. What she really needed was somebody who'd take her home, tie her up and lecture her in Latin.

'You're terrible,' Lucy said.

'And you're an adulterer – technically, at least.'

'I don't do technical. I can't even change a fuse. Oh, I forgot to tell you – Lizzie's married.'

Glenys's jaw dropped. 'You forgot? How can you forget? Is it that cardio-thoracic bod from next door?'

'Yes. And I think it'll work, because they're good friends. And she can change a fuse. It was one of those sudden and beautiful things, yet they act as if they've known each other for ever. I think it's possible to remember someone from the future.'

Glenys tutted. 'You don't half talk some crapola, Lucy.' She looked at her watch. 'Mrs Styles is very late.'

'Yes, I noticed that too.'

'And I think that daft bloke of yours is flattening his

nose against the window of a dump where the coffee's three quid a cup and counting.'

Lucy turned and looked at him. It was clear that she couldn't take him anywhere, because he had no idea of how to behave. Perhaps he needed a playpen? She beckoned, and he came in. Waitresses and counter staff stood still while he approached. 'Don't worry,' Lucy advised the whole establishment. 'They let him out just for one day.'

He sat down and winked at a very pretty girl in a frilled apron. 'Do they let you take your uniform home?' he asked. 'Because you could use the apron and the— Ouch.'

'She doesn't take the ouch home,' Lucy said with mock severity while delivering a second slap to his hand. 'Bring him a cappuccino with sprinkles, dear. And allow me to apologize for my father's behaviour.'

Glenys fled to the ladies' room, a hand on her mouth failing to hold back laughter.

'Is she all right?' David asked innocently.

'She just needs somebody to take her home, tie her up and talk to her in Latin.'

'Oh. That's OK, then. I can do the Latin, but I'm no good with knots. Anyway, I'm spoken for. Give us a kiss.'

'I can't. You're my father.'

'Right. Now, where's Mrs Wotsit?' He smiled insanely at the girl who brought his coffee. She placed it on the table, withdrew her hand quickly, and dashed away. David took a sip, allowing the moustache deposited by froth to remain on his face. He then asked had the earth moved for Lucy last night, as she wiped his face with her napkin.

'Yes,' she snapped.

'You can't wait here all day, Louisa.' He picked up a menu, saw the prices and put it back. 'Daylight robbery,' he muttered.

Glenys returned. She greeted David before informing Lucy that she had phoned the house, and there had been no answer. 'I'll try the mobile.' She dialled. 'Hello? Mrs Styles? It's Glen— it's Gloria. Yes, that's right. I'm waiting in the Boule Miche.' A long pause followed this introduction.

Glenys frowned. 'Really? Oh, dear. Shall I visit you at home, then? I may be able to shed a little light on your predicament.' She tapped the table with her fingers while Trish Styles spoke. 'Good grief, that's terrible. Try to calm down. Did you say second on the right? Thanks. I'll be there shortly.' She severed the connection. 'He's gone walkabout. She was up by eight o'clock, and there's been no sign of him. The poor woman's halfway out of her mind. She found a noose hanging from a tree, and a chair nearby. Alan's the only one who could have put it there.'

David immediately became serious. He had come along as chauffeur and cabaret, because he knew full well that Louisa was taking today seriously, but he could no longer lighten her load by acting the fool. The father of her children had absented himself after preparing a noose, presumably as a tool for suicide. 'Will he be in a pub, Louisa?'

'I've no idea. Lizzie says he's stopped drinking, but it's one day at a time, isn't it? I'm coming with you, Glenys.'

'And I'm coming with her.' He pointed at Lucy before going to pay the bill. A noose? Why would a man kill himself while living with a woman who had millions?

Money was important to Alan. David told the girl at the till to keep the change for tips, then followed his two companions into the street.

He tailed Glenys until she found the address. An electric gate slid open, and both cars entered the grounds. They drove at funereal pace until they reached the columned entrance. The place was so grand and sombre that it put one in mind of an impossible ménage à trois comprising a palace, a museum and a crematorium. 'It's massive,' Lucy breathed. 'Makes Tallows look like a cottage. I'm scared, and I don't know why.'

'Stay cool, love. We've got to find your old man after Glenys has done the difficult deed. Shall we wait here?'

She pondered. 'No. I want to be there for Glenys and for Trish. And you can be there for me.' They left the car and walked hand in hand towards uncharted territory.

Avoiding poor Trish hadn't been difficult. He'd just walked round the exterior walls of the house, making sure that wherever she was, he wasn't. He couldn't face her. Would he be able to face her after the meeting in the Boule Miche? She didn't go. But the meeting came to her, and Lucy was on the committee. He'd heard her voice, and he was going to hell in a muck wagon; going to prison today. Underneath the calm exterior, Lucy was after revenge.

There was nowhere to run. He wished he'd stayed away from the house, wished he could be with Damien, because he was the only human allowed to embrace the haughty, ill-tempered miniature camel. Were they camels? He'd never bothered to find out. He thought they might be from South America rather than Africa, but he wasn't sure. But at this moment, he needed to bury his face in that woolly and slightly smelly neck. Damien knew about suffering – it was in his eyes.

Leaving the grounds of Styles was out of the question. First, he would be seen. Second, he had a tenner in his pocket and, for the first time since his op, was completely devoid of hope. He would buy a half-bottle of good whisky if he got out. Not that it mattered. One small binge could make little difference, while going to jail in a state of sobriety was not a good idea.

He sat on the ground and leaned against the building. There was no way out, since Howard Styles had been extraordinarily thorough when it came to security. Wherever Alan went, he would be seen. If he ran full pelt towards the rope, those inside would cut him down in good time. There was only one thing for it. He had to go in and face the music. Not yet, though. No, not just yet.

It took them half an hour to return Trish to a state in which she could absorb and respond to what was being said. At the beginning, she was convinced that Lucy had come to get Alan and take him away, while Dr Vincent intended to section him as insane. 'He doesn't drink any more,' she screamed several times.

'I'm a cancer doctor,' David explained, 'and I–'

'He hasn't got cancer. My husband was the one with cancer.'

'I work with children. Mostly leukaemia.'

'He's not a child.' Trish glared at Glenys. 'Why did you fetch these people here? I thought you were something to do with Howie's business, a bit of conveyancing work or something of that nature. False pretences, you used to get in my house. You even changed your name.'

Strangely, it was the wife who managed to comfort her. 'Glenys thought there was something you should know about Alan. I feel the same. Dr Vincent is my fiancé – he drove me here. In a car, not with a whip,' she added in an attempt to lighten the atmosphere. But the lame joke fell on stony ground. 'We mean you no harm, honestly. And I haven't come to get Alan back, dear. We don't love each other – I'm with this lovely man now. Please, just listen to my lawyer friend here.'

'I don't need to know anything about him,' Trish said, her heart allowing in a crumb of hope. Lucy didn't want him back. She was engaged to another man, so Alan was still free. 'I love him no matter what. As long as he doesn't drink.'

Glenys spread paperwork on the kitchen table. 'Here's what we've come to show you, Mrs Styles. He stole most of my client's money, forged her signature, and mortgaged a house that's been in her family for generations. I'm so sorry to have to give you such bad news, but we are trying to act in your best interests and the facts are there in black and white. These are photocopies for your perusal. He committed fraud on several occasions over the years.'

Trish cast an eye over the items on her table. 'I thought it might be something like that,' she said. 'But he'll not go to jail, because I'm going to clear his debts.'

'What?' Glenys looked at Lucy, then at Trish. 'The mortgages?'

Lucy leaned across and patted Trish's hand. 'The man's hopeless with money – always was. When I took

373

power of attorney, I sold plant worth a lot more than he knew. With a bit of help from my own estate, I cleared the fraudulent mortgages. That man is the father of my three children, and I couldn't just sit back and let him go to jail. So the Halifax has no claim on him, and all his commitments have been honoured. If he would call in at Tallows occasionally to pick up his post, he'd know all this.' She turned to David. 'Find him, please. None of us wants his neck in a noose.'

David left the house.

'He's not bankrupt?' Trish asked.

'He's not. But in a way, it would be better if he were bankrupt, because this could all happen to you. I was married to him, so—'

'So you let him do it,' Trish accused her. 'Well, I won't. Any new business will be a partnership with me at the steering wheel. You should have stopped him.'

Lucy sighed heavily. 'Look, my children are all that matters to me. When they were grown, I took command, retrieved my money and left him. By that time he was pickled in whisky and beyond the point at which negotiation could be useful. I chose my way. We all choose our own way, and those of us with children perhaps choose differently.'

'Sorry,' said Trish.

'It's all right, I know how you feel. I'd go to the ends of the earth for David, but don't tell him. Look.' She pointed to the window. 'Here they come, two fools for the price of one.'

Alan came in first. He stood and stared at the floor.

'It's OK,' Lucy said. 'No one's here to hurt you. We came to protect Trish, and I'm sure you know why. Look at me. Look at me, Alan.'

He raised his head. David stood by Alan's side, two men staring at a solid block of female power.

'I discharged you, and I thought you would have been told. What about your mobile? Didn't your lawyers let you know that no fraud charges were coming your way? You're my children's dad, for goodness' sake.'

'I changed my SIM card. Lizzie has my number, but no one else – apart from Trish.' He paused. 'She got married. My little girl married?'

'Yes.'

David decided to take charge. 'Right. I gather that you two ladies have done what you came to do? So we should go and leave Alan and Trish to talk. This is their business now, not ours.'

A buzzer sounded. 'Sorry I'm late, Trish. It's Eric.'

Glenys jumped up. She knew that voice. 'Eric Simmons? There have been developments, Eric,' she told the machine on the wall. 'Wait there, we're all coming out now.'

'My accountant,' Trish explained.

'I know him, so I'll keep him out of your way while you talk. Good luck, anyway.' Glenys dashed out, leaving behind a very bemused Lucy.

'We'll be off, then.' David took Lucy's arm.

'Just a minute,' Alan called. He blushed, and the words didn't arrive easily. 'Thanks, Lucy. I never treated you right, and I wish I could pay you back.'

'You can. Take good care of Trish if she still wants you. By the way, you look miles better. I know you can beat the booze, Alan. With Trish behind you, anything's possible. That is one strong little woman. Depend on her.' She handed him a card. 'Phone me if you need to – either of you.'

Outside, David leaned casually against the car. 'You're quite a sensitive little flower underneath, aren't you?'

It had been a crazy day thus far, with no time for reflection. But she stood for a moment and felt a moment of pure fear invade her heart. Life was so fragile. If anything happened to him, she would know what he had gone through after the loss of Anne. 'I love you, little David Vincent, and I couldn't possibly live without you. Liverpool tonight, I think. Our work is not yet done.'

'To the bat poles,' he suggested. 'We have a city to save.'

In the car, Lucy used her phone. 'Glenys? What are you up to?'

'Erm ... yes, Mr Charnock. I have your file on my desk.'

'Is he married?'

'No.'

'You can't talk, can you?'

'No, Mr Charnock.'

'Is he handsome?'

'No.'

'But you like him, and you've always liked him.'

'That's right.'

'Bye.'

'What was all that about?' David asked.

'No idea. She thought I was Mr Charnock.'

David decided not to bother asking who Mr Charnock was. He slowed down near the gate and waved at Glenys. She was in the company of a medium-sized man in a grey suit.

Lucy wound down her window. 'See you, Glen. Bring Mr Simmons to supper soon. Or Mr Charnock ...'

David drove on. Lucy was up to something. She was usually up to something these days, because she'd been up to nothing for so long. Her next something went under the name of Lexi, and it was going to be quite an eventful evening if said Lexi put in an appearance. The boot of this car was crammed with stuff that would make the evening a very happening time. 'Where shall we live?' he asked.

'Your house and mine. Mine when you're in Liverpool, yours when you're in Lancashire. You need me to look after you, and I need you because you can reach high shelves.'

'And your bed-and-breakfasters?'

'Carol. She can't wait to get away from Dee's kids and Our Beryl. By all accounts, Our Beryl is the devil on wheels. She has the whole of Bootle organized. Everything is in her charge, and she runs the area from her gilded chariot. MS. Like Moira.'

David thought Carol was quite terrifying, though he kept that to himself, because Carol was much loved by Louisa.

'You're smiling,' she said.

'I'm happy.'

'Are you, indeed?'

'Yes indeed. I am indeed.'

'Oh, right. Don't worry, I'll soon put a stop to that.'

David laughed. She would never change. She must never change.

Moira had her husband back. At last, he had told her everything, and she had forgiven him. She was anxious, though. What if the creature burnt down their house? Apart from that piece of disquiet, she was happier than she had been in months. The shaking was minimal and, apart from permanent face pain, she was relatively symptom-free.

They had lit a little gel fire in the wooden house's living room fireplace. 'I can smell autumn,' Moira said. 'Damp, earthy and a bit sharp. Did you look round Tallows? Isn't that one fabulous house?'

'Yes. Where did it get its name?'

She told him about the original owner of the house on Chandler's Lane. 'Before paraffin wax and so forth, candles were often made from tallow – animal fat. He bought the whole area – the lane remains unadopted to this day. And a chandler was a candlemaker, so there you have it. But Lucy's forebears took the house on about a hundred or so years ago, and now Lucy and David are going to use it for his patients.' She looked round the room. 'I've fallen in love with Lucy's shed.'

'It's cute,' he said. 'Do you fancy a cup of tea?'

'Yes, please.'

As he set the kettle to boil, he took in the cosiness of the place and decided that it was like being a child again in a playhouse with his friends. But now he was with just one, and she was the best friend he'd ever known. He found some biscuits and carried the tray through to the living room. She was exactly where he had left her, but she wasn't . . . she wasn't right.

Tray, mugs and contents hit the floor, bouncing, crashing and spilling all over the place. She wasn't breathing. He picked up the phone and dialled 999 with the instrument on speaker, barking out orders and address, making damned sure they knew he was a doctor.

She had not been down for three minutes – he hadn't left the room for long, and Lucy's kettle was rapid-boil.

Three minutes. A brain that lacked oxygen for any longer was damaged. He found a thready pulse, made sure her mouth was clear, and decided that the Heimlich move was no use, since she had choked on absolutely nothing. He ran back to the kitchen, found a knife and a ballpoint pen, and returned to his wife. After lifting her from the chair and placing her on the floor, he took the pen apart. 'I'm sorry,' he whispered before drawing the knife across her throat. He parted skin and subcutaneous tissue, punctured the cricothyroid membrane, and inserted the outer layer of the pen into her airway.

'I've done a primitive tracheotomy,' he told the man on the phone. 'Now, send that bloody ambulance, or I'll have all your jobs!'

'On its way, sir.'

Her chest was moving slightly. She hadn't been eating – this was one of those occasions on which even her own saliva became a threat. The heart was making some effort, and air was going in via the tube, because he could hear it rattling slightly. What now? He was a bloody doctor, and he didn't know what to do next.

They came eventually. Paramedics worked until she was stable enough to be carried on a stretcher. By the time they were in the ambulance, Richard felt near to collapse. Then he heard them. She'd had an infarction. 'What?' he cried. 'There's nothing wrong with her heart. Her BP's fine, and her cholesterol's a damned sight lower than mine.'

'Stress and pain,' said one of the medics. 'Is it MS?'

'Yes.'

'Well, you did your best. Let's get her to A and E as quickly as we can.'

The siren wailed. Richard picked up the pen casing with which he had saved his wife's life. She now had a proper tracheotomy and equipment that announced her status second by second. A heart attack? That wasn't supposed to happen. Didn't she suffer enough with the rat-faced, sly, evil-minded disease named multiple sclerosis?

In his mind's eye, he saw her struggling to walk through the hallway at home, went with her through doors behind which sat occupational therapists, speech therapists, experts in swallowing, people who knew sod all about double incontinence and the dignity it stole from the sufferer. He saw her in Sainsbury's, a can of low-salt, low-sugar baked beans in a hand, witnessed the involuntary jerk of the limb that sent the same tin flying through the air into the next aisle. He saw her weeping with the pain, watched while she dashed away tears and painted on a smile for him. Just for him. For her husband.

Moira showed no sign of regaining consciousness. They fought long and hard in the hospital, and Richard never left her side. But, after the second heart attack occurred, he pulled himself together. Staff were preparing to shock her yet again, and Richard held up his hand. 'No,' he said quietly. 'She's had a happy week and a day that was almost pain-free. I don't want her to die, but that's selfish. There are times when she can't swallow, can't talk, can't walk, can scarcely breathe. Tonight, she gave me a history lesson about the house where we were staying. She was as bright as a button today. Let her rest.'

A long pause followed. 'Are you sure, Dr Turner?' the main man asked.

'Am I hell as like! But I'm certain of one important thing. She'll have no more suffering if you just leave her alone.'

The consultant crossed the room and placed a hand on Richard's shoulder. 'Her heart is badly damaged. You're right. With this trouble on top of MS, she'd be very ill. Even if we did manage to get her back ... Shall I call it?'

'Yes.'

The man removed half-moon spectacles and dragged the back of a hand cross his damp forehead. 'Time of death, eleven thirty-five p.m. Thank you, team.'

One by one, they left the room until only Richard and the consultant remained. Both exhausted, they sank into chairs and stared at each other. 'GP?' the specialist asked.

Richard nodded. 'Yes.' He paused for a few seconds. 'She was with me all the way through my student days. When we married, she was the most beautiful woman you could wish to see. Her hair was so long she could almost sit on it. I used to brush it for her. She loved that, said it was nearly as good as sex. Remarkable skin, huge eyes, and a waist so small – she looked breakable. I watched her eroding. I saw her becoming truly breakable. And broken.'

The medic reached out a hand. 'I'm Guy, by the way. Guy Morris.'

'Richard.' They shook hands. 'Why have they been bombing Iraq when the money could be used to cure stuff?' Richard asked.

'Because they *can* bomb Iraq.'

'And they can't cure MS?'

The man raised his hands in a gesture of hopelessness.

'God knows what they might manage if they concentrated. Day centres for the disabled are being closed or charging huge rates. That keeps the people in wheelchairs tucked away out of sight in their own homes. Their allowances have been slashed mercilessly – who knows how many are dying due to lack of attention and help? As for the diseases, I've no idea what's being done. There's a lot of begging via TV advertisements, so that says a lot. Charities are all we have left.'

Richard looked at his wife. She wasn't twitching, wasn't gasping for breath or talking rubbish. No longer would she need those painkillers that gave her chronic constipation; no longer would he slip her a Valium 5 to calm the shakes while worrying about the same drug further impeding her breathing. 'She can't choke now.'

'No, Richard, but you might. Get counselling. I'm serious – this is a big thing, a monumental happening. It's my opinion that she would have been dead within weeks, but we'll never know.'

'And I must live with never knowing. Yet we do know, Guy. We know her life, however brief, however long, would have been unbearable.'

'Absolutely.'

Richard stood up. He had to go. Simon, Stephanie and Alice needed to be told that they were motherless. But first, he had to go back to Lucy's little park home and clean up that last cup of tea that had not been enjoyed by him and Moira.

'I'm done here, so I'll drive you,' Guy offered.

'I'll get a taxi.'

'No, you won't. Trust me, I'm a doctor.'

Richard smiled grimly. 'I want her back in Crosby as soon as possible. This is foreign soil for us.' He kissed the cooling forehead of the woman who had supported him through thick and thin, then followed Guy out of the hospital. He was alone deep inside. There was a hole in the region of his stomach, and it would never be filled. Thirty years of their life together was being wheeled down to the morgue to be placed in a fridge. She didn't mind the cold. Heat had troubled her, especially since the MS had entered the secondary progressive stage. 'I don't know how I'll manage without her. She might have been a cripple, but she was an amazing one. Very funny, almost mischievous. And all she ever worried about was me. She'd done such a good job on the kids that they turned out great, very focused and positive. Our son married recently, and he'll be shadowing someone like you, but at Guy's. With your name, you should be working there.'

The driver said nothing. He knew Richard needed to talk, to vent some of his misery as soon as possible.

'My girls are at medical school in Edinburgh, one in her first year, the other in her second. Yes, Moira was a brilliant mother.'

At last, Guy Morris spoke. 'When you wake tomorrow, for the first few seconds, everything will be OK. Then it will crash in on you, so don't be alone. Things change after the funeral. They don't heal, they just shift.'

Richard turned to look at the driver. 'You've been through this?'

'Yes. I lost my wife last year. It's a long, long process, but life goes on, as they say. I live alone, though one of my wife's friends does my cooking and housework. She's a nice woman. I'm working my way up to asking her out for dinner.'

'And you're still in counselling?'

'Yes, but on the other side of it. Now, I listen to people who've had a loss. Not easy with my hours, but I always phone them back as soon as possible. It's a bit like Alcoholics Anonymous – give and take.'

They pulled into the driveway at the west side of Tallows. The back garden was illuminated by lights that came on at dusk and turned off at dawn, and they walked all the way down to the park home. Inside the little wooden house, Richard stood and looked at the mess. Guy picked up the knife and looked at the floor. It had been a clean job, because there was very little blood. He shifted everything while Richard sat and stared at a dead fireplace. The gel pots lasted just a couple of hours, so they had burnt out ages ago. 'I can't stay here,' he said.

'I have some pills,' Guy told him. 'You will take some and sleep. No way are you driving tonight. I shall stay with you and, in the morning, you will not leave here until I've filled you up with caffeine.' He stood up. 'I'll go and make a sandwich – I just did a twelve-hour stretch. Phone your children while I'm gone.'

Richard stared at his phone. At this moment, his kids were happy. Simon, in Lucy's house with his new bride, was ecstatic about life, about Lizzie, about London. Steph and Alice were up in Edinburgh, possibly drunk, probably hanging round with other students, laughing, joking, singing terrible songs. They were young and carefree, and he was about to put a stop to their joie de vivre. But it had to be done.

He would tell Simon first, as he was the oldest. It had to be done, and he mustn't cry. They had just one parent now, and he must not let them down.

*

Lexi made her way through the darkening streets. She had learned her lesson – flat shoes, dark clothes, don't talk to anyone, walk at a steady pace. Why was she doing this? Life was looking up, she'd been out for a drink with Tom Rice, and she knew the job was hers. But Richard Turner had got to her. He had pretended to love her before throwing everything in her face. She was common. She was unsuitable. She was on the warpath.

This was her swan song, and it would be colourful. She carried a final letter for his wife, plus a can of purple paint. It was going to be her finest hour.

David made doubly sure that he had disabled the outside light before joining Lucy in the dining room. They sat in twilight, each staring at a bank of small screens loaned to them by the father of a boy with leukaemia in remission. The man was a specialist in domestic and industrial security, but David wasn't. He'd done his best, and the equipment had been tested by Lucy who had played the fool in front of all three hidden cameras. They seemed to work, and they performed in near-darkness, so the pair crossed their fingers and waited.

'What time is it?' Lucy whispered.

'Five minutes later than the last time you asked,' he replied.

She sighed. 'I'm bored.'

'Oh, diddums. Shut up and keep still.'

Lucy shut up for about three seconds. 'The front door's ajar?'

'Yes.'

A few more seconds limped by. 'David?'

'What?'

'You remember that killer conker you had?'

'Vaguely.'

'There was nothing vague about it. It wiped out your whole class and twenty-three of mine and Diane's. It was a deadly bloody weapon. The Americans and the Russians argued about it.'

'Right.'

'Was it concrete?'

'No.'

She poked him in the ribs. 'Tell me.'

'Bog off, Louisa. We all have our trade secrets.'

'Tell me. Please.'

He pressed her to the floor and lay on top of her. 'Do you think we've time for a bit of Chopin?'

'No. But if you don't tell me, I'll tickle you.'

He kissed her long and hard, then dragged her back into a sitting position. 'Right,' he said. 'Here we are, behind a sofa with three television screens. We are positioned thus in order to catch a bad woman. And you want to tickle me, so that will give her warning not to venture into the house and on to *Candid Camera*, because I'll be laughing like a drain.'

'OK. I won't tickle you.' They separated. 'Tell me about the conker, then.'

'No, Louisa.'

'Then tell me who stole my wedding ring from the soap dish in the shed.'

'I claim the Fifth.'

'You stole it.'

'I didn't.'

'So who did?'

'Moira. She stole it for me, OK?'

'All right. I won't ask about the wedding ring you're having made specially. Don't trust one woman to keep a secret from another woman. So, if I let you off about the wedding ring, which is to be a wedding-cum-engagement ring all in one piece, and I don't know anything about it, tell me about your conker.'

David fought back a force ten gale of laughter. 'Never ask a man about his conkers. It's far too personal.'

'What time is it?'

'Shut up.'

'I love you, David. Tell me about the conker.'

He allowed a long sigh to escape. 'Vinegar, slow heat in the oven, clear nail polish.'

'You bastard.'

'That's me. Hush.'

Camera one showed Lexi outside. She was rattling a can before spraying the wall. David hung on to Lucy. 'Leave it, hon. She hasn't done enough yet.'

Camera two saw her pushing the front door inwards. After standing still and listening for a while, she picked up some items from the coat stand shelf, then ventured into the living room. The third camera caught her stealing Moira's jewellery.

Lucy shot from the dining room like a bullet from a gun. David felt transfixed as he watched his fiancée knocking Litherland Lexi to the floor. She was using her fists, and was probably doing damage that would show. He jumped up in order to intervene and, just as he entered the next-door living room, tripped in near-darkness over a stool that had been kicked into the doorway. Lucy was so engrossed in her revenge that she didn't notice. David clambered to his feet and switched on the lights. His left knee hurt like hell. 'Louisa?'

'What?'

'Stop. Right now.'

There was something in his voice that cut through the anger like a hot knife in butter. She stopped. Silence reigned for some time. Then Lexi tried to put back the jewellery she had stolen from Moira's little folding table, and the money she'd lifted from the hall. Lucy came back to life in a split second. Like a trained boxer, she beat her fists into the woman's chest and stomach. David, in pain and temporarily stunned, could only watch while his Louisa took it all out on this one woman. Lexi had done wrong, but she was in receipt of at least two decades of pent-up fury.

He grabbed the maelstrom and eventually contained it, though he was awarded several powerful blows during this difficult process.

Worn out, Lucy turned in her lover's restraining arms, and it poured out of her. Language David might have expected from a chain gang flowed from her lips in a steady stream. 'You're dead, you whore. There's another of your sweet letters for Moira, isn't there? In the hall where you left dog shit, you filthy, diseased bitch.'

The language had improved slightly, thought David as he pushed Lucy into a chair. He inhaled deeply and spoke to Lexi. 'We have you on TV. We have you with money from the hall, and jewellery from this room. The wonderful woman you tried to destroy is not here. By the way, our cameras work in darkness, so I have you spraying the wall as well as stealing. You'd better bugger off before Louisa gets a second wind.'

'And you have her beating me up.' Lexi thrust forward a determined chin.

David was ready for this one. 'I'm sure a court will take our side, madam. Moira, the poor sick woman to whom you sent all those filthy letters, didn't deserve any of this. Her husband intercepted every piece of your disgusting literature, so don't pride yourself on having upset Moira, because we are here to protect her. She's a bright, intelligent, strong woman, and her friend here was righteously angry with you for the letters, the graffiti we still haven't seen, the dog dirt and now the thieving. His car isn't here, so you thought you were safe. You thought he'd mistakenly left the door unlocked. You will never again be safe. We know people who know you.'

'I'm leaving the room for a mo,' Lucy announced. 'It's OK, I must just wash her off my hands. But first I want to get the letter she wrote to an absentee.' She pulled away from him and went to retrieve the envelope. She returned, and after opening it she scanned the contents and spoke to Lexi. 'I would advise lessons in basic English,' she snapped before handing the paper to David and marching out into the hall.

'What is the matter with you?' he asked the cowering woman. 'Why can't you get on with your life and leave these people alone?'

'He said he loved me and liked being with me.'

'And that's excuse enough for you to put dog excrement through the front door?'

Lexi hung her head. She was bloody injured, and something wanted doing about this lot here. The woman was a raving lunatic for a start, and this chap was too . . . too posh. 'I want to go,' she advised the floor.

He told her what he knew Louisa wanted. The film, including her attack on Lexi, should go to the police. Louisa would take her chances, as this was her first offence – if, indeed, it might be labelled an offence – and she might get a warning, a fine, or a suspended sentence. But Lexi would go to jail, since she already had a record. 'Her sole aim is to get you locked away so that Moira will be safe.'

'I've got a new job.' Lexi swallowed painfully.

'Tough.'

The phone rang. He heard Lucy talking while he glared at the seated offender. A couple of minutes passed before Lucy arrived at the doorway. She was pale, shaking and, at first, unable to speak. 'What's the matter?' he asked.

Lucy opened her mouth, but no words emerged.

'Louisa?'

At last, the syllables began to limp from her tongue. 'Simon's phone's switched off,' she managed. 'They're out. They were out when we got here, weren't they? There was no one in my house.'

'Yes. I expect they're with some of Simon's friends from the hospital.'

She slid down the wall and sat where she landed. 'Richard says we're not to tell Simon. He wants to do it. We have to wait up till they come back.'

'OK.' He scratched his head. 'And?'

'She died.'

'Who died, sweetheart?'

'Moira did. Tonight.' She looked at her watch. 'Last night now, I suppose. That beautiful soul has gone.'

It was David's turn to go into shock. 'Did she choke?' he asked after a few moments had passed.

'Two heart attacks. Richard was with her. He's back at the shed, and a doctor's looking after him. But he wanted to tell Simon first, because he's the oldest. He asked what we were doing in here, and I said we were getting rid of rubbish.'

Both stared at Lexi, who was weeping. 'Bugger off before I let my lioness loose again,' David said quietly. 'She may be on the floor, but she's still growling. Even I don't trust her mood at the moment, and I'm engaged to marry her. Go on – get lost. If you're very, very lucky, this may be the end of the matter. We've things to do, and we haven't time to waste on you.'

Lexi rushed out.

They sat together on the carpet, sharing a silence that became a partnership, because they held on to each other like a pair of young animals looking for warmth. There was no need for speech, since she knew his thoughts, and he knew hers. A taxi pulled up. Lucy knew it was a cab, because diesel was noisy. 'Go,' she whispered. 'Just tell him to phone his dad. Leave Lizzie with him – he'll need her.'

Alone, she stared at Moira's chair with the little shawl draped over the back. On a work table, embroidery silks shared space with pastels, watercolours and a multi-coloured quarrel of knitting wools, waiting for the good days when hands were steady and pain was bearable. 'I'm glad Richard was with you. I'm glad you liked my little play house, and pleased that you enjoyed your week.'

This house would be dead without Moira. She had put up a damned good fight against the ravages of her illness, had been strong, cheerful, stubborn and persistent. The woman had filled the place, not just because of all the equipment she required, but with the breadth of her character, the quirkiness of her personality. 'I feel as if I knew you all my life, Moira.'

David came back. 'Your boys are with them. They've gone up into the gods.'

'Did Simon make the call?'

'I didn't stay. It was right to leave him with his wife and his peers.'

It was moments like this one that told Lucy why her love for this man was so real and at a depth that would never be reached by mere words. They had laughed and joked about the act of lovemaking, but when it came to abiding love, the man was pure Beethoven. And that, from Lucy, who was a great fan of Ludwig, meant something.

'We'll go back shortly,' he said. 'If they need us, they'll find us.'

'In my bed?'

'Of course. First I must paint out the B A S T U R D on the front of this house, and I need to shift the surveillance stuff. I think Richard should not have to see any of that.' He smiled wanly at her. 'Yes, your bed. Where else would we be of comfort to each other?'

He was right again. Where else should they be?

Christmas

It was cold on the steps. Built from concrete to hold back the Mersey after valuable real estate had fallen into the river, they completed a monochrome picture on this special day when the Christian world celebrated the birth of a holy child.

The dog didn't mind the cold. Samson leapt about like a puppy, threatening the waves, coming back several times to deposit weed, a dead crab and a condom at the feet of the man who had brought him here. A dull, heavy sky hung low over a boiling river whose chief colours were pewter and darker greys. Even the crests on beating water looked like the aftermath of washday, sepia foam landing rhythmically on the stretch where Vikings had disembarked to claim territory. Blondell had built all the villages – Great Crosby, Little Crosby, Blundellsands and Thornton. 'I see no ships,' Richard said before ordering the dog to heel.

It wasn't his dog. He had borrowed it as an excuse for leaving a house filled by people, coloured lights, gaily wrapped packages and dozens of cards that celebrated a day he didn't want. Christmas had arrived early this year. Unlike Easter, it wasn't a movable feast, so he was the one out of step. Again. London. Carpets and kindness. How long had he been back from that place? One day at a time? So many days squashed, forgotten, obliterated.

He turned to look at houses newer than his own. This was Blundellsands; this was the area Blondell had grabbed for himself, and it was valuable. Million-pound residences all in a row, fairy lights everywhere, trees in gardens illuminated by garish décor. What a bloody mess.

No. He was the mess. He could remember way, way back, but recent days, weeks and months had been compressed into a folder marked *Bad*, and he had disposed of it. 'They say it's temporary,' he told his canine friend. 'But I think I've lost it, old son.'

Samson, who had enjoyed a good upbringing, made a polite little noise in his throat. The house to which he begged to return had been interesting today. Scents of last night's cooking had hung in the air, and he wanted to taste all that had been promised.

'OK,' Richard sighed. 'It's all right for you. You don't have to pretend to be human.'

They began the walk back to Mersey View. Richard didn't want to face the hopeful smiles, the dinner, his children. Harley Street had been acceptable, because he hadn't needed to try, since it was just tufted Wilton and politeness and strangers. And expensive. Here was real, and he wasn't ready for reality.

'I have insight into my own condition,' he told Samson. 'That's what they said, anyway. In other bloody words, I should pull myself together.' He liked this dog. Moira had ... Moira had liked this dog. 'Let her in, Rich,' he ordered himself. 'Go there. Be there. Think about your wife. And for everybody's sake, grieve, and let go.'

'He's out there running round like bloody Heathcliff in a mac.' Carol Makin folded her arms across a bosom that was overly ample. 'I've gone out of me way for him on Christmas Day, and he's not here. I'll kill him when I find him, I will. I'll bloody crown him with me roasting tin.'

Lucy decided yet again that Carol was an unusual woman. She talked like an overgrown street urchin, yet she had read just about every classic on library shelves. Heathcliff in a mac? That was a very accurate description of Dr Richard Turner, who had stopped being a doctor, had stopped being a father – had stopped being.

'Shall I go after him?' David asked. 'After all, he could be leading my dog astray.'

Paul laughed, though the sound contained little merriment. 'That dog knows nothing about astray. The trouble with Labradors is they're too good.'

Carol turned on him. 'Oh yes? Ho flaming ho and a happy Christmas all round? You should see my rug. Well, you shouldn't, because it's in the bin. Pigs in blankets?' She turned to Lucy. 'Our Dee done best pork sausages in bacon. Lovely, they were, but the flaming dog made away with half of them. The birds down Bootle is having a lovely Christmas. Don't talk to me about bloody Labradors. I don't care if I never see one again in–'

Samson chose this unfortunate moment to enter the house and run to Carol. He loved Carol. She was a foodie, and she often gave him illegal scraps when David wasn't looking. 'Hello, pet,' she said, thereby making herself a total liar. 'Who's my lovely boy, then?'

Richard came in. Carol blinked, because she could scarcely bear to look at him. He appeared not to have enjoyed a good wash in twelve months, while his beard was nearly thick enough to accommodate a family of house sparrows. 'Where've you been?' She was one of the few people he heeded, so she made sure she addressed him loudly and clearly.

'Beach,' he said.

'Sit,' she ordered. Dog and man sat, the former waiting for food, the latter waiting for nothing.

'Stay,' she added before leaving the room.

The dog looked at his borrowed master, and the man looked at the dog.

David smiled to himself. Sometimes, canines went where humanity feared to tread. He grasped his wife's hand and looked at her twin sons. They sat as still as a pair of statues, because like everyone else they didn't know quite what to expect from the next few minutes.

Simon and Lizzie slipped into the room. They stood behind Richard's chair and shared the pregnant pause.

Carol entered bearing a box. She was clearly unamused, as she was cursing under her breath about something or other, but that was not unusual for her. She dumped the box in Richard's lap. 'Happy flaming Christmas,' she spat. 'I only had it two nights, and that was enough. It's a bastard.'

Richard opened the box, and everyone's breath was held. 'Hello,' he said. 'Did you eat a rug? Where are the sausages?'

Lucy allowed a long sigh of near-relief to escape. David had spoken of traumatized teenagers who communicated through Samson, whose bruised minds healed through Samson. She watched while Richard lifted a miniature Samson from the box. 'A bastard, eh?' he said.

David waved the paperwork. 'He's a close relative of my dog, and he's good stock. The Queen's gun dogs share ancestry with these two. But even good stock chews its way to new teeth, I'm afraid. He's nine weeks, and he needs one more shot from the vet. Apart from that, he's good to go.'

Richard lifted the small dog and allowed it to nuzzle his neck. He stroked a satin ear before handing the puppy to Samson. 'There you are, lad. Train him.'

Carol dashed a few tears from her third chin. Watching the doc deteriorating hadn't been easy. She'd caught Dee crying her eyes out, and Dee was tough. It had been heartbreaking, mostly because he'd never really mourned. After the funeral, other doctors had taken over the practice, while he'd taken to sitting around doing nothing. The two girls had come down, with permission from their university, to look after Dad, but they'd got nowhere with him. And he was such a good-looking bloke – it was a damned shame. 'Doc?' she said, her voice cracking slightly.

'Yes?'

'Look after that hound. She would have liked it. Moira would have loved a dog like Samson.'

The room was still and silent. 'She would,' he said. 'You're right.'

'And if you look after the dog, it'll look after you.'

'Yes.' He examined the puppy. 'It's a boy. I'll call him Henry. Come along, Henry. You must meet the cat.'

It was as if the world had stopped. Steph and Alice

arrived from next door, since everyone was to eat in number 32 Mersey View today. 'Where is he?' Alice whispered.

'Outside with two dogs and a cat,' replied Lucy.

They all filed into the dining room and stared through the window. The inevitable had happened, and poor little Henry was learning the hard way that cats didn't negotiate, they dictated. 'That won't last,' said Lucy. 'Smokey loves dogs.'

And it happened. Richard sat on an old swing and cradled his puppy. Although he was facing away from the house, all inside could tell that he was sobbing, because his back shook.

'That's the start,' David announced. 'Like Churchill said, God bless him, this isn't the beginning of the end. But it is, perhaps, the end of the beginning.' He placed an arm round his wife's shoulders. 'Is Alan definitely coming?'

'Yes. So is Trish. Tomorrow. That's step two. But the pup broke the ice.'

There wasn't a dry eye in the room. The dinner went on hold, and even her majesty could wait if necessary, because everyone here had lived through Richard Turner's hell. The trouble was, most of the populace expected a doctor to be on top of things all the time, but David knew better. He had lived in a dark place himself, and he didn't want to see Richard enduring a decade of nothingness. David had organized the Harley Street clinic and the dog; he had decided to talk to Alan and to invite him and Trish for Boxing Day. 'Who's a clever boy, then?' Lucy whispered in his ear.

'Early days, my darling. I'll go and carve that massive bird before Samson sets his sights on it.'

Lucy went to stand at the back door. She smiled to herself. Richard was drying his tears on a nine-week-old puppy, and that, too, was a very good thing. If a man had no tissues, using a little dog as a handkerchief was thinking outside the box. An inch at a time, he would be dragged kicking and screaming from the container into which he had locked himself. 'I won't give up on him, Moira,' she whispered as a single flake of snow landed at her feet. 'None of us will.'

Boxing Day was sharper, clearer. The sun put in an appearance, its rays bouncing from a thin coating of hoar frost that had descended in the night. It was cold. Lucy slipped from the embrace of her husband, pulled on a dressing gown and went to the window. 'We now have Heathcliff and Henry in a mac,' she said. 'Richard's got his pup peeping out of the collar. Henry can't be allowed on pavements till he's had another injection.' She sighed. 'And another busy day. Come on, lazy-bones.'

'No Chopin this morning?' he groaned.

'Not even chopsticks. Did he write that? Shut up and get up, David Vincent.' She went to have a shower, her mind running through today's menu and things that still needed to be done. Most of it was ready, but she prided herself on a good table, even when it offered just a buffet. Shirley and Hal had gone to their retirement home, so Ian, the new gardener, was to bring his family, while Carol and Dee were accompanying the formidable Beryl. Dee had refused to fetch her children, had muttered darkly about some things being unfit for human consumption, so Lucy had left it at that.

David joined her. 'It's all right,' he said. 'I'm just in

the queue, no Chopining about, and definitely no Tchaikovsky. But don't turn round, or I might get carried away.'

She turned round with deliberate slowness. 'Bog off,' she said. 'I've salmon to poach.'

'I married a poacher? Can't you buy your salmon from a supermarket like everyone else? Do you have to go out with fishing tackle and—' A wet sponge hit him in the face.

Lucy left him where he was and pulled on a robe. She fought the urge to laugh, because he was capable of going from sublime to ridiculous and back in a split second. This was what happened when women married spindly little lads who turned out to be the spit of John Lennon, but taller. If he ever stopped being a nuisance, she would be very sad.

It was even colder than yesterday, but it was certainly brighter. Richard walked on sand while delivering a monologue to his new friend. The creature was warm, soft and pretty. He could not remember contact with any other being since … since September. It was the heat of one little body that had finally threatened to melt him. It was the trust in brown eyes that made him talk.

He told Henry about the world, the water, the sky. He showed him the steps, flags that forbade swimming, the coastguard station. 'They rescue human idiots. I shall have to rescue you from Carol, because she'll take your little deposits a lot more seriously than I do. And that, Henry, is the longest speech I've produced since … since Moira died.'

No drop of booze had passed his lips today. Last night, in his cups again, he had neglected this little chap and had been forced to pick up several tiny piles of dog dirt. Lucy and David were wise. So was Henry. Intelligence had been inherited from superior Canadian wolves, while prescience, too, appeared to be present. Henry was a wolf. Every dog, no matter what its size or shape, was ninety-nine per cent wolf. This one was a godsend.

'The drink stopped me feeling. Now, I have to feel. Because people are waiting for me, you see. Friends are caring for my patients, the girls have lost a whole term and, when I was in London, I refused to see my only son. I saw him eventually, but he must have been hurt. They lost their mum. Technically speaking, Henry, a wife is replaceable, but a mum isn't. I've been selfish.'

She wasn't replaceable. He had no desire for women, no need for anyone. Lucy was still beautiful, but she wasn't what he wanted. Without Moira ... 'Moira's gone,' he said.

The puppy bit his chin, which was already fragile after the first shave in days or weeks – Richard couldn't remember. 'No biting,' he said before lowering himself on to a step. The Mersey was happier today. It looked cleaner. This was how life was meant to be – a series of changes, a different backdrop every hour, every moment. And he had to tackle it. He had to deal with it himself, because he knew only too well what drink could do.

The pup was like a mobile hot water bottle. He tried to wriggle out of prison, but the master held him back. 'Soon,' he promised. 'For now, it's just gardens, Samson

– we have to trust to luck there – and that terrible cat. We've puppy food at home. Let's get back. We have to start living.'

All six offspring from the two houses had been sent out for the day. After phoning several people, Simon had found an all-festive-season-come-as-you-are-but-with-bottles party in the digs of one of his ex-colleagues, so they went off happily with cans of lager and bottles of wine. They would be back in a day or two, they assured Lucy and David.

Staff and their families had been and gone, and enough food had been saved to entertain Trish and Alan when they arrived.

Exhausted, Lucy and David cuddled up on the big sofa to watch the recording of yesterday's Queen's speech. 'I'd hate her job,' said Lucy when the programme ended. 'Having to be nice to people all the time, never expressing a true opinion, dancing to the tune of a nation, no politics allowed, dress up every day, no privacy.'

'The Queen Mum had politics.' David laughed. 'She was a grand old girl, wasn't she? She said the best parliament to have was Conservative, but with a very large Labour opposition. Yes, she knew her onions. And her horses.' They were filling in time, talking just to kill the silence.

The doorbell sounded, and Lucy jumped to her feet. 'Do I look all right?'

'You've two buttons undone. Anyone would think I'd been interfering with you,'

'You have been interfering.'

'Yes, but there's no need to advertise. And you'd

better not tell QE Two. It's probably high treason or something.'

Lucy opened the door. For the first time in many years, she was pleased to see her first husband.

The front door was ajar, so Alan walked in. Through another door on the right, he saw a man sitting on a chair, a puppy chewing his shoelaces. 'Richard?'

'Yes?'

'I'm Alan. Lucy's first husband. My second wife's next door, and they're talking legs off donkeys, so I thought I'd come and introduce myself.'

Richard stared blankly for a few seconds. 'Sit down. Sorry about the pup. He seems to like you.'

Alan picked up the wriggling mass of black fur. 'We keep donkeys, Trish and I. Rescued, they are. And Damien – we kept him. He's my llama. He was supposed to go to Yorkshire, but I thought no, why should we do that to a defenceless animal?'

Richard almost smiled. 'Would you like a drink?'

Alan shook his head. 'Teetotal. Have to be. I'm a recovering alky.'

'Ah. I meant tea or coffee.'

'No, ta. I'm drowning in the stuff as it is. Two bloody wives in one room? The kettle's never been off since we arrived.'

Another silence followed, then Alan cut to the chase. He took paperwork from a pocket, showed Richard the state his health had been in. 'I had this good, quiet wife, and I never appreciated her. And I must have drunk thousands of pounds in whisky.'

For the first time, Richard allowed himself to laugh.

He told Alan about Lexi, about the way that quiet, good wife had knocked seven shades out of her. 'I've been quiet myself, so they think I hear nothing. I hear. And Lucy all but killed her. She can be quite fierce, actually. Fortunately, it all stopped short of police, otherwise our quiet Lucy might have got herself a record.'

Alan thought about that before expressing the view that Lucy hadn't cared enough to be nasty about him and his girlfriends. 'But she took her money back. Then she kept me out of jail, you know.'

'They've sent you to stop me drinking, haven't they?'

'Yup.'

Richard explained that he'd been on a binge, but it was over. He was one of the lucky ones. He could go back to his nightly dose of Scotch intended to help guard against atheroma. 'My wife died,' he said. 'I blacked it all out deliberately, and I used spirits rather than drugs. Inform the Mothers' Union next door that they don't need to be concerned.'

Alan told Richard about his weeks in Easterly Grange, the drying out in solitude, the surgery, Trish. Richard spoke about London and how time had become distorted. 'I reckon I lost two months somewhere along the line.'

'But you haven't lost yourself, doc. You can lose your way without going crackers, you know. I was very odd. Drying out's no bundle of laughs. But I made it. You'll get through this. My mam used to say if a bad thing doesn't kill us, it makes us stronger.'

'Yes.'

When Alan had gone, Richard took his puppy into the garden. He explained at length about defecation and the need to find a place suitable for the results of this activity. 'I'm a doctor. I have patients. They don't want to come to a house stinking of pee and poo, do they?'

The dog wagged a pathetic string of a tail. Already, he knew why he was here. This man had food. He would give food to his dog and, in return, the dog had to work. Henry didn't know what his specific tasks would be, but he was ready to learn. He skipped sideways in an attempt to show his willingness, fell over dinner-plate paws, and rolled about in a way that was undignified, to say the least of it. But he shook himself and pretended that the move had been intentional.

Richard laughed at the canine clown. He laughed till he cried, and he allowed the tears to flow. In time, he would be all right. The girls could go back to Edinburgh, Simon and Lizzie would return to London, and Richard must begin the process of building himself up again. Moira would want him to be well.

As he dried his face on a tissue this time, he noticed a lonely flake of snow on the dog's dark fur. 'Moira,' he said. 'I will be all right. So will our children, Lucy, her kids and David. You can stop worrying now.'

extracts reading groups
competitions books new
discounts extracts
competitions events
books new reading groups
extracts discounts
events books
extracts new reading groups
new title
interviews
events
extracts
discounts
new books events books
events new
events
discounts extracts discounts
www.panmacmillan.com
extracts events reading groups
competitions books extracts new